Beauty and the Brit

Also by Lizbeth Selvig

Rescued by a Stranger
The Rancher and the Rock Star

Beauty and the Brit

LIZBETH SELVIG

AVONIMPULSE
An Imprint of HarperCollinsPublishers

Excerpt from *The Rancher and the Rock Star* copyright © 2012 by Lizbeth Selvig.

Excerpt from *Rescued by a Stranger* copyright © 2013 by Lizbeth Selvig.

Excerpt from *The Cowboy and the Angel* copyright © 2014 by Tina Klinesmith.

Excerpt from *Finding Miss McFarland* copyright © 2014 by Vivienne Lorret.

Excerpt from *Take the Key and Lock Her Up* copyright © 2014 by Lena Diaz.

Excerpt from *Dylan's Redemption* copyright © 2014 by Jennifer Ryan.

Excerpt from *Sinful Rewards 1* copyright © 2014 by Cynthia Sax.

Excerpt from *Whatever It Takes* copyright © 2014 by Dixie Brown.

Excerpt from *Hard to Hold On To* copyright © 2014 by Laura Kaye.

Excerpt from *Kiss Me, Captain* copyright © 2014 by Gwen T. Weerheim-Jones.

EPub Edition SEPTEMBER 2014 ISBN: 9780062370174

Print Edition ISBN: 9780062370198

JV 10 9 8 7 6 5 4 3 2 1

*This book is dedicated to the circle of real Davids in my life:
Cyrus David—my beloved father-in-law, who taught
me truths about life both here and in the hereafter
I could not have survived without, and who is
waiting at Heaven's gate for us to join him;
Jan David—my husband, who changed the entire world
the day I met him and still lives as if his only goal
on Earth is to make my life happier and easier;
Adam David—my son, who enriched my life from the
moment he came into the world with his kind and
hilarious personality, and shows me every day what it
means to be gifted with a truly gentle and peaceful spirit;
And our littlest angel David—my first grandson, who
taught us about loving through ultimate sadness and now
holds the hand of great-grandpa Cyrus David while he
plays guardian angel to his little sister, Evelyn.*

Acknowledgments

IT DEFINITELY TAKES a village to write my books! And my village is filled with the most amazing citizens:

Tessa Woodward: the nicest person, and the most encouraging and talented editor I could ever ask for. Thank you for urging my stories into becoming wonderful novels, for always loving my characters, and for never yelling at me when I'm four hours later than I say I'll be.

Elizabeth Winick Rubinstein: half agent, half friend, who makes me feel ten feet tall whenever I talk to her, but who will never let anything slide that isn't good enough. Thank you for finding me.

My mom, Grace Feuk, who starts every book with me, listening to tentative concepts and reading the first shaky pages, and then making everyone she knows read the final product. Just . . . thank you with all my love!

My critique partners: Ellen Lindseth, who brainstorms like crazy and talks me off of ledges when I don't want to write anymore; Laramie Sasseville/Naomi Stone, who makes me write active sentences so my writing doesn't drag and then cheerleads to the end; and Nancy Holland, who watches my language and characters like a hawk—thank goodness!

My Alaskan muses, who still never fail me: Morgan Q. O'Reilly, Maxine Mansfield, and DeNise Woodbury know how much I rely on their opinions and expertise and support.

Jennifer Bernard: thank you for being unfailingly honest and more helpful than you'll ever know. And for holding my hand and guiding me through the minefield that is publishing.

Candis Terry, that goes for you, too.

So many thanks to Joy Miller from Warrington, England. (Who knew you could make a lifelong friend in three weeks on a cross-England hike?) Thanks for answering all my British questions on topics from language usage to Queen's Scouts!

And, most importantly, thank you to my readers. I still can't believe you aren't any of you my mom but you still read my books. It's mind-blowing! And I love you all.

Chapter One

"I CAN'T BELIEVE you've been in this country ten years and this is your first game of hoops. Sad, man. How'd they even grant you citizenship?"

David Pitts-Matherson ignored the jibe and crouched in front of his friend. Dr. Chase Preston looked very little like a physician at the moment. He dribbled the ball slowly, intense as Kevin Love, the bounce echoing through the cavernous gymnasium.

"Chatter on, mate," David replied with a practiced sneer. "I'm a fast study."

"Sure y'are. I'll go easy on you anyhow, Limey, so you understand what you're studyin'."

David feinted left and then right, his shoes squeaking on the polished wood floor. The fake worked. He batted the ball from Chase's hand and headed down the court, his dribble admittedly sloppy. When Chase reached him in three long strides, David stopped, took hurried aim, and let the ball fly. It missed the basket and the back-board by a foot, careened off a caged clock, took a hearty bounce, and skittered into a wall.

Chase doubled over in laughter.

"What was *that*?" he crowed. "Thing had about as much control as a fart in a fan factory."

David choked, his own laughter wheezing free in a fit of coughing. He might have a noticeable accent, but as far as he was concerned nothing took the prize for sheer outlandishness like Chase's Southern drawl and resulting phrases of lunacy.

"Nice steal, though." Chase wiped his eyes. "We'll work on the shooting."

David retrieved the ball, dribbled three or four times, and took a jump shot. The ball banked off the backboard and swished neatly through the net.

"No need."

"Did I ever tell you how much I hate British arro-gance?" Chase grinned and captured the ball, dribbled it to the free-throw line, turned, and sank the shot. "Nothin' but net."

"Did I ever tell you how much I hate Americans show-ing off?"

"Yup. You have."

David laughed again and clapped Chase on the arm. Not quite a year before, Chase had married David's good friend and colleague Jill Carpenter, and this was the second time David had overnighted with Chase at Cross-roads youth and community center in Minneapolis. He was grateful for the camaraderie, and for the free lodging on his supply runs to the city, but mostly for the distraction from life at the stable back home in Kennison Falls. Here there were no bills staring up at him from his desk, no finances to finagle, no colicky horses. Here he could forget he was one disaster away from . . . well, disaster.

It also boggled his mind that he and Chase had an entire converted middle school to themselves.

"All right, play to thirty," Chase said, tossing him the ball. "Oughta take me no more'n three minutes to hang your limey ass out to dry."

"Bring it on, Nancy-boy."

A loud buzzer halted the game before it started.

"Isn't that the front door?" David asked.

"Yeah." Deep lines formed between Chase's brows.

The center had officially closed an hour before at nine o'clock. Members with ID pass cards could enter until eleven—but only did so for emergencies. David followed Chase toward the gymnasium doors. Voices echoed down the hallway.

"Stop pulling, Rio, you're worse than Hector. He's not going to follow us in here."

"It's Bonnie and Rio Montoya." Surprise colored Chase's voice. "Rio's one of the really good ones. Sane. Hardworking. I can't imagine why she's here."

Rio? David searched his memory but could only recall ever hearing the name in the Duran Duran song.

"Don't be an idiot." A second voice, filled with firm, angry notes, rang out clearly as David neared the source. "Of course they're following us. They might not come inside, but they'll be waiting, and you cannot handle either of them no matter how much you think you can. Dr. Preston's on duty tonight. He might be able to run interference."

"They won't listen to him. To them he's just a pretty face. Let me talk to Heco. You never gave me the chance."

"And I won't, even if I have to lock you in juvie for a year."

"God, Rio, you just don't get it."

"You're right, Bonnie Marie. I don't. What in God's name possessed you to meet Hector Black after curfew? Do you know what almost went down in that parking lot? Do you know who that other dude *was*?"

Chase hustled through the doorway. "Rio? Bonnie? Something happen?"

David followed five feet behind him. The hallway outside the gym glowed with harsh fluorescent lighting. Chase had the attention of both girls, but when David moved into view, one of them turned. A force field slammed him out of nowhere—a force field made up of amber-red hair and blazing blue eyes.

Frozen to the spot, he stared and she stared back. Her hair shone the color of new pennies on fire, and her complexion, more olive and exotic than a typical pale redhead's, captivated him. Her lips, parted and uncertain, were pinup girl full. Her body, beneath a worn-to-softness plaid flannel shirt, was molded into the kind of feminine curves that got a shallow-thinking man in trouble. David normally prided himself on having left such loutishness behind in his university days, but he was rapidly reverting.

"Rio? You all right?" Chase called, and she broke the staring contest first.

David blinked.

"Fine," she said. "I'm sorry to come in so late. I needed a safe place for this one."

The teenage girl with her couldn't have been more her opposite. Model slender and taller than Rio, a pair of dark eyes and a fall of glossy black hair showed a rich Latina heritage.

"Very funny," the teen said, her lip curled in disgust.

Chase gave an easy chuckle. "Not our sweet-tempered little Bonita." The teasing in his drawl coaxed a smile from the girl. "All right, now. You both look terrified as june bugs in a twister. What's goin' on?"

"About five minutes ago I broke up a transaction that included this one here. Paul and his asshat *amigo*, Hector, are beyond pissed off. I don't think we should go home, at least for a few minutes."

Chase folded his arms. "It was smart to come. Do you want a place to stay for the night?"

"No, no." Rio dismissed the question. "Once we're home we'll be fine. They just need some time, a chance for everyone to cool off."

Chase nodded. "Let's sit here awhile, then, and I'll be glad to take you home. But I'd feel better knowing what's really going on."

"What's going on is that Rio came busting in on my date with Hector like Buffy the Vampire Slayer." Bonnie's laugh was half a step from hysterical. "She clawed at him so hard she left scratch marks that will definitely leave scars down Heco's face. That's what made him furious."

"And what does Paul have to do with this?" Chase asked.

"He was there," Rio said. "He ran off with Hector after Boyfriend's car drove away."

"Boyfriend?" Chase's features transformed instantaneously from concerned to fully alarmed. "*He* was part of this 'transaction'? Is that what you meant?"

Rio nodded.

"That's it. I have to have a talk with your brother."

David listened to the exchange, amazed. He already knew how effective Chase's people skills were from his reputation back in Kennison Falls. He'd heard the stories about his work with inner city kids two days a week, but he'd never seen the calm, serious community leader in action.

A crash, like a chair clattering across the floor, made all four of them jump. It reverberated from the lobby, followed by a foul expletive and the quick beat of running feet. Seconds later a handsome Latino man hurtled around the corner, eyes half-crazed.

"Rio, where the hell are you?" He caught sight of them and slowed to a walk, jabbing his finger through the air as he approached. "Damn it, *Manita*, I could kill you. Do you know what kind of a mess you caused out there?" He spoke with a slightly exaggerated Mexican accent.

"Don't you 'little sister' me in your fake Spanish. This is a mess you started, assh—" Rio cut herself off. "At least your real little sister is safe. No thanks to you."

"I was handling it."

"Handling it? Bonnie was in the car with him. Do you have some *special* kind of shit for brains? Get lost, *Inigo*. I'm starting to think *Paul* is dead to us."

Rage twisted his features, and he lunged forward. David tensed instinctively, recognizing the look of a man momentarily unhinged. Paul made it two steps, and David slid sideways into his path, throwing one arm straight out, clotheslining the young man midleap. Paul's feet shot out from under him, and he landed on his back, but not before hooking David behind the knees. David slammed the deck flat-backed, and the air left his lungs in one sharp exhale. Paul flailed around, attempting to right himself.

David forced himself upright, coughing as his lungs reinflated. Rio reached out a hand to her brother. Paul slapped it away and scrambled to his feet. To David's shock, she offered her hand to him next. With only the slightest hesitation, he took it.

If he'd expected her grasp to be light and feminine, he'd been quite mistaken. She clasped his hand firmly, planted her feet, and pulled him up, keeping her eyes on his as he rose. Her head reached the bottom of his lip.

"Thanks."

To his further shock she smiled. "Nice tackle. Are you all right?"

Behind her, Chase held the wriggling, still cursing brother by both shoulders.

"Brilliant," David said. "Dusted the floor, but none the worse."

Her mouth gaped. The accent caused that all too frequently, something he found slightly ridiculous.

Paul pulled toward Bonnie, and Chase spun him away. "That's enough, Mr. Montoya. Lead the way to my office. Ladies, let's get this straightened out."

Rio ignored the directive. "You're Br—"

"Bruised up?" David cut her off with a teasing wink. "I'm not, though. Honestly. Please don't worry."

"Worry?" She scoffed although her eyes remained wide. "I'm trying to figure out what the Duke of Edinburgh is doing in a place like this."

"I see. Well, since the Duke of Edinburgh is Philip, husband to Queen Elizabeth, I'd say you don't need to worry about that either. But I appreciate the mistaken identity."

She wanted to laugh. He could see it in the quiver of her lower lip and the sparkle trying to overtake the anger in her eyes. Even the weak little smile she'd offered seconds ago had transformed her face; he'd have loved seeing the full-blown version. Instead she battled back the forces of mirth and tightened her lips.

"You Not-Duke-of-Edinburghs all look the same to me." She shrugged. The joke in the middle of her crisis touched him. That took strength. "Thank you, whoever you are, for stopping Paul. He wouldn't have hurt us on purpose, but he'd have knocked me down."

"Glad I could be of service."

She slapped one hand over her mouth—to hold in the laughter, as evidenced from the return of the sparkle to her eyes. When she got control she shook her head.

"I don't believe for one minute you aren't a duke. Nobody talks like that."

"Evidently I do." He stuck out his hand in a proper greeting. "David," he said. "Not to be confused with Philip."

"Rio, short for Arionna," she replied. This time her fingers slipped like satin into his handshake, trailing tiny jolts of pleasure across his palm. "And now I need to go see what the doc thinks I have to do."

He had a suggestion. Stay away from her brother, stand there, and keep talking to him.

RIO SLIPPED INTO Chase's spartan, yellow-painted office, mostly unadorned except for a bookcase full of books—Crossroads' bare bones lending library. Although not many books found their ways back once lent. Chairs had been pilfered from other rooms, and everyone had a seat except Doc Preston, who perched on the edge of an old, black metal desk. Bonnie sat several feet away from Paul, who slouched sullenly on a metal folding chair. Rio sat beside Bonnie, far too aware of David-Not-Philip taking up a post by the door.

"First of all," Chase said. "The extra person back there is David Pitts-Matherson, a good friend from Kennison Falls."

The small town in southern Minnesota where Doc lived. Rio spun to look again at the duke. The stuffy, hyphenated name fit the first image Rio had had of him—a little stiff, a lot extremely hot man. But now that she'd glimpsed his inner laughing-eyed joker, she couldn't reconcile anything hoity-toity with him.

"I think you need a better class of friends, Doc." Paul practically spat the words.

Rio glared at him. He'd dropped the fake accent he used on the street, something that drove her insane.

"I'm sorry to have met on such violent terms," David said.

Rio wasn't sorry. Few people took Paul Montoya down anymore because he was the gang leader's right-hand man. David had done it as easily as stepping off a curb.

And his voice made her see, a little bit, why women dragged their drooling tongues on the ground over British accents. They wreaked havoc on a person's nervous system.

On the other hand, she'd lost her self-control a couple of times now over the accent, and losing control annoyed her. She took in her brother and sister, the former tight as a time bomb, the latter slumped into her folding chair. She had no time to slobber over men from a different league and class.

"Tell me where you were going tonight, Bonnie." Doc's perpetually kind voice eased some of the rigidity from Bonnie's posture.

"Hector said we were going to meet a friend of his. Said the guy was totally cool and had a sick collection of albums. He knows I love new music. But we didn't go to Heco's place. We met his friend in the school parking lot. We were just starting to talk about favorite groups and stuff, and we were sitting in the back of his friend's car because he had an expensive new sound system in it. That's when Rio showed up."

"That's when Rio saved your little ass," Rio replied.

"Whatever."

"Paul." Chase turned to him. "Were you part of this?"

"No, man. I just found out Hector was dealing with Boyfriend. I went to tell him to leave Bonnie alone. But my stupid idiot of a sister had to bust in and humiliate everyone. Now we're all in trouble."

"How's that?"

"Aside from getting a fist in my face after she left?"

"What?" Rio stared more closely at her brother. Sure enough, she could see the faint outline of a lump blossoming beneath his right eye.

He sneered. "They punched me out when they thought I'd narked to my sister. But that's the least of it. You had to get into a damn physical fight with Hector, and now he's vowed to pay you back."

"Oh, what's he going to do, Inigo?" She used his street name derisively. "Come and scratch my face, too?"

"You underestimate him. He's real mad."

"I've lived here for twenty-six years. I know how to handle a threat from Hector Black."

"Not this time."

Paul bore the same olive-skinned Mexican beauty Bonnie did. Both had inherited the dark hair, eyes, and classic bone structure from their mother, her papa's second wife. Rio had missed out on that beautiful mix of chromosomes and gotten instead a set of spliced genes from her Irish mother's family. She literally *was* the redheaded stepchild.

But Irish or Mexican, stubbornness ran rampant through the Montoyas' bloodstreams. If Paul, obstinate since birth, thought this mess was her fault, it would take lightning and a voice from the Almighty Himself to change his mind. Losing his mother seven years before hadn't helped, but age had done nothing to soften him. She turned to Chase.

"When I realized Bonnie had defied the rules and gone out, I had to follow. In all honesty, that's something she doesn't normally do. Then, when I saw her actually get into that car, I don't know whether I was more angry or panicked. Hector, who isn't the freshest tortilla in the pack, is the one who let slip who was in the car, and I know girls who go off with Boyfriend don't come back."

Chase turned stern eyes on Bonnie. "What do you think?"

"I think I could have taken care of myself." Bonnie's defensiveness was trying to turn to defiance. She crossed one leg over the other and shook her foot in frustration, slapping her rhinestoned flip-flop against her sole like a castanet.

"Bonnie, I'm not sure *I* would want to try and take care of myself in a locked car with a guy like that." Chase raised his brows.

"She didn't have to attack Heco. I would have gotten out."

"But you wouldn't have." Rio kept her voice calm with effort. She needed to be the parent right now, not get drawn into a pissing contest. "Hector was physically blocking me from getting to you and blocking you from getting out so, yes, I absolutely fought him. If he's mad as hell, so be it. I'd do it again."

She turned finally to her brother. "And you can protest all you want, but you were not going to stand up to Hector."

"You'll never know that, will you?"

She held her tongue with difficulty.

"Are you positive you three don't want a place to stay tonight?" Chase looked from Paul to Rio.

"I'm positive." She had faith in her locks, one of the few things she'd splurged on in the old house she'd inherited from her mother's meager estate. She also had faith—she had to—that Paul carried enough street cred to get them through this. She sighed, burying her pride with effort to ask for one more thing. "If I could just be sure she gets home safely," she said, inclining her head toward Bonnie, "we'll be fine after that."

"Is your car nearby?" Chase asked.

"No, it's at the house. It was faster to run the three blocks."

"Will Hector retaliate?" Chase turned to Paul.

"He could. Send his boys to threaten her."

"Aren't *you* one of his boys?" Bonnie leveled her gaze at Paul, showing anger with her brother for the first time. "If Heco loves me like he says he does, he won't hurt you or Rio."

Paul sank even more deeply into his chair, his features swimming in sour annoyance. "I'll handle it."

"I can get you home," Chase said. "I'm still not convinced I should leave you there."

"It'll be fine." Rio sat on the edge of her chair. "I'll take Bonnie to school tomorrow before work. *You*, Inigo, will make sure she gets home afterward. Safely. Do you hear me?"

"I don't know. I doubt I can be trusted." He glowered.

"You might be an idiot." She glowered back. "But I know you love your sister. Just keep her away from that scumbag Hector for one hour tomorrow. Can you do that?"

"I'm right here, dumbasses." Bonnie straightened in her chair. "Quit making plans for me like I'm a kinder-gartner or I'll leave and take care of myself."

Weariness fell on Rio like a thick, suffocating blanket. Her lungs wanted one minute of simple, stress-free breathing, but she couldn't get one *breath* that didn't contain the stifling, gang-ridden, fear-scented air of Minneapolis.

"Fine." She threw up her hands. "You're right. We can't do this without your cooperation, so if you want to go trust your future to Hector, we'll back off. I don't want to pull you out of any more cars, rooms, or God forbid, a drawer in a morgue, so let me know as soon as possible and I'll get on with my life, too."

Bonnie snapped her mouth shut.

"That's enough." Chase stood from his seat on the desk. "Paul, take Bonnie and get something to drink from the kitchen. Rio, hang on a second."

When the two had shuffled from the room, Chase knelt in front of her chair.

"I'm sorry." Exhaustion sent her head into her palms.

"No apologizing. We've focused completely on Bonnie and Paul, but it's you I worry about. This is not a small gang scuffle, honey, this is serious. Maybe it's time for you to get some help."

She popped her head up, adrenaline surging. She'd worked her butt off the past seven years at every restaurant or dive that would hire her, and she'd never had to ask for assistance, steal to get by, or sell herself.

Over Chase's head, she caught the eyes of David-Not-Philip. The warm-cocoa gaze shone with sympathy, and her face flamed, knowing how he was seeing her and her family. Despite his kind eyes and her schoolgirl attraction, his cool, quiet demeanor aggravated her. She was holding her world together with sheer will and sarcasm, and he was observing from the corner like a visitor at the zoo.

She forced her attention back to Chase. "I appreciate your concern, but I can handle things."

"Don't stretch yourself too thin." He placed one hand on her knee. "You've been mom, sister, truant officer, and rescuer for a lot of years. You're too special around here to lose to burnout—or something worse."

"Thank you." His words warmed a cold spot in her heart. "I've dealt with Paul's friends a long time."

"I know better than to argue with you." He stood. "I have to be here another forty-five minutes. Can you hang tight? I'll take you home then."

"Whatever we need to do."

David moved from the corner for the first time. "I have my car out back," he said. "Why don't I just run you home?"

Rio turned back to him, her pulse rising one tiny, excited half beat. The man shocked her every time he opened his mouth. "I couldn't make you do that."

"I understand if you're not comfortable with a stranger after what you've been through. But I'm certainly happy to help. You said you have to work in the morning, that's all."

She could think of ten reasons having this man drive down Lake Street to her neighborhood at this time of night was a bad idea. Aside from the fact he'd show up like a spotlight in a coal mine, he could get lost, he could get his car keyed, he could find Hector lying in wait and get his English ass handed to him . . . and she'd have to rescue him right along with everyone else.

"It's not a bad idea," Chase said. "Less time for Paul to get antsy and leave to go solve things on his own."

That point was worth considering.

"I'd be honored to do more than stand around gawping."

Honored? She sighed. She didn't want to be responsible for him out on the streets, but when that patient smile slipped onto his lips, her brain tilted off balance yet again.

"All right," she said, before she could stop herself. "But let me warn you, where we're going isn't an English garden. It's about as un-pretty as it gets."

"It's quite all right." He nodded, unperturbed. "I'm sure I've seen worse."

She remembered her manners just in time to stop a snort of disbelief.

Chapter Two

"THERE, ON THE right. With the outside light."

David peered down the dark street in the direction of Rio's outstretched finger. "The two-story, just there?"

"Yes."

He found an empty spot along the curb and executed an impressive parallel park for a Brit from Yorkshire.

"I can't see if anyone's there." Bonnie, in the backseat, pressed her nose to the window.

"No lights in the house," Rio said. "Doesn't *look* like Paul's come back."

The young man with whom David had crashed to the floor half an hour before had disappeared as soon as Chase had turned his back. David's gut clenched. First the guy had, if Rio's story was to be believed, nearly allowed his young sister to be prostituted. Now he'd run out on keeping them safe. Brother or not, Paul Montoya was a lowlife if ever one had crawled out of the primordial ooze.

He swallowed the anger. There was nothing he could do about the girls' brother, so he concentrated on getting them safely to the house the three siblings shared. It had been left to them after their parents' death, he'd learned. He searched the dark, tree-lined street. At least Rio's small house had a well-lit sidewalk and seemed secure.

"This is nice," he said, hoping to put a little lightness back in Rio's face. "You made it sound as though you lived in a carton in the middle of the street."

She offered a rueful smile. "It's not a lot bigger than that, but at least we have locks on our carton. Some people don't."

"I don't see anyone lurking about." David automatically scanned the overgrowth around the house foundation looking for movement in the shadows. "But let's get you in as promised."

"You don't need to do that." She faced him with the frank, sapphire stare that had fascinated him at first sight. Her entire spring-loaded body fascinated him, with its lithe, wary grace and rich, paprika hair so different from her siblings' black curls. "You probably don't want to leave this car unattended."

"Why ever not?" He laughed. "It's a Subaru not a Lamborghini."

"Is it stolen?" she countered. "Has the odometer been tampered with? Does it have a single scratch on it? Believe me—this might as well be a Porsche made of platinum out here."

Her seriousness made its impression and he nodded. "All right, so noted. With that in mind, I'll take two minutes' worth of chance."

Exiting the car into the unseasonably cool, early-August night, he stared up through the boulevard trees and made out ragged wisps of clouds bearding a waning moon. He gave his upper arms a couple of warming scrubs and hurried around the front of the car to where Rio had already thrown the passenger door open. When he offered her a hand, she stared as if she had no idea what he wanted. As if she hadn't been treated like a lady in a long time.

Bonnie, on the other hand, beamed when he reached for her hand.

"You know, I wouldn't do this chivalry thing in front of the punks around here." Rio's eyes clearly mocked him as he guided Bonnie protectively to the front of their parade of three. "I can't imagine what kind of field day the Whites and Browns would have over such eccentric manners. Not to mention with you if you opened your mouth."

"Are you making fun of my accent?" After ten years in the United States, he was used to the attention his voice drew and, thanks to BBC America, people gave it readily.

"Just keeping it real. Around here, they'd call your accent 'pansy-assed' and give you a beating for fun."

Was she just trying to shock him now? He wasn't shocked, but he was confused at the way she'd grown ever cooler and warier. "Well, thanks much for the warning," he said. "Clearly I need to keep very quiet while I walk you to the door."

A quick, amused light flared in her eyes, and she allowed her sensuous mouth to twitch upward. "You should be a lot more nervous than you are. That's all." She turned and headed for the house.

"You live here," he replied. "If you're not afraid, why should I be? I'm just a possible deterrent to someone jumping out of the bushes."

"All the more reason not to look or sound like a dude from *Men in Tights*."

"Ah," he replied, smiled, and raised the pitch of his voice slightly to quote. "But they'll listen to me because, unlike some other Robin Hoods, I *can* speak with an English accent."

Bonnie giggled. Rio stopped and stared as if he'd just belched in church. He laughed and took her upper arm gently, continuing toward her door. "It's from the movie?" he offered. "*Robin Hood: Men in Tights?*"

"I *know* that. I just think you must be insane."

"Inappropriate perhaps. Not insane. A bit of levity on a tense night, sorry. I don't mean to make light of your fear."

"Hey." She pulled free of his hold. "You said it yourself a minute ago. I'm not afraid. So don't think you have to be any kind of superhero."

He grinned at her ruffled feathers. Her hair, piled on her head like thick, maroon silk, shone in the light from the porch, a few stray strands hinting at its length. He wasn't sure what to make of her. On the one hand she was wise enough to seek sanctuary when she needed it. On the other hand, she clearly had her act—or her foolish bravery—together.

She moved like a gorgeous, jungle-raised cat, watchful and smart, graceful but far from tamed. She very likely *didn't* need him to play bodyguard. Nonetheless her unexpected and fascinating presence in his life had his interest temporarily piqued. No way was he shirking this responsibility.

They reached a four-step stoop. Brick-red paint flaked off the cement in sharp-edged chips. Bonnie pulled open the aluminum storm door revealing a worn but solid wooden inner door. Rio jangled a small ring of keys and isolated one, but before she could insert it into the lock, the door swung open under Bonnie's hand. For the first time since he'd met her, Rio's skin drained of color.

"I locked that door." Her voice didn't shake, but it lowered to a croaking whisper. "I always lock the door."

An unwelcome flash from his days patrolling in Basra overtook him, and he swept Bonnie behind him. "I'm going in first," he said. "Stay here until I call you."

"Are you nuts?"

Her indignant cry dispelled all thoughts of wartime. He chuckled despite their tension. "Probably." At her intake of breath he glanced over his shoulder. "I'm not nuts. Just let me have a look 'round first, right?"

He stepped into a tiny entry foyer maybe six feet square. The room beyond was dark and quiet. Cocking his head, he listened before sweeping one hand along the wall to his right in search of a light switch. When he felt nothing obvious, he half-turned. "Is there a light—?"

He banged into Rio not two inches behind him.

"Ow!" she cried, and rocked backward. "Cripe sakes!"

He grabbed her to keep from tripping like he'd done with her brother. "I told you to wait outside."

"It's my house, excuse me to pieces."

She was so close wisps of her hair brushed his chin, and the heat of her words tickled his throat. The soft touches made her seem vulnerable when she was the furthest thing from vulnerable he'd met in a very long time. He cleared his throat and released her. "We've definitely lost any element of surprise we might have had. Where's the light?"

She scooted around him, brushing torso to torso far too intimately. A moment later light flooded the entryway as well as the room beyond. David blinked and then lost all control of the situation when Rio pushed into the living room and searched the perimeter like a bloody narcotics dog.

"No one's here," she announced. "But I see Paul's cap. Wasn't that the one he was wearing tonight, Bons?"

A battered San Diego Chargers hat lay on a threadbare sofa. David remembered the incongruous California team logo.

"Yeah." Bonnie tossed her fabric bag purse beside the cap.

"My butt-headed brother left the door unlocked." Rio shot an exasperated glance around the room. "He's not detail oriented, to put it mildly."

"Can I look around with you to be sure?" David asked. "You know Chase will grill me on whether you got in safely."

A dubious look crossed her face, but she must have decided he was right. "Fine. Look around down here. I'll check upstairs."

He'd already figured out enough about Rio Montoya to know that if she wanted to check upstairs, Heaven help anyone she found awaiting her. She disappeared up an interior staircase, her footsteps echoing on the uncarpeted treads.

"Can you show me the rest of what's down here?" he asked Bonnie.

"Yes. Come on, the kitchen's back here."

Memories of moving through small, dark houses in Iraq hovered like ghosts. David couldn't help but compare this small, neat home to the quickly abandoned, often ransacked Iraqi dwellings he'd been ordered to enter in search of insurgents. Tidiness ruled here, although it couldn't hide the worn state of the furnishings. Traffic paths crisscrossed the faded blue carpeting, and the upholstery on the mismatched sofa and three chairs needed repair.

The walls seemed freshly painted, however, and were filled with artwork. Two companion landscapes of barren, rolling hills and distant mountains hung side by side. A line of wild horses appeared in the distance on each picture, and David smiled.

Half a dozen prints around the room followed the theme, depicting similar isolated spaces. He didn't know if they indicated a love for such scenery or just inexpensive artwork that sort of matched. They reminded him of places he'd camped during his youth.

The same neat shabbiness greeted him in the kitchen. A beat-up wooden table and four chairs stood in one corner. The cupboards were a thinly veneered chestnut brown, and the linoleum was a faded gold and cream pattern of swirls. Most curiously, piles of old, dog-eared books covered three of the stove's four burners.

"Nobody's upstairs." Rio popped in behind them.

"That was quick. Are you some sort of superhuman speed searcher?"

"We haven't got a full second story. So although I do have ninja powers I can call on if needed, this only took forty-five human seconds."

The mix of impishness and snark in her voice was downright sexy. Her features—so perfectly shaped—beamed with sassy satisfaction. Despite the outward smile, however, her eyes remained sharply vigilant. She might pretend to blow off the whole check-the-house mission as ridiculous, but she hadn't taken her upstairs search lightly.

"Wise choice to conserve superpowers," he replied, refusing to acknowledge a wave of desire to hold her close and protect her from having to be so strong. "Never know when you'll need them for something important."

He glanced at the grayish-blue walls and saw three multi-color paint samples, the kind from a home or decorating store, taped beside the room's only window.

"Redecorating?" He pointed.

"It's on the wish list," she replied matter-of-factly. "Next extra forty-five dollars I have for paint."

"I like the lighter gold color," he said, and smiled inwardly when she stared.

A tiny, attractive smirk formed on her lips. "You don't act like an interior designer."

"Oh? Does an interior designer act a certain way? Or was that an insensitive, stereotyped slur against men who appreciate how to pick paint colors?"

She didn't miss a beat. "Not men in general, just proper English *dukes* who appreciate how to pick paint colors." She rattled the knob of a door David assumed led to the basement, gave a satisfied nod, and faced him. "I mean, who doesn't like a guy who knows his golds?"

"I train horses," he told her. "But in my spare time, I'm finishing the inside of my older house. I've spent far too long looking at paint samples, actually."

She'd frozen in place, her hand still on the doorknob, her mouth parted in surprise.

"Anything wrong?"

"Did you say you train horses?" Her severe eyes gentled. A childlike excitement lightened the already-bright blue of her eyes.

"I do."

"Do you *have* horses?" Bonnie's eyes did the same bright dance.

"Several. You're into horses, are you?"

"I love them, but you should see Rio's room!"

"Oh?" David chuckled, and a flush of pink crept up Rio's face.

"No. I don't think you should." She glared at her sister.

But Bonnie tugged on his jacket sleeve. "Come on. You wanted to check the whole house."

Rio followed, flustered in a way he hadn't seen even when discussing gang retribution. The reaction piqued his curiosity, but one thing he understood was personal boundaries. He'd lost enough of his own growing up in his father's shadow.

"Show me your room if you like," he said to Bonnie. "Rio needn't show anyone her space."

Her eyes shone with gratitude, although he wondered if she realized it.

Vivid turquoise paint adorned the walls in Bonnie's room at the back of the house. Posters and magazine pictures of celebrities formed most of the artwork. On the wall over her bed, however, were the horses—posters of prancing, dish-faced Arabians, a fanciful winged horse with a star-studded background, and a unicorn with its head in a maiden's lap.

"You don't have an Arabian horse, do you?" It sounded like she might ask for his autograph if he did.

"Unfortunately, no. I have two rather naughty thoroughbreds and two warmbloods."

"Warmbloods?"

"A cross between normal light horses and heavy draft horses," Rio answered, standing in Bonnie's doorway, a cross between a proud sister and a rabbit ready to bolt.

"Right," he said, pleasantly surprised. "There are many warmblood breeds. I have an Irish Draught and a Hanoverian."

"That's so awesome," Bonnie said.

"Little girls in the city wish for horses, because we can't have them."

"Show him your horses, Rio." Bonnie crossed the room. "You have an awesome collection." Rio shook her head. "Come *on*." Bonnie took Rio's hand. "You should be proud of them."

"Bonnie, he doesn't care."

"She has, like, a hundred Breyer horses. You know them?"

He knew of them. His mother had collected similar molded horse statues, much to his father's bemusement. Why had she needed fakes when she had real ones down the garden path? It was impractical. And practicality had almost been a religion in their home.

"I haven't got a hundred—" Rio mumbled.

"You don't need to—" he said at the same moment.

"But you have the really rare one," Bonnie persisted.

"Aw, give us a look then," he teased. "I'll have tunnel vision—only what you want me to see."

"Whatever." Rio sighed.

Across the short hallway she flipped on the light and ushered David into her room.

He had a hard time keeping his promise not to take it in. Rio's room, a pale, paint-chipped blue, was less coordinated than Bonnie's. The double bed's four posts were spindly and old-fashioned, and her nightstand was simply two wooden produce crates, painted and stacked one atop the other. The open range theme continued with a stunning eight-foot-wide panoramic poster of horses grazing beneath a mountain range.

Above her bed hung two prints of cowboys leaning muscled and shirtless against stall doors and hay bales. They were the kind of cowboys he doubted actually existed—but, then, what did he know from cowboys?

Another wall held a neatly arranged collection of eight horse portraits, all palominos, the largest one of a stereotypical wild stallion, standing vigilant on a sunset butte with his flaxen mane and tail fanned in the breeze.

"If I were ever lucky enough—that is what I'd get."

"Accept no substitutions?" He winked at her.

She actually laughed. "Well, around here you can't charge for substitutions. People would go broke." Her smile faded. "That was a restaurant joke. I work at a restaurant."

He had a feeling it was more than a joke. She'd likely settled for many substitutions in her life.

"Honorable work. Underappreciated."

"But, look, look. This is the cool stuff." Bonnie bubbled like a teapot and turned him in place to face an eclectic assembly of bookcases and shelves nestled against the wall opposite her bed. A stereo system took up one large shelf, but true to Bonnie's promise, the rest of the space was filled with model horses. Dozens of them in every color and pose. Prominently displayed in the middle was an orangey-brown stallion on a wooden stand, its regal head straight up and alert. A western saddle adorned its back, and slender brass chains created draping reins.

"He's really old," Bonnie the de facto tour guide explained. "Our grandmother found him at a garage sale for only two dollars. Now I think he's worth a couple of hundred."

"So the story goes," Rio added, her full soberness back in place.

"He's quite something." David peered at the figure. "And it's an impressive collection. How many do you have?"

Rio considered a moment. "Maybe eighty," she said. "Only a half dozen were bought new. The others came from thrift shops or garage sales. I don't collect them for the value. And I'll never sell the old guy so I don't care what he's worth." She gave the little orange horse a stroke along the neck. "One of my sillinesses from childhood."

"My mother collected model horses, so I don't think they're silly. She still loves hers."

Bonnie threw her sister a hip bump. "Told you he'd be impressed."

"I am. You've made a warm and personal home here," David said. "Chase said it came from your parents."

"From my mother's side," Rio acknowledged.

"Rio calls it our nest egg, because we're going to sell it when I'm done with high school. We'll own it totally then because there are only ten payments left."

"Bonnie!" Rio stared in obvious dismay at the personal revelation.

"But it's an amazing plan." Bonnie ignored her sister's consternation. "After we sell it, we're moving out West and having all our own horses. We watch the ads for land all the time. Rio's been planning it forever. Haven't you?"

A new flush spread across Rio's cheeks.

"That's not something you go blurting out," she admonished. "Some things are private."

Young Bonnie had a few underdeveloped social filters, although not a mean bone as far as David could tell. Nonetheless, if the plan was true, it was impressive.

"It is a good plan. It takes intelligence and patience to plan your future."

"It's a someday plan," she replied, her tone factual and unemotional. "We're lucky to have this house, so even though it could be a ticket out of the city, I don't want to misuse it."

"You'd like to leave the city?"

"Sure. Leave and never come back. Some day."

"So the Western landscapes on all the walls were a clue." He smiled.

"I guess it would be silly to deny it." She swung her attention back to Bonnie. "It's late, you little blabbermouth, better make sure your homework is done. Traumatic night or not."

"And"—David took his cue—"it's time for me to leave you ladies to it. You're obviously quite safe here. I can go back and tell Chase you're tucked in."

He wasn't sure what this micro-insight into Rio Montoya's world revealed about her: strength, courage, vulnerability for a start. And the dreams of horses and moving West added a further level of attraction.

"Thank you," she said at the front door. "It was nice of you to get us home."

"My pleasure."

"It was nice to meet you!" Bonnie was the first to offer her hand.

A residual chill transferred at her touch as it dawned on him what had almost happened to this bright little bird. For all she'd grown up in the same place as her sister, she was so much more innocent and wore an unspoiled air Rio didn't possess. He looked back to Rio's steady, unemotional gaze.

"If you ever have a wish to visit the horses, you'd be welcome at my place. Kennison Falls isn't that far away—an hour and a half drive, perhaps. Plenty to do there. See what stable work is like, take a ride perhaps. Test out that good plan of yours."

He stopped, aware he was not only channeling his pathologically hospitable mother but on the verge of sounding like an infomercial. Bonnie's face broke into a grin. Rio shrugged with wistful pragmatism.

"That's very kind of you. In many ways, though, an hour and a half might as well be four days."

He nodded. In truth, it would probably be better not to mix his world with hers. He couldn't think of two more opposite places.

"The offer stands. It was lovely to meet you both."

"Will you come back to Crossroads?" Bonnie asked.

He smiled. "I come to the cities now and again. Meanwhile, you stay out of strange cars, right, love? Even if good music's involved?"

She smiled with a touch of, but not nearly enough, self-consciousness. "I will."

He looked back to Rio and, again, had an urge to protect her, despite the fact that she wanted no protection. "Stay safe."

Her smile was far more sardonic than her sister's. "Somehow, I always do."

Three minutes later he pulled from the curb and watched the Montoya sisters' porch light fade in his mirror. She'd gotten to him, the stoic and protectively sarcastic elder Montoya. She was not like any woman he'd ever found attractive before.

Not that he'd ever see her again. Still, he hoped with all his heart his gut fear for her was nothing but the last wisp of those old ghosts.

Chapter Three

THIS HAD TO be a nightmare.

Rio stared at the chaos around her and tried to make sense of the voices. So many voices—rendered into dissonant babbles and shouts by the hiss of the fire monster that had awoken her twenty minutes ago. Like a dragon, red and black, evil, crackling, belching smoke, it devoured her life before her eyes.

No. That was wrong. Their lives were intact. She'd gotten Bonnie out safely. Paul wasn't home. She'd rescued her cell phone and her ancient laptop. She'd gotten the fire department here in good time and given them all the information they'd asked for.

She swayed on her feet watching her home burn and told herself their lives were all that mattered.

Held back from the disaster by a snarl of fire hoses and swarms of efficient firefighters, there was nothing more to be done except stare in disbelief at the flames devouring the roof. She didn't even know what time it was. She'd paid no attention to the clock when the thick veil of smoke had choked her awake.

Bonnie sat on the boulevard grass beside her, shivering despite the thick blanket given to her by one of the firemen. She stared, her eyes wide but expressionless.

The horror did mesmerize. Their house had stood ninety years in this spot, and Rio had done her best to keep up the one material thing her mother had left in her care. It wouldn't spontaneously combust. This fire could not be an accident.

Pajama-clad neighbors gawked and murmured in little groups. Few of them had approached her. Neighbors didn't get too close since Paul and Hector had grown so attached.

Hector.

He wouldn't. Even he can't be that evil.

She let her head fall forward into her palms. Oh God, this could not be happening.

"Rio? Bonnie? Girls, are you all right?"

She recognized Chase Preston's troubled Southern drawl before she saw him. Before she could answer, Bonnie released a cry and jumped to her feet, throwing herself into Chase's arms with a sob.

"Aw, honey, honey, I know. But thank God you're both out here." He locked her into a safe embrace and caught Rio's eyes. "Are you really okay?"

"Yes."

No.

Then she saw David. The world around her slowed for a few blessed seconds while her stomach took an unexpected dive for her toes. He stood behind Chase, the concern in his eyes blazing to match the fire. It seemed like mere moments since he'd been standing in her room and Bonnie had blurted out their life plans, giving him possession of secrets she'd never told anybody. Because she'd never thought to see him again, she'd let the embarrassment go. At his surprising appearance here, she felt even more vulnerable than she had four hours ago.

"Rio." He spoke into her ear, and she blinked, unsure how he'd moved to her side without her noticing. "This is shocking. I'm so awfully sorry. I'm sure it's too early yet for authorities to know what happened?"

The direct question calmed her. She appreciated him not asking again how she was.

"I don't know. I . . . I have a suspicion, but only because of what happened earlier."

"Do you think your brother was involved?"

That question took her aback. Paul? Even if *Hector* was involved, Paul's friendship would never extend to something this vile.

"No."

"Good. Perhaps one suspect eliminated." He allowed a gentle, bittersweet smile, which she recognized as understanding.

"It wasn't an accident."

Saying so out loud for the first time ripped through the layer of numbness protecting her from her feelings. Tears of anger and the first edgings of fear welled in her eyes. Averting her gaze, she swiped the moisture away.

"Aw, it's all right, love. Didn't you only just tell me

how much of your future is wrapped up in this house? You're allowed to cry. It's not weakness."

His accent touched her, wrapped around her heart with less formality than earlier, but calm drifted further from her reach. Was she so transparent he could see how to obliterate her control with a couple of understanding words?

Shit.

She didn't do physical displays. She needed to follow her instincts and shove him away, buck up, and take care of her crisis. Instead, she didn't even object when he wrapped his arms around her the way Chase had done with Bonnie. Her tears won, and she sobbed.

For a minute it was a relief—to let him shore up her wobbly knees and his broad chest to obscure the sight of the fire. To weep for things she was losing as she stood there. David didn't move except to tighten his arms. He didn't speak or use his power to take advantage of her, but power was what he had. Power to surround her, insulate her, let her believe it wasn't her fault she'd lost control.

His scent dulled her fear like anesthetic. His chest, rising and falling beneath her cheek, pulled her focus from the disaster and put it on him. A thought crept insidiously through her brain: she could hide within this stronghold for a long time and get used to it. The very idea slapped her back into reality. She didn't know this man. To let him take away her fear and her focus was dangerous—fear and focus were her only weapons.

Drawing self-control back around herself like a cloak,

she slipped from his embrace and crossed her arms tightly around her middle, covering the flimsy T-shirt she wore as pajamas. As soon as she had escaped his embrace, however, she found she had no desire to escape his presence. Even without the drugging fog from his scent and his touch, he exuded calm protection.

Chase placed a hand on her arm.

"We don't need to stand here and watch, honey. We can go back to Crossroads and wait. The police can come talk to you when the fire is out."

"Please, Rio, please, let's go. I can't stand this anymore." Bonnie's tear-tracked cheeks and wild eyes conveyed her fear.

"Sweetie, I know." Rio cupped her sister's face with her hands. "But I can't leave and not be sure they're doing all they can. We could take you across the street to the Hansons'. Look, they're in the front yard. I'm sure they'd let you sleep on their sofa."

"No! They're nice, but their house ... is—" At the word "house" she covered her face.

"Why don't you take Bonnie back to Crossroads?" David turned to Rio. "I can stay here if you'd be all right with that."

"It's not necessary. I don't want to make you stay."

The thought of remaining alone with David, but without Chase as a buffer, slightly terrified her. Yet the thought of David leaving left her stomach hollow. She didn't really want to face the firefighters, the police, and the flames on her own.

"You aren't making me do anything. We don't need to

know each other that well for me to act as another set of ears and eyes."

Again his smile was kind and unforced. He was right about two things. One, they didn't know each other at all. Two, at this point it didn't matter. Nothing worse could happen to her.

"All right, thank you," she made herself say. "Bonnie, it's fine if you go with Chase. I understand why you don't want to watch."

Bonnie considered a minute and then nodded.

A weight lifted from Rio's chest. Bonnie, at least, would be in good hands. If the staff at Crossroads had a strength, it was providing a safe environment for kids.

For a long, silent moment they all stared back at the house. Flames lit the windows of Rio's bedroom and the living room, turning them into fiery eyes, malevolent and cruel. Firefighters with axes crawled over the half of the roof not engulfed in flames. Smoke hissed from high-pressure water meeting tenacious fire.

"You'll stay at the center tonight," Chase said, finally. "Don't worry about any other plans yet. After the fire is out, we'll think about the future. You know we'll help, right?"

"I do know, Chase."

He and Bonnie left, and the only way Rio could make the watching tolerable was to study the firefighters, who moved through the disaster scene in choreographed precision. Their instructions were terse and efficient, their movements were never wasted, and all their efforts were immediately effective. Not a single one of those attributes applied to her life.

"Are you cold? Can I fetch you a blanket or find a sweater?" David asked, when their silence had stretched to several long minutes. "I can run somewhere quickly and get you something hot to drink."

She turned her attention to him, even though meeting his eyes after her crying jag was one step from humiliating. He wore a plain white undershirt, disheveled as if from sleeping in it, and to her mortification, a starburst of wrinkles surrounding a damp spot on his chest made it clear where she'd fallen apart in his embrace.

"I'm fine." Her voice came out tight although she didn't intend it. "I'm not going to lose it again. You really don't need to babysit me."

"Bloody lucky," he replied, his voice light. "I'm nobody's idea of a good nanny. I've just never seen a house fire in person before, and it's terrifying. I have no idea what you must be going through. When in doubt, a good Englishman always rings for tea."

A reluctant smile found its way onto her lips. "Tea and a sweater. Probably the best offer I'll get any time soon, but I'm fine."

"You're sure you aren't cold?"

She shook her head. The air temperature hadn't even registered with her. "I'm sure."

"All right. But don't be brave on my account."

They held their vigil for another half hour. She grew accustomed to his presence, even pointed out when she noticed the flames had stopped chewing through the roof and when more firemen took time for short breaks because they seemed to be making headway. She stayed close to him, although she didn't want him to know it was mostly because he kept her mind from panic and her body warm without a blanket.

"Miss Montoya?"

Rio looked away from the scene at her blackened front door where a fireman was emerging from the now-dark house. She met the eyes of a square-jawed, sixty-ish man who'd introduced himself much earlier as the captain.

"Yes?"

"I thought you'd be interested to know what we found along the side of the house, half-buried beside the foundation."

He held up an ancient-looking metal gas can with a melted plastic spout. He might as well have parked one of his trucks on her chest. David swept an arm across her back, just as her knees turned to soup.

"Steady, love."

She grasped his arm automatically. "That's proof, isn't it?" Her voice croaked from her constricted chest. "Somebody did this."

"We can't say anything for certain yet," the captain said. "There'll be further investigation. But if you don't normally keep a gas can next to your house, I'd say this points strongly toward arson."

"He's gone completely crazy." Rio stared at the embers of her house.

"Who has?" David asked.

"Hector Black. He's a puny little leader of a small, mean street clique. They can't even truly be called a gang.

This, along with what he tried to do to Bonnie, is beyond his usual scope. It's like he's trying to get noticed."

"The authorities will sort this, Rio. Try not to worry." David looked helplessly toward the captain, who nodded.

"Worry? What more can happen to worry about? I'm pissed as hell."

He drew back, his dark eyes surprised. "Well, I'm proud of you, then, aren't I?"

"Proud?"

"You haven't been one to curl up and whimper. I'm not sure how you're doing it."

Rio wasn't either. Most of her was numb. Her chest hurt. But what choice did she have? What choice had she ever had other than to fight on? It still annoyed her that she'd broken down in front of him at all.

Before she had to form a response, the phone she'd hastily stuffed into the waistband of her sleep shorts vibrated next to her skin. She pulled it out, stared into its outdated, not-smart screen, and saw the indication for a new text. Her heart thundered.

"It's Paul," she whispered, and opened the message. But when she read it, it confused her—it didn't sound like her brother.

So the can surprised you. Hope you know the doctor can't keep Bonnie away from me.

She swiveled her head wildly. Whoever it was, was watching. He knew she'd just seen the gas can. He knew Bonnie wasn't here.

"What is it?" David searched with her. She handed him the phone, her throat too tight to speak. "Your brother is here?" He dropped his arm from her shoulders and all but leaped into the street, his eyes, narrowed and alert, sweeping the neighborhood. There was nothing.

"I don't believe he'd do this to his own house. I don't."

But the message had come from his phone.

Rio's strength finally deserted her. She never in a million years would have thought Paul capable of such an awful crime. Or of such hatred of her. They were only half siblings, but they'd been there for each other all their lives. And he had always adored Bonnie, his full sister. Rio couldn't fathom what had changed. She clutched her churning stomach.

"Rio? Rio, come on. We need to get you to someplace warm and safe. You can't find answers until you have some place to think. The fire is nearly out. Let me take you back to Bonnie and Chase."

There was nothing to do but obey. Now her life did feel as though it had ended. A house was just a thing. Safety, however, was right up there with health. If you didn't have it, you couldn't live. Until this moment, the only thing that had kept them all safe was their status as family. As much as it seemed impossible beyond words, Paul had just destroyed that.

She buried her face in David's T-shirt once again and let helplessness steal the last of her pride.

Chapter Four

RIO STOPPED PICKING at the fraying hem of her jeans and stared out the windshield at a long, tree-and-pasture-lined driveway. Pristine brown fencing surrounded jewel-green fields, and the glossy horses dotting them should have had her in ecstasy. Instead, only the numbness of the past five days ruled her emotions.

Jill Preston guided her Suburban across an actual bridge over an actual stream and approached a fancy wooden sign painted with black-and-gold lettering. "Bridge Creek Stables." Rio couldn't quite reconcile the surroundings with her expectations. If this was where David lived, it was a very far cry from the horse farm-slash-dude-ranch she'd pictured.

Bonnie, on the other hand, had oohed and ahhed the entire way from Minneapolis to Kennison Falls. Any memories haunting her from the week since the fire were invisible at the moment. In fact, the girl had been frighteningly ditzy since that night, swinging from inconsolable weeping to manic excitement.

Rio hadn't cried since embarrassing herself in David Pitts-Matherson's arms. She could have. She'd had plenty of time for nightmares. But her crying wouldn't make Bonnie feel safer or solve the countless issues facing them. So she'd dug in and channeled her terror into problem-solving, as she always did.

Jill caught her eyes, and Rio managed to return the encouraging smile with a polite one of her own. She didn't speak. All she had strength to do was ride this crazy train she'd been forced onto until the conductor kicked her off. Unfortunately she wasn't sure their current destination was the right or smart one.

Chase had immediately found a group shelter home for her and Bonnie, and Rio would rather have stayed there, kept her job, and searched out a new place to live. But cryptic, semi-threatening messages from Paul's phone had continued and eventually found them at the supposedly safe place. *We know you both are at Rose House. You can't hide from us.*

After Chase talked to the police, insisting the girls had to get out of the city until the gang's anger cooled, he'd offered his home in Kennison Falls as a safe place. Jill would be there as a buffer, and it was nearly two hours from Hector. Rio had agreed, reluctantly, for Bonnie.

But yesterday the plans had changed again. Chase and Jill lived in an old farmhouse, and several water pipes had unexpectedly burst. It wouldn't be a quick fix, he'd reported sadly. Even he and Jill would be staying elsewhere while large sections of the house's aged plumbing got replaced. David, however, could save the day. He had a huge home and had more than willingly offered it.

David.

No matter how much Rio wished she did, she had no other options, especially since she hadn't told anyone the whole story. When the fire had taken away their house, Bonnie had dismissed it. "We have insurance," she'd said. "We'll just move earlier than we planned."

Rio had spent the entire week while at the shelter trying to make that hope a reality, but the reality was, there was no future out West anymore. No dreams even for after high school. The house had not been insured.

Jill pulled up in front of a mansion. Rio forced the lump in her throat downward where it couldn't choke her. She hadn't seen David since the fire. She dreaded seeing him now—still sensitive to how many of her fractured emotions he'd seen. She clearly remembered his offhanded offer of assistance should they ever need it—an offer she was certain he'd never expected to be honoring.

Surprise.

"You're sure he's ready for us?" Rio couldn't think of anything more intelligent to ask.

This man had to be wealthy beyond her fantasies. Three of her little houses would have fit inside the two-story white dream home wrapped with a porch and decorated with gables and scrollwork.

Jill nodded firmly. "He's looking forward to having you. As you can see, the house is plenty big enough."

No shit, Sherlock, Rio thought a little unkindly.

"This is where we're staying?" Bonnie scooted across the backseat to press her face against the window. "Ohmygosh."

"I'm really sorry you couldn't stay with us," Jill said. "I'd have loved having you. But this house is nearly a hundred years old, and wait'll you see it. It was in pretty rough shape when David bought this farm ten years ago. He spent the first four years fixing up the outside so it would look good for his business. Then he started inside. It's very, very nice; you'll be comfortable here."

Bonnie pushed her door open and stared like Alice arriving in Wonderland. "This is the most beautiful place I've ever seen."

It probably was. Bonnie had never been out of Minneapolis.

"It's *very* temporary," Rio reminded her. "So remember we're guests."

"At least it isn't a depressing safe house prison." Bonnie hopped out of the car. "And Hector won't find us."

It was worth being here just to have Bonnie free of Hector. Rio steeled her heart and repeated her warning to herself. This was not a home. It was charity. Charity she intended to repay.

A warm breeze caressed her face when she stepped from the car, as if true August had awaited them here in the country while the city shivered in unseasonable coolness. Turning in place, she took in the surroundings. Fifty yards from the house, the driveway opened into a large yard connecting a complex of buildings. A neat white-and-green barn stood closest, and she assumed the tan metal-sided building that dwarfed it was a riding arena. As she admired the flower beds, the tidy lawns, and the grove of shade trees in which they stood, two riders led horses out of the barn door.

"Look!" Bonnie pointed.

A trickle of disappointment slid through Rio's stomach. Neither rider wore jeans or cowboy boots, the cowgirl uniform she'd dreamed of owning, along with her own horse, since she'd been a kid. Neither of these horses wore a big, cow-roping saddle. There wasn't a Stetson in sight. Instead, the two girls wore form-fitting breeches with inner knee patches and prissy black helmets.

"You'll find this is a busy place." Jill stood beside her. "Never a dull moment in the barn and arenas, but the house stays pretty private, so you'll be fine there."

Rio simply stared.

"Everything all right? You look a little shell-shocked." Jill touched Rio's shoulder. "I'm so sorry. It must be overwhelming."

Rio finally responded to the kindness in Jill's words and nodded. "I'm a fish on the sand here," she admitted. "I was imagining more jeans and dust."

Jill laughed. "Don't worry. You'll find plenty of those, too."

Bonnie apparently harbored no disappointments. "I love those riding breeches! They look super-hot."

"Super-practical," Jill amended. "I'll find you a pair to borrow. You'll see."

"Honest?" Bonnie looked at Rio as if for confirmation of this amazing promise.

All she could do was shrug again. If Jill did find Bonnie a pair of breeches, it would at least make three pairs of pants the girl owned. Between fire, smoke, and water damage in the house, neither of them had been left with much wearable clothing.

"I'll get you set up inside," Jill continued. "David could be finishing a lesson. He'll find us."

Rio quit listening when a third person emerged from the barn. For an instant she watched casually, but then his movements, his wave of thick, dark hair, and a smile visible across the distance shocked her into recognition.

David.

She took him in, and her heart fell in disillusionment. In tight-fitting breeches, a pale green-and-white striped polo shirt, and tall black boots hugging his lower legs all the way to his knees, he looked as un-macho as the two stylish women who'd just passed by. If Rio could have created a picture that screamed "I am the opposite of a cowboy," this would have been it. For once, even Bonnie was quiet.

And yet, as the length of his confident stride carried him closer, the contours of his thighs and breadth of his shoulders erased anything she'd mistaken for effeminate about him. Her disenchantment faded enough to make room for curiosity.

"Rio. Bonnie," he called out. "I'm glad to see you've made it safely. How was the ride down? Construction traffic?"

Jill shook her head. "Easy peasy."

"Brilliant." His accent and warm smile gave the word an onomatopoeic brightness.

He faced Rio directly, and her memories of him turned to pale shadows. The real man, with his sculpted cheeks and rich, glinting brown eyes, turned her heart and pulse into a marimba band, drowning her disappointment further with the fluttery music of gut-deep attraction. Tight riding pants and all, he was flat-out gorgeous. How could she have forgotten?

She tore her eyes away, already annoyed. Why did the man turn her brain to mush?

"Any word on Paul? Or Hector?"

"He's sent more text messages," Bonnie answered for her. "But we don't think it's really him."

That was true. Something had never felt right about the messages. Paul, in his gang persona as Inigo, often blustered, but he didn't threaten pure violence. Paul in his role as a brother, especially to Bonnie, could even be tender.

Anger, deep in the pit of her stomach, rose to a familiar boil. The longer she'd thought about it, the more Rio believed Paul could not have sent the messages. Deep down, she knew it was Hector who'd shattered their life.

And yet, they were the ones in hiding.

Awesome.

"Let's hope the police will find the answer," David said. "Meanwhile, let's get you into the house. I've cleared the afternoon so I'm at your disposal."

At your disposal? Who said that? Rio buried her anger again. David was back to being as genteel as a duke and as polite as the diplomat she'd seen in him days earlier. She half-expected Jeeves the butler to come waddling out of the mansion and call her "miss."

"You didn't have to change your schedule for us."

"It hardly would have been chivalrous to make you wander around an unfamiliar place by yourselves. There are lots of nooks and crannies here where new-comers can get disoriented. We should also do a bit of grocery shopping. Stock the pantry with some of your favorites?"

He was only being wonderful. Welcoming and open. But his offers suffocated her like more smoke from the fire. It would take forever to repay him for this, but she had to take the help for Bonnie's safety. Her stomach ached. She'd always been able to scrape her way out of tight spots, but this time she'd been squeezed to the point of helplessness for one of the very rare times in her life.

"I . . . appreciate this." She stumbled over the words, knowing she needed to sound at least a little grateful. "Bonnie's pretty excited."

Bonnie normally railed against Rio speaking for her, but the girl was too immersed in a theme-park state of mind to care. "This is *so* cool!" she said for the hundredth time.

"Okay, I've got to get home, so you guys enjoy the tour of the house and barns." Jill got an enthusiastic hug from Bonnie, and accepted a perfunctory one from Rio without questioning the lack of enthusiasm. "I'll be back to teach in a few hours," Jill continued. "I'm guessing Chase wants to come and say hi, too. He was so worried about you."

It dawned on Rio that she knew nothing about Chase's life outside of Crossroads. She knew Jill had her own horses and taught here with David. But what was the old farmhouse they were fixing up really like?

"Everything okay?" Jill asked.

Rio pulled a smile from somewhere deep. "Sorry. Tell Chase thanks for helping set all this up. Thank you, too."

Jill waved a dismissive hand. "This is no trouble. See you later, David."

An awkward silence filled the void Jill left behind. David stood alone before them in this new reality, truly the only port in this storm. Unlike when she'd first met him, however, he seemed much less harmless than at the community center or even at the fire scene. Here she was in his domain where, breeches and all, he definitely ruled. His dark good looks only enhanced the picture. With hair mussed from the breeze and a small vee of skin at the base of his throat messing with her equilibrium, she noticed his maleness far more than when she'd been in her own space. The danger wasn't that David Pitts-Matherson would ever hurt them physically. Emotionally . . . that was where she felt a deep, nameless peril.

"Let's take your things inside," he said. "Please forgive the state of the house. It's very much a work in progress."

There wasn't anything to forgive. Dark pine wainscoting and a welcoming shade of sage green greeted them in the entryway. Three large oil paintings of horses caused Bonnie to squeal in delight yet again.

Past a stairway with an open railing, the living room was comfortable and masculine in the same woods and greens. Deep-cushioned furniture, upholstered not in cliché leather but in a rich burgundy print, looked rich but inviting. Bamboo flooring glowed a burnished gold beneath thick area rugs.

"Books and telly in here any time you like," David said. "Kitchen's this way."

At the kitchen doorway, Rio nearly lost her composure for the first time. She'd never seen the like, even in the diners where she'd worked. The expanse of granite countertop seemed big enough to land small aircraft. Stainless gleamed from the appliance surfaces, and a few dishes sat in the sink. When she caught sight of the shiny stove, tears filled her eyes. Her stacks of cookbooks, some from her grandmother, most discovered at garage sales or used bookshops, had been destroyed in the fire. Gone, like the Breyer horse . . .

Mortified, she held back a ripple of nausea. She'd spent so much time trying to instill a philosophy of nonmaterialism to her siblings, and here she was mourning the loss of her things more than the loss of the house itself.

"Here now." David's warm voice drew her away from the memory pit. "I'm sorry. Let's skip this for now."

"No." Rio squared her shoulders and stiffened, angry at her breakdown. "I'm just fine. Once in a while I just remember something we lost."

"What was it just then?"

She stared into his cocoa-brown eyes and almost allowed herself to sink into their sincerity. She shook free of his spell. "Cookbooks," she said shortly. "Nothing important."

Attractive creases formed between his thick brows.

He thought a moment. "Is that what was piled on the range?"

She shrugged. "They were all of them old and generic."

"But did you use them? You like to cook?"

"She's a great cook." Bonnie had prowled through the room and returned, an eager puppy exploring a new world.

"When I had time and money." Rio tried to convey indifference. "I rarely had them both together."

"I think most of us can identify with that."

She knew he meant his quiet smile to show camaraderie, but irritation rolled over her, and her good intentions to stay calm and aloof dissipated. This man had no idea what it meant to run out of either commodity. If he could blithely clear his afternoon schedule of work and create a home that looked like this, he had nothing in common with her microscopic bank account or the forty-plus-hours-a-week job at Calvin's Diner she'd just had to quit. She turned her back on David and Bonnie and gripped the handle of her donated suitcase.

"Where do you want us to take our things?"

"Right this way," he said. "There's a bathroom on this level through there." He pointed to a hallway door on the other side of the living room. "It and my room and office are beyond."

He led them to the front staircase made of more burnished wood and studded with pristine white balusters. In spite of herself, Rio ran one hand along the polished railing as she climbed the steps, reveling. This was so different from the narrow, enclosed staircase in her old house, which had been scarred and painted and functional, period. She loved elegant staircases.

"Now you'll see how much there is left to do on the house," David said, when they reached the hallway at the top. "Believe it or not, there are eight rooms up here, albeit small. One day I'd like to put in some skylights. Until then, this long hallway is dark and a bit dreary, I'm afraid."

True enough, the hall was windowless and held only doorways, but with light beige walls and pictures lining its length, it was hardly dreary.

"Two bedrooms up here are finished. The others are still in original condition. There's another bath. It's ugly but clean."

His eyes apologized. Rio held back a grunt of disdain. He'd just described the bathroom she'd used for the last twenty-six years. He turned to the right and led the way to a corner room facing the front of the house, decorated in spring green and white. A beautiful quilt in greens and yellows with touches of blue adorned the double bed. Bonnie gaped.

"This has to be the most gorgeous room I've ever seen! Oh Rio, look. Look at the flower pictures."

The décor was luxury beyond anything Rio could ever have afforded. The delicately striped green-and-white curtains were pretty but not frilly. David Pitts-Matherson clearly had deeper talents than raising horses and filling out tight pants.

"It's yours for now if you wish," he said.

"Really? Oh, really?" Bonnie spun around the space once and flipped her suitcase onto the bed. "Thank you!"

She stopped short of throwing her arms around David's neck.

"Yours is right next door." He caught Rio's eyes, his smile underscored with friendliness.

"Yeah!" Bonnie stopped her room-ogling and grabbed Rio's upper arm. "I can't wait to see what yours looks like."

"Hers" looked like a page out of a decorating magazine. What Bonnie's spring-fresh room was to airy neutrality, Rio's was to masculine serenity. A soothing dove gray covered the walls, and classy blue, gray, and maroon striped drapes hung floor-length at the window. Like the green room, this one faced the driveway, barns, arenas, and off into the fields.

The quilt on the bed was even more intricately designed than the first, in stars and log cabin blocks of blues and whites and reds. Rio stared at the richness of the space, both entranced and terrified. The colors touched her, yet David might as well have placed her in a room hung with gold tapestries.

"I'm afraid this one is a bit less pretty," he said. "Fit a little better for a fellow, I reckon."

"Stop apologizing," she heard herself say. "This will be fine. It's . . . beautiful."

Reluctantly, she set her case on the floor next to the bed, not daring to place anything on the amazing craftsmanship of the quilt.

"Not much cohesiveness between rooms—each is its own little theme park, isn't it?"

"Just shows you have an amazing talent for decorating," Rio said.

"Me?" David's eyes filled with amusement. "Good Lord, no. I can frame a room and hammer up drywall, but the rest is one hundred percent my mother. She comes from England once or twice a year and drives the people at the decorating shops into padded cells. She'll be here the middle of November, in fact."

"So when you picked the color chip in my kitchen . . ."

"It matched the floor." He shrugged. "My mother tells me it's important, the matching part." He hesitated, then spoke hesitantly. "I truly am sorry about your kitchen. I know I said it, but I do understand being here isn't the same."

One point for him. She nodded without replying.

"C'mon, then," he continued. "Let me show you the rest of what's up here so you'll know."

The bathroom was only a little ugly. Aged, shrimp-colored tile lined the tub surround and rose halfway up the rest of the walls. The glazing on a classic, pedestal sink had cracked over the years, and the linoleum had bubbled slightly in a few places. But, just as David had said, it was spotless, and it smelled like fresh citrus. Fluffy white and blue towels hung on a long towel bar, and a white wicker shelf unit held more linens. A pot of bright silk flowers up on one shelf added a cheery spot of color. David's mother, Rio assumed, had made the best of the old room.

"I use the bathroom downstairs," he said. "So this is private for you ladies."

"I thought you said it was ugly!" Bonnie laughed. "It's pretty."

Thank goodness for bubbly Bonnie saying all the right

things. Rio couldn't rid herself of the slight sourness in the pit of her stomach every time she opened another treasure trove of a room in this immense house. She barely knew what to say about anything.

"These last rooms are just as they were when we bought the house," David explained, leading the way down the hall. "A bit less dusty and filled with my own storage but unchanged from probably fifty years ago. The house, according to the original deed, is eighty-nine years old and was quite the showplace in its day."

It's quite the showplace now. Was he so jaded he couldn't see what he had?

One more room faced the house front. Its walls bore faded flowered paper and the floor was stacked with neat plastic bins along with a folding table and a sewing machine in its case.

"Mum uses this as her sewing room when she comes," David said. "The bins are full of fabrics, I guess. I don't come in here much."

"How long does your mother stay when she visits?" Rio had to wonder about a woman who specialized in drive-by interior decorating.

"A solid six weeks. Long enough to indulge her decorating fantasy-of-the-moment and get a bit of visiting in, as well. She's quite a girl is Mum."

Rio swallowed back the slightest twinge of envy. She'd been four when her mother had died, and she remembered her mostly from stories and pictures.

"This room is purely storage." David opened a door on the opposite side of the hallway.

The small, white-walled room had a sloped ceiling, a small window facing the back, and was filled nearly floor to ceiling with cardboard boxes and random pieces of furniture. The not-unpleasant scent of age filled her senses.

"It's my version of an attic," he explained. "I don't even remember what's in some of the boxes. There's a trunk in the corner came from England ten years ago. Shows you that, unlike my mother, I'm basically disorganized."

After showing them more rooms, each a different size and filled with a random assortment of junk, extra beds, exercise equipment, and horse tack, David pushed open a door at the end of the hallway. "The last room," he said. "Completely untouched although it probably has the most potential, as an office or lounge or some such thing."

The room was slightly bigger than the other bedrooms. Bare hardwood covered the floor, and the walls bore faded, purple-ish paint. Although the sloped ceiling reduced the back half of the room to three-quarters height, three windows brought in an abundance of light, and half-height bookshelves lined the back wall. A single bed covered in a quilt of periwinkles, purples, and turquoises stood on one side, and a large antique wardrobe served as a closet.

The barren space seemed to call her name. "This is beautiful."

"We call it the nothing room," said David.

"Could I stay in here instead?" she asked, before she could lose the bold nerve.

"Here?" He seemed honestly astounded. "But there's nothing to it."

"There's character. And a bed, and a place to put what's in this suitcase. We aren't going to be here long, and I'd rather have the ... sparseness."

"Of course," he said, still nonplussed. "You're welcome to it. But you know you can stay, you must stay, until the threat toward you and Bonnie is gone. Don't you want something more comfortable?"

To her, this space was steeped in more comfort than any *Better Homes and Gardens* room she'd already seen, as if it was perfectly suited to holding her tiny suitcase of possessions and her enormous trunk loads of mental junk.

"This is plenty comfortable."

"All right then." He swept his arm toward the room. "If you want it, it's yours."

"Do you have a plan? For this room?"

"Ah? Not in the near future."

"I thought maybe if you had a paint color chosen I could paint for you."

He turned in place to face her squarely. "Look here, love. Are you taking this bare room and offering to work for it out of some wrongheaded idea that you don't deserve simply to be here and be safe? You don't have to earn the right to be here."

He rested his fingers on her upper arm as casually as the word "love" flowed from his lips. The touch meant nothing, and yet her stomach filled with frenetic butterflies. A mix of spicy musk, sawdust, and faint farm odors befuddled her, and for an embarrassing moment she found no words—she only stared and swallowed. Then annoyance with herself returned and, ducking from his touch, she hardened her features and stared him down.

Long, long ago she'd learned not to accept free help. Free help equaled ulterior motives and ulterior motives usually required payment due later.

"I don't do charity well, Mr. Pitts-Matherson. We'll earn our keep, and we'll be out of your hair as soon as I know the police have Hector Black in custody."

He half-chuckled. "Please don't backslide into the 'Mister' title. Nobody even calls my father Mr. Pitts-Matherson. My great-grandfather, perhaps, the one who saddled us with the mouthful."

He so charmingly ignored her point, Rio couldn't decide whether to laugh or scowl harder. "Do they call you Dave? Or Davy?"

"Not if *they* want an answer. It's David. Or, if you must, Hey You."

She gave in at last to his incorrigible charisma with a small smile. "Hey You. I need you to understand that we're not here as charity cases. We're grateful, but I'll find a way to get back into a place of our own just as soon as possible. And, like it or not, I'll somehow work off our room and board."

For a moment he looked ready to argue further. At the last second, he nodded. "All right. Under one condition. Tell me *you* understand that I do not view either of you as a charity case and we agree today is a free day. You both unpack, and I'll show you around the place. We'll go into town, get acquainted with the area. No fires, no Hector, no police, no worries. Even your brother doesn't know where you are, right?"

"Yes," Rio said. "Since he took my car, it's safer for all of us if he can't find me."

"Then everything's good for now. I'll fetch your case and leave you to it."

Bonnie tripped back to her pretty green room, and Rio buried a twinge of envy at her sister's ability to forget and adapt. "I can go get my own suitcase."

"If you like. But I'm happy to do it."

All at once the whole situation—this amazing house, with this seriously attractive man she didn't know a thing about—seemed ludicrous. Who was he? What was she doing here?

"Why?"

"Why what?"

"Why are you 'happy' to get my suitcase? Why are you perfectly okay with having two city girls running from trouble invade your house?"

He laughed without hesitation. "I don't know any differently, Rio. Before my parents married, my mother and grandmother ran a guesthouse in northern England. When she married, Mum continued with her own version of the same in Kent. I grew up with guests coming in and out all the time. It seems perfectly natural to take in visitors."

A very, *very* slight weight lifted from Rio's shoulders. He was serious. And although the situation sucked, at the moment her life was as calm and safe as it had been in a while. She made a conscious effort to diffuse her anger.

"Rio? David?" Bonnie emerged from her room. "What was that you said about no police?"

Rio's heart skipped a beat at the pale confusion in her sister's eyes. Gone was the effervescent excitement. "What's wrong?"

"Why do you ask?" His eyes narrowed.

"There's a squad car sitting right out front of your house."

Chapter Five

AT THE SIGHT of the black-and-white cruiser, Rio's first reaction was relief. They'd found Hector and Paul. This whole exercise here at David's was moot, and she could go back home—or at least back to her neighborhood, start looking for a new place, and get her job back.

"This might be good news," she said.

Bonnie remained sober. "Police are never good news."

The attitude saddened Rio. Bonnie had never had run-ins with police. Even so, the place she'd lived all her life had shown her that help only came when something awful happened.

"I guess we'd better see what he wants," David said. "No worries. I'm sure Rio's right."

By the time they filed out the front door, the police officer, along with his gun, flashlight, and nightstick, stood frowning at the house.

"Good morning, Officer." David extended a hand. "You must be our new chief. We haven't met yet. I'm David Pitts-Matherson."

"Tanner Hewett," he replied crisply. "I replaced Chief Gunderson six weeks ago."

"And how is he doing?"

Chief Hewett scowled a little impatiently. "I haven't kept in touch with him, I'm afraid. I'm here on official business, Mr. Pitts-Matherson."

Without a blink at the curtness, David nodded. Bonnie stepped closer to Rio, and the fact that her sister still needed her calmed Rio's rising nervousness.

"What can I help you with, Chief?" David asked.

"I've been in touch with the Minneapolis PD who alerted me to the presence of one Arionna Montoya and her sister, Bonnie Montoya." Hewett's eyes swung slowly to Rio. "Can I assume you are Miss Montoya?"

She knew plenty of city cops, some wonderful and helpful, others suspicious and tough. This one's tone raised the hairs on the back of her neck. "Yes, I'm Arionna. This is Bonnie."

"Ran into a little trouble in the city, I hear."

"My home was set on fire. In some places that would be considered more than a little."

She'd learned long ago that using sarcasm to a police officer was unwise no matter what. She walked the line now, but, to her shock, David offered a sidelong smile of support.

"Have you come with news about the men involved in the fire?" he asked.

"I'm afraid there's been no sighting of the accused or Miss Montoya's brother."

Rio gritted her teeth. "The guilty, do you mean?"

"Miss Montoya, around here nobody is guilty until proven so. I came by to let you know we're aware of the situation and of why you're here." He turned back to David. "You do fully understand what you've taken on?"

"I understand my guests need a place to remain in safety until the men who started the fire in her home are caught."

"Miss Montoya, I've heard you were involved in a heated altercation with Mr. Black before the fire that may have contributed to him seeking revenge," Chief Hewett said. "I hope you'll work to keep your profile low here. Once we find these boys, there'll be a lot of questions for you as well as for them."

She didn't know how to respond. It sounded more like a threat than a promise of protection.

"Like, why would we want to do anything else?" Bonnie stepped out of her shadow. "We don't exactly want them to find us."

"Shhh, Bons, it's fine," Rio said.

"We definitely don't want them to find you first," Chief Hewett agreed. "This is a quiet place, and I'll be watching closely to make sure your big-city crime doesn't find its way to Kennison Falls."

Rio's mouth fell open.

Her big-city crime? Damn it, she hadn't even wanted to come here. Her neck hairs bristled again but a light touch on her arm startled her, and she looked into David's composed features.

"The town will remain quiet, Chief," David said. "With your help, of course. Can I assume that if we have any problems we can come directly to you?"

"Of course. But Miss Montoya, if you do hear from either Mr. Black or your brother, I expect you to contact my office immediately. We don't want problems escalating."

"Of course." Her mimicked retort came out more mockingly than she intended, and the chief's eyes pierced her with distrust.

He opened the door of his patrol car. David smiled pleasantly.

"Thanks for your time, Chief Hewett," he said. "I appreciate it."

Appreciate? She added brownnosing sycophant to their host's list of personality traits—this one not his most attractive. Once the cruiser had turned slowly around in the farm's gravel driveway and rolled far enough down the driveway so its driver couldn't see them, Bonnie stuck her tongue out.

"Ass," Rio muttered under breath.

"Quite so." David snorted, equally quietly.

His agreement surprised her. As did the pleasant expression on his face. Her insides roiled at the injustice of the veiled warnings, and yet David Pitts-Matherson looked as if he'd just shared a beer with a buddy.

"You seemed to get along with him just fine."

"I don't know him," he replied. "He strikes me as an arrogant sod, but it seemed wise to avoid antagonizing him while we need his help."

Rio backed down, chastened. She'd thought exactly the same thing, and still she'd let her underwear not only bunch but start chafing. She knew better.

"You're right," she mumbled.

"Rio." His voice pulled her eyes back to his. "This is a small town. Everyone has his or her own way even though as a rule they're all pretty friendly. Hewett is new, and he's trying to look tough. Ignore him."

His words didn't excuse, but his voice held certainty and promise that all was fine. Suddenly, his fitted riding pants and the black leather boot tops rising up the length of his calves seemed tough, protective, and anything but wussy.

"Thank you," she managed, still not willing to give up her wariness. "All police are nervous when it comes to gangs. I shouldn't react to one cop's skepticism."

"But he was a condescending jerk." Bonnie still watched the dust from the cruiser, her lip curled.

"He was," David said. "Let him bluster. At least he'll be on the lookout for us."

True enough. Better a cop with a tough attitude than one who didn't care at all. Hector was acting like a big-time gang leader even though he was no such thing. Mean, yes, but hardly important. Maybe a rigid hand was exactly what a street punk too cruel for his britches needed.

"Right, then." David smiled. "I'm going to change from my riding clothes, and after you unpack let's go have a look 'round town. We'll stock the kitchen, and if you're hungry for lunch, there's a nice café with excellent food."

"All right!" said Bonnie.

The familiar twist of resentment clenched in Rio's stomach. Lunch at a restaurant would mean another bite, beyond grocery shopping, out of her meager savings, or more charity on his part. She wanted neither. Since the fire, she had, maybe, two hundred dollars in her dwindling account, most of which had been earmarked for utilities, groceries, and back-to-school supplies for Bonnie.

She didn't need the utility money any longer . . .

Her throat constricted.

And she had no idea where Bonnie would even go to school or when she'd start. In Minneapolis school started after Labor Day, five weeks away. Please, God, she thought. Let them be well away from here in five weeks' time.

Gravel crunched in the driveway again, and Rio looked up half-expecting to see the chief returning. Instead, a green Ford Focus with a slightly scuffed door pulled toward them, bass thumping from its radio. The driver stopped, rolled down his window, and turned down a blaring rock song.

"'Lo, Dawson. Thanks for the noise abatement." David grinned at the good-looking young man who stuck his elbow and head out of the window.

"No prob. Just dropping her off."

David bent his knees and peered into the car. "Hey, Kim. Lesson today?"

"Yup." A cheery voice carried to them from the passenger seat. "A show and a Pony Club certification in the next month. Thanks for letting Jackson stay here while we work on everything."

Rio had no idea what the conversation meant, but she recognized the awe on her sister's face as she fixated on the young driver. He looked vaguely familiar, with bright brown, David-colored eyes and wide handsome cheekbones nearly sculpted into adult handsomeness. Dark sable hair cascaded in gentle waves to his shoulders. He gave Bonnie a careless, friendly wave. Rio gave her a tap on the ankle with her toe. "Stop staring," she whispered.

Bonnie grinned for the first time in fifteen minutes.

"Kim, hang on," David said, as if he'd just had a brilliant idea. "Jill's not here yet. Have you got a moment? There's someone I'd like you to meet."

"Sure."

The passenger door opened, and a blond head appeared on the other side of the car. The girl looked to be about Bonnie's age, but she was the bright, sweet-and-lovely, pretty counterpart to Bonnie's dark, sultry beauty.

"Do you still need me?" the kid named Dawson asked.

"Nope." Kim tapped on the car top. "Get out of here. Thanks for the ride. And I get the car tomorrow."

"Yeah, whatever."

Dawson waved again, the Focus exited in the tracks of the police car, and Bonnie, her cheeks pink, wordlessly watched it go. Bonnie's discovery that batting her long lashes had a powerful effect on males was what had gotten her into trouble with Hector. Rio would have loved cloistering her somewhere far from the opposite sex, but since that was impossible, at least Focus-driving Dawson looked a whole lot safer than Hector or the Boyfriend.

"Bonnie, I'd like to introduce you to Kim Stadtler." David's proper manners were back. "Kim, this is Bonnie Montoya."

"Hey, Bonnie! Welcome to Bridge Creek."

"And this is her sister, Rio. They'll be guests for a couple of weeks. Visiting from the city."

"Rio. That's awesome," Kim said. "I've always wanted a prettier name."

"Short for Arionna." Rio smiled, unable to resist the girl's unpretentiousness. "And I'll trade you. Kim is pretty in my opinion. Rio's just weird."

"Done! Nice to meet you, Kim," said Kim.

"I'm going to change for a trip to town," David said. "Could you take Bonnie and Rio on a little tour of the barn? Introduce them to Jackson." He looked at them. "If you don't mind waiting to unpack."

"Sure," said Kim.

"Sure," echoed Bonnie.

Unlike with crazy Chief Tanned Hewett or whatever his name was, Rio felt welcomed by Kim. And she didn't have to make a word of conversation as Kim and Bonnie fell into an easy chatter about their ages, horses, and the "awesome place" that was Bridge Creek.

"Awesome" barely described the stable's facilities. Kim led them through a twenty-four-stall barn with polished wooden stall doors, a neatly swept cement aisle, and fancy name plaques on each stall. Behind the barn, Kim pointed out two indoor arenas, one small and one much larger, and to the fields beyond the pastures filled with odd-shaped obstacles she called the cross-country course.

They followed Kim along a lane between several paddocks and slipped through one of three gates along the lane where she introduced them to a beautiful, light-brown horse with dark-black legs and a white stripe down its face. Rio swallowed back her first twinge of envy.

"This is Jackson," Kim said.

Fifteen minutes passed while Bonnie willingly let Kim instruct her in all things barn- and horse-related. She set her to work on Jackson's dusty sides with a stiff-bristled brush, and Rio stood by reaching now and then for Jackson's muzzle, letting him nibble at her T-shirt, forgetting about the life she'd run from for a few magical moments. She tasted, fleetingly but in person, the life she'd fantasized about for twenty years.

"Omygosh! Isn't this just the kind of barn we're going to have?" Bonnie burst the fantasy.

For one instant Rio wanted to shake her sister. Couldn't she figure out how dead that dream was now? But she caught herself. There was no point in rubbing Bonnie's nose in reality at this point. It would all hit the fan soon enough.

"We're moving out West to our own ranch when I'm done with school," Bonnie continued, in a shortened version of the story she'd told David just days before. "Rio's been planning it since *she* was in high school."

At the prompt, Rio remembered the name of the town: Bear Falls, Wyoming. They'd stopped there for lunch on one day of the Boys and Girls Club trip she'd won in a raffle back in tenth grade. She'd seen some of her country's most iconic sights: Mount Rushmore, and the Crazy Horse monument, and Wall Drug before reaching Devils Tower with the group. But it had been the ad in the window of a little real estate office next to the Ma and Pa café in Bear Falls—population two hundred and twenty-seven—that had captured her imagination.

Two hundred acres, house and barn, with outbuildings. Needs some repair. Wooded and secluded. Suitable for horses or cattle.

"That's so strange." Kim's cheerful voice brought Rio back to the present. "Ever since my mom got remarried a year and a half ago, my stepdad has offered to let us move to a bigger farm, but Mom refuses. So they're just fixing up our old place. It's kind of cool, everything's getting updated. Like David's doing here and Jill is doing at their house. But I think it would be fun to move somewhere new. Where are you moving to?"

"It's going to be a while until that happens," Rio said.

"Probably Wyoming." Bonnie ignored her. "There are always farms and land for sale. We can't wait to get away from the city and have horses of our own."

"That's a pretty perfect dream."

"It's not a dream, it's a goal."

Bonnie parroted the promise Rio had been drumming into her head since their father had died. Now the words of that promise pierced like daggers.

"Sure." She forced a smile. "We've just had a little setback."

"Setback?" Kim asked.

"We had a fire at our house in Minneapolis," Bonnie explained. "That's why we're staying here until we can find a new place."

"Oh my gosh! That's awful." Kim stopped working on the horse and turned fully to Rio. "I'm so sorry."

She clearly meant every sympathetic word. She was very hard not to like.

"Thank you."

"So, do you guys ride?" Kim asked. "Can you at least have some fun while you're here?"

"I've never ridden," Bonnie said. "Rio has once or twice, but only in Western saddles."

Kim grinned. "Western is awesome. But if you try English, you'll never want to do anything else."

The two girls launched into the new topic. Rio tuned them out and turned to watch a dark-gray cat leap gracefully up and over a stall door. Another cat, this one a wiry calico, joined the first. One stall door just down the aisle hung open with the front end of a wheelbarrow sticking out of it and tuneless whistling emanating from inside. A very short hallway off the tidy aisle led to the smaller of the two indoor arenas. So amazing. So opulent.

The acreage for sale in that real estate window so long ago had seemed worth a fortune to sixteen-year-old Rio. The surmised costs of this horse palace boggled her mind.

"Did you get the penny tour?"

She turned at the sound of his voice and did a double take that shamed Bonnie's earlier Dawson-gaping. Jeans now set off David's long legs and hugged his waist like a lover's embrace. A soft, white, button-down shirt had been tucked in but left open at his neck, and the sleeves were rolled up to his elbows. His thick brown hair curled in damp waves, and he smelled of pine and spice.

"I'd think you'd have to charge much more than a penny for this place," she replied, and immediately regretted the slight judgment in her tone.

He frowned. "My bank creditors would like me better if I did book tours and collect money. And gave it all to them."

She knew he meant nothing by off-handed jokes about money, but the man could not be hurting no matter what he said.

"Well, my bank creditors are crap out of luck," she said.

Discomfort shadowed his face. "Yeah. Rio, I'm sorry."

She shrugged, swallowed away the omnipresent lump in her throat, and changed the subject. "If we're going to town, maybe we should go."

"Right. Good," David said. "A short drive is all."

"Could I stay here and watch Kim's lesson?" Bonnie asked. "I'd rather do that."

"I don't think so," Rio said. "You need to stick with us and help pick out what you want."

"You know what I eat," she said. "You shop at home. Please, Rio, just let me hang out here."

"It's okay with me," Kim said.

"It's up to you, of course," David added, "but she'll be fine. Kim and Jill will watch over her well. She might as well get to know the place."

The one thing Rio had figured to have some control over, some sense of home with, had been Bonnie. What had happened to the scared teen hiding from the police chief? Here she was, jumping into the pool without Rio as a life preserver.

Grow up, Rio. You always say you never want to be her mother.

"All right, if you're sure." She looked to Kim.

"Absolutely."

Rio turned warning eyes on her sister. "Be careful."

"Duh."

David chuckled.

Rio could already see how Bonnie, with her extrovert's personality, might take quickly to Bridge Creek. Rio felt slightly ill at ease in a place where nobody seemed to be on guard or at least on watch for danger to erupt.

"What do you think? Shall we go? Leave the little girls to their gossip?"

That's when it dawned on her she was about to head off alone with the man, his muscles, and his accent. She glanced hopefully at Bonnie, but her sister didn't even look up from her newest lesson on how to pick up a horse's foot. There was no hope she would change her mind about coming to town.

"All right."

"Do you need anything from the house?" David asked, when they'd reached the yard. "Take as long as you like. There's no hurry."

"I should grab my purse."

"I'll bring the car 'round to the front."

The butler-esque phrase seemed to clear her head. Or maybe it was just being out of the barn where his delicious masculine scent couldn't scramble her brain.

She faced him. "You're going above and beyond for us, and I can't thank you enough. But I hope you won't keep waiting on us hand and foot. I'm not used to that."

He frowned. "I know you're not. You're used to making your own way, and I respect that. But you'll find we do for each other around here. And you have an incredible number of things to figure out. They don't all have to be sorted this minute, but when you need help we'll be here. Go grab what you need," he finished. "See you in a couple of minutes."

She made her way back to the stark room she'd chosen and was pleased with the sense of comfort the empty space still gave her. For one moment it was like standing on a blank canvas, no blemishes, nobody else's marks on it, no expectations of what should be on it or in her life.

Her shoulders relaxed slightly.

One problem at a time. She could learn to do that. The only truly immediate problem she had was how she was going to survive a closed-in car ride with David Pitts-Mattherson without his presence and that voodoo scent he wore turning her logical brain to mush.

Her logical brain was all she had left.

Chapter Six

DAVID SHIFTED IN the leather seat of his Forester and glanced at Rio, who, with her chin in her palm, had lost some of her rigidity. If she wasn't comfortable in his presence, at least she seemed resigned rather than resentful. Now if only he could bring back the smile he'd seen exactly twice since meeting her. It wasn't fair that such a stunning woman should have to wear this guarded a look all the time. From what he remembered of her rare happy face, it turned her into a radiant beauty. And him into jelly.

Not that he could blame her for wearing the weight of the world on her slender, angry shoulders.

"Not much to see until we get a bit closer to town." He broke the silence and nodded to the expanses of corn and wheat fields.

"It's incredible," she replied. "I forget there's this much empty space in the world."

"After living in the city, this must seem barren. There'll be houses here soon, though. Land is getting sold acre by acre."

"That's sad."

"We're just far enough from large cities that it's taken a while for the growth to reach us. But Faribault and Northfield, the biggest cities in this area, are spreading outward."

"Until just now, they were foreign names on a map." She turned to him, her eyes big and blue. "This could be Mars."

He grinned. "You might be even more convinced of that after meeting the *townsfolk*." He drawled out the word with an exaggerated American accent.

It had taken him plenty long enough to fit into the quirky community—not that small English towns were any less strange—but he'd grown to love the people and this place he'd called home the past ten years.

"I've already met the local law. I'm a little afraid to show my face."

She turned a grimace into a passable smile, and his pulse thrummed. He'd been right about the smile. It set off her rich russet hair like sunshine set off a lake.

"Don't worry about him. The word is this job is a bit of a step down for our Chief Hewett. He arrived thinking this is the lawless West, and he's the man to clean it up. He'll mellow out. If your brother and his mates happen to show up, they'd not get far. Kennison Falls manages to take care of its own."

"I'm not one of its own, though."

"That'll change, I promise."

"Oh my gosh!"

Her cry and gasp nearly made him swerve. He stared at her and then toward the "Welcome to Kennison Falls" sign, and he did swerve. Straight onto the shoulder and to a stop. In front of the sign stood a very large vehicle shaped like a giant hot dog.

"What the devil?" He laughed.

"Wonder Weenies," Rio read off its side, and for the first time in his experience, her sapphire eyes flooded with mirth. "Seriously? This is the home of the Giant Wonder Weenie?"

"Never seen it before in my life." David stared at the bright monstrosity. "There's a sign on it."

"'Weenie Feed Fund-raiser for the Kennison Falls Library Association,'" Rio read. "'August twenty-first and twenty-second. Sponsored by The Loon Feather and Bert's IGA.' Friends of yours?" Her wide, sweet lips parted into an enchanting bow.

David swallowed. So many of their conversations had taken place under such dark circumstances; he'd never studied how appealing her lips were when they moved. How their plump fullness fit perfectly on her slightly cherubic face.

"The Loon Feather is a town institution—a great restaurant and meeting place. Bert's is where to go and complain about politics or the weather while you're picking up your groceries. I'd reckoned to bring you both places."

"I'd definitely ask to go to the Weenie Feed if it was sooner than August twenty-first. Now, that's a meal worth leaving the big city for."

So, she could joke about her situation—given the proper circumstances. He tucked the knowledge away and put his foot back on the accelerator.

"It's only two weeks from now. Maybe we can get you to the Weenie Feed."

"I certainly hope not," she said, her smile leaving her eyes and freezing in place as the momentary cheeriness dissipated.

THEY ROLLED ALONG Main Street, and Rio knew David watched her, assessing her reactions. His gaze sent relaxing, almost physical, starbursts of tingles across her skin—a sensation she could definitely get addicted to—and she took in the appealing downtown under the narcotic haze of pleasure. She didn't want to like what she saw, but the small town ambience was so different from the harshness pervading the streets of her city neighborhood. Here charm bloomed like the flowers in the storefront window boxes, and a dozen or more businesses had adopted blue-and-white striped awnings that gave the whole main street a coordinated sweetness.

She read the business signs: "Dewey's Gas 'n' Garage," "Joey's Barber Shop," "The Curly Cue Salon," "Mamie's Attic," "The Bread Basket."

"How the heck do you pronounce *that*?" She pointed at a white sign hanging from a post before a street front law office. The names VOSEJPKE and HORESJI looked like letters tacked against the wood by a three-year-old.

David chuckled. "I feel for you. There's a lot of Czech

heritage along with the Scandinavian. Give 'em a try." He slowed enough so she could look closely.

"Vo-sej—" She shook her head. "I haven't got a clue."

"*Vo-sayp-kah* and *Ho-rish*."

"I just decided I could never live here." She allowed herself a quick laugh that relaxed something inside. How could she hold on to pure anger in a town with a Wiener Mobile and words containing consonants that should never get near one another?

"There's the police station." David pointed out a small brick building.

"Is there much crime here?" Rio asked.

"I expect there's crime everywhere," he replied. "But in a town of nine hundred, everyone knows most everyone else. There are four officers, two just part-time, and I think they deal mostly with thefts, vandalism, curfew violations, underage drinking. But in the ten years I've lived here, there hasn't been a murder in town, and our gangs consist of factions of kids from the different small towns that feed into the same bigger school district."

"No wonder the chief took an instant dislike to me. I'm the worm in his perfect apple."

"Hey, none of that chat." David glowered, his voice stern in genuine admonition. "You're nobody's worm, Rio. I don't know you well, but I know that. You're tough and brave. Don't let him get you to belittle yourself, even in jest."

His gentle scolding warmed her even as it shocked her. David had struck her as so passive, so amenable to every situation. His protectiveness—of her, no less—even in this back-door kind of way, made her feel safe for the first time.

"Thank you," she said quietly.

His scowl vanished. "Believe me, this town is nice, but it's definitely not perfect. Except, maybe, for that place. The Loon Feather, just across the street."

She took in the pretty corner building with its gray brick walls that all but glowed in the afternoon sun, and the striking mural of a loon carrying its chick on its back that took up nearly an entire side wall.

"My gosh. It's all so pristine. Everything shines. Do they repaint it all every night like they do at Disneyland?"

"Hardly. It's 'pristine' because pretty much everything we've passed so far, even The Loon itself, got nailed by a category four tornado two years ago this month."

Her jaded disdain for the picture-perfect town turned to guilt. "Oh! I'm sorry. That explains the newly planted trees and the empty lots. It must have been pretty bad."

"Devastating, yes. Not everyone has been able to rebuild, sadly, but thank God nobody died, so it also made everyone a bit closer. Disaster can bring out the best in people."

Slight swelling closed up her throat. She sympathized with those who hadn't been able to rebuild. She knew the feeling—an empty future weighed almost more than a person could handle.

"Are you hungry?"

She forced down the lump at the base of her esophagus. She'd spoken to all the bank people and insurance representatives she'd been able to reach in the five days she'd been at the shelter. She could do no more until after the weekend. Meanwhile, she wasn't about to start leaning on his charity already. She'd leaned on him so literally and with such weakness the night of the fire. He didn't need to keep seeing her as a poor needy woman.

"I'm fine just getting a few things at the grocery store."

"All right, what I meant was, would you join me for lunch? I know where you'll get a proper welcome to town—friendlier than the one from our new constable."

"That wouldn't take much." She raised her brows. "I'd get a cheerier reception from the town undertaker."

"Undertaker?" His unexpected laugh was infectious. "I doubt they even call them that in Dodge anymore."

"What does a proper-speaking English duke know about Dodge?"

His brown eyes took on a rich, velvety sparkle, and he adopted a passable Southern drawl. "Why, you'd be surprised, Miz Rio. Even dukes can learn lower-class ways given enough time."

She tried to hide a smile and execute a nonchalant shrug. "Fine, you're on. Take me to this super-friendly place. If the greeting isn't as good as you say, you're paying."

His brows knotted again. "I'm paying anyway."

"I can—"

He held up a finger. "This was my idea. It wasn't my intention to make you spend extra money your first day. Get the next one if you like."

He'd done it again—protected her from herself. He'd

allowed her to save her meager funds and yet save face. The man was sharp. Or truly kind. Or slick-tongued. She honestly couldn't tell which.

Five minutes later he led her into the wood-and-calico interior of what he reiterated was the town's favorite gathering place. She stood face-to-face with a large, neat birdcage, well-appointed with hanging toys and mirrors and occupied by two cockatiels, one gray, one white. A printed sign outside the cage read, "Cotton's new phrase is 'Have some pie.'"

David laughed. "This phrase is brand-new. Effie's going for shameless promotion now. Brilliant."

Rio frowned. "I don't get it."

At that moment the gray bird tilted his head and trilled out a familiar song she knew came from some old television show. When he finished, the white bird gave a short whistle and hopped across its bar. "Howdee, Stra-jer."

Delight bubbled through her. "Oh! That's so cool."

"Meet the official greeters of Kennison Falls, Cotton and Lester. Lester's the singer, and he'll remember which song he sang for you. From now on, you're with the Andy Griffith team. Cotton used to do nothing but stare—now she's cock o' the run. Can't stop her talking."

"Wekkom, kom in," the bird said.

"Told you you'd be greeted properly," David said.

Enchanted, Rio put a knuckle up against the cage bars. *The Andy Griffith Show*. That's what the tune had been. "Do you have a song?" Lester bumped his beak against her skin but didn't bite.

"Same one," he said. "Everybody is one of two. Andy's

theme or 'The Colonel Bogey March.' You know, *Bridge on the River Kwai*?"

"Insane," she said. "It seems like it has to be faked somehow."

"Not at all. Canny little birds, these. Survived the tornado. They keep everyone cheerful without fail." He leaned toward the cage. "Cotton. Have some pie. Have some pie."

"That means something?"

"It's what they're teaching her to say next. Say it every time you come in now, until she knows it."

"Have some pie?"

"Hav, hav," said Cotton, and Rio laughed outright.

In the mostly empty main café, David walked straight to a table against a far wall filled with shelves that held classic old coffee and cookie canisters. Each table in the room bore a different calico or print fabric tablecloth and contrasting napkins resulting in a delightful hodge-podge.

"Why, hello, David. It's a surprise to see you here in the middle of the day."

A tall, trim older woman with sun-worn cheeks and an impressive gray braid that hung over her shoulder and nearly to her waist held out two menus.

"Claudia?" David lifted his brows. "Likewise. How did you get pressed into service?"

"You haven't heard yet. Effie took a tumble in her garden yesterday and broke her hip. They're talking replacement. We're scrambling to fill in for her."

"That's dreadful!"

Rio immediately caught the true concern in their voices.

"It is. Meanwhile, I took today as hostess and waitress. Gladdie will take tomorrow. Karla will stay on until she has to start teaching the last week of August. We'll manage. Now tell me. Who have we here? The new resident from Minneapolis is my guess. Hello, dear. Rio, isn't it?"

Rio stared, flabbergasted. How did this grayed, lined woman-left-over-from-Woodstock remotely know who she was? The too-easy familiarity gave her a dull stomachache, although she didn't see a shred of malice anywhere in the woman's smiling face.

"It's all right," David soothed, reading what must have been a fabulous example of disbelief on her face. "News moves swiftly through a small town. You'll get used to it."

"Awesome." She held her tongue against further retorts. She didn't need any more enemies. Then again, she didn't need an entire town keeping watch on her either.

"Claudia Lindquist, may I introduce Arionna Montoya? Rio is preferred, though, yes?" He looked to her for confirmation, and she nodded. "Rio, this is one of our . . . what are you, Claudia? The original town mum, I should think."

"I'm certainly ancient enough." The woman's laugh rang musically. "Very pleased to meet you, Rio. Welcome."

"Thank you. Glad to meet you, too."

Only she wasn't. Claudia Lindquist knew too much already, and she'd learned it too quickly, reminding Rio of her step-grandmother—a woman she'd be pleased *never* to see again.

"So, what'll it be, dear ones? The only things we don't have are Effie's pies. I'm afraid nobody can re-create those. But Tiffany over at The Bread Basket has sent us some cheesecake. It's a pretty good substitute."

"Tiffany's chocolate cheesecake," David said with a grimace of pleasure. "Glad not to have to choose between that and Effie's pies. Okay. Give us just a sec?"

"You got it, handsome. Rio, if you want that cheesecake after lunch, it's on us. Sort of a welcome-to-town offering." Claudia turned for the kitchen, her braid swinging back over her shoulder.

"You're wrong. This *is* Disneyland. She's just in costume, isn't she?"

"I told you not to judge a town by its new police chief. And don't worry about everyone knowing you. The network around here makes satellite technology look like two tins and a string. The town will take you in and keep you safe if that's what you need. It's a good place."

She could barely imagine a good little place anymore. Her home had been a good little place.

"I'm sure it is."

"Rio." He reached a long-fingered hand across the table to where she toyed nervously with her napkin. When he covered her hand with his, she tried to draw away, but a sweet spark of comfort raced through her and she changed her mind—not liking that she had. "I don't pretend to know what you're going through. But give us a chance to help. It hasn't been long enough yet to get everything sorted, but we will."

"We?" She did withdraw her hand then, although it

left her feeling torn and cold when his warmth was gone. "What do you mean 'we'? Look, I am thankful to be here, don't get me wrong. But you don't know me. I don't know you. This whole situation is just a little weird, don't you think?" She held up her hand when his mouth opened. "Rhetorical question. The point is, I will figure out what to do next. Don't spend any time trying to solve my problems—you don't need to do that. I don't want you to do that."

To his credit, he seemed to take no offense to her tone. "I promise you nobody will make your decisions for you. I only mean that we'll do everything we can to make you feel comfortable here until you can go back to Minneapolis."

How did he do that? Defuse everything. Give her nothing to fight. Her strength was in her ability to push back, to solve, to be tough. In defense she changed the subject.

"Effie must be the regular cook?"

"The owner," David replied. "And the pastry chef. Her pies are locally legendary. Her husband, Bud, is the main cook. Our high school music teacher, Karla Baxter, works here over the summer, but she's got to head back to school soon. Effie normally hires short-term help over the winter. Looks like it'll need to happen sooner."

A bubble of a thought rose in Rio's mind, and for the first time her churning brain stopped treading water. She'd spent the last eleven years of her life working in diners and restaurants. Four different eateries, although they'd all been a fair amount sleazier than this one. The best had been the most recent, where the food had been decent and the tips actually helpful. If she only had a way to get from David's house into town . . .

"What?" David's quizzical grin caused her cheeks to heat. She hadn't meant to let her musings show on her face.

"Nothing. Just remembering the life of a waitress. It's not an easy job, really."

"That's what you were doing?"

"Yes."

"And all the cookbooks you lost in the fire. Did working in restaurants have any connection to them?"

She lost all words. Nobody ever made that link. She'd had two kitchen managers over the years who'd been her secret role models. Only one, Florin, a German student working his way through culinary arts school, had seriously shared his knowledge with her. There wasn't much haute cuisine you could create in a burger joint on Lake Street, but she'd loved the few things she'd picked up during her stints as a line cook.

"I like working around food."

"I pretend to." His smile turned self-conscious. "I learned to cook in Scouts."

"Like, Boy Scouts? Seriously?" Her mood lightened again, this time at the mental image of stiff, proper David Pitts-Matherson in a khaki shirt and kerchief grubbing over a campfire.

"What, you don't think I could have been a Boy Scout?"

"Anyone can be a Boy Scout. My brother was a Boy

Scout. For about twenty seconds." She grinned at him. "Is that where you learned to ride a horse?"

"I learned to *ride* from my father, the Olympic champion. I learned *Scouting* from my mother, the Yorkshire girl who wanted me to love the outdoors. She was even a leader for a time."

"I suppose you'll tell me you were an Eagle Scout, too."

"We don't have them in England. We have Queen's Scouts, but no, I wasn't that dedicated. I was a bit of a rebel, liked to go off and survive on my own."

"Say what?" Her disbelief couldn't be contained.

None of his information meshed with the picture he presented. A loner? She'd only known him for a few hours, and he seemed like a guy who could calm a storm at the center of a failing universe.

"Well, my father would be pleased you don't find me the type. Predictable and by the book, that's what he'd rather have from me."

"Your father sounds kind of rigid."

"That, love, would be an understatement."

They ordered, and despite her initial reluctance to let David pay, Rio found herself digging into a hot Rueben sandwich like a starving trucker. They'd eaten plenty well at the shelter, but something about the laid-back atmosphere and the peaceful, homey décor of the restaurant acted like an appetite stimulant. Rio stuffed the entire meal down before she knew it. When Claudia brought two pieces of cheesecake without even asking, Rio groaned.

"I'm gonna need a hospital gurney and medics to wheel me out of here."

David laughed. "Aw, it's just a little piece of cheese-cake. One moment of celebration that you're here safely. Fellas like it when women don't eat like little butterflies."

"You're evil." She pushed her fork tines into the velvety chocolate. "Attractive or not, pigging out isn't my usual style."

"Who said anything about a pig? No pigs here—just chocolate."

"Evil," she repeated over her stuffed mouth.

When she finished, despite feeling exactly like the stuffed pig David said didn't exist, she knew she wanted the recipe for the cheesecake. It had been a long time since she'd been so completely indulged.

"I'll bet Tiffany would share it," David said when she voiced the desire. "She's given out other recipes."

Small towns, she thought. Probably no big secrets in the recipe world either.

"Are you going to be in town long?" Claudia asked, when David had paid and Rio stood, rubbing her stomach as if it were bruised.

"I honestly have no idea. There are a few details with the house to figure out ... the house in the fire," she added, not sure how much Claudia knew.

"I heard." The older woman clucked in sympathy. "I'm so sorry. Well, I hope you stay a good long while. Come back anytime."

Rio almost blurted her question then. Almost wondered out loud how much help the restaurant needed. But she had no way to get here every day. No real chef skills. No idea how long she'd be able to stay and work. She certainly didn't want it to be long.

"Thank you."

"Right, then, cheers, Claudia," David added.

"You devil with that accent. You come back soon."

"Can't stay away."

The air sat still over the main street, hot but not oppressive. It hadn't been this warm in Minneapolis for weeks—how could sixty-five miles make such a huge difference? Rio lifted her eyes to the pure blue sky, amazed. No wires, no crumbling roofs, no obstructions.

"Feeling any better about this place?"

"You know that weird magical land in the old musical that shows up only once every hundred years or so? That's 'this place.'"

"Brigadoon?"

"That one."

With a laugh, he started down the sidewalk. "Maybe so. Regardless, let's go 'round the block to get to the car and walk off a calorie or two of that dessert."

A good idea, she had to admit, even if she did feel like her belly needed a sling, and walking sounded gross. A nervous flutter joined the sense of fullness as she fell in beside him. It wasn't his presence alone causing the little butterflies. It was this time-wasting attitude he seemed to have. Nothing seemed vital. They'd left two teenagers alone with horses. They had shopping to do. She had to get unpacked. Bonnie had to . . .

Had to what?

For the first time in countless years, it hit her that she didn't *have* to do anything, not get to work, not figure out what to make for dinner, not keep track of Paul. She was aimless.

She stopped dead in front of a store window she hadn't noticed on the drive into town. Tattoo art from the sweet to the skeletal decorated the plate-glass window, and letters in gold gothic typeface read "Th-INK Designs—Art for Your Skin. Nora Pint, Damian Pint, artists." The few designs on display captured her. She loved tattoos—not so much full body ink or even heavy sleeves or cuffs. But a beautifully rendered picture—

"Strange what people will do to themselves, isn't it?"

She met his eyes, and the peaceful calm just starting to return boiled back into defensiveness. "What do you mean?"

"What's that phrase—whatever floats your boat? I think skin is quite nice on its own, so why shove needles full of ink into the cells trying to look prettier or tougher?"

"Oh?" An acerbic bite laced her words. "You mean like this?"

She turned away from him, hooked a thumb in the back of her waistband, and dragged it down three inches.

Chapter Seven

THE PALE SWATH of skin Rio exposed stopped the vital flow of air to David's lungs. Or so he truly believed. He'd seen a woman's backside before. He'd seen many tattoos. But he stared at the exquisite picture she presented, and his body tightened as if she'd stripped to nothing.

The horse's head and body formed a heart shape a full four inches tall and at least that wide. It was the most unique tattoo he'd ever seen. The fine, chiseled head was centered at the small of her back and its mane swept up and left to create half the heart. The horse's back and tail formed the other half. What enticed him most, however, was the end of the tail—the point of the heart, that disappeared below the seat of her jeans. Her thumb hid the top of the cleft between her cheeks. He'd never given a rat's bum about anyone's tattoo, but this one he wanted to follow with his eyes, his fingertips, maybe partway down with his lips . . .

His breathing resumed with an audible hitch. Heaviness hit painfully behind his fly, and heat rose in his face over such a shallow reaction. "That's . . . amazing."

"You never know who you might insult, do you?"

To his disappointment she lifted her waistband back up and smoothed her purple T-shirt back in place.

"I'm sorry. I had no idea . . ."

"I have others, too." She ignored his too-late apology, and her eyes blazed, a little disproportionately to the situation he thought, but he let her continue. "Would you like to get them out of the way, as well, so you know exactly what kind of person you're dealing with?"

She yanked up the right leg of her jeans, and David closed his eyes as her ankle and long, smooth calf appeared along with an owl on a branch. Once again, the artwork astounded him.

"Rio, I . . ."

"And here." She started to tug at the neckline of the T-shirt, her face now a flushed pink that only set off the blaze of her incredible hair.

"Stop, Rio." He grasped her upper arms and held her as he'd have held a raging child. She wriggled for a moment, then stood quietly, looking at the ground. "I'm truly sorry. I did not mean to insult you, but you're right, I was insensitive. All I've ever known were military tattoos, and they were only a way to commemorate something I had no desire to remember. I've paid no attention to artful tattoos, so I admit to ignorance and prejudice. Yours are beautiful."

To his astonishment she stared at him, angrier than ever, her fists clenched at her sides.

"Now you stop it! Stop . . . smoothing everything over. Stop taking away everything I can cling to that's maddening. Stop—" The anger melted in a flood of real tears. The first he'd seen except for the few at the fire scene.

"Here now." Awkwardly, uncomfortably, he took her into a hug. It was one thing to offer words of encouragement, even apology. It was another entirely to touch her this way. Especially when his body was confusing the hell out of him with its reaction to the stupid horse tail.

"I'm sorry," she sobbed. "I don't really give a crap if you like tattoos."

He chuckled at the defiance that swam up through her sadness. "I know."

"The owl is supposed to remind me to keep my head, stay smart. There's nothing anywhere right now that makes me feel remotely capable. I can't do or fix anything. I can't even stop from crying. I don't cry."

"Even when you've lost most of your physical world? C'mon, love, give yourself a break. Allow yourself to grieve."

She relaxed in his arms. A wave of flutters joined the heaviness in his body, and tenderness melted him like a hot breeze. "You were in the army?" she asked. "Is there anything you can't fix with all your worldly experience?"

"There are so many things I can't fix," he said. "So I try to concentrate on what I can do. Just as you do."

She pulled away, but her movements had softened, and she stayed close rather than step away from him. He could see the struggle in her eyes—her fierce need to survive on her own terms warring with her need for help.

A smattering of freckles danced across her nose. They were so faint in her unusual, deep-toned skin he hadn't noticed them before. She didn't look like the typical, fragile-to-sunlight redhead. In fact, in spite of the tears she stabbed at with her slender fingers, she didn't look fragile at all.

"I'm fine," she said simply.

"I think what's needed is to get the shopping done and head back to the house. You'll feel better once you have your things unpacked."

"And know Bonnie hasn't gotten into trouble."

"Does she get into trouble often?"

A range of emotions he couldn't read flitted through her eyes before she wiped her nose a final time. "No. It's just Hector. I don't know why Paul introduced Bonnie to him; he's never wanted her involved with the gangs. He must have owed Hector something big."

"If I'm honest, I have to admit I wasn't too impressed with your brother. When he abandoned you and Bonnie the other night, I thought it cowardly."

"You're right." Her lips thinned.

"Tell me about you three. How did you get such a unique name and that red hair when the other two are so . . . opposite?"

They fell into step with each other again, leaving the tattoos and all the emotions they'd unleashed behind.

"We had different mothers."

The bluntness startled him. "Really? Bonnie is your half sister?"

"Yes. She and Paul are full siblings, but we've never

paid any attention to that. We're family. My mother was a fair-skinned Irish girl named Colleen Flannigan. She gave me a name she thought would offset the Montoya. She died when I was four, and my dad married again almost right away."

"Paul and Bonnie's mother?"

She nodded. "Dad was a quarter or three-eighths Mexican, the rest, he used to tell us, was tough, loyal stray. When I was little I actually thought it was cool to be part stray. Portia, though, was Latina through and through, and gorgeous. Bonnie looks a lot like her."

"But she's not around anymore either?"

"She never wanted children. Paul was an accident. Portia managed him because her mother, Yaya we called her, watched us most of the time." Her features eased slightly in absentminded amusement. "It may be too much information, but Portia made my father get a vasectomy. Almost six years later—surprise."

"No bloody way."

"Yeah." She gave a little ironic snort. "Dad adored Bonnie, but for Portia that was one child too many. She stayed two more years, but she hadn't signed up for motherhood, she said. Dad had failed her. So, she left. I think she lives in Nashville now, but that's hearsay."

"And your father? Chase told me you've been on your own for quite some time."

"He was killed in a truck accident when I was seventeen. He'd been paying Yaya to stay and watch us while he was driving cross-country. By the time he died, I'd figured out a few ugly truths about my step-grandmother, like the fact she wasn't with us because she loved us but loved Papa's earning potential. I never knew how to tell my father without worrying him. When I was eighteen and emancipated, I kicked Yaya out. I don't know where she is."

The story amazed him. Most eighteen-year-olds he knew today were obsessed with themselves and their smartphones not the welfare of their families. He himself had certainly been a selfish teenager, and it had taken the British Army to whip him into shape.

"That has to have been hard."

"Sometimes," she agreed. "I miss my dad. He worked a lot, but when he was home it was like Thanksgiving and Fourth of July all rolled into one."

"This explains a lot about why you've got too much responsibility. It doesn't seem fair."

"My life was what it was, and is what it is. Life is a series of puzzles. And now there's another puzzle to solve."

Her pragmatism had a sad, or maybe just weary, edge to it. His heart fell a little harder, and once again he fought an urge to hold her. She should be falling in love, living her dream in Wyoming. Instead she'd already raised two kids and was dealing with . . . this.

"When you see the picture once a puzzle is completed, it's usually worth the work," he said. "For all the work you're putting in, this one must be terribly intricate and beautiful."

Rio's mouth curved into its rare full smile. "You didn't really say that!" She laughed. "Not many *girls* could come up with lines like that in the middle of a conversation. Did you learn poetry in Scouts, too?"

He'd been inordinately proud of making her smile, but that flash of ego burst at her teasing. "Maybe my mother just raised a sensitive, new age guy."

She laughed again. "Well, she did a fine job then. You're sweet."

Sweet? Fantastic.

He'd seen her face when they'd met that morning, the way she'd taken in his riding clothes with surprise. He knew why. Not only didn't he look like the bare-chested cowboys she'd had hanging in her bedroom, he had a perfectly decorated home, and now he'd shown her he was a girly-lines sort of bloke. He worked hard to bury stereotypical macho attitudes because of his chosen profession—dealing with the public and mostly females at that. But "sweet" when someone like Rio Montoya said it pretty much signaled the kiss of death.

A tone from the pocket of his jeans cut off the thoughts, and his heart fell. His mother. Her call schedule was normally as regular as Old Faithful, but this wasn't on that schedule. There was either an emergency, or some new, disastrous plan that included him.

"Sorry," he said to Rio and answered the phone. "'Lo, Mum."

"Surprise, sweetheart!" Stella Pitts-Matherson's thick North Yorkshire accent had softened over her years away from the dales, but it still rolled round-voweled, bossy and friendly from across the miles.

"This is a surprise. Anything wrong?"

"Nothing at all. In fact, everything is quite wonderful, and that's why I'm calling."

"Good news is always welcome."

"Oh, that's lovely. I hope having your dear old mum visit is considered good news, because she's on her way to you."

"Pardon me?"

"I'm coming early, love. I'll be there day after to-morrow."

"Mum!" His heart dropped in full dread. "This is perhaps the worst moment you could choose. My big annual show is coming up in just weeks, I've got houseguests, there's no time to work on decorating—"

Not to mention the lack of a single extra quarter to dole out for that purpose.

"Houseguests?" Her voice turned even chirpier. "Who's there? Anyone I know?"

"Absolutely nobody you'd know." He rolled his eyes at Rio, who smiled back despite no comprehension. "And they've only just arrived, in fact. Could your visit be moved back just a month?"

"Oh, I know it's rude of me," she said. "But I have a surprise for you—a traveling companion of my own."

A man? David hoped beyond hope his mother had found someone on whom to lavish at least a little of her abundant energy. He adored the woman, but she could be exhausting.

"Brilliant. What's his name?"

"Oh, not a him, sweetheart. It's a lovely surprise. We'll take the unfinished rooms if you have guests already. And we'll stay out of the way."

He couldn't imagine his mother staying out of the way were she on hallucinogenic drugs.

"Of course you're always welcome, Mum. I just know there won't be a lot of time."

"It's fine, love. I have things to work on while you're busy. You know I don't require entertaining. It's just always wonderful to see you.

That much was true. His mother created her own entertainment. He was tired already.

"And you, too, you old blouse." His fifty-seven-year-old mother laughed at the age insult.

"Who raised you, you cheeky little bugger? Be nice. Can you write down the flight information or shall I send it?"

"Text it if you would."

"All right. I will see you in two days' time. I'm an old woman aflutter."

"So, Mum, who's the companion? What's—"

"Don't worry, you'll get along fine." She brushed him off. "Just someone I ran into by chance. Love you."

She was gone—after blowing through the past five minutes like a sudden squall leaving nothing changed and everything different.

"Well, *that's* the dog's bollocks," he said, and Rio peered at him curiously.

"That sounded sarcastic so I'm thinking it can't mean anything good."

"Oh, it was sarcasm all right. My mother. Coming two months earlier than planned."

Her face made its mercurial morph into concern. "Oh David, we'll be in the way."

"You will not. You've seen the house. I have countless bedrooms, and she'll take the unfinished ones. I'm just sorry she's bursting in on you and Bonnie. She's a bit of a force of nature, that one."

"Sounds formidable."

"Yes. She's quite lovely and no mistake, but not much stands in her way. I could have told her no, but she'd have shown up with a tent and pitched it in the back garden."

"Did you know your accent gets heavier when you start talking faster?" The lightness returned to Rio's eyes.

"Sorry. I try not to let that happen, but I don't hear it."

"It's—"

"If you say sweet I'll clock you."

"Sexy."

The word hit him like a piano falling unexpectedly from the sky. She smiled, clearly joking, yet a flash of candor shot through her blue eyes. American women tended to focus far too much on his accent. They fawned over his odd phrases and giggled over pronunciations. But an utter lack of guile in Rio's face sent excitement coursing through David's body. She was the most different sort of person he'd ever met. He hoped her little glints of humor were truer markers of her personality than the sadness that pervaded her eyes and words the rest of the time.

Chapter Eight

LOADED DOWN WITH four stuffed grocery bags, Rio followed David and his four equally overfilled bags into the house. She listened for Bonnie, but the rooms were silent. Part of her couldn't help but worry, but when the opulence from the shopping trip overflowed onto the center island in David's kitchen, she had a hard time concentrating on anything but nagging nausea. She'd never bought eight bags of groceries at a time in her life. David had just plunked down a hundred and ninety dollars for everything from salad greens to three thick New York strip steaks—"to celebrate your arrival."

"I still can't believe this," she said, surveying the mound of food.

"It'll last us a good week," he assured her.

"A week? This stockpile better last at least a month."

She was used to buying things as needed and stretching supplies to the breaking point. A seventy-five-dollar spree was a huge shopping trip, and rare. Extravagant items like a bottle of wine and a bag of frosted animal cookies, especially purchased at the same time, were seldom on her list.

He simply smiled and directed the stowing of supplies so she could learn the layouts of the cupboards and refrigerator. By the time they'd finished, she was surprised at how the activity had relaxed her. Once she couldn't see the purchases all at once, her guilt over receiving so much bounty dissipated, and her curiosity over the perfectly appointed kitchen space took over. It was like stocking the pantry in Wonderland.

"A job well done," David said.

"This is a lot for you to take on."

"It's good to do a proper shopping. Now you can make yourself at home, eat when you wish, help yourself."

"And you're going to start showing me what you need help with around here."

He leveled a blue gaze at her and sighed. She steeled for a lecture. He'd admonished her enough times already about equating acceptance of his hospitality with the need to pay him back.

"Tomorrow. Today you are getting settled. Remember?"

"Yes."

"It's only one-thirty. Don't you want to come out and play with the horses a bit?" His resonant voice enticed her with its hint of playfulness. "Or, if not, why don't you get things sorted upstairs and then just have a wander about? You've been nothing but responsible all day; you can let go. What would you do if you were still at home?"

"Be working."

"Of course you would be." He set his hands on her shoulders, spun her toward the kitchen door, and gave a little push to get her walking. "But not here. Not this afternoon. For today only I'm dictating what you do."

"Excuse me?" She tried to be angry, but there was too much of a twinkle in his eye.

"Stop arguing and listen. You're going to go upstairs and unpack your case. You're going to come back down and *then* check on your sister. After that you're going to do nothing of import. You have the rest of your stay here to muck about in the barn and find things to help with."

"But I—"

"Nope. I have spoken."

She moved along at his urging, masking a smile with a scowl. She had to admit she reveled a little in the unfamiliar experience of having someone else take charge.

"Are you always this tyrannical?"

"Hardly ever."

She actually believed that. A streak of overaccommodation ran through nearly every action he took—from taking her and Bonnie in, to allowing the rude police chief to have his say, to letting his mother come barging in with no notice.

"Fine. I'll unpack my twelve things like an obedient guest. You'll let me know, I assume, if my sister is lying under a tractor or a horse somewhere?"

She glanced over her shoulder to see his head and his shoulders shaking in amusement.

"Why are you so worried about her? I guarantee you, there are plenty of kids around here along with Jill, who can keep her safe in a barn. Bonnie is fine. Let her have a free afternoon, too."

Her spine stiffened, and she stopped, turning back to face him. "Look. One thing I won't let you do is lecture me about my sister. You don't know her. Groups of kids are her downfall. She has an IQ to die for, but I promise you, emotionally she's nobody's Einstein."

Skepticism fogged his bright eyes, but the familiar David Pitts-Matherson surfaced. "You're right. I don't know her. You can certainly go check on Bonnie any time you wish."

For a few seconds she stared at him, as frustrated as she'd been at the café earlier. The man's control of his backbone slipped around like a transmission going bad. He had the ability to engage her like no one she'd met in years and, unnerving as it was, she forgot the world when he locked wills with her even in fun. But he couldn't seem to sustain it.

"I'm fine if you check on her." She continued toward the stairs again, shorter with him than she should have been but tired of analyzing him.

If he cared she'd been curt he didn't bat an eye. "I will do that. I've also got a few things I can work on if you'd like some time to yourself. Or come find me anytime, and I'll officially show you 'round the place."

She purposefully pushed thoughts of him to the back of her mind once he left. Why dissect the personality of a person she'd known one day? She'd had enough men in her life to know they were barely worth analyzing as a gender. Good or bad, what you saw was generally what you got.

Her room hadn't grown any less stark, and she still didn't regret her choice. Her suitcase, filled with a few changes of clothing and personal hygiene products she'd been given at the women's shelter, sat on the single bed. She ignored it while she explored the space more thoroughly than she'd been able to with David and Bonnie standing in the doorway.

The purple-gray walls opposite the windows were faded. She didn't mind them as they were, but a new coat of paint wouldn't hurt either. The mostly bare bookshelves along the back wall held an eclectic smattering of books and oddities. She squatted to examine a pile of a dozen children's books and found a copy of *The House at Pooh Corner,* a set of Narnia books, and eight, small red-covered books all with titles that included the name William. *Just William, William the Outlaw, William the Pirate, William and the Masked Rancher.* She mused over David being the type to keep children's books. She supposed . . .

She spun a miniature globe on its axis, sifted briefly through a basket of seashells, and turned over an old Magic 8 Ball without asking it a question. "Better not tell you now," she read.

"Fine, I don't want to know anyway," she replied, scoffing at the soft echo in the room.

She opened a door to find a tiny empty closet. Then she pulled open both doors of the large, oak wardrobe.

The bar inside held at least two dozen hangers, far more than she'd need, and two garment bags hanging against one side of the cupboard. She slid them curiously to the center. Unzipping one, she found a sequin-spangled, royal-blue gown. The other bag held a cocktail dress in stunning black and white. Like every woman, she'd eyed such dresses in stores, but there was no call for a diner cook in inner city Minneapolis to own one.

Nor for a sexy male to own two.

She studied the gown and chuckled as she spread the bodice. These were definitely not David's unless he'd once been five-foot-five and a solid D-cup.

After zipping the bags back up, it only took a few minutes to hang her things beside the garment bags and stash underclothing in the two drawers at the bottom of the wardrobe. She carried her personal items to the bathroom. They hadn't had wealth at their old house, but she and Bonnie had had their girlie creature comforts—nail polishes, makeup, jewelry. At the shelter the loss hadn't seemed real. Here, stripped to toothbrushes, shampoo, conditioner, and some tampons, the sparseness of her new existence smacked her with full force.

Yet again she shoved growing despair aside. Dwelling on the losses helped nothing. She would find a way to earn money again. If David wouldn't give her work, she'd hitchhike to town.

Back downstairs she prowled the living room, studiously avoiding David's bedroom, peeked into one more guest room, neutrally decorated, a small office, and a half bath. Finally, inexorably, she was drawn back to the kitchen. Like her sparse room upstairs, it filled her with comfort. Simply standing beside the island and staring at the gleaming appliances made her long to turn every stove knob, open every drawer, and explore all the cupboards she'd merely glimpsed when putting away the groceries.

And then she caught sight of the three copper bowls, hanging on a rustic brick wall between two cupboards and glistening like newly forged treasure. She'd missed seeing them earlier, and stroked the cool metal. It was so silly, but she'd coveted a set of bowls like this forever. She loved copper for no practical reason except that she did.

The discovery of the bowls released a flood somewhere deep inside that sent bubbles of excitement effervescing through her body. One by one she opened cupboards and drawers, and each yielded more five-star kitchen booty: every shape of baking pan, a kitchen store's worth of high-end cookware. She squealed over a drawer that, in addition to the standard measuring cups and spoons and normal kitchen utensils, seemed to contain every cool gadget she'd ever wanted to own. When she picked out a heavily weighted wire whisk Julia Child would have panted over, her eyes moved to the largest copper bowl and her breath caught at the audacity of her next thought.

She opened the refrigerator and took closer stock of the contents. It held standard fare—condiments, milk, the cream and cottage cheese David had just bought. The pink, perfect steaks he'd been so excited about for tonight's dinner occupied one shelf, but next to them she caught sight of another package of meat—this one chicken. She lifted it out. The use-by date . . . yesterday.

One of her excited little bubbles burst into annoyance. This was just another indication of how much money the man had. Two pounds of chicken pieces had no business going to waste in a refrigerator. Forget the starving children in China; there were people down her old block who would have loved the ability to simply purchase five dollars' worth of chicken.

Without hesitating, Rio tore into the shrink-wrap and sniffed the meat. It had been in the coldest part of the fridge, and it smelled perfectly all right. Resolutely she set the package back on the shelf and closed the refrigerator door. Then she started ransacking the cupboards in earnest. The steaks could wait their turn. The old standby her father had called Junk Stew was now on the menu.

She had no idea exactly how much time had passed when she heard voices at the back door. She hadn't even known there was a back door.

"Rio?" Bonnie's call rang through the kitchen.

Shocked that she hadn't thought about her sister once in the last—Rio checked the clock on the microwave— two and a half hours, she glanced around the kitchen, which was now far from pristine. Her heart thumped in nervousness, knowing it was highly possible David might be annoyed at what she'd done. But a thread of contentment mitigated the worry. She'd never had such an amazing space in which to spread out and play with her food. The flour dust, the juice-covered cutting boards, the pile of chicken fat and skin waiting to be thrown away, all made her happy. Happy to the point where she didn't really care what David thought.

"It smells awesome in here!" Bonnie entered the kitchen and grinned.

She'd seen Rio's cooking messes before. David, on the other hand, who followed in jeans and stocking feet, stared like he'd been thrown into a new dimension.

"And to think I was worried about you," he said.

"You told me to *stop* worrying for the day," Rio tossed back. "I got distracted on the way to the barn."

"Evidently. I didn't intend for you to slave away in the kitchen just because we went shopping."

"I know. And I have something to say about that, too." She fixed him with a stern look and crossed her arms. "We could have held off shopping for days. Do you know how much perfectly good food I just rescued from the realm of kitchen science projects?"

His features twisted with a hint of sheepishness, and the tic of contrition at the corner of his mouth made her want to touch it, which threw her planned lecture into a jumble of disorganized thoughts.

"Judging from the amazing smells, I'm guessing quite a lot—and I'm also guessing the rescues were successful."

"I don't know. We'll see."

All she noticed as he moved into the kitchen were his amazing looks and, far more weirdly than that, his shoeless feet. Their shape, swathed by a pair of thin white socks, was large and masculine.

Stupid. She was supposed to be lecturing him on waste. Instead she was losing her mind.

"I definitely didn't expect a home-cooked feast,"

he said earnestly, catching sight of a pie cooling on the counter. "This is amazing."

Her cheeks warmed, and the heat drifted down to her stomach. "Thank the week-old chicken." She found her lecture, but none of the admonishment she'd intended to spice it with. "And the potatoes sprouting eyes, and the eight pounds of what the bag said were State Fair apples starting to wrinkle."

"Oh no. I forgot about those. A student brought them. But only a week or so ago," he added hastily, the attractive little apologetic tic returning. "She said it was an unusually early harvest this year and I should try them."

"They'd have been fine if they'd been in the refrigerator rather than the pantry."

"I told you. I only dabble in cooking. I'm really quite uneducated."

"All right." She narrowed her eyes, but averted them when a smile threatened. "Then this is your first lesson in not wasting food." She hesitated. "But I apologize for making a mess. I'll clean it up."

"You think I'm the least bit worried about the state of the kitchen? It's brilliant to have it look used for a change. I'm only sorry you felt you had to work. I wanted you to relax."

"She probably did," Bonnie said, padding in behind David after leaving her own shoes at the door.

"Yeah. I . . . guess I did." The truth of her own revelation surprised her.

David studied her a few seconds, seemed to see she

meant it, and rubbed his palms together. "All right, fair enough. So can I ask what's on the menu?"

"Junk Stew for starters."

"Yum!" said Bonnie.

"Which is?" asked David.

"Pretty much anything you can find to put in the pot," she said. "I had the chicken, I found a hunk of kielbasa, carrots, celery, onions, a little broccoli, some peas, and frozen corn."

"Our dad used to make it," Bonnie explained. "He would put just about anything in it. Even sauerkraut once."

Rio exchanged wrinkled noses with her and they laughed.

"Sounds awful."

"It kind of was."

"What else we got?" The phrase sounded positively Americanized.

She pointed out the apple crisp beside the pie, another glass baking dish topped with mashed potatoes and filled with a green bean hot dish she'd memorized from an old cookbook—the one she'd miss most she'd decided—and a pot of water ready for the broccoli she'd found yellowing in the refrigerator crisper drawer.

"It's only four-thirty." Regret tinged David's voice, and he drew a visible breath through his nose. "But I'd gladly have a go at eating early."

"I'm going to make biscuits for the stew and cook the broccoli," she said. "Twenty minutes more. You two could set the table."

"Set a table?" David chuckled. "The last time I did that it had something to do with my mother being here."

"I find that hard to believe for a proper duke," she teased.

It was easy to relax now that she knew David wasn't going to freak out over her kitchen takeover. And that Bonnie had survived her afternoon.

"What *should* be hard to believe is the duke supping with the scullery maid." He raised his brows.

"I'd be happy to serve him in his chambers."

"Oh no. You don't want to see his chambers."

In some weird, deep down place that wasn't true. Very inappropriately, she did want to see them. "Then you'd best get over yourself, Your Highness."

"English History One-Oh-One," he replied. "No 'Highness' unless it's royal, and I am not. You may address me as Your Grace."

She sputtered and then burst out laughing. It felt nice. "Yeah? You can kiss my grace, buddy."

"Rio." He surprised her by grasping each of her upper arms and bringing his face close to hers. He smelled of wood shavings and horses—subtle and masculine. "If this were day two of your stay—I would."

He let her go, and she nearly staggered backward. He winked, oblivious to what his unexpected touch had done.

"I . . ." She turned back to the stove, struggling to show as little frazzle as possible. "You . . . go wash up, the pair of you. And hop to on the table."

Bonnie rolled her eyes at David. "This is only a little of how bossy she can get."

Like the laughter, bossy actually felt pretty good. It dispelled the rampaging butterflies in her belly.

"She's the cook," he replied. "I guess she gets to make the rules."

"Darn right," Rio replied.

David contributed a bottle of white wine that came, he said, from his micro cellar of thirty or thirty-five bottles of wine, which had been stocked almost exclusively with gifts from people who knew far more about choosing good wine than he did. Whatever his lack of expertise, however, the Riesling he poured during supper was delicious. He offered to let Bonnie taste some with Rio's permission, but Rio unequivocally refused. She wasn't about to start their stay here off on that foot. Bonnie protested but, once again, in his calm-the-waves way, David simply produced a bottle of sparkling grape juice. His mother, he told Bonnie, was pretty much a teetotaler, so he always kept juice on hand. Bonnie was in good company.

Rio, on the other hand, was hard put to stick to one glass of wine. It was a glass more than she'd had in ages, and even though she sipped it, savoring the mild fruitiness despite wanting to guzzle it like the indulgent treat it was, the warm buzz filled her head, mellowed the conversation, and encouraged more friendly laughter. Bonnie talked about school and classes and where she'd thought about going to college if they moved West. The impromptu cooking session was feeling like a grand success when David pushed his plate away once his third helping of the stew was gone.

"This was brilliant! You are a kitchen wizard."

She smiled with happy wooziness and drained the last of her wine. "Nah. I can follow a recipe, and I've memorized a handful of our staples. Give me a pound of hamburger and some noodles or potatoes and I can make it look good."

"And taste good," Bonnie added. "You *are* a great cook, Rio."

She and Bonnie normally got along fine, but lately she'd spent so much time acting like a parent, such praise between them was rare. Maybe Bonnie was showing off, but regardless the compliment was nice.

"I concur, so far," David said. "I'm reserving judgment for after the pie."

"It's one of her specialties," Bonnie said.

Rio brought the pie, still hot, to the table and handed David the knife.

"Cut the pieces however you want them. Who's here to tell us they're too big?"

"You always tell me." Bonnie grinned.

"Oh, go for broke. It's your reward for complimenting the chef."

"Really? Awesome." She scooped out a giant slice as did David. Rio had eaten so much at lunch she barely had room for a sliver and opted for watching David's reaction. It didn't disappoint.

"This is just wrong," he moaned through a mouthful, smacking his lips. "Nobody should eat decadence like this."

"Stop trying to suck up." Rio laughed. "It's just apple pie."

"It's an Effie Jorgenson–caliber pie," he corrected. "Around here, that's the highest compliment we give."

Despite herself, Rio's chest swelled with pride. She opened her mouth to brush off the praise with solid Minnesota false modesty, but a loud knock at the back door halted her. David's brows puckered, and he stood. A moment later he ushered Kim Stadtler into the room.

"Would you like a piece of pie?" he asked. "You're missing out if you don't."

"No thanks." Kim smiled. "I'm just here to invite you guys, Bonnie and Rio especially, on a trail ride. Jill's taking some students out to the park to give the horses some fun."

"A trail ride?" Bonnie's fork clattered to the plate, the uneaten pie forgotten.

"Who's going?" David asked.

"I talked Dawson into it." Kim winked. "Chase might be coming over. Becky Barnes, Angie, Deena, a couple of others."

"You should go." David looked at Bonnie and then at Rio. "That's a great group."

"Will you come?" Bonnie asked him.

"I could get you out of my hair and get a little paperwork done." He winked, but Rio wondered how true the sentiment was.

"I don't know if we're ready to jump on horses and go riding," she said, although the idea sent her pulse skittering with excitement. "Shouldn't we at least practice a little?" She turned to David. "Bonnie's never been on a horse, and it's been years for me."

"But I have been on a horse." Bonnie exchanged a secret smile with Kim.

"You what? When?"

"I put her up on Jill's horse, Sun," Kim replied. "We rode all over the big arena. She did great."

Rio's instinct was to grab her sister and run to the nearest padded room. They'd talked about owning horses their entire lives, but dreaming about horses and jumping willy-nilly onto the back of one were two different things.

"Without . . . permission? When I wasn't here to—"

"To what?" Bonnie demanded, her complimentary voice gone. "To watch over me? Rio, stop worrying, for crying out loud, and start having a little fun of your own."

"I'm not your mother, Bonnie, but I'm responsible for you."

"Stop being so responsible then."

She loaded one last giant bite of pie onto her fork and stuffed it into her mouth. When she'd finished it, she wiped her mouth and stood.

"I'm going," she said. "Come along for crying out loud."

Hiding the sting from Bonnie's words, she shrugged tightly. "Sorry, it's fine. Go ahead."

"It's an easy ride," Kim added. "We'd love to have you come, too. Honest."

"Thanks," Rio said. "But I'd like to clean up here. Maybe a rain check?"

"Sure."

When the girls were out the door, Rio scowled and picked up the wine bottle. She was just being stubborn now, and probably stupid, but she poured another half glass. The first gulp warmed going down but it didn't curb the bite of Bonnie's words. They'd just lost everything; why couldn't she see that all Rio wanted in the world was to protect what was left—namely *her*? To her shock—again—David placed his hand over hers, cupping the wineglass and her fingers in his large, warm grasp.

"Do you always drink when you're angry?"

"Never!"

"Don't start now."

"Okay, wait just a frickin' minute. You have nothing to say about it. You are not my—"

"I feel responsible for *you* while you're here."

The words shot straight into the wound Bonnie had left. Rio sucked in a breath.

"That's low, twisting my words to suit your argument. I've asked you to stay out of our business."

"I don't want to get in your business," he said softly. "I am an impartial observer."

"David—"

"Rio."

"Oh what?" She huffed out a breath at his quiet insistence.

"Come riding with us. Why deny yourself just to prove you had a point?"

She hated that he could get into her head so easily. For someone who loved to back down from conflict, he didn't seem to need avoiding conflict with her. Maybe the wine, maybe plain exhaustion, made her hold back another stubborn refusal.

"Are you going?"

"I'll go if you go."

She snorted. "How ridiculous is that?"

"Maybe I want to poke a bit of fun at your riding."

"Excuse me?" Her heart hammered in disbelief.

"Rio, c'mon," he chided. "Stop taking everything so seriously. I would never tease a new rider. Your sister was right. You should have more fun."

There was not much she could say to get out of the activity after that. He helped her put the food away, marveling that they still had the casserole and an entire apple crisp for another dinner.

"Leave the dishes," he admonished. "You cooked. Bonnie and I can clean up later."

"That's very liberated," she said.

"No, not at all." His eyes shone with the fun she was growing to recognize. "I have an older sister who was liberated with a capital "L" I'm quite afraid of girls actually."

"I don't believe you. What's her name?"

"Penelope."

"Penelope Pitts-Matherson?"

"Penny. She was Peepee and nothing for it. A tragedy. And I heard rumors that I was originally to be Phillip. Nickname for that over there is often Pip. Pip Pitts-Matherson. Nice."

Once again he'd dispelled the tension. Rio giggled as she left the house. The afternoon had heated things up, and even though it was approaching six o'clock, the temperature had to have been in the eighties. Rio breathed deeply, pulling in the scents so different from what she'd been creating in the kitchen. Grass, animals, and hay mulled together in the warm August air—an outdoor feast for the nose.

"I'm not really dressed for riding," she said, as they neared the barn. She could hear voices from inside, laughing, calling.

"We'll get you a helmet," David replied. "And I'll bet Jill has a pair of heeled boots to lend you. She's brilliant at having loads of equipment around for emergencies. Otherwise? Your jeans are . . . perfect."

The way he hesitated over "perfect," with emphasis not only from his accent but his eyes, heated the wine in her bloodstream. Her head swam a little with the thought that he might mean it as a compliment. Heck, she decided, she might as well make it perfect as long as she was going to fantasize.

Chapter Nine

"YOU CAME!" BONNIE threw her arms around Rio's neck as if there'd never been a single cross word. "And David, too."

Rio hugged her back, but didn't get out a reply before Bonnie was off to join a gaggle of girls, where she chattered as if she'd known them for months instead of minutes. Typical Bonnie.

There were five teenagers along with Jill, Chase, and David. And herself, as good as a sixth child, she thought, nervous as she stood at the fringes watching the activity. How did Bonnie already look like she knew what she was doing?

"Would you like to see your horse?"

David materialized beside her, and she breathed a sigh of relief. He held out a pair of pull-on, ankle-high boots.

"Okay."

"And try these. They're Jill's extra paddock boots. If they don't fit, well, fake it for now."

A moment later she'd doffed her running shoes and tugged on the boots. They were half a size too large, but they'd work.

"They feel fine," she said. "Thank you."

"Sure. C'mon."

He led her to a stall and slid the door, which whispered open on sibilant rollers. Jill could feel her eyes widen at the gleaming horse in front of her. "Holy cow," she murmured.

"More of a holy horse, wouldn't you say?" he teased back. "And, actually, he is as close to heavenly as I've got. This is Tully. Short for Tullamore Dew. Like the good Irish whiskey."

"Hello, Tully." Rio forgot her anxiousness even though the stunning animal towered over her. She touched his muzzle and then stroked his neck and sides. He shone like golden brown liquid.

"He's Irish Draught—an old friend now at nineteen. He's big, and he's fast if you want him to be but not if you don't. We've had him do pretty much every job on the place, so he's well trained. You'll have a great ride with him, I promise."

"He's beautiful." Rio turned back to the horse. "You're beautiful, aren't you?" Tully snorted and lipped her fingers. Rio laughed, enchanted, all shreds of anger, fear, sadness, gone. For the moment she had a horse. She turned back to David. "Thank you."

"I'm glad you're coming with us."

It took solid strategic planning to get nine horses tacked up, nine people mounted, and three dogs underway. Jill and Chase's little black-and-white dog, Angel, the sweetest, smartest dog Rio had ever met, led the pack. Kim and Dawson had brought their handsome golden retriever, Roscoe. And Fred, a Corgi mix that belonged to David's only employee, Andy, who lived in a small apartment above the barn, trotted right along on stumpy legs that didn't look as if they'd carry him across the farm much less for an two-hour trail ride. David assured her that, short legs or not, Fred would outlast them all.

Tully's big-strided, rocking walk was only one of the hundred sensations rushing at her like a tsunami when Rio rode out of the stable yard and into the pasture at the rear of the group with David. Sitting astride the big gelding seemed as natural as she remembered from her only two riding excursions ten years before. She relaxed into the comfortable Western saddle and let her hips roll and her spine undulate with the motion.

Her stomach effervesced with delight, the hot evening breeze reached through the vent holes in the helmet David had found for her, the collective crunch and stomp of thirty-six hooves muffled the chatter from the kids ahead of her.

Out of habit she watched Bonnie closely for the first fifteen minutes. Her sister rode in an English saddle, with no horn, no heavy stirrups, and no deep, padded seat. She seemed secure enough, and Rio marveled. The little socialite was taking to riding like she took to everything else she put her brain to—effortlessly.

"What do you think?" David had kept mostly silent as the group left his property. Now they headed through an open field two abreast on a grass track, and he drew beside her on the gray gelding he rode—a tall, gorgeous thoroughbred named Going to Bedlam he fondly called Gomer. "Are you glad I made you come?"

She allowed her mood to shine through a smile. "Yes. I didn't expect to get to do something like this."

"You can't avoid horses around this place. We're all nutters. We play with them, work with them, talk about them. You'll find out fairly quickly if you're a deep-down horse fanatic."

"What's not to be fanatic about? Do you all know how lucky you are?"

A fan of smile creases appeared beside each eye. "Nobody takes this for granted. You'll see the hard work that goes into an evening like this."

"I didn't mean to imply I thought it wasn't work . . ."

But, truthfully, she had. Deep inside, beneath the thrill of this experience, lurked jealousy. A touch of envy because these people had been born into circumstances where work could pay for fun like this instead of where work couldn't quite pay all the bills.

She shoved the ungracious thought aside. Before the fire she hadn't had a bad life. It hadn't been easy, but there had been good nights with Bonnie and Paul and friends. When they'd prided themselves for making it. On their own.

"I've been watching you. You're a natural on that horse."

"Me?" At that silly compliment, her mood soared. "I'm not doing a dang thing. Tully's doing all the work. Bonnie—she's the one. Not even using a big, safe cowboy saddle."

"Ah." He lowered his voice. "But here's where my eye is more practiced. Bonnie's doing great, and she'll learn to be a good rider, but if you watch closely you'll see the stiffness in her shoulders and how she's leaning a little forward and clutching on the reins for balance. That's all perfectly normal new rider stuff."

"I guess." Rio did see.

"You can't see yourself, of course, but feel how loose your lower back is? How easily your knees can move out from the saddle?"

She flapped her knees like wings. David grinned. "You aren't asking him to do much of anything yet, but you're not getting in his way either. You're a born cowgirl."

"Easy in a big, safe saddle."

"No, that's not it. You're not afraid. You're listening to the horse."

She let the compliment settle around her, accepting it for what it was—something she'd never before experienced.

"Where are we going?" she asked.

"To the far end of the state park. Butte Glen is just a mile from town. There's a secluded spot not really meant for camping, but we know the rangers and have unwritten permission to be there. The public isn't allowed, but local hikers and riders can go if they know about it. It's a nice spot a little over an hour away. I think they brought drinks and snacks."

"Ugh." Rio wrinkled her nose. "I've done nothing but eat all day."

"Too right."

The ride to the secret spot passed in a delightful haze. The teens, all of them Jill's students except for Dawson, chattered like squirrels. Rio did as David directed and let herself enjoy the serene ride through fields and woods. Once again the lack of concrete and overhead electricity struck her as almost magical and solidified the knowledge that moving from the city permanently one day was the right dream for her. It would take longer now, but somehow, at this moment, she still believed it could happen.

They dismounted in a clearing with trees scattered through the space to make tethering spots for the horses. David showed her how to tie a quick-release knot with the halter rope Tully wore beneath his bridle. The number of straps, ropes, reins, and buckles had Rio's head spinning, but David promised she'd get it straight before she knew it.

"How do the legs feel? The first time you spend an hour on a horse it doesn't matter if you're an athlete or a couch potato, your muscles are gonna yell at you."

She moved away from Tully's side and laughed. Nothing hurt, but her legs performed as if they'd been tied around a barrel for a day. "I see what you mean. Am I walking funny?"

"Not yet."

"How comforting."

The kids formed a haphazard circle around a well-used fire pit. Rio eased onto the grass not far from Jill, noting Bonnie had snared a spot right next to Dawson, but she clearly wasn't the only one who saw his raw, youthful sex appeal, and Dawson laughed and flirted with ease. He was Kim's stepbrother and that was really all Rio knew. She pried the fingers of concern loose from her mind. If there was a safe place to flirt, this was it.

David, who'd disappeared momentarily into the woods, returned with his arms full of wood. He winked when he got to the fire pit and let the bundle tumble to the ground.

"I happen to know where we keep a secret stash of approved firewood."

"David's our chief fire builder," Jill said. "He can actually make flame from sticks, but we let him use a match."

"You really, really were a Boy Scout?" Rio asked.

"Really, really."

"He was an army Boy Scout." Jill patted him on the shoulder. "Tell her."

A slight shadow flickered through David's eyes, and he shot Jill a semi-dirty look. "She thinks it's a big deal," he said. "I acted as my unit's survival expert, but we all learned how to survive over there."

"Over there?"

"Iraq. Most of the time we were in Basra. Occasionally we'd send patrols out into the desert. We all knew how to build fires. Not a big deal."

Something about the casual way he dismissed the topic while deftly setting up tinder and kindling for a fire belied a more serious truth. His actions appeared instinctive, as if building a fire were a sport he'd trained for just like his riding. When he had a log cabin shape around the center, he pulled a small box of stick matches from his pocket, struck the match head, and gently set the flame into his pile of dry leaves and small branch tips. They flared. David cupped his hands and blew gently, urging the brand-new fire to catch the slightly larger twigs.

Rio stared a moment at his pursed lips, swallowed, and turned away.

What was wrong with her? She was letting David scramble her nerve center wherever they went. He still wore jeans and the button-down shirt. Now the top two buttons were undone, and as he brushed down the fabric to get rid of the wood residue, Rio caught a glimpse of smooth skin dusted with dark hair. He thwarted her attempt to look away again by stepping from the little blaze and taking a seat beside her.

"Ta-da," he said. "Grog make fire."

An unladylike snort escaped her, causing him to grin. "Impressive," she said.

"I should hope so."

Jill appeared with two small plastic cups. "Here. We smuggled in the newest bottle of wine from that vineyard west of the cities."

"A vineyard in Minnesota?" Rio took the cup.

"Surprisingly, there are quite a few," Jill said.

"Got a white and a red." Chase came up behind Jill with two uncorked bottles. "Which for you, Rio?"

"Ah, white. Please."

"Red for me." David held up his cup.

"Kim's mom sent hot chocolate for the kids," Jill added. "It's decadence all around tonight."

"What's the occasion?" Rio took a sip of the wine and swirled it in her mouth as if she knew what she was doing. It had a sweet bite to it. "Nice. It tastes icy, like the grapes shivered for a while."

That garnered laughter.

"Occasion?" Jill looked at the other three and they all shrugged. "You and Bonnie are as good a reason as any."

"Excellent occasion." Chase raised his glass. "To Rio and Bonnie. Welcome to the infamous Bridge Creek Stable trail rides."

"And to Minnesota wine at the end of the summer." David raised his cup.

"And, to a huge thank-you," Rio added, something she'd likely not have done if she hadn't already been buzzy and warm from the wine at dinner.

She sipped and let the moment overwhelm her. Chase had always been someone to look up to, not a peer. Jill was a blond-haired, brown-eyed beauty who made Rio's red-haired, dark-skinned coloring look like something out of a comic book—the kind of person Rio might detest if she wasn't one of the nicest women on the planet. And here they all were, accepting her as an equal. If nothing else, the abundance of wine helped dispel the disbelief.

The girls and the dogs started a silly game of hide-and-seek with Dawson, and Rio watched for a few minutes, more than bewildered. Dawson was seventeen, Bonnie and Kim each sixteen, Becky, and Deena just fourteen.

In Minneapolis, Dawson would have been far too cool for such ridiculous behavior, and the girls wouldn't have been caught dead tossing leaves at one another and darting in and out of the woods. In and out between cars as they cheated traffic on Lake Street, maybe.

She shook the negativity out of her mind and tried to revel in the reality of kids playing something wholesome in a place that wasn't crime-ridden.

A shriek of fright ground the game and all conversation to a halt. Becky Barnes, a darling, round-faced girl with a swath of bright purple in her hair, dashed out of the woods, her hand on her chest. "God, he scared the crap out of me," she swore.

The uniformed figure followed Becky into the open and a pall slammed over the little party. Chief Tanner Hewett stopped and stared as if he'd stumbled upon a woodland orgy.

"I'm looking for Arionna Montoya. Seems I've found her."

Angel barked twice, wagged her little black-and-white tail and sat expectantly in front of the chief. He ignored her. Roscoe and Fred each gave a woof. Dawson grabbed the golden.

"I'll start by asking what you're all doing here breaking at least six laws I can see without taking another step."

"Good evening, Officer." David stepped forward first, his voice of reason firmly in place.

Rio's stomach churned from where it had sunk to her toes. What dire thing would make the authorities come all the way out here after her? Even if they'd found Paul or Hector, they could have waited until she was home. Unless someone was dead . . . But then why was the man carping on about rules? Her mind whirled.

"We're just having a little outing with our students," David continued. "They worked hard all day and this is a nice way to relax."

"By trespassing on non-equestrian designated trails, having a fire in an unauthorized area, and allowing dogs to run off leash." He pointed at several of the pop cans scattered by the fire. "Littering. Any alcohol?"

David's eyes turned flinty even though his voice lost none of its calm. "Chief Hewett, I believe you'll find that once we leave there'll be no trace we were ever here. The park rangers' office has full knowledge we use this spot on occasion."

"A lot of things around this town got blessings they shouldn't have. If I let you party here, I'll have to let anyone who wants to party here. This is not a campsite. I need to ask you to leave."

"Chief, come on." Chase moved in beside David. "Many years of goodwill don't have to be destroyed by a hasty decision. This is a safe place for us to bring the kids and the horses for very short periods of time. It's been going on for ten years without incident. I promise you, we don't cause trouble."

"You don't sound like you're from around here."

"I'm sure from here now." Chase held out his hand. "Dr. Chase Preston. I started the new clinic south of town."

Hewett nodded curtly and shook with equal brevity.

"Glad to know you'll have some influence getting things rounded up here then, Doctor."

He swung his gaze to Rio, and something in his superior attitude flipped a switch inside. She stalked toward him and stopped a foot from the badge on his light-blue uniform shirt.

"You said you came looking for me. The others aren't doing anything wrong, so ignore them and let's talk."

For an instant Hewett stared in disbelief. The smile that followed wasn't warm.

"Very well, Miss Montoya. They found your car, a '98 Ford Taurus, abandoned in a lot at Fort Snelling State Park. The keys were under the floor mat along with a piece of paper that read, 'Return to Rio Montoya.' Any idea how it got there?"

Her heart slipped into a desperate pounding against her rib cage. "Of course not. I haven't seen it in nearly a week. What about my brother? It had to have been Paul."

"You think your brother abandoned your car?"

"He was the last one to have it, as far as I know."

"Well, the Minneapolis PD has impounded it. They'd like you to come and make an ID."

Rio recoiled. If Hector wasn't in custody, she wasn't going near the Twin Cities. If he had any kind of eyes on the Taurus, he could follow her to Bonnie.

"I can describe the car right down to the VIN number," she said. "I don't need to see it."

"You need to claim it in person if you want it back. And if you're pressing charges, you'll have to give a statement."

She pressed a thumb and forefinger into the corners of her eyes. She'd been asked about pressing charges when she'd reported the car gone. Having the police pick up Paul would get him off the street for a while. On the other hand, he had taken a car he often used. Minneapolis police had bigger fish to fry.

"I'm not pressing any charges." She looked at him directly. "I'm also not coming to Minneapolis until I know Hector Black won't be following me back here to my sister."

Hewett nodded. "All right, Miss Montoya, but I patrolled the inner city of Philadelphia for ten years, so I know how this works. He's your brother. You'll protect him. Just remember that when you're asking us to protect you."

She'd seen plenty of altercations between police and gang members. If this guy had been a beat cop on a gang street, he'd not been a popular one. Not with his veiled sarcasm and barely concealed accusations.

"Chief, do you know my story? I mean, really know it? You haven't asked once what I need, or even hope for, so please don't judge me on how I treat my brother."

The stoniest angles of the chief's severe face softened. "Point taken," he said. "Look, if your friends get packed up and clear out, I'll forget the violations. And if you'll come with me for a few minutes to fill out a vehicle description, I'll send it on to the MPD and see what can be done to get it out of impound. If you pay the fee, perhaps a detective can get it to a safe spot."

"Fee?" Rio stared at him. "But it was taken without my consent."

"I'm sorry. If you're filing no complaint, then it's simply your responsibility. I think it's only a hundred and fifty or two hundred dollars."

"Only—" She cut herself off. She'd undo whatever strides she'd made if she pushed. As annoying as Hewett was, he wasn't at fault for this. Turning to David, she forced a smile. "I'll go do this and be right back. I'm sorry."

"There's no way you're facing this alone," David said. "I'll come along."

"You don't need to do that."

"You won't even know I'm there. And you'll have someone to walk you back."

The cruiser stood about three hundred yards through the trees on a wide dirt hiking path. Hewett didn't speak as Rio wrote out a description of her old burgundy-colored Taurus. She enumerated the dents and rust spots she knew like her own face and noted the license plate and the VIN numbers. They were things you memorized when you lived in a place where car theft wasn't just something on the news. When she finished, the chief thanked her.

"If I were to come back in half an hour, you'd be gone, correct?" he added, curtly.

David nodded without speaking. Hewett got into his car and backed around in a tight circle. Seconds later he was gone. Without warning pure unadulterated anger made Rio's legs buckle in weakness, and furious tears filled her eyes. She couldn't even keep her messed-up life away from these people who'd been so kind. Because of her, they'd lost something important to them.

She bowed her head. In two long strides David wrapped his strong arms around her. Just as he had at the fire.

"Rio. It's all right. You were absolutely bloody marvelous."

Marvelous? She'd gotten them all in trouble. She jabbed away her tears and lifted her eyes to his. They shone in the low sunlight slanting through the evergreens.

"I—"

He stopped her words with his lips.

All she could do was squeak in surprise before the wine, the emotion, and the softness of his mouth made her go weak in his embrace.

Chapter Ten

THE SHOCK OF her tongue against his swept away all David's regrets over the rash action. Hints of wine flavored the kiss and melted in his mouth with a rush of heat and urgency. The slap he expected for his rudeness didn't come. Instead Rio liquefied in his arms, as unlike the Rio he'd grown to know as anything he could have made up himself. And almost as soon as her bones went soft, she solidified again and reached into the kiss like it was a life ring.

A thrill nearly like pain sliced through his lower belly. She scrabbled closer, brushing her breasts, her lower stomach up his body, her fingers pulling at the back of his shirt as she massaged his spine in time to the pulsing exploration of their tongues. Her own sweetness burst through the wine, and she tasted like abstract things—bravery, and seriousness, and searching. Their mouths sipped and sampled until thrills spun into sparks that ignited a timeless reaction.

She groaned, which only intensified the hardness of his body. He needed to stop, but the moment owned itself. Their exploration lost all boundaries—racing toward unknown territory with willpower in its wake.

It was Rio who halted it.

Violently, she tore away and shoved at his chest. They panted at each other, her eyes as wildly bewildered as he felt. The lavender T-shirt she'd worn all day now twisted around her torso and crept up her waist. When had he made such a wreck of that? As she tugged it into place, he caught a flash of color on her side. She covered it too quickly for him to make it out. Another tattoo?

Another flash to his already-uncomfortable groin.

What the devil? He'd meant it earlier when he said tattoos never turned him on.

"I'm sorry," he said quickly. "I don't make a habit of kissing girls who barely know me. I really don't." He ran a hand across the back of his neck. His own shirt had been pulled partially free of his jeans. One of the front tails hung loose. The other clung in place by an inch of fabric. "What just happened?"

"I—I don't know. You started it." For an instant her tough, fight-back sharpness threatened to return.

"I admit it. But I most certainly didn't plan it."

Her posture drooped; her wall stayed down. "I didn't plan it either. I'm sorry."

"Why sorry? It was a bloody good kiss."

He tried a smile and attempted to lift her chin so he could study her eyes. The moment between them was definitely gone, however, and she brushed his hand away.

"I was so pissed off at Hewett that when he left I lost it. You just happened to come along."

"Did it really feel that scientific?" He took a step back and studied her eyes. Large and sapphire. Wide and guileless. They reflected uncertainty.

"It's all science. Biology. Hormones mixed with anger."

"Fine then," he teased. "We at least alleviated the anger, right?"

At that her eyes took on a more familiar, wary toughness. "No. The chief only came out here to bait me. That'll piss me off for a long time."

David ran his hand inside his waistband, tucking his shirt back into place. "It explains a lot that he's from Philadelphia."

"Only that he was probably not a well-liked cop. Antagonism isn't the way to handle gang problems. Of which he seems to think I'm one."

"You defused him. You seemed to know just what to say, and yet you didn't give in to his taunts. I thought about clocking the man."

"You? I can barely see you hitting a punching bag."

He placed a hand over his heart. "You wound me, madam."

She turned away and gave her T-shirt a last adjustment then she swung back to him, her features determined. "Nothing happened here that can't be explained by overreaction. I made a mistake. You got me at a weak moment. Whatever. Nobody needs to know about this. Please don't tell Bonnie."

Bonnie. After only one day of watching and listening, he knew Rio took her role as mother figure overly seriously. She needed to keep track of her sister, true, but Bonnie was more a crutch. For what wound he didn't quite know.

"That's unkind," he said. "Do you really think I would march out of here to kiss and tell?"

She seemed taken aback, as if she'd never considered he would know how to be discreet. What sort of people had stung her to make her so constantly wary?

"I don't know you," she said. "But no, I guess I don't think you would."

"And I won't. Ready to go back?"

"Yes."

On the way to the clearing she stared at the ground, silent with a pinched, serious face like someone who'd witnessed a crime. He stopped her. "Was it that bad?" he asked.

She looked him in the eye. "You know it wasn't."

"I do." He wished he could kiss her again just to feel her body relax against his. To maybe make her smile again. "So don't look as if you nearly got mauled by a bear, okay? Smile or somebody's bound to ask."

She nodded. "You're right."

The pop cans were packed away, and the fire had been smothered fully with sand and dirt when Rio led the way back to the others. Nobody looked upset. Dawson still had the younger girls at his beck and call. Jill and Chase looked up from beside the dead fire.

"All's well?" Chase asked.

"Fine," Rio said.

"She wrote down the car description and handled Hewett brilliantly."

Bonnie perked up at that, her eyes bright with hopefulness. "What'd you do? Did you tell him off?"

"She did not," David said. "We should all learn to talk to authorities like she did."

"She's bailed Paul out enough times. She knows how."

"I'm sorry I got you all into trouble," Rio replied. "You'd still be able to use this spot if it wasn't for me, and Bonnie."

"Hold on, do you think we'll stop coming here just because of that?" Jill stood with a laugh. In two strides she reached Rio and gave her a hug. "We might be upstanding citizens in our real lives, but in secret we're all lawbreakers. This has been a spot for horse lovers in the area forever. A new police chief isn't going to change that. We have friends in low places, as the song goes."

For the first time since Hewett had shown up, Rio's face eased into a smile.

"I hope so."

"We'll plan our next ride on the way home." Jill winked.

"Hear, hear," David agreed, and Rio smiled one more time.

It was the last easy moment between them. On the way home she lost a little of the natural sway to her back that had captivated him earlier. She laughed a bit too easily with everyone but him, and still she radiated dangerous levels of everything that had attracted him from the first moment he'd laid eyes on her: prettiness that sparked at unexpected moments into fiery sexiness, tightly held emotions that burst without warning into showers of delightful humor, a smile that could crack a guarded heart.

He'd made a mistake in kissing her. For a woman who seemed like she might have trust issues, there probably wasn't a worse thing he could have done. Yet he'd kiss her again in a heartbeat to have her taste on his lips and her sexy, curvy body in his arms.

He had no idea why the kiss had happened in the first place. His mother and sister had raised him with more sensitivity than that. Katherine certainly had taught him more self-control.

Katherine.

He rarely thought of his ex-fiancée anymore. There was no sting after nine years except the tiny but everlasting sense of injustice. She'd been decorum personified—the perfect girl who would have made the perfect wife. According to everybody. But the failure he'd borne home from Iraq had affected everyone, Katherine most of all. The changes in him—the buried emotions, the purposeful non-confrontation that made him, according to her, too passive—had rendered him imperfect husband material. The wedding had been called off. He'd heard she'd married a year later, but he no longer remembered her married last name.

He didn't regret the path his life had taken, but Rio Montoya certainly was a sudden swerve off the straight and narrow. He'd never regret helping her, but he did regret his rising attraction. He had too many personal storm clouds brewing to let a beautiful woman spike his hormones and distract him. Except the kiss had been amazing.

"Hey, Limey. You sleep-riding?"

David jerked in the saddle at Chase's voice, surprised to find him riding beside Gomer.

"Sorry, mate. Just planning the chores for tonight."

The sidelong glance he got was more than skeptical.

"I told Jill I'd ask if you wanted to track down Pete Bosworth at the park headquarters tomorrow sometime. We'd best head off a complaint if we can and make our case about tonight. Got any free time late morning? I have a couple hospital visits first thing, then nothing until afternoon."

"I'll make time. Say when."

"Eleven?"

"Done."

"Everything all right? Nothing happened with Hewitt back there, did it?"

David waved his hand. "He was a bit of an arse, as he has been all along, but Rio put him in his place quite respectfully. She surprised him, but that's it."

"I've known her for the last six months." Chase let his eyes drift to Rio's red ponytail, hanging from beneath her helmet. "She's a unique woman. What she's done to keep her family together the past ten years is nothing short of miraculous. Thanks for helping her out."

"Of course. It's no trouble."

"She seems to like you. You could do worse, my friend."

"What the hell is that supposed to mean?"

"I dunno. I have no idea why I said it." He shrugged, winked, squeezed his calves, and trotted up to find his wife.

A LOT OF "should haves" assailed Rio the next morning when sunlight filtered through the window closest to her bed and fell across her eyes. She flung one arm over her face, but her mind leapt immediately out of sleep. She should have slept until noon after the night of wine, more wine, and two and a half hours spent on a horse. Not to mention the hour and a half afterward learning to feed horses, wipe down tack, and sweep barn aisles. Instead she peeked at the bedside clock and saw exactly what she suspected. 6:30 a.m.

She rolled to one side and groaned. At home she'd loved to sleep in when she could. Bonnie always told her she was a creature of the night, choosing the lunch to dinner shifts at the diner, reading late, keeping vigil during the deceptively quiet wee hours.

Well, she should have kept better vigil here. She should have run from David Pitts-Matherson when she'd had the chance—pushed him away decisively and unequivo-cally before that stupid kiss had been allowed to start.

Only there'd been no warning. One minute she'd been weeping over the stupid police chief, the next she'd been drowning in a musk-and-spice sea. What had she been thinking? She had a strict policy where men were concerned. They were vetted and practically interrogated before she consented to even a first date. The policy had served her well over the years. Guys knew not to mess with her. It was that kind of caution she was trying like mad to instill in her sister, and she was having a tough time of it. Some example she'd been last night. Rio didn't know David from any other pie-loving customer at the diner. He seemed like a nice guy. He liked her cooking. So what?

When had she made a decision to fall just because? Just because he was kind. Just because he had the sexiest accent she'd ever heard. Just because he could kiss like every fantasy she'd ever had.

She threw off the quilt to stop the internal list-making, and the instant she swung her legs out of bed, the just be-causes, the chief of police, even the memory of the kiss all vanished. Because every muscle from her upper abs to the one that moved her pinky toe protested like striking workers on a picket line.

"Jiminy Christmas," she blurted to the empty room.

She stood and winced. Her legs moved like wooden posts with pain receptors. Tiny little muscles she'd never known existed squeaked at her from her torso. Lumbering around for her clothes, she almost had to laugh. Twenty-six wasn't old enough to be this affected by a new activity. She was a wimp.

No sound greeted her at the bottom of the stairs, and she assumed she was the first one awake. Her muscles loosened as she padded toward the kitchen. Maybe she'd have enough range of motion to manage a pot of coffee.

"Good morning!"

She jumped. David stood beside the center island, a

mug already in his hand. He was back to breeches, this morning's pair a deep mocha brown, and her thoughts went careening out of bounds. Memory of the errant kiss flooded back at the sight of his thighs and butt so . . . showcased. Any thoughts of English riding pants being unmanly were permanently buried.

"Hi. It's so quiet I didn't realize anyone else was up," she said.

He grinned and pointed across the room. "Actually, you're the slug-a-bed, I'm afraid. Meet Limpy Lucy over there. She's been up a fair few minutes now."

Rio chuckled at the sight of Bonnie seated at the table, her head resting on her folded arms. "Hey, you," she called. "How goes it?"

"Kill me now." Bonnie's muffled words made both Rio and David laugh out loud.

"I told her what's needed is a bit of the hair of the dog. She needs to come on out and saddle up."

"Oh God," Bonnie moaned again.

"I have to agree." Rio shrugged. "That sounds awful to me, too."

"Ahh." He sipped his coffee, and the rich, black aroma eased her pain. "Got you, too, did we?"

"Hah. My toenails hurt."

His laugh rang through the kitchen. "You a coffee drinker, cowgirl?" He reached for a mug in the cupboard beside him. "Happy to pour you some."

"Yeah, I learned to drink it working late at the diners. We always had a cup in hand. If nothing else it was a decent weapon to throw if a jerk came by."

"I'll be sure and remember that. Anything in it?"

"Milk?"

"Cream?"

"Holy decadence. I'd say no, but I think I worked off enough calories last night to justify it."

"I like how you think."

The banter soothed her. His nonchalance calmed the earlier rush of hormones and erased the awkwardness she'd feared.

"Want me to make breakfast?" she asked.

"No, love. You go and sit with your sister. I can handle breakfast. Everything else, bets are off. How about I hire you as our chief cook while you're here, but I'll take the mornings."

"You'll let me cook to help pay our way?"

"Let you? I'll beg you to cook."

"Will you pay me to stay in bed?" Bonnie lifted her head and curled her lip.

"Out West they'd call you greenhorns." David opened the refrigerator. "Here's the deal. You two have the next twenty minutes to wake up those city slicker muscles, and then it's time to see how the real horsemen do it."

"I thought this was a mansion spa we were coming to." Bonnie yawned and smiled for the first time. "Can't I just be a guest at this dude ranch?"

"Hey, even at dude ranch guests head out to gather the cattle. I have no cows, but I have a barn full of cats you can try to herd."

"That's supposed to be hard, but if I don't have to get on a horse to do it, I'll figure it out," Bonnie said.

Rio grinned in surprise. When had Bonnie developed that quick sense of humor?

"And you two want to go out and start your own ranch," David teased. "Well, ladies, welcome to your reality check."

"I thought he was a nice guy at first," Rio said.

"Yeah. Me, too."

The easy chatter lasted through breakfast, and Rio cleared the dishes afterward. Her abs stung when she bent forward. Her inner thighs burned when she squatted to reach the dishwasher soap under the sink. But somehow, after the easiness and teasing between the three of them that was now a two-for-two precedent at mealtime, the pain felt more like a badge of honor.

And David never said a word about the kiss or even hinted he remembered it before he headed out to start his day.

Chapter Eleven

THE BARN AT 7:15 a.m. was a noisy place. Snorts, stamps, whinnies, bucket rattling, and a few solid wall kicks were Bridge Creek's equivalent to rush-hour traffic. David kept thirty-seven horses on the place, twenty-six of which were in stalls overnight. He, Rio, and Bonnie were the first humans to arrive, and Fred greeted them as if he hadn't seen them only hours earlier.

"Andy doesn't come down to start cleaning stalls until eight," David said. "I like being the one to feed and let everyone out in the morning. It's a good time to plan the day, check the horses myself, make sure everyone's okay."

"This is a lot of work." Rio looked at the long row of stalls and the eager faces behind the bars.

"It's a lifestyle, that's for bloody certain."

The matter-of-fact statement rang with resignation, something she'd not heard in his voice before. David the easygoing, the acquiescent, the cheerful breakfast chef suddenly had a stoic resignation in his eye and a grimmer set to his mouth.

For the first time since the kiss, she let herself study the full, artful swell of his lips and the texture of his skin. A single shot of latent desire darted to her core and pulsed there. She knew too well now that those lips could be as talented as those of any bad boy she'd ever met, and as gentle as any touch she'd ever conjured in her fantasies. But until this morning they'd never looked hard. Something subtle had changed his mood between the house and the barn.

He led them to a closed door near the front of the barn and unlatched it. The smell of malt and molasses, and pungent grain wafted from inside. He flipped on a light and pointed to a chest-high box on wheels.

"The magic feed wagon," he said. "Push it out and every horse in the place is your best friend. And they'll all tell you so."

The wagon sported two tip-out bins each filled with grain. Above the bins was a deep drawer filled with plastic separators and a few small buckets of powders.

"Every horse has a card by his or her stall that tells exactly what he gets. Ready for equine nutrition one-oh-one?"

He was a patient, interesting teacher, explaining exactly what each supplement did, why the horse got it, and how to remember what was what. Bonnie studied the feeding process with the same intensity she studied schoolwork. If only she'd taken as much painstaking effort to keeping her social life under control, Rio wished.

Feeding the horses was rhythmic and repetitive, and the sounds of contented snuffling in grain buckets filled Rio with a sense of well-being and accomplishment. Feeding time had another bonus. The barn cats showed up—popping out of hiding spaces like they'd heard an enchanted piper. Six felines—that Rio could count—hopped onto stall doors, twined around ankles, and sniffed at the grain that inevitably fell. David stroked them when they sat within reach and talked to them if they called noisily enough.

"They get fed after we're done with the horses. They're trying to hurry us up."

"Do they ever come into the house?" Bonnie took a break from graining to sit on a hay bale and scoop up a gray-and-black tabby. "Hello, baby."

"Nope, strictly barn cats. They're all happier outside. They have food and an ample supply of mice."

"Living mousetraps. Could have used one myself on occasion."

At that moment one of the mouse-trappers in question leaped onto the cart, sending Rio back with a surprised squeal. The little mottled cat meowed with much more lung power than should have been possible for its size, and Rio laughed.

"Hello to you, too. You're a unique little thing."

"Sort of a smashing cat with that tortoiseshell black-and-orange mix," David said. "She's one of an abandoned litter we found just down the road about six months ago. There were five and we found homes for all the others. Thirty-one here never interested anyone. She's got a pretty devilish personality."

"Thirty-one?"

"Short for October thirty-one," he replied. "She looked so Halloween-ish when her coat started to gloss up, and she's always up to something tricky. Cliché names like Goblin or Spooky were nixed."

"But a number?"

He shrugged "It stuck."

The cat was a stunner. The Halloween colors were evenly striated across her body except for solid black around her nose and two funny patches of orange-stripe over her eyes. Rio touched its head, and the half-grown cat lunged, wrapping its front legs around Rio's hand. As soon as its claws came out, however, they retracted almost immediately, and Thirty-one meowed and pressed her head into Rio's palm.

"Look at you, goofball," she said. "Are you trying to trick me into believing you're a tough cat? I think you're a little faker."

She scratched behind the dark ears and worked her way under the cat's chin. A purr vibrated up through her fur.

David's brows lifted. "In all this time that may be the longest anyone's petted her."

"That can't be true."

"You've usually got about thirty seconds before she turns on you. You must have some sort of touch."

The little Halloween cat seemed to be melting under Rio's fingers. She slid onto her side and closed her eyes.

"You're making it up. I have no knowledge of cats. Am not a cat person at all. She seems perfectly sweet."

"I'm telling you, it's a miracle," he teased, and went on to his next horse.

Rio picked up the cat, nuzzled it for a few seconds, and put it on the floor. "Go on, now." She finished the next horse. Seconds later the little cat sprang back up on the cart. "Goodness, hello again. What's this about?"

Two more attempts to get Thirty-one to stay on the ground failed. By the time Rio was done with the first row of stalls, her new friend was a permanent passenger. When all the feeding was finished, the cat trotted beside Rio like a dog. Something about that pleased her inordinately. She'd never had time or money for a pet even though she loved animals. The idea that maybe an animal might adopt her was another heady experience.

Like David's kiss.

Dang. The floodgates opened again, and she looked to where David stood with Bonnie, discussing a horse over its stall door. Her stomach danced like one of her maternal ancestors' Irish jigs. Usually a man who looked like David—tall, dark-haired, perpetually outdoorsy with a physique like a fine-tuned instrument, knew he was attractive. This man was sexy without trying.

And she was out of her element.

By the time Andy showed up at eight o'clock on the dot, the horses had been turned out and the cats fed. Thirty-one no longer followed Rio looking for food, and David had put muck forks in their hands and set them to work cleaning stalls.

Rio was busy reminding herself to watch what she wished for when Andy Manning, a fit, thirty-something man with a limp, a blond buzz cut, and slow, deliberate speech, greeted her cheerfully. He leaned over a stall door to watch her fork clods of manure clumsily into a wheelbarrow.

"Does this mean I can quit my job now?" He grinned.

"Please don't," Rio groaned, her muscles crying after just two stalls. "I'm so not good at this."

"It takes time to get fast. But I'm kidding. You don't have to do this as your job. David said he's just letting you see how to run a barn."

"Do you normally do all these stalls by yourself?"

Andy nodded. "Twenty-six stalls take me three or four hours depending. It's good work. I like it."

He spoke like a man with a slightly less-than-average IQ, yet his eyes were quick and intelligent.

"I've almost finished three, and I think if I had to clean this whole place by myself I'd finish at midnight and have to start right over again. You have my undying respect."

He beamed as if she'd given him a medal and went on to talk to Bonnie. Rio heard her sister laugh and Andy tell her she was doing a fine job. He seemed like a nice guy, and he was easier on her equilibrium by far than David. She wasn't sure where David had gone, but it was almost a relief to have him out of sight.

She'd finished five stalls by the time he showed up again. He startled her like Thirty-one had, but he with a silent, sudden presence, leaning casually against the open door of the stall she was finishing.

"My gosh," she cried. "What are you, ninja barn owner?"

"Sorry." The tightness from that morning was gone, yet he stared at her as if he'd never seen her before.

"What?" she demanded.

It was her turn to be less than cheery. Now any muscle that hadn't hurt from riding screamed at her if she moved. She stank like horse poop, and she had stripped to the tank top she'd put under her T-shirt. Oddly enough, the horse smell didn't bother her. The angry muscles, however, no longer felt like badges of accomplishment.

"They're actually quite pretty, aren't they?" A curious smoky veil faded out the blue of his eyes.

She stared back. "If I knew what you were talking about, I could agree or disagree."

"The tattoos."

"Oh!"

She stared down to where the delicate white, blue, and lavender-shaded feather along the inside of her right breast swooped up from beneath the rounded neckline of her tank top.

"I'm sorry." He hesitated, measuring his words. "I was unkind yesterday."

"It's fine. You don't have to like tattoos."

"In the army I saw plenty of, how should I say it kindly? Unfortunate ones. It wasn't fair to judge by those standards."

"I was picky about mine. I knew I wanted beautiful art. They represent a lot of savings and, some would say, wastefulness."

"How many do you have?"

She hesitated. "I have six."

His eyebrows twitched a fraction higher, but he nodded and scratched his nose self-consciously. He looked positively cute in his awkwardness.

"Are they showable?"

She smiled and couldn't help arching her own brow. "Not all of them."

His Adam's apple bobbed. Warmth flooded her cheeks.

"I expect that was a rude question considering my actions last night. I never apologized."

She looked instinctively down the barn aisle.

"It's all right," he assured her. "I sent Bonnie back to the house to get something to drink. I wanted to say I'm sorry."

"We're adults. I didn't exactly run screaming, David."

"No. And I was glad you didn't. Although tell me nothing happened during that kiss and I'll feel a lot better."

Over the two days they'd known each other, the only thing she'd grown slightly self-confident about was teasing him, and suddenly she couldn't even do that. So *much* had happened during the kiss she didn't dare open her mouth.

He nodded. "That's what I thought."

"It was a stupid thing for us to do."

"Oh, I don't know. I hate to call it stupid. Impulsive, yes."

"It was that."

"I meant what I said. I don't make a habit of kissing women who didn't ask to be kissed. I want you to think I took for granted I thought it was something I could do."

"Thank you."

What else could she say? That she wanted him to kiss her again, but even harder and more deeply? Because she did. Standing there alone it would have been easy for either of them to step forward. She could do it just as well as she could wish for him to do it . . .

For a long, anticipatory moment she held her breath.

He stepped back and the tension dissipated.

"I actually came to ask if you want to take Bonnie into town and show her around. She didn't get a chance to get oriented yesterday."

"Yeah, I guess. If we can move well enough to get there."

"I'll drop you at the pharmacy. You can hobble in and buy yourself some muscle rub."

"You're so thoughtful."

"My middle name—as they say. Stop mucking now and let Andy finish. He's bored." He turned away, then back. "Rio?"

"Yes?"

"What I really wanted you to know is that you're safe here. Bonnie is, too. I don't want to have jeopardized that feeling on your first day."

"Oh David. You didn't."

He nodded his thanks. "We can leave in half an hour if that's enough time."

"Sure."

He walked away, leaving her heart wishing he'd left her feeling just a little less safe.

SENIOR CITIZENS WITH walkers could have beaten her and Bonnie in a race up Main Street, Rio thought, as they limped past the small-town shop windows hoping nobody thought they were wounded homeless. They passed a yarn and fabric shop with gorgeous quilts in the window called Sew for Ewe. They spent a relaxing half hour in Grandy's Book Store, right next to the boutique Rio had seen yesterday. She showed Bonnie the tattoo parlor, and they squinted through the window. There wasn't much to see except one wall of tattoo art and a table with a pile of notebooks on it.

"I'm almost ready for another tat," Bonnie said. "But I don't know what I'd get."

"Then wait. They need to mean something so you really love them."

"I guess."

"Ready to meet David and Chase at the café?" Rio asked.

"It would feel good to sit down." She rubbed her hip.

"Still want to have our own barn?"

"I'd like to have this one. Holy crap—it's gorgeous."

"Yeah."

"Kim says it's impossible to make money boarding horses. She thinks even David struggles sometimes."

Rio sighed as they approached The Loon Feather's corner-facing door. She'd like to have David's struggles. He didn't have to tell Bonnie—very soon—that there'd be no money from the house with which to pursue a ranch. He didn't have to tell Paul that because of his stupidity there was no place for him to live. No place for any of them to live even once Hector was no longer a threat.

They entered the cool, blue-and-green interior of the

café, and a clear wolf whistle rang through the entryway. Bonnie glanced around herself, confused. Rio laughed.

"Check this out, it's pretty cool," she said.

They were cooing to the two cockatiels when the gray-haired woman Rio had met the day before greeted them.

"Rio! You're just in time to beat the lunch rush. Welcome back."

"Hi. Claudia, right?"

"Right. And this must be your sister?"

"I'm Bonnie." Always gregarious, she stuck out her hand for Claudia to shake.

"Can I get you a table?"

"We're meeting David. Along with Chase Preston."

"Wonderful. Two handsome men dressing up the place. And good ones, too. That new doctor of ours is about the nicest man I know. And David? They just don't come any more ethical or good-hearted. Or fun, for that matter."

"They've helped us a lot," Rio acknowledged.

Claudia led them to a table with a brightly colored cloth patterned in lighthouses. She took their drink orders and disappeared behind the counter.

"This is nicer than where you used to work," Bonnie said. "Everything's so clean."

Rio laughed at the exact words she'd said to David yesterday. Slowly she relaxed. Long hours weren't foreign to her, but work this physical was. It had hurt to sit in the chair at first, but she'd finally stopped feeling like she couldn't even lift a fork.

She roamed the room with her eyes, and they lit on a

printed sign beside the cash register across the room. The fine print wasn't readable, but the "Help Wanted" across was clear. All the tension returned to Rio's body.

It didn't make any sense for her to think about a job here. She wasn't going to be in Kennison Falls long enough to be a worthwhile employee, since there were only five weeks left until Bonnie needed to be back in school. Nonetheless, the idea of having at least a little seed money was as enticing as water to a desert traveler. What harm would there be in getting some information?

"Hullo, girls!"

David's cheery, accented *"gerls"* snapped Rio back to attention. She smiled as David, Chase, and Jill trooped in and took seats. Claudia headed for them, too, a Diet Coke and a lemonade in hand.

"The gang's all here," she said. "Taking drink orders. What'll you have?"

"So you really are pulling yeoman's duty, Claudia," Jill said. "I'm so sorry about Effie. Chase went to visit her this morning."

"How's she doing?" Claudia asked.

"She's uncomfortable," Chase said. "But you know Effie, she's like you and your sister. Tough Norwegians the lot of you. She'll do just fine after the hip replacement."

"How are you doing with all these hours?" David asked. "You've got all your own projects at home."

"Oh, we're fine for now." Claudia swung her long gray braid over her shoulder. "Gladdie did the supper shift yesterday so I could get my gardening done. Karla's doing double duty. The kitchen's okay with Vince and

Bud cooking. I have to say, I don't know how Effie does it. She must have the stamina of three Vikings. We've advertised for help. Karla only has three weeks left, and Gladdie can't work as many hours because she watches her grandson two afternoons. It would be nice to have one more set of hands."

"I could help."

Five pairs of eyes turned to Rio, and she winced inwardly before turning to Claudia. The offer had simply slipped out.

"Rio, no, you don't have to—" David began.

"I could use a job, you know that."

"Are you serious about this, dear?" Claudia asked. "Do you have any experience?"

"Eight years at three different restaurants in Minneapolis. I'm not a chef, but I've worked on a couple of grill lines. I've waitressed, and I've handled the till."

"Goodness me, we have an expert right under our noses."

"Now hang on a sec, Claudia." David stared at Rio, and she braced for a fight. But, though she expected condescension, she saw only concern. "It's not my place to tell you what to do—"

"That's right."

"But I don't want you to do this because you have some daft idea you need to pay to stay at my place."

"That's part of it," she admitted. "But I have other reasons for needing to work. Besides, you just heard her say how they need an extra pair of hands right now. There's one catch." She turned to Claudia.

"Yes?"

"I honestly don't know how long I'll be here. And you probably want to know exactly what happened back in Minneapolis. If I'm not the best choice for this. I'd understand."

"Sweetheart, if you could give us a week, just so we could get through next weekend's library fund-raiser and interview someone who wants a more permanent position, we'd be grateful. Could you come back tomorrow and we'll talk about details?"

"I . . ." She hesitated. "I think so. I'll need to impose on someone to help me get my car. It's in Minneapolis."

"We'll help you," Jill said.

"You didn't want to go into the cities," David countered.

"I do now." With a firm look she stopped any further protest and nodded at Claudia. "What time would you like me here?"

"Mid-morning between the breakfast and lunch rushes? I'll talk to Effie, too, and let her know. You can meet Karla and Gladdie, as well."

"All right. I'll be here."

"And just like that, Heaven has answered our prayer." Claudia patted her on the shoulder. "For that, drinks are on the house." She chuckled. "I've always wanted to say that. Too bad we aren't talking whiskey."

Chapter Twelve

AFTER LUNCH, FOR which David and Chase split the bill, Rio's confidence flagged when she realized she had to face Chief Hewett and find out how to get her car back. David insisted on taking her, and he sent Bonnie back to the stable with Jill, who had to first drop Chase at his clinic. Rio's head spun at all the finagling. She was used to making a decision and carrying it out. By herself. Depending on other people, and watching them have to change their plans because of her, made her feel like she'd lost all control.

All the more reason to suck it up and talk to Hewett, even though the man probably wouldn't walk across the street to greet her unless she was in some kind of trouble.

The Kennison Falls Police Department was far from ostentatious. A small, brick-front building housed a sixties-era lobby with two brown Naugahyde benches and a handful of uncomfortable-looking chairs. At a chest-high counter with a small array of monitoring devices behind her, sat a woman of about forty with a broad, cheerful face and curly black hair.

"Hey, Faith." David greeted her. "Anything big going on today?"

"Somebody egged Miller's barn last night. Two kids lit a handful of Black Cats in the Dumpster behind the grocery store. And Lillian kicked Ezra out again."

David snorted. "Happens about once a month," he explained. "Ezra is eighty-six and likes his boilermakers and *Playboy* magazines. Lillian is eighty and can handle the alcohol, but not when that brown-wrapped magazine is delivered. She sends him to the Motel 6 ten miles away and tells him to stay out."

"That's the police blotter? For real?"

Rio honestly couldn't believe this was the sort of thing there was to discuss at a police station. At the precinct nearest her in Minneapolis, it would have been racially motivated graffiti, .38-caliber bullets, and a pimp selling a girl.

David touched her arm, his face full of empathy. She wondered what her face was saying and worked to make it blank even while she reveled in the warmth of his touch. She liked that his fingers imparted safety but not possession. When he dropped his hand, the spot felt empty. She cleared her throat.

"I'm here to see the chief."

"I'm not surprised." Chief Hewett appeared from around a corner with familiar toughness in his face but sans his bulky utility belt. "I heard you've already been over to the State Park office and talked to the ranger."

"And you'd already beaten us there," David replied. "But we're here about an entirely different matter."

"Oh?"

"I've decided I need my car after all," Rio said. "I'm willing to pick it up, so I need to know what I have to do to get it today."

"Must it be today?"

She eyed him suspiciously. "I need to use it tomorrow morning."

"Fine. I'll have it to you by 9:00 a.m."

"You?" She was flabbergasted. "You'll get my car? Why?"

"Because you made a good point, I don't want you leading Hector Black here, accidentally or otherwise. I have someone who'll drop the car off in Faribault fifteen miles north of town in the middle of the night, and someone else who'll bring it here."

More convoluted scheming.

"I would never purposely lead him back here."

"No. But If Hector Black or your brother is trying to find you through the car, maybe the police can lure one of them out. If not, the car's yours and we all stay a little safer."

"Keep the riffraff out, right?" Rio asked a little more sarcastically than she should have.

"Exactly." Tanner Hewett was a handsome man beneath his wall of anger. She wondered what had made him so unpleasant. "But there's also your safety. There's never been a murder in Kennison Falls, so the records say. I don't plan to have you be the first."

A statistic? That was all he cared about?

"Fine." She picked a small sticky notepad off Faith's desk. After scribbling quickly, she peeled off the top paper and thrust it at the chief. "This is my cell phone number. I'd like to know the minute you have the car."

"I can do that for you."

The man was an enigma. Half antagonist, half seemingly willing helper.

"Thank you. What will I owe you?"

"We'll work that out when I've got the car."

The idea of paying out close to two hundred dollars still stung, but with the hope of money coming in, the prospect wasn't as terrifying.

"I appreciate your help, Chief Hewett."

"I want this situation resolved, too, Miss Montoya. The sooner I don't have to worry about gangs from Minneapolis finding out about our little town, the happier I'll be. I'm hoping this will speed up the process of getting you home."

Her jaw worked soundlessly. Of all the arrogance . . . Just about the time she was willing to give him the benefit of the doubt.

David touched her again, this time on the shoulder. She lifted her eyes to his and found an angry light she'd never seen in them before. He leaned close to her ear, and breath tickled the soft skin of her lobe. "Ignore his tone. Like you did last night. It'll be okay."

Shivers flooded her system. He pulled away, leaving the comforting scent of his aftershave.

"That would be good for all of us, Chief," she managed to say without rancor.

David smiled, coolly. "Thank you from me, as well," he said. "And you and I will be in touch on our other issues."

"Yes, we will." The chill hadn't left Hewett's eyes either.

"I think you'll find our group is more than willing to find some legal way to compromise. We love that space, so we'll all work it out."

"I'll look forward to the interactions."

Once outside again, Rio let out a huge breath she hadn't realized she'd been holding. "Wow."

"He's quite a fellow, our new chief."

"Quite a fellow? He's an arrogant asshat."

He snorted. "Usually arrogance comes about because of some insecurity."

"Are you always so understanding? You compromise on everything, even that little spot you all want to keep using. Why back down?"

"Because he's right. We were breaking the law. We just always had permission before. If he's not going to give his, then we run the risk of losing it completely if we counter him."

She made a rude snort.

"You feel the same way," he continued. "I know you do. I saw it last night. You didn't antagonize him when you could have. You knew it would do you no good."

He was right. Still, his reasonable tone rankled. "You can read my mind, can you?"

"You're pretty open and honest, love. It's an attractive quality. Something I could use a little more of."

"You? If you've ever told a lie in your life, I'll clean ten stalls tomorrow morning."

"I'll tell Andy to come in later."

He chuckled and put his arm around her shoulders to guide her away from the station door. "You're a breath of fresh air around here, you know. Come on, I've got horses to ride, and you've got one more afternoon of vacation if you're hell-bent on taking a job."

"You don't really think I'm crazy?"

"I do. But I also understand."

"Do you?"

"I'm beginning to. You'll be more stressed if I make you relax."

Yeah, she thought. He'd hit that nail on its head.

FRED WOKE DAVID from a deep sleep with frantic, watchdog barking that only meant one thing—there were people around. But at 5:45 a.m.? He crawled from bed and cracked his blinds to see a pair of headlights swing past the house and shine toward the barn. Frowning, he grabbed a pair of jeans from the floor next to his bed. Rummaging in the gray, predawn dimness through a basket of unfolded laundry, he found a T-shirt, and as he yanked it over his head, the blinds lit up again from the outside. A second glance revealed a second car.

"Bloody hell," he mumbled.

It didn't occur to him what might be going on until he was in the foyer slipping a pair of running shoes over his bare feet.

"David?"

He glanced back up the stairs. A disheveled Rio eyed him uncertainly. "Is it possible this is my car?"

"I'm about to go find out. You should stay here in case it's someone you don't care to meet."

She rubbed her eyes and yawned absently. "I'm pretty sure if Hector or Paul had found us, they wouldn't drive up in two cars with their lights blazing."

Good point. He stared, entranced by the vulnerability sleepiness gave her, and dry-mouthed at the careless sexiness she clearly didn't know she exuded. A worn pair of cotton sleep pants covered in hearts hung low on her hips. A minty-green, spaghetti-strap, knit shirt thing clung to her torso and left her soft breasts outlined by the dim light. She pulled on a lightweight hoodie as she came down the rest of the stairs, a pair of flip-flop sandals slapping softly against her soles.

"All right," he said. "Let's go see what's going on."

He held the door and she ducked under his arm. Soft strands of her burnished hair flopped in messy disarray across the top of her head. He desperately wanted to smooth it. He refrained.

Over the roof of the state-of-the-art arena, the one to which he'd let his father add every bell and whistle, streaks of purple and gold heralded the sunrise. Two car doors slammed. Rio pointed.

"That's my car."

Two shadows moved toward them, and David couldn't miss the tall, solid physique of Dewey Mitchell, who ran the local gas and service station. It made perfect sense to have Dewey involved, David thought. He imagined there wasn't much trouble Dewey couldn't get himself out of.

"Sorry to wake you." Dewey's laconic voice cut through the morning air. "We were hoping to leave the car and go so it would be here when you got up."

"It's no trouble at all," David replied.

"It was cool. We were kind of part of a sting." A younger man trailed Dewey, one David recognized as Gladdie Hanson's grandson Joey, who'd been working at the garage all summer.

"A sting?" Rio asked, her voice no longer sleep-soaked.

"Rio, meet Dewey Mitchell. Dewey, this is Rio Montoya, the owner of the Taurus."

"Nice to meet you." Dewey's big grip engulfed Rio's pale hand, but she shook firmly. "This is Joey Hanson. Got him to come along and be my getaway driver. I'm sorry to say, the fellow the police are looking for never showed up."

"Showed up where?"

"The way I understand it, the Minneapolis police had a plainclothes officer take your car from the impound lot around one this morning and drive it to Rosemount, 'bout twenty miles from here. They left it sit there about four hours, and then Joey and I went to pick it up. Guess they watched it pretty closely, thinking somebody would try to find it to find you?"

"That's crazy!" Rio looked from Dewey to David.

"I admit I laughed when Chief Hewett first asked me to help with this," Dewey said. "It seemed like maybe he'd been watching too much *Law & Order*."

"No lie," Rio agreed.

"But turns out it was really the Minneapolis police thought this up. They want this guy, too. Guess he's been moving around outside his normal area, held up two convenience stores, and disappeared again. All Hewett had to do was find a person to bring the car back."

"I'm sorry you had to get involved." A tinge of the Rio-hardness David was coming to recognize rising behind the words. "I don't mean for other people to be a part of this."

"It was cool," Joey said. "Really."

"Well, you got the car," David said. "Thank you."

"Yes. Thank you." Rio's voice thinned.

She stepped away and took a walk around her car, stopping on the far side to squat and disappear from view.

"She's awfully young to be in such a fix." Dewey looked to David.

"She's older and tougher than she looks," he said. "Impressive girl, actually. Her brother is friends with the bloke wanted for arson. Personally, I'd like to know why a two-bit thug is so interested in her. It doesn't make sense. But this is a start to solving the puzzle, I guess."

"I'm glad we could help." Dewey stuck his hand out. "We don't need anything else."

"Nice of you, mate," David said. "Are they compensating you for the trouble?"

Dewey blew out a dismissive breath and waved his hand as he turned. "Civic duty. It's just what you do."

David stood back as Dewey and Joey said their good-byes to Rio, hopped in the second car, Dewey's gray

Sonata, and drove off. He waited for Rio to finish her slow inspection of doors, glove box, and boot. When she returned to his side, she held one piece of paper—the note Hewett had described: "Return to Rio Montoya."

"It's Paul's writing, for what it's worth."

"Does that mean anything, do you think?"

"Only that he's been in the car recently. There's a new dent on the driver's door and a scratch along the lower half of the driver's side rear door, so somebody played a little rough with it."

"I'm sorry."

She shrugged. "It's an inner city car. It shouldn't look pretty. It just pisses me off that Paul is part of this."

"Come on, love, let's go inside. I know you drink coffee. Do you drink tea?"

"Herbal tea. Sometimes."

"I'll see what I can find."

Chapter Thirteen

DAVID BROUGHT THE tea to the deck off the back of the house that faced a stand of hardwoods ringing the property. Dawn made the trees to the west glow. He would have fallen for the land his farm sat on even without the buildings. The rolling mix of pastureland and woods made it one of the prettiest places in the area. The fact that the house and barns had been ready to update had made purchasing it irresistible.

He wished Bridge Creek wasn't at such a crossroads. The recent economy had wreaked havoc with luxury businesses like his. And his father's working visit the previous summer had been an enormous drain on his meager savings. The bells and whistles on the new arena hadn't been covered by the insurance money he'd gotten to replace the one lost in the tornado. Two years ago already. How could that be?

"This is nice."

Rio came through the patio door with two mugs. Her hair still tangled in crazy waves, but her features had softened, and her vulnerability had returned. He set his pot of hot water on the small table in front of a double rocking lounger and sat. She sat beside him.

"It is. Perfect sunrises. A little wildlife hops and past now and again."

"The only wildlife we regularly see in the cities are squirrels and birds."

She poured tea from the pot into the two mugs and lifted hers between cupped palms. He liked watching Rio inhale, close her eyes, and lift her bare feet up to tuck them beneath her. Her knee brushed his thigh.

She needed this haven. This escape. It was the reason he'd let her perception that he was wealthy go unchallenged. He normally didn't appreciate being lumped into the category of gentry, even though he'd worked very hard on his ten-year plan to turn Bridge Creek into a showpiece that could attract top level riders. He'd saved. He'd allowed his mother to pour her time and talents into the place. He'd allowed his father to use his name to start building the facility's reputation.

But he was out of funding, out of options, out of ideas after the past few years' big hits. He could still afford to go out to dinner. Still afford to shop for groceries certainly. But his budget was stretched. Rio didn't need to think she was any more of a burden than she already did. She wasn't a burden. Neither was her sister. One good thing his eccentric mother had taught him was that people came first and that, somehow, Heaven would provide.

"Earth to David."

He blinked. "Sorry. I'm afraid I was just thinking that today's the day my mum is arriving."

"Do you know when?"

"Mid-afternoon, according to her messages. I'm not to pick her up. She wants her own car so she will rent one. I guess we'll just have to be surprised."

Her eyes gave away neither anticipation nor dread. "Are you sure we're not in the way?"

"I am sure. I'm not saying you won't want to run screaming."

"Are you trying to scare me?"

"No. There's no way to describe Mum, that's all. Like I told you, she's adorable and vexing all at once. The main reason she and my father split up is because they were mutually uncontrollable. He couldn't control her with inflexibility and firmness, and she couldn't change him with sweetness and stubbornness."

"Sounds like they should have been soul mates forever."

He laughed at the wry humor in her voice. "In an odd way they still are. There are still fireworks when they're together. The explosiveness is more fun now that they're divorced."

She settled deeper into the rocker. Her left leg remained folded beneath her, but she planted her right sole on the cushion and hugged her knee and thigh while sipping her tea.

"Mmmmm." She closed her eyes. "What's this?"

"Some minty cocoa thing. I grew up on stout Yorkshire tea so this stuff is a bit anemic. It smells good, though, and it's good for guests."

A thump punctuated his explanation, and both of them looked to the cat padding across the deck after having jumped from the railing.

"Thirty-one!" Rio said.

David eyed the bundle hanging from its mouth and tried not to laugh. "Uh, Rio, be warned—"

The cat dropped the dead mouse on the decking in front of them, looked up, and let out a yowl that announced her presence to the whole farm.

"Ohmygosh!" Rio screeched like a girl in a cartoon and twisted on the seat right into his chest. She buried her eyes, and he wrapped both arms around her.

"It's just—"

She was laughing, and this was no giggle but an enormous, rolling guffaw complete with gasps for breath. He held her, her body shaking uncontrollably against his. She'd landed so spontaneously in his arms that it seemed the most natural thing in the world. She pulled away to wipe her eyes.

"I'm sorry." She coughed. "I did *not* see that coming."

"I warned you about the mice."

"You did." She unrolled herself from the ball she'd become and groaned. "Ow. I still can't move fast. I think my legs hurt more than they did yesterday."

"My poor little greenhorn."

Her smile sent his pulse on a free-for-all. Having her so genuinely happy—or seemingly so—made his worries feel lighter. The young orange-and-black cat meowed again and leaped onto the chair.

"She brought that as a gift, you know," he said.

"I do know." She pulled the kitten onto her lap, and David marveled. The animal was pretty but had won no friends. With Rio scratching its belly, however, it acted like God's gift to personable cats. She lowered her voice to a sexy coo. "Thank you, sweet little Thirty-one. You're beautiful and thoughtful, but can I ask a favor? Since dead animals aren't my favorite thing, how 'bout you just bring yourself next time?"

The cat whirred like a little trolling motor.

"You have a way with her."

"Nah, she just found a kindred spirit." Rio nuzzled the cat.

Having Rio as a kindred spirit would be nice, he thought. But nothing could be further from the truth. She was his opposite in so many ways—a fighter, unafraid to speak her mind, protective, and focused. All qualities he pulled out only if he really needed them. Even so, she felt perfect, half-leaning on him as she fondled the cat's ears.

"What do you have in common with a little cat like that?"

"We're both oddly colored. We're both a little leery of the world. We'd both kind of rather be alone . . ."

She trailed off as if embarrassed, and David seized the opportunity to straighten and take her by both shoulders to turn her toward him. The cat hissed like a cobra and swiped at him with claws unsheathed.

"Hey now!" Rio picked up Thirty-one and held her in front of her face. "I like him, so you be nice."

David reached to stroke the kitten, and it hissed again.

"Right. We'll have no more of that." Calmly he took Thirty-one by the scruff of her neck and held her the way a mother cat would. "You can play with Rio later. It's my turn."

He reached through the deck rails and set the cat on the grass. She protested plaintively. Then he bent over, grasped the tip of the dead mouse's tail, and picked it up.

"Gross." Rio grimaced.

"I'll toss it into the trees over there," he said. "The mouse equivalent to a burial at sea."

"My hero." Her voice carried to him, deadpan.

He got rid of the mouse, then ran his fingers under water from the hose coiled just off the back step of the deck. He joined her again.

"Why did you really shoo away the cat?" she asked.

"Other than the fact the little puma was going to slash me open and feast on my pancreas?"

"That itty bitty thing?"

"She's taken to you. If you're not careful, you'll have a nasty bodyguard cat on your hands."

"Do I need a bodyguard?"

"Do you want one?"

That stopped her a moment. She pursed her lips. "You said it was your turn to *play*. I'm wondering what you meant."

"The truth? I'm feeling decidedly unmotivated to work and that scares me a bit. So I'm trying to figure out why you make me want to ignore my chores, drink girlie tea . . . kiss people without warning. This isn't me."

"Funny you should say that . . ." Her words trailed off.

"What?"

She sighed. "I'm not sure who I am here either."

"Look." He lifted one hand and caressed her knuckles gently with his thumb. "We wouldn't think this was strange if we'd met through a friend or at a pub and we were attracted to each other. And I'll admit there's definitely attraction. On my part."

"Mine, too. It would be silly to deny it. But I'm not going to be here that long."

"A little while—until you're safe."

"So what are you asking?" A tinge of playfulness crept into the question. "To date me? To kiss me? To . . ."

"See whatever of your tattoos you're willing to show me."

"I . . . what? Seriously?"

The question sent her features into such confusion that he laughed. "Is it so unbelievable that I'm intrigued? You said you have six. How can I help but wonder what they are?"

She cocked her head and studied him with a suggestive smile, as if deciding his worthiness. "I can show you some of them."

"What will I learn from them? About you?"

"It's more what you won't learn—where the feather goes. Or the horse's tail."

He leaned closer. "Awww, c'mon."

She only shook her head. "I can show you the moon." At his raised brows she glowered. "Not that kind of moon."

"Would you show me the horse's head again?"

She smiled indulgently and swiveled in place. Bending forward, she pulled down the waistband of the cotton sleep pants, and this time David wasted no time in shock. He examined the art on her back with wonder. He hadn't noticed the subtle golden shading in the horse's dished face and arched neck, or the delicate strokes of pure white ink in its sweeping mane and tail. The palomino she'd said she wanted.

An urge he refused to control made him extend his finger and trace the flowing, heart-shaped curve of the horse's tail. She twitched, and he heard her tiny intake of breath. He tamped down the heat it ignited, frustrated that he still couldn't see the end of the tail or the point where it curved to meet the mane. The desire to follow below the waistband of her heart-covered pants nearly wrecked his self-control, but he dragged his finger from her skin.

She shrugged off her lightweight sweatshirt and exposed the skimpy knit top that served as her pajamas. "I can show you this one." With the deliberateness of a striptease, she slipped the string strap from her right shoulder and let it fall to her elbow. "Pull the fabric past my shoulder blade."

He tugged gently on the fabric, his fingers clumsy with the task. The tattoo he exposed just beneath her shoulder blade extended down and toward her side—a black-and-white image of the moon and stars, dark and bright at the same time. Striking and beautiful.

"Damn," he said. "That's a stunner, isn't it?"

She straightened and spun on the seat again, pulling her sweatshirt back around her shoulders. The soft knit

T-shirt stretched across her breasts, and their perfection pressed out in relief against the fabric. The outline of one nipple beckoned like a signal light. He caught her by both upper arms as he had in the park.

"Attraction," he said. "Fascination. Red hair. That's all."

"I'm not wearing a bra," she added, as he lowered his mouth. "It could be shallow male lust."

"Trust me, you're not half-wrong," he whispered next to her mouth. "But we promised we wouldn't do this again, so if you tell me to stop I will. I'm shallow but not irredeemable."

She made the final move into his kiss and managed to surprise him.

Her hands grasped either side of his head, and she angled her mouth so it fit better against his. Weaving her fingers through his hair, she played with the pressure of their lips, opening and closing hers with butterfly-like nibbles. He followed her lead and cupped her ears, massaging his thumbs just in front of them, causing her to melt closer and open her mouth. Their tongues collided in sweet, mint tea goodness, and she smiled behind the kiss, sighing in acceptance. The vibrations carried tremors all the way to his gut. Her fingers dancing in his hair sent goose bumps bursting across his scalp.

He pulled slowly away, drawing out the kiss and touching her bottom lip with the pad of his thumb after they parted. "The first kiss might have been a fluke," he said. "Isn't that what we said?"

"Uh-huh." She blinked a couple of times as if coming out of a stupor.

"What do you think now?"

"I think you're dangerous. You shrivel my brain and turn me as boy crazy as my sister."

"I could like being considered dangerous."

She stood and slowly licked her swollen lips. "You could have gone further," she said. "I practically flashed you a neon welcome sign. And if you'd touched me, like I was praying you would, I'd have liked it. But you didn't." A wistful smile lit on her lips. "I didn't know I needed you to be a gentleman—they're hard to find these days. Thank you. I'd better go get ready for my job interview."

Brilliant. He was a gentleman. He knew there was fear and vulnerability she wouldn't admit to under her toughness. Still, what had playing the gentleman gotten him? A kiss and extreme physical frustration. It was a bloody good thing she couldn't read his ungentlemanly mind.

Chapter Fourteen

RIO GOT TO the end of Bridge Creek's long driveway, stopped her car, and dropped her head forward onto the steering wheel with a thump and a groan. She still couldn't believe what a freaking idiot she'd been. David had to think she was ridiculous.

I'm not wearing a bra. She'd really announced that? As if she had to tell a man who could teach master classes on the art of kissing something so obvious. As if you advertised something like that at all.

Not to mention *I'd have liked it if you'd touched my boob, but thank you for being good.*

Seriously, where was her brain? She never acted this stupid around men. Around anybody. It was only him, and it had started before they'd ever kissed. Now that they had, apparently her head was a quivering mass of dead and dying brain cells.

And apart from opening her mouth allowing stupid

to come out, why would she thank a man for respecting her? As if he should have a choice. As if she'd had no choices in the matter, and gotten lucky.

She pounded the steering wheel. The problem was, she didn't *want* to think about female empowerment. All she truly wanted was to relive David's kiss, because the only thing that had made her feel powerful in a very long time was the unbelievable current that ran through her body when her lips meshed with his.

A crush. Women got them on their rescuers all the time. Only this didn't feel like a crush. It felt like something inevitable and cosmic, despite how ludicrous that sounded in her head. With a final groan of frustration she pulled herself together and continued to town, passing the Wonder Weenie Mobile still beside the "Welcome to Kennison Falls" sign.

She stepped into the main restaurant and got a shot of warmth. David had called it the heart of the town. It wasn't hard to see why. Every eclectic detail called out "welcome home."

"Good morning, Rio!" Claudia passed her with two plates of eggs and pancakes, her long gray braid swinging jauntily. "You're right on time. Do you drink coffee?"

"I do."

"There's a pot next to the counter over there. Pour yourself a mug and settle into the booth in the corner. I'll be right there."

"Okay. Thank you."

"Good morning again."

A vaguely familiar voice hailed her, and she turned

to see the man who'd delivered her car. In the light his features showed him to have a serious expression but a friendly eye that softened what could have been an intimidating face. High cheekbones and a thick, sable mustache camouflaged handsomeness that would be easy to miss. Rio smiled back easily.

"Hi, Mr. Mitchell."

"No, no. It's Dewey," he said. "How's the car running, then? Okay? I didn't have time to check it over but it seemed to drive all right."

He had a tinge of Minnesotan in his words, something Rio, a born-and-bred Minnesota girl herself, rarely heard. Yet he made the accent charming, without sounding like a Coen brothers film.

"It seems fine, thank you. And it's full of gas, too. I'm sure it wasn't found that way."

He shrugged. "A little gas to get you going. It's not a big deal."

"I appreciate it, though."

He smiled. "Well, bring 'er in if she has any problems. I'm happy to take a look if she needs a little tune-up."

A sense of unreality threatened to overwhelm her. Niceness filtered through the air here like a weird sort of perfume. The people she worked with in Minneapolis were nice, too, but not like this. This was unicorns and kittens nice, not normal, "hello, have a nice day, see you later" nice.

"That's very"—she stumbled over the word "nice"— "kind of you. Everyone's been so welcoming."

He lifted his coffee mug in a mini-salute. "We're

all right most of the time. Sounds like you'll maybe be helpin' us out, too?"

Laughter sneaked up and lightened her heart. There wasn't any point anymore in being surprised at what people knew around this place.

"Maybe. For a little while," she admitted. "So I'll see you around then?"

"Here every day at break time."

"Good. And, thank you again. It helps a lot to have my wheels back."

"I figure, who can survive without tires and an engine, right?"

She gave him a thumbs-up and turned back for her coffee, to find Claudia with a mug already poured.

"Oh!"

"You'll fit in just great around here," Claudia said. "Chatting with the customers like that? They love it."

"I swear this place is covered in pixie dust or something. It's like having coffee in Cinderella's Castle."

"Not at all. It's just different from the city is all. You'll see soon enough."

Rio took the coffee and followed Claudia to an isolated booth made from handsome wooden logs. There were other booths, but this one stood out as unique.

"This is Bud's Booth," Claudia said. "Effie's husband built the original that was destroyed in the storm. He, Dewey, and David, actually, rebuilt it. The first thing you have to know is that it's always kept open for anything special that comes our way. If a couple arrives looking like they need to be alone—put 'em here. If someone looks sad—put him here. If there's an important meeting—it goes here. Somehow, it's almost always available when it needs to be."

"Wow, a magical booth."

"Just one of the services Effie provides." Claudia chuckled. "I think you'll find this is quite a place, honey. Little special things everywhere."

Rio stiffened. Being called "honey" never failed to give her a painful tweak. Even after ten years she could hear her step-grandmother's grating voice float in from the past, "Honey Rio, trust me. I know what's best."

"I'm sure there are," she said quickly, dispelling the memory.

They talked after that about Rio's experience, about what she wanted to do, and when she was able to work. The matter-of-fact conversation flowed more easily for Rio and allowed her to keep her emotional distance from the warm, fuzzy Claudia, and returned her sense of control. Rio understood schedules, restaurant rush times, and sharing duties. They were things she could control and negotiate.

When Claudia brought her to see the kitchen and introduce her to Effie's husband, Bud, the owner and main chef, and to Vince, one of The Loon's three cooks, Rio could comment on the state-of-the-art facility and prove she knew her way around a grill. After her flood of questions, Bud seemed impressed.

"You might be dangerous to hire," he said. "You know too much. We'll be obsolete."

She shook her head in certainty. "I know about frying

up greasy burgers and grilling patty melts. I think you'd have far more to teach me."

"She's hired, Claudia," he said. "She's polite and knows how to suck up. That's a rare combo. Welcome aboard, Rio."

She started unofficially then and there. After filling out paperwork, she shadowed Claudia, learning the cash register and the credit card system. She took a handful of orders and watched as Vince and Bud whipped up the sandwiches and burgers. The crowd filtered in as it approached noon, and at twelve-thirty Karla Baxter arrived for her shift and greeted Rio like a long-lost sister.

"Thank goodness you came along," she said. "I've been so concerned about school starting. I didn't want to leave everyone in the lurch, but I have no choice."

"I think it'll be fun," Rio said.

"We're all family. We've been pulling together a long time."

That made it all the more strange to Rio that she was so quickly accepted. Families were usually tight-knit and slow to let outsiders infiltrate. Yet, the small crew welcomed her patiently and with good humor. She wasn't even officially on the payroll. The five hours between her arrival at The Loon and 3:30 p.m. flew past.

"I think we've stuffed enough information into your poor brain for today," Claudia told her after Rio rang up her first bill on her own. "You're a quick study."

"It helps that I've done this before," she replied. "Just never in such a nice place. I think I'll enjoy working here."

"I'm so glad. And I think we'll enjoy having you. Now, you're all right with the day shift? Four days this week. My sister Gladdie will take Friday, and I prefer the evenings because it gives me the days to get my work done at home."

"That'll be just fine."

"Then we'll see you tomorrow at nine. You'll meet a couple of the other girls who help at busy times throughout the week. They'll all head back to school in three weeks, too, so they're very part-time."

"I'll be here. Thank you, Claudia. This will help me out a lot."

"It's mutual, honey."

Rio let the "honey" go. Claudia's endearment wrapped her in warmth, so different from Yaya's rankling condescension. When she reached her car, she realized the embarrassment and confusion of the morning with David had ebbed away. She also realized, a little bit to her surprise, how much she enjoyed hanging around a restaurant. At home it had simply been her job. She'd never minded going to it, but she'd certainly never considered it something she liked. The atmosphere at The Loon Feather gave her a sense of accomplishment and place. She looked forward to returning.

Before starting the engine, she pulled her phone from her purse and checked it out of habit. Her thoughts careened to a halt when Paul's name appeared above a text message.

Her heartbeat doubled. She hadn't heard from him—or whoever it was—in over three days except for the sign in her car. With trembling fingers she tapped on the message. Her mouth dropped open.

Clever to sneak the car out of the lot in the middle of the night. I don't know where you are yet, but I'll find you and Bonnie before you can find me. Inigo sends his love.

She dropped the phone like it was a snake and gasped for air. The confirmation it wasn't Paul sending the messages both relieved and terrified her.

But why was he going to the trouble?

Hector was a two-bit gang member. He simply couldn't care this much about a teenager he'd dated fewer than half a dozen times. And if he was angry about the scratches from Rio, well, he'd burned her damn house down. What more revenge could there be? This whole terrorizing gig made no sense.

Her high deflated. Hector *had* been watching the car. Rio didn't know how likely it was he really could find Bonnie. He was a small-time thug with few connections. On the other hand, he was mean, and he was resourceful. He'd evaded police for more than a week now.

She shouldn't worry, but all at once she couldn't wait to get back to David's and check on Bonnie. Or maybe she should first go back and quit this job. How could she look out for her sister if she wasn't with her? On the other hand, how could she ever get Bonnie out of there if she didn't have money? She rubbed her eyes for a painful moment. Five minutes earlier life had been hopeful for the first time in many days. Now reality had scuttled her ship again. You really couldn't escape who you were. Even in unicorn and puppy land.

Sure enough, at Bridge Creek something seemed off. Searching the yard, however, gave Rio no clue as to what it was. There was no evident panic. Several cars were parked beside the barn. She pulled in beside a shiny new, green Nissan. It could have belonged to anyone, but she eyed it suspiciously. Cars at the barn were always dusty and filled with riding paraphernalia. This vehicle was pristine.

Neither Bonnie nor David was in the barn. At the house, she crossed the deck to the back door and opened it to the sound of voices carrying through the empty kitchen from the living room. Puzzled, she made her way to the doorway. The moment she caught sight of a short, plumpish woman with the loveliest silver-streaked black hair she'd ever seen, Rio knew who she was and also who belonged to the perfect car outside. She'd completely forgotten about David's mother's arrival.

Mrs. Pitts-Matherson sat beside Bonnie on the deep-cushioned sofa. For once the girl wasn't the main focus of the room. That seemed to be David and another woman, seated on the love seat opposite the couch. They bent over a book, the woman, slender and elegant even seated, spoke rapidly in a very Julie Andrews–esque accent. A glistening fall of satiny, dark chestnut hair hid her face.

"Do you remember this day?" She tapped the book and patted David's thigh. "I was quite awful about having to go on that hunt with you, but you talked me into it so sweetly, and I ended up having such a marvelous time. I never forgot that."

"I do recall it vaguely." David's voice held a note of uncertainty, and Rio's very first impression was that he'd be happy to get away.

But then she put her arm briefly around his shoulders, squeezed once, and smiled tenderly. Rio's stomach slid to her toes, surprising her with the force of her jealousy. Mrs. Pitts-Matherson looked up then, and confirmed her identity without saying a word. Rio saw exactly where David had come by his smile and warm cocoa-brown irises.

"Why, hello," she said. "Here's another face at the party. Is this your sister, pet?" She glanced at Bonnie.

"Yeah, it's Rio. Hi!"

David's head had popped up, and he caught her eyes with a slightly sheepish grin.

His mother stood and crossed the floor with a strong, sure stride that emphasized her bulldog sturdiness. She wore crisply creased black dress pants and a yellow shell beneath a pretty yellow, black, and lavender summer blazer. Rio had never seen a more beautiful bulldog.

"I'm Stella Pitts-Matherson." She held out her hand. "We've heard so much about you already, Rio. Your sister has been delightful company, and I'm pleased to meet you."

Stella's accent was thicker, heartier, less refined than David's.

"It's nice to meet you, too. I'm glad you got here safely."

"Always good to settle here after the long trip. It's such a welcoming home away from home."

"I understand you had a big hand in that. David says you're the master decorator, Mrs. Pitts-Matherson."

"Pish-tosh, call me Stella. I just like to play."

"Right, Mum, this is your full-scale living dollhouse. Admit it."

David stood. For an instant she imagined a hint of smokiness and a secret smile when he looked at her, but he was all calm business again before she could be sure. The other woman stood. Her height nearly matched David's, and her elegant navy-blue suit and crisp white blouse hugged a model's body. Rio might as well have come from slaving in a coal mine for her own rumpled appearance in comparison.

"Hello, Rio, good to meet you." she said in that incredibly perfect accent. "I'm Katherine Wentworth, a very old friend of David's. That is, I guess if a former fiancée can be considered a friend. Pleased to meet you."

Katherine? Of course she was Katherine. She was Kate Middleton, Kate Winslet, and Kate Hepburn all rolled into one stunning package. With an open, inviting smile to top it all off.

But fiancée?

"I haven't seen Kate in nine years," David added. "Had no idea she was coming, isn't that something? She and Mum recently found each other and planned this surprise." A slight tinge of shell-shocked wideness in his eyes made Rio feel better.

"I assume it's a good surprise," she said quietly.

"It's a dream to see him again," Kate said. "I've been married and widowed since we were together. When

Stella told me David was living in the States and had never married but followed in his father's footsteps, the pull was simply too strong." She threaded her hands between David's upper arm and torso and hugged possessively. "I'll always love this one. It's good to find out he's well."

David extracted himself with a smile. "It's great to find out you're well, too, Kate."

"Although, he's lost so much of his accent," she teased. "You sound positively Yank-ish, love."

"I consider it a compliment, thanks." He took a step toward Rio. "How did it go at The Loon Feather?"

"Ah . . . great. Actually, I took the job."

"And it's something you want? You'll like the job?"

His questions were so sincere she finally relaxed and returned his earlier smile gratefully. "Everyone there is so nice. Yes. The job will help a lot."

"All right then."

A buzz from her back pocket where she'd stuffed her phone made her jump. The earlier text from Hector had been forgotten in this latest surprise. Now she quailed at the thought of another threatening message.

"Sorry." She pulled out the phone trying to hide her worry.

David's thick brows knotted.

When she opened the text she laughed in relief. "It's from Karla Baxter at The Loon Feather. I guess I forgot my sweatshirt there."

"But you didn't think that's who was contacting you." David held her eyes with his.

At that moment she knew she'd planned to show David the text from Hector. She'd known he would care. Part of her crazy reaction to him from the first moment they'd met was the sense of him, more than the farm, being a safe harbor.

But now there were ripples in the still, safe waters that were David.

"There aren't that many people who call me," she said. "I always wonder who it is."

A five-second stare-down followed and David turned away first, but he clearly hadn't gotten the answer he wanted.

"Rio, guess what I get to do?" Bonnie stood.

"I'd love to hear." She looked to the others. "I'd be very happy to make dinner. It's nearly four o'clock, and you both must be ready to drop. I can do something with the beautiful steaks David bought yesterday and have it ready by five."

"You don't have to cook," David said. "We talked about ordering a good old American pizza. I can go pick one up—it'll take half an hour tops."

"You don't want to leave your mom and Kate. I honestly don't mind cooking. Your kitchen is fun to work in."

"I could at least grill the steaks."

"Okay. That I'll let you do."

"Well, thank you." His eyes lit with their familiar, good-natured sparks.

The give-and-take, the compromise, the teasing partnership all served to calm Rio's emotions and quell the little bubbles of jealousy still percolating in her chest.

"Let me get cleaned up a little and I'll be back," she said. "I'll let you know when it's time to grill."

"Okay."

"It's great to meet you both," she said to Stella and Kate. "I'll be more sociable at dinner. C'mon upstairs, Bonnie. Tell me your news."

Chapter Fifteen

BONNIE FOLLOWED TO Rio's room chattering nonstop. She'd gotten to ride in a lesson with Jill, who'd promised she could take more if she'd come back to her place and do some work there, and if she'd groom for her at David's big show coming up in two weeks.

"Groom?" Rio asked.

"Help her by getting her horses ready and taking care of them after she rides. And helping her get ready, too. Watching and helping is a great way to learn how to show. I want to do a show later in the fall."

Rio's heart lurched. She was excited for her sister and, as always, envious of her extroverted personality. But she didn't want Bonnie to take any of this for granted. They simply weren't going to be here that long. Just long enough to . . . She took a deep breath.

"That's awesome," she said. "It's fantastic you're able to work off what they're letting you do. But don't get too invested in things here, Bon. We can't stay that long."

"I'm just having fun," she said. "I know as soon as things are cleared up with the house, we're going to move."

"Still want to?"

"Well, sure. It would so cool to create a place like this. I really like English riding."

The bed creaked when Rio sank onto the mattress, her heart in her throat. "I have something to tell you," she said quietly. "It's not good news, and you'll be really angry with me."

"Heck, I'm always mad at you."

"No, this is more serious than me telling you what to do when you don't appreciate it."

"What's wrong?"

"Last month, a final balloon payment came due on a second mortgage Dad took out before he died. I've been paying that off just like everything else, and it's been fine. But I couldn't quite swing the huge amount, because I also had to make the insurance premium payment, so I made a choice. I let the insurance payment on the house lapse until I got all the house payments caught up. I was going to pay the insurance up this week."

Bonnie could be immature socially, but she had brainpower to spare, especially when it came to numbers. She grasped Rio's meaning immediately.

"You're telling me our house wasn't covered by insurance?"

Rio nodded. Tears threatened the corners of her eyes.

As aggravating as Bonnie could be at this age, she was all Rio had. Nothing in the world could have made Rio hurt her on purpose, but the pain on her sister's face blossomed swiftly.

"I'm so, so sorry," Rio said. "When we were at the shelter, I used every spare minute to talk to the bank, to the insurance company, to the city. I haven't quite given up yet, but it's not looking good. There might be some assistance to help pay off the property taxes for the year, and I'll have to try and sell the lot, although in that neighborhood it could be tough. I don't know, Bons, we might have to find us a really inexpensive place back in the city and start over again."

"No." Tears slipped from Bonnie's eyes first. "It can't be true. You've promised this for so long."

"I know, I know. I told you you'd be really disappointed in me."

"I . . ." Bonnie plopped onto the bed next to her and covered her face with her hands.

She sobbed quietly, and Rio didn't move to comfort her or make any excuses. No words could remove the sting or fix the hurt. Rio, not Bonnie, had screwed up this time.

And then Bonnie did the most extraordinary thing. She gave a last sniff and straightened, wiping her face with the back of one hand.

"Shit happens, you know?" she said.

"What?"

"You didn't do it on purpose. This tanks your dream, too. So why don't we just stay here?"

"Here, as in this house?"

"Sure.

"No, no, that's not a good idea at all!" Crazy visions of the two of them doddering around with David, his mother, and his ex-fiancée for the next twenty years while Rio scrimped for dream money hit her like a bad smell.

"I'm sure David would let us work off room and board."

"Bonnie, that's not what he's in business to do. Besides, we need to get you back so you can finish school."

"They have schools around here, too. Kim is my age, I'll bet she goes to school." She rode the line between teasing and sarcasm. "And we don't know where Hector is. Can I really go back to South? Wouldn't he find me there if we go back?"

Of course she was right. Rio shivered again when she thought about the text from Hector. *I'll find you and Bonnie before you find me.* Since she'd made it a day of disclosure, Rio sighed, pulled out her phone, and showed the text to Bonnie.

"I can't believe I thought he was a closet nice guy," Bonnie said. "It's just, he wasn't mean to me, ever."

"How many times did you go out with him?"

"Four."

"Anyone can play nice for four dates. I only hope Paul didn't know his plans from the start."

"I don't think he did."

"You need to stop being merry sunshine over everything." Rio breathed a little easier. "You trust too much and never see the negative."

"But sometimes I wish you could see the positive. I

wouldn't mind going to school around here. We could make it work. If we can't stay at Bridge Creek, maybe someone else has a room. There's always a solution."

She stared at her sister. "When did you get so wise?"

"When you stopped treating me like a little girl and told me the truth. And listened. So, about five minutes ago."

"I don't know what we're going to do. I don't want you to put your heart on the line here. If they do find Hector, going home might be the best thing."

"Maybe. Meanwhile, you could take the same advice. I've seen how David follows you around with his eyes."

"He doesn't."

She only shrugged. "I just wish Dawson would do what David does."

Oh no, he'd better not. Rio was careful, this time, not to say out loud the words screaming through her brain. She forced teasing into her voice. "I think my first idea about leaving here sooner rather than later is the right one."

"C'mon. Dawson isn't like Hector. I know that for sure."

Rio remembered the moments in the woods before Chief Hewett had broken up the trail ride party, when Dawson had been so sweetly flirting with all the girls.

"Maybe. But can you blame me for being gun-shy?"

"Don't be. You know his dad is Gray Covey, right?"

"Excuse me? Gray Covey, the singer?"

"Yeah! He married Kim's mom about two years ago."

Gray Covey was one of the most popular rock stars in the world. He wasn't considered all that current with kids, but he had a widespread fan base and plenty of decent songs. Rio shook her head in disbelief. This place grew more Wonderland-like with every passing minute.

"I've changed my mind again," she sighed. "Just marry Dawson—he must be coming into some rock 'n' roll money pretty soon."

"Okay. Deal."

Bonnie laughed, and although Rio's heart still didn't know the answers, it was temporarily lighter.

R IO. R IO. R IO. Rio. Rio. David couldn't get her name or thoughts of her out of his head. He hadn't been able to since their kiss on the deck the morning before, but he hadn't had one minute alone with her since.

He strode toward the barn, hoping no one in the house but Bonnie had seen him leave. She'd told him Rio had already gone outside. Which was odd, he thought. Then again, from whipping up delicious meals spur-of-the-moment, to disappearing at 6:30 a.m., to kissing him senseless and then seeming embarrassed by it, Rio defined unpredictable. For the life of him, he couldn't say why that quixotic trait attracted him, but he hadn't been able to concentrate on anything except his reactions to her, even after his mother had driven in from the airport with the shock of a lifetime.

And Rio's face yesterday when Kate had introduced herself . . . Kate wouldn't have caused more shock if she'd claimed to be a three-headed alien and then proved it. He understood. Nobody was more flabbergasted by Kate's presence than he was. More unnerving yet was the fact he'd thought of her out of the blue only days before.

Kate had clung to him like a shadow last night, through dinner, dessert, and the entire evening until Rio had excused herself and headed for bed. Kate apparently intended to spout memories the whole of the six weeks she planned to stay.

Thanks a million, Mum.

"She's lonely, love," his mother had confided, after Kate had retired to the room Rio had rejected that first day. "She's going to help me at the bed-and-breakfast back home to get away from her memories. She jumped at the chance to visit the States, and you should have seen her eyes light up when she heard you're single."

He'd nearly let her have an earful at that, but his mother was nothing if not brilliant at ignoring him. She was here after all, at the busiest time of the year. From the end of August until October, David had no time to entertain even family. And there was the matter of his unhappy financial state, which he'd reluctantly admitted to his mother the last time she'd gone off on her latest decorating ideas.

"I know things are tight for you in the economy here," his mother had said last night. "Maybe Katherine is a godsend."

Since Kate's father and husband were both gone now, she'd been left a wealthy woman.

He knew his mother didn't intend to sound like she was pimping Kate out for her money. Stella Pitts-Matherson was no stranger to shoestring budgets and hard work. But still, David cringed at the thought of Kate thinking he'd ever be after her pocketbook.

The instant he entered the barn he heard the gentle swish and thud of shavings hitting a wheelbarrow. Andy wasn't down yet, but Fred trotted down the aisle, his tail like the rotor of a helicopter that might just carry him away in excitement.

"Rio?" he called, as he stopped to pat the dog.

"Down here."

He found her filling the wheelbarrow in an empty stall. Thirty-one balanced between two bars of the stall door and hiss-growled like a jungle monkey when he arrived.

"What in the world are you doing here so early?" he asked, ignoring the cat.

"I couldn't sleep. So I came out here to talk to Tully and one thing led to another. I've already fed them. I texted Andy and asked if it was okay. He said half an hour early wouldn't hurt them."

"You could have asked me."

"I didn't want to bother you. You were up late visiting."

He moved into the stall and leaned on one wall to watch her work. Thirty-one gurgled evilly. "Gerroff, y'little terrorist." David growled back at her. "I'm not going to hurt her."

Rio giggled. "I swear I don't do anything to make her like me."

"Where's Ducky?" He looked for the horse that normally occupied the stall.

"In the empty stall down the row. I don't know where everyone goes, so I didn't let him out."

"You don't have to work this hard around here. I keep telling you."

"I know. This is cathartic, though, and my muscles aren't so sore today."

"I don't mind mucking stalls either."

"Mookin'." She grinned. "Doesn't sound very Yank-ish to me."

"Oh, don't you start. I'm a man lost between two worlds. Have a care."

"Did you know she was coming?"

"I did not."

"She's gorgeous."

"Yes. Always was. She's got a bit of mature beauty now, too, but between you, me, and that muck fork, she's on the thin side of attractive for me."

"Seriously?" She seemed genuinely surprised. "No sparks for your old fiancée?"

"After the shock wore off, it was nice to see her. But no. Nine years is plenty long enough to lose a spark."

"Why? Didn't you marry her, I mean."

She braced the fork tines on the stall floor and leaned on the handle, every millimeter of her face engaged and interested without a speck of judgment. She shone like a flame-colored rose in the sunlight.

"She threw me off," he said. "Said I'd changed too much after I got back from the Middle East."

"Was she right?"

"She was. Iraq changed everyone who went."

"Were you all right? Were you injured?"

She'd surprised him again with her abrupt switch in focus, honing right in on him and setting questions about Kate aside. He considered kissing her again.

"No, no, nothing like that. It made me a little less open, I guess. I learned to avoid fighting because I'd seen too much of it, but Kate said I'd turned into someone who didn't care about anything anymore."

"I know that's not true. I'm living proof."

She was living proof all right, that a man's fantasy could be curvy and ponytailed and tattooed—and honest, tough, and stubborn. He studied her faded jeans, her small but clever hands, and her bright blue eyes waiting for his reply. His heart swelled—a sensation he didn't remember having for a woman before, not even Kate all those years ago.

He couldn't stand her closeness, her natural beauty, her features still soft from sleep, any longer without reacting. "God, Rio, can I kiss you again?"

Her lips opened, then closed, and she giggled. "Really? Twice we just pounce on each other and suddenly he asks?"

"I'm trying not to give away that I've been thinking about it ever since yesterday morning. I was afraid I'd truly offended you since when you left you seemed, unhappy?"

"Only with myself. For sounding like such an idiot."

"You did?"

"Don't make me repeat it." Her hand shot out and grasped the front of his T-shirt. "And don't be so polite. I liked the surprise when you just did it."

She dropped the muck fork and made no protest when he pushed her backward until her back flattened against the boards of the stall wall. Bent over her, he felt protective, powerful, wanted. A sharp thrill sped down the cords of his neck when her fingers ransacked his hair, and his stomach tightened when she opened her mouth in invitation and waited for his tongue to enter. She *hmmm'd* against his lips and squeaked a little when he ran one hand up the side of her hip to the indentation of her waistline.

He didn't ask whether she'd still like it better if he didn't touch her. He'd either read her correctly yesterday and was doing so again now, or she'd slap him. Either way, his fingers slipped around to her stomach and up her rib cage to the swell of her breast where he fingered the mini-erection of her nipple.

No slap.

She mewled in enjoyment. He lipped her chin and trailed his kisses to her neck. She hunched her shoulders and laughed. "If you could feel my goose bumps, you'd be awfully proud of yourself."

"Who says I can't feel them?"

"I'll bet a lot it's not like I can."

She flexed her fingers against his scalp, dragged them down his neck and across his shoulders. The lightning flash of gooseflesh down his spine rocked him forward so their pelvises meshed. "I'll take your bet," he whispered.

Her hands continued journeying while her mouth plied his with soft urgency. When her fingers reached his waist they curled against the back of his shirt and gathered the fabric until it pulled free of his breeches. Eagerly she burrowed under the hem to touch his skin.

"Nice," she murmured against his lips.

"This is highly unorthodox," he groaned back.

"Oh, if that doesn't sound like my duke. Unorthodox, indeed, Your Grace—"

"David?"

The voice from the barn door pulled a squeal from Rio, and David cut it off with his mouth, then pulled away and replaced his kiss firmly with his forefinger. "Kate," he whispered. "What in God's name is she doing here this early?"

Rio dragged his hand away and kissed his fingertip. "Maybe she couldn't sleep either."

He grinned while stepping back and putting his shirttails to rights. Just as in the woods, they'd managed to make each other completely unpresentable without doing much of anything.

In his rational mind he knew there was no sanity in this attraction, yet he was like a randy schoolboy around her. People often called him proper, but Rio Montoya had snogged the proper right out of him.

He asked with raised eyebrows if she was ready, and she nodded. "We're down at the end of the aisle," he called. "Last stall on the right, Kate."

He poked his head out the door in time to see her glide into the barn like a swan, long-necked and elegant. As he had yesterday, he waited, expecting his pulse to elevate the way it had before he'd left for Iraq. Or, barring that, for his heart to reshatter in his chest the way it had when she'd broken their engagement the year after he'd returned. Neither happened.

Ducking back into the stall, he squared his shoulders. "We don't have to hide this, you know."

Her blue eyes softened into puddles of wonder, but she shook her head again. "*I don't understand this sneaking kisses like horny tenth-graders after only four days.*" She echoed his thoughts. "Nobody else will get it either."

"Hello. This is a rather aromatic place to start the morning." Kate appeared at the stall door just as David grasped the handles of the wheelbarrow.

"The smell of Heaven on Earth, Kate, don't you remember?" David smiled and she stepped aside as he pushed the loaded wheelbarrow out the door.

"It's been a while since I've spent time around horses. Good morning, Rio. Has he really got you mucking stalls, too? After cooking and cleaning up last night?"

Was she being condescending? He couldn't hear it, but he was a complete clot about women's subtext, and these two together worried him.

Rio only shook her head. "No, it's really the opposite. He's tried to tell me I don't need to work around here, but he's done so much for my sister and for me, I really want to help. Besides, being around horses has always been a dream of mine. Even the smell is still a novelty."

Kate laughed. "You're a nicer woman than I am. Well, I came to tell the both of you that Stella has breakfast ready."

"Good heavens, you and Mum weren't even out of bed half an hour ago."

"Of course we were, love." Kate waved her hand dismissively. "We took our time in the bath is all. Still a bit of jet lag. We'll be positively useless come one or two o'clock. Take us while you have us."

"I'm not touching that line." He laughed. "Fine. I'll dump this and then we'll come in. Okay?" He turned to check with Rio.

"Sure."

"When do you start working at The Loon?" he asked her.

"Monday. Ten to four-thirty. But I need to make sure that's okay with you. I agreed to the day shift so Claudia can stay home after I'm trained and take care of her garden, but that means Bonnie has to occupy herself here. I don't want to assume she can roam around mooching lessons off of Jill or—"

"Hey." David set the wheelbarrow back down and turned to her. "Stop worrying about her. You've seen to it she's a great kid. She'll be no trouble."

"Thank you."

"That's our David," Kate said. "Generous to a fault."

It was the first annoying thing Kate had said. "Hardly," he said. "Rio and Bonnie have more than earned their keep since day one."

The instant the words were out he wanted to kick himself. First of all, Rio didn't have to earn her keep as far as he was concerned. This was a safe place for her to stay, end of discussion. Second of all, he and Rio were sneaking around like they were the criminals. He didn't want her to think for one moment that was part of earning her keep. He tried to catch her eye, but she was sifting soiled shavings meticulously through her manure fork.

"Of course I didn't mean to imply it was a hardship. Just that you'll stop to help anyone."

A loud, plaintive mew kept David from telling her to stop talking. He looked down and found Thirty-one had reappeared.

"What a beautiful little cat!" Kate squatted.

"I'd be very careful with that one," David said. "It's like a Hydra. Practically grows a second evil head for anyone except Rio."

"Don't be ridiculous. She's adorable."

Kate stroked Thirty-one's arched back and David rolled his eyes. Obviously the animal was a feline feminist that simply hated men. But then Kate picked her up, and Thirty-one immediately stiffened.

"See?" Kate said and took a step toward David. "She's—"

In a snarl of pumpkin and ebony, Thirty-one spat and twisted out of her arms. Kate shrieked as the claws left launching marks, and David bit his lip to keep an I-told-you-so grin from showing. To his surprise, the cat twined around his legs twice before zipping over to Rio and performing the figure-eight around her ankles, as well.

Rio picked the cat up and it settled into her arms. A warped sense of pride wound through David's chest.

"Well, honestly, that's the strangest thing I've ever seen." Kate rubbed her forearms. "I should say she seems to be your cat."

"We've adopted each other," Rio replied. "I don't think she's really anybody's cat but her own."

Kate nodded in bemusement and touched David lightly on the arm. "I'll go tell your mum you're on your way. She's doing up some porridge and eggs."

"Okay. Your arm all right, then?"

"It'll be absolutely fine, David. You tried to warn me after all. See you in the house."

She waved at Rio and headed back out of the barn, her long-legged designer jeans and her perfectly tucked-in, tight-fitting yellow T-shirt somehow just a little too perfect.

Chapter Sixteen

THE WEEKEND SHIFTED Rio's life paradigm yet again. Only two weeks ago her future had seemed so solid. Now she'd taken a job she could never keep, to start saving to pay property taxes on a useless lot, and keep gas in her car, so she could get to the job, just to start . . . She halted the vicious circle of thoughts. Bonnie was right. She should be happy to be here.

The place was perfect, after all. She loved being so close to the horses. She loved that one stupid, mean little cat had taken a liking just to her. She liked that there was quiet at night, and she liked David. A lot.

But she missed being anonymous. In the city, people she cared about knew her, and the other four hundred thousand paid no attention to her whatsoever. She passed hundreds of them every day, served some of them lunch or dinner, shopped next to them, and honked at them on the roads. But they didn't care if she came or went.

In Kennison Falls, all she'd have to do was sneeze and somebody would broadcast her case of the flu.

And what had begun as she and her sister bunking in a quiet little corner of a very big house had become, overnight, a season at court with Katherine and Stella. Kate was friendly, courteous, nice enough. But she had the intimidating presence of someone who owned a room simply by appearing in its doorway.

Then there was Stella. David had been right; his mother was a force of nature. Her schedule-keeping for the household was a wonder to behold. Two rooms were immediately chosen to be decorated, a list of friends she'd made over her years of coming to the States was drawn up, and talk began to surface about guest lists, while she tried to pin David down on a day for a gathering at his house.

"You can't do anything here until after the show, Mum. I'll be painting jumps, setting arenas, and making course maps. There's no time for partying. I warned you on the phone."

"Of course, love. But you needn't spare a thought to anything I do. Plan the show. After so many years with your father, I know how that goes. It's in two weeks if I recall. Give me the calendar, then, and I'll work around things. You won't even know we're here."

"Promise?" he'd asked.

Luckily Rio spent little time in the house with either woman over the weekend. The moment she finished helping with barn chores on Saturday morning, David invited her to ride the John Deere Gator with him and Andy around the cross-country field to inspect jumps, and from that moment on she not only saw how true it was that life before a show was crazy, she was hooked on learning all she could about putting on a three-day event.

She'd watched the Olympics and seen riders and horses fly over ridiculously large jumps, but she was utterly clueless about the details. David eagerly explained everything. For the first time she saw him in full command of his domain, pointing unquestioningly to the next project, outlining exactly what needed to be done, handling hammers, screwdrivers, and cordless drills with the same expertise he did his horses.

Bridge Creek's cross-country course ran through twenty acres of rolling and wooded fields and was filled with unique and sometimes frighteningly massive solid obstacles. David and Andy worked like a pair of surgeons, tightening wobbly legs on oversized picnic tables, replacing slats on an inclined fence he called a tiger trap, and securing giant ropes on a log that hung over a two-foot-deep ditch.

Andy, who, just as in the barn, moved with a limp and sometimes needed to be reminded what he'd been asked to fetch, brought out the best in David's patience and humor. Rio wondered what his story was but still didn't feel comfortable asking. Fred followed them gallantly, never far from his owner, never averse to a random belly or ear scratching.

Four hours passed in a flash, and when David announced they were nearly done, Rio was assailed by disappointment.

"The water complex is all that's left," he said. "What

do you think, Andy? Should we take our lives in our hands and let Rio drive this last bit?"

She'd been nagging them for the last hour to let her behind the wheel.

"I dunno. She might be a worse driver than I am."

"Aw, c'mon," she groused. "Just because you drive like you have a wooden leg."

Dead silence enveloped the three of them. David and Andy exchanged pained grimaces, but just as Rio was about to panic, the pair burst into laughter.

"I thought you knew," Andy said. "I don't have a wooden leg, it's titanium."

He pulled up the hem of his jeans and exposed the shaft of a prosthetic leg rising from his work boot. Rio nearly sank to the ground in embarrassment.

"Oh God, Andy, I'm so sorry. I'm so, so sorry. I didn't know." Tears beaded in her eyes.

"It's okay, Rio," he said in his deliberate speech. "Really. You didn't say nothin' wrong. I like it when people tease me like I'm just a normal guy."

"You are a normal guy, Andy. Oh jeez, I . . . I'm really sorry."

She was. She'd had no clue he was missing a limb and had never thought to ask kindly if there was anything she should know or do to help or—

"Hey, love, don't cry."

Strong, sun-heated arms came around her, and full-fledged tears rolled down her cheeks. David held her and chuckled, the sound reverberating beneath her ear. Andy patted her awkwardly on the shoulder.

"Don't you dare feel sorry for this jammy old dogsbody. I pay him a bloody fortune, and even though he's worth every cent, he does live the life o' Riley."

Rio pulled away and wiped her face, remnants of embarrassment warming her face faster than the sun had been doing all morning. "I have no idea what you just said."

Andy laughed. "He's insulting me and complimenting me all at the same time. I'm used to it."

"Don't you dare insult him." Rio punched David lightly in the arm. "I just did it plenty well all by myself."

"Neither of us insulted him. A dogsbody is an old-fashioned term for a gofer. Andy does my bidding regularly. And jammy just means lucky. He's dead lucky to have me, I can tell you that right now."

"I let him think that. He'd be lost without me and my wooden leg."

The two growled and threw a couple of fake punches at each other. Rio's heart melted a little at the obvious affection.

"Don't you tease me," she said. "I feel bad enough."

"We told you not to," Andy said. "If you want to beat yourself up you can, but don't blame us."

That was when she understood that although Andy spoke slowly and sometimes missed a beat, he was far from stupid.

"Fine. I no longer feel bad. Do I get to drive?"

"I've got both my good arms," Andy replied. "I can hang on tight enough."

"I'll hunker down with the tools in the back. Should

be safe enough unless a hammer gets loose and cracks the old loaf."

"Why are you talking like such a foreigner all of a sudden?" Rio slid into the driver's seat and turned the key. The Gator growled to life like a high-end lawn mower. "You're usually understandable."

"Trying to impress the pretty bird," he said, and gave her neck a private little squeeze. "Is it working?"

Shivers chased each other down her back as David swung himself gracefully into the small bed of the utility vehicle. She swallowed. Everything he did was graceful. His legs beneath his worn jeans were powerful and athletic. His arms were buff but not bulky. He moved like an agile pack leader out here—confident, strong, not as intimidating as a wolf, but lithe and smart like a coyote.

"The water complex is right over the hill," he said. "Onward, driver."

The Gator jerked at her first unsuccessful attempt to finesse the accelerator. Andy crossed himself. David quietly muttered, "Our Father, which art in heaven." Rio jerked the accelerator again, purposely, and laughed so hard she snorted. She couldn't remember the last time she'd been part of such unabashed and genuine teasing. The lightness threatened to lift her right out of the seat.

The water complex was a massive pond with crazy banks, beachlike edges, and jumps of different heights placed all around the sides. In the middle of the water stood a jump built to look like a suspension bridge. The whole thing was probably a hundred feet in diameter. Rio stopped where David indicated and sat back.

"Now, this jump is intimidating."

"Nah," he replied. "Not from the back of a horse."

"You said that far too casually." Rio climbed out of the seat. "What do we do here?"

"Make sure the log jumps haven't come loose. Check the banks, make sure the reveting is tight. Then we can go back for late lunch."

"I'm all for that," she said.

"You're a natural ranch hand, aren't you?" he asked. "We've been out here a long time with only water to drink. Not a peep or complaint from you."

"Why does this surprise you?" she challenged. "Because I'm a wimpy girl?"

"Precisely." He wrinkled his nose in a scowl.

"Chauvinist. Come on. Tell me what to hold."

As it turned out, only one of the jumps needed shoring up, a four-foot-diameter tree trunk set into the edge of the pond and held in place with a huge frame of railroad ties. One of the giant lag bolts holding the frame tight had loosened, and the log had rolled out a couple of inches leaving a gap right where a horse would take off to jump over it and into the water.

"Horse steps in that gap and he's a goner," Andy said.

"We can winch it tight with the Gator, hold it in place, and see if we can reach the bolt from underneath."

"If not, it'll take a little more effort. We'll have to pull the log out and reset the framing."

David gave his temple a rub, the first sign of stress Rio had seen all afternoon. "Let's pray it doesn't come to that," he said. "That's a daylong job and no mistake."

The log pulled tight easily, and David stretched out on his back, half under the log to reach the bolts. Rio stared as his shirt rode up to expose his navel and his jeans dragged down to taunt her with the trail of hair disappearing beneath the fly. His beautiful, long legs, sexy and strong in breeches, looked equally tantalizing in his work jeans.

"Bloody Nora!" He cursed suddenly from his burrow, and Rio sputtered. "I can't reach the bolt head with my whacking great hand."

He made a few more contortions that lifted his hips, twisted his torso, and only served to tighten Rio's gut and dry out her mouth completely. When he finally inched his way free, he let his head flop back on the ground and blew a sigh through his lips.

"Want to try it, mate?" he asked Andy.

"I will. My hand isn't any smaller than yours, though."

"Let me try." Rio shrugged. "My hand's smaller."

"It's a bit dank under there." David sat up and grunted to a stand. "Back of your shirt'll get dirty."

"Oh, well, then, forget it." She shot him an evil look.

The underside of the log smelled of wet moss and mold, but she ignored it and groped for the bolt with her fingers. Hefting David's crescent wrench, she wrangled the jaws around the nut and gave it a turn. It spun loosely. After five or six rotations she finally felt it grip, two more and it tightened. With a last hard grunt and twist, she got it as tight as she was able.

"I think I've got it," she called.

Once she stood next to the men, she surveyed the jump. The gap had disappeared.

"Nicely done, love. You just saved us a huge job."

"Yay me." Pride expanded inside her. "I hope I got it tight enough."

David took her hand and led her to the top of the jump. He bounced up and down on the broad barked surface and got her to join in. "It feels perfect."

Rio jogged in place beside him, grinning, until her foot came down on the very edge of the jump. With a screech she headed off the log. Strong, quick hands found hers, but her balance was too far gone. She landed butt-first in the water and screeched again as it closed around her chest.

David landed on his hands and knees beside her, the splash harmonizing with his yelp. The water would only have been thigh-high standing, but his flight position sent his face for a full dunk. When he erupted back up, he gasped and shook his soaked bangs out of his face.

"Blast!"

He looked like an affronted cat made to take a bath. Rio covered her mouth. His shirt, now plastered to him, outlined his pecs and flat masculine nipples. He wiped his face and slicked back his hair with fingers that flexed and showed off the ridges of tendons and veins in strong and sexy hands. What would they feel like slicking the water off of her? She didn't even recoil at the thought. He was just too beautiful for her, or any woman, to feel guilty about ogling. When he looked at her, still on her rear in the brownish water that smelled of mud and rain, his eyes widened.

"You're all wet," he said.

"Yeah, but your *face* is all wet."

He turned to her on his knees, the water rising to just cover his crotch. Without warning he scooped his hands through the ripples and splashed a micro-tsunami into her face. "And now yours is, as well."

"Oooooh!" She stood swiftly and shoved a wave back at him.

Moments later he was on his feet, and she tackled him around the knees, plopping him right back down. He grasped her jeans, and it was her turn to land flat on her face. Uproarious laughter made her gulp at the exact wrong second and she inhaled a snout full of water.

Choking and gagging, she staggered to her feet and bent over, hands on her thighs. She held up a hand in surrender when he came toward her.

"You okay, there?"

"N-no." She couldn't catch her breath for laughing through her aching lungs. "You, you, tried to drown me."

"Right. Well, I can give you some mouth-to-mouth if that'll make up for it."

A clanging from outside the pond made them both look up. Andy banged the wrench lightly on the front grill of the Gator. "I don't wanna see mouth-to-mouth!"

"Not even to save her life?"

"If she's in that much danger, I'll do it," Andy said. "Don't trust you."

David grasped her hand and started for the bank. Still wheezing, Rio let him drag her onto the grass.

"What was that about?" Andy asked.

Warm, sweet, sunshiny air sent shivers of delight through Rio's body. She hadn't realized just how hot and sweaty she'd gotten working in the sun. It felt glorious now.

"Just a bit of a swim."

David finger-combed his hair again, pulled out the front of his green T-shirt, now nearly black with the water, and twisted the excess from it.

"Felt nice. Sure you don't want to try it, too?" Rio coughed up the last of the water, following David's lead and wringing out her shirt.

"Don't think so. You two look like drowned puppies."

"Well, then, perhaps we've finished this job for now."

"Do you want me to drive us home?" Rio started for the Gator. "I'll go fast enough to dry us off." She brushed a leaf from the top of David's head.

"You two sit in the back." Andy brushed past her and climbed behind the wheel. "Me and my wooden leg are driving back."

"WHERE HAVE YOU two been?"

Stella met them in the kitchen fifteen minutes later, fussing as if she'd had the entire county looking for them.

"Had a little run-in with the water complex," David said. "No worries, though. We fixed the prelim log."

"You're sopping."

"Have you only just noticed?" He toed off his paddock boots.

Rio kicked off her squishy tennis shoes and pulled off

her socks. David followed suit. They both rolled up their hems, the denim heavy and disgusting. She stared at David's feet with their straight, even toes. Good gosh, was there nothing about him that was ugly?

"David!" Kate entered the room and stared.

"Hullo, Katherine," he said. "Fancy a swim?"

"I most certainly do not."

"Kate, pet, run and fetch some towels out of the bath," Stella directed.

"Don't be daft, Mum. We're perfectly capable of making it to our rooms."

"And drip on the wood floor? Don't you be daft, young boyo. Hang on."

David rolled his eyes at Rio, who considered ignoring his mother and traipsing directly through the precious kitchen. But Rio was a guest. David was the one who needed to stand up and walk through his own home—nasty wet or not—but so far he didn't counter his mother either.

Kate reappeared with an armful of fluffy blue and green towels. Stella took one and made for Rio like she was approaching a child after a bath. Out of the corner of her eye, Rio saw Kate do the same to David. Her stomach clenched as Kate lifted the towel and began to rub David's head.

"Off with that shirt," she said to him.

"Here, here, love." Stella wrapped a towel around Rio's head, as well, blocking her view and keeping her from seeing whether David complied with Kate's directive. "Whatever possessed you to climb in the water jump?"

After a vigorous toweling Rio finally found air to

speak. "We more fell in. We were testing how solid the log was and I slipped. David rescued me."

"But she wouldn't let me give her mouth-to-mouth resuscitation, more's the pity." David's voice came muffled through his own towel.

"David, really, how rude is that?" Kate sounded imperious for the first time. "What a chauvinist."

"Am I? Well, Rio, I apologize."

"Not a problem." She started to giggle as Stella draped a towel around her shoulders, then bent to squeeze her pant legs with another. "Andy offered, and I turned him down, too."

"I see." Kate arched a brow. "Are we quite well then?"

The royal We? Rio held in a burst of laughter with effort, nodding but not daring to reply.

"All right." David pulled Kate up from where she squeezed the excess water from his hems, as well. "We're perfectly fine, and we won't drip too much on the floors. We just came in to change and find something to eat. I've got three lessons to teach this afternoon, and then we've got some of the kids staying to paint a few stadium fences."

He turned to Rio. She noticed with relief he hadn't removed his shirt. She had the completely unreasonable desire that Kate not be the first of them to talk him into stripping.

"What say, my girl? How are you with a paintbrush?"

"I've used a few." Warmth filtered through the dampness of her clothing at his attention, but then he turned to Kate, as well.

"And you? Did you bring anything you can slum in to help paint?"

"I can find something."

"Good. Mum?"

"I've painted more fences in my time than you've jumped," she teased. "I'll paint you all into a corner, mark my words."

"A painting party it is then."

He stepped around Kate. Rio followed him, not quite as buoyant since he'd included Kate in his invitation. He didn't look at either her or Kate as he led the way out of the kitchen. But as she followed she couldn't help but notice Stella narrow her eyes.

Great, Rio thought. Just peachy. David's mother hated her.

Chapter Seventeen

RIO HOBBLED THROUGH her first two days at The Loon Feather, stiff as old leather after David took her, Bonnie, and Kate riding following the painting marathon. They had jump standards and rails in rainbows of amazing, bright colors, but Rio only knew that pain was back with a vengeance.

The only thing that gave her pleasure was Kate being in the same world of hurt. Such pettiness also caused guilt since Kate was perfectly nice. It was just that Stella wanted to make sure David remembered how nice.

Tuesday afternoon, once the town regulars were gone and a local book club had settled in with pie—from The Bread Basket across the street—Claudia pulled Rio into Bud's Booth with a cup of coffee and two cookies.

"What do you think now that a few days are under your belt?" she asked.

"I really like it." Her reply was honest.

"You're doing such a good job. Do you think you're ready to work on your own tomorrow?"

"Do *you* think I can handle it?"

"I have no doubt. I also have another favor to ask."

"Sure."

"This weekend is the Wiener Feed Fund-raiser for the library. The one we're using the crazy hot dog car for. I'm hoping you might be willing to take a shift selling hot dogs each day. I'll take one and Karla will take one, but my sister has to watch her youngest granddaughter again."

"I'm happy to help."

From the entryway, Lester let out his wolf whistle announcing guests. Rio smiled when she reached the entryway and found Bonnie beside Dawson, with a kid-on-Christmas-morning grin on her face.

"Hi, Rio! We're here to meet some friends."

"Hi, Bons. Dawson. Come on in. Still look like rain out there?"

"Yeah. The clouds are getting darker."

She settled them at the largest table where their friends could join them and took their drink order. She didn't know if this constituted a date or if they were just early to a group gathering, but she was happier than she'd have believed she could be to see her sister hanging out with a boy.

By the time Rio was ready to leave for the day, a contingent of eight Kennison Falls teens had gathered. They were an innocent-looking bunch and yet typical teens. Bonnie stood out slightly, her complexion one shade darker than the others, her eyes so wide and slightly exotic, but somehow she fit beside Dawson with his thick sable hair and hooded brows like they'd been a planned pair. Bonnie threw back her head and laughed, sucked on her malt straw, and looked happier than Rio had seen her in a long time. For a brief moment the events of the past two weeks seemed worth it. Maybe, if Bonnie got a few tastes of what normal felt like, she'd reach adulthood without too many scars after all.

Rio left to her sister's surreptitious wave good-bye and Claudia's wish for luck the next day. Outside, the August heat wave hanging ahead of the coming thunderstorm left beads of sweat on her forehead and between her shoulder blades as she walked to her car a block from The Loon. She had barely unlocked the door when she heard her name—in a shriek that chilled her damp skin.

She turned. Bonnie tore down the sidewalk toward her, hair flying.

"Rio!" she sobbed when she reached the car. "Look. Oh God, he found me."

She held out her cell phone and Rio read the message.

It's been a long time, chica, and you haven't taken time to let me know you miss me. Hope you aren't finding new boyfriends while we are apart. Text me. Tell me you can't wait to see me on your doorstep. Your Heco.

"Oh Bonnie."

Rio's heart lodged in her throat. She didn't know why Hector had waited until now to contact Bonnie on her phone. She'd prayed he'd lost her number and Paul had removed it from his phone.

Bonnie threw herself into Rio's arms. "Don't let him find us."

"He doesn't know where we are, Bons, I promise."

"I didn't used to be afraid of him, but now I am."

"It's all right if you're afraid. It keeps you smart. Look, give me your phone for a little while. I'm going to visit the police chief."

"I don't want to text him back."

"Absolutely not." Rio released her sister. "I want you to forget about Hector for now. You have new good friends, so go on back to them and continue having a good time. You'll be fine."

Bonnie straightened and brushed her hands roughly over her stained cheeks.

"I'm sorry I panicked," she said. "It's the first he's used my phone, and it freaked me out."

"Hey, I'm freaked out, too. I'm worried that he's using Paul's phone, but we haven't actually heard from Paul."

"I hope he's okay."

"He's fine. He's just being an idiot." Or so she hoped. "Look, the police are going to find Hector eventually. Until then, you were right the other night when you said we should just stay here for a while. School starts in a little over two weeks. I'll find out what it will take to transfer you here."

"Really? Oh Rio, thank you. I've been so worried about going back to South."

"I'm sorry. You shouldn't have to worry." She took a steadying breath and gave Bonnie an encouraging smile. "Go back. Can Dawson get you home?"

"Yes. If he doesn't think I'm a complete freak for running out of the restaurant over a text message."

"He won't. You'll figure out what to tell him."

She got one last hug from her sister, who then headed back to the haven of friends. That's when Rio began to shake.

"I NEED TO see Chief Hewett," she said five minutes later to Faith at the station desk, who picked up her phone, spoke a few words, and hung up. "You can go right to his office," she said. "Down the hall and first door on the left."

A shiny brass sign left of that door read "Tanner P. Hewett, Chief of Police." The chief looked up before Rio could knock.

"Good afternoon, Miss Montoya. Come in."

The contents of a folder were spread across his desk. His blue uniform shirt was neatly pressed, and he wore a tie, although the knot had been pulled six inches from his throat. His spiked, sandy-colored hair was slightly mussed, as if he'd been worrying it.

"What can I do for you?"

She entered his sparse, white-walled office. The edge she'd come to expect in his voice hadn't surfaced yet. She held out Bonnie's cell phone. "I wanted to show you a message that just came to my sister."

He took the phone and studied the message quietly. When he looked up, steel shuttered his eyes.

"Do you have any idea why he's still threatening her?"

"No. We don't think it makes sense."

He sighed. "Is this the only communication you've had with him?"

"I got a text last Thursday. He knew the car was taken from the impound lot."

"And you didn't think that was important enough to tell me?"

He was right. She'd promised to let him know. "I did, actually. I'm sorry. I should have come in; I've just been so busy . . . No." She met his eyes. "I was . . . nervous. I know you don't like me."

"What makes you say that?" He sounded genuinely surprised.

"The warning that you don't want big city troublemakers like Bonnie and me around has been crystal clear. But I'm sorry. I didn't come to accuse you of anything. I knew I had to show you the messages. Maybe the Minneapolis police will want to know, too."

"They will. Believe it or not, we have been in regular contact."

"Oh. Well, thank you. That's all I wanted."

He straightened in his chair and indicated she could sit in one of the two facing his desk. "Will you tell me what was in that last message you received? I'd . . . like to know."

"Yes, I can show you."

She handed him her phone and he studied the last several messages. "Have you responded?"

"No. I don't know how realistic it is for someone to trace cell phone calls, but I don't think it would be smart to engage him anyway."

"And you're absolutely right."

"I am worried about one thing. Hector's been using my brother's cell phone all this time. I assume my brother is fine, but if you ever hear ..." She hesitated over the awful thoughts in her mind.

"I'm sure if anything had happened to your brother, the police would let us know. My guess is Mr. Black is using the phone hoping you'll contact Paul."

"Or he stole it."

He acknowledged the possibility with a nod. "I know this is your sister's phone, and she probably won't want to be without it. But if I could hang on to it for twenty-four hours, I'd like to try and get a subpoena for Mr. Black's and your brother's cell phone records."

"She'll understand." Relief spread over Rio's worry.

"Bear in mind, things don't happen in real life as quickly as they do on television shows. This isn't *CSI*."

"I live in the heart of the city. I know how long things take with the police." She had a harder time keeping the bitterness out of her voice this time. For a second he tensed as if he had a retort of his own, but he composed himself.

"I'll do my best to get this back to you tomorrow."

"That's fine. Thank you."

"Anything else?"

She shook her head.

"I'm glad you brought this to my attention. I'm ... sorry you've felt you couldn't come to me. I'll do my best to help locate your brother and Mr. Black."

She wasn't sure how to respond. It was almost easier to be wary of the man. "Thanks."

He paused, then spoke reluctantly, as if he rarely explained himself. "I know you think I don't understand what's what around here, but all too often I've seen crime seep out from the city and overrun pristine little towns like this one. I didn't ask to come here, but now that I have, I don't want to see bad things happen. It's a nice enough place."

High praise from the cold chief, Rio thought.

"I've been here less time than you have, Chief Hewett, but I already agree with you."

He nodded and let her walk out the door.

By 1:30 P.M. on Saturday, JW Kennison Memorial Park, two blocks south of Main Street, looked to be packed with every resident in Kennison Falls. Rio had learned Fallsians loved their community parties, and this cause—money for library books—was dear to them. People missed having a full library building after two years of housing books in a tiny room above the Belly Up, one of the three bars in town.

The Wonder Weenie Mobile held two cooks barely comfortably, and even with an exhaust blower and a small metal industrial fan above the three-foot roller grill, sweat ran down Rio's spine and plastered her thin bandana to her head. When she leaned out the small window on the side of the giant hot dog to take her next order, the line that had been ceaseless since she'd entered the wiener at 11:00 a.m. had grown so long she couldn't tell where the end melted into the general crowd.

Her four-hour shift would be done by three, but Bud planned to stay, and she had no idea where he got his stamina. He handled all the grilling and still remained endlessly cheerful and full of jokes and laughter. Bud Jorgenson definitely loved food, loved people, loved his job.

Rio didn't know many people, but she saw every single one of those she did. Chief Hewett, more cordial than usual, and one of his officers ordered their dogs early. Dewey Mitchell ordered three at once. Jill and Chase showed up with an elderly man who limped slightly and smiled crookedly.

"Rio," Jill greeted her with genuine affection. "I'd like you to meet Robert McCormick. He owns the farm we moved into last October. He's kind of our keeper."

"That's for ding-dang sure," the man retorted. "How do you do, Rio? I've heard an earful about you."

"I'm really sorry." Rio laughed.

"Yah. Well, I'm sorry we couldn't have you and your little sister at the house. Things still ain't right, all torn apart. You wouldn't'a liked it much."

"Thank you, Mr. McCormick. Your offer means a lot even if it didn't work out."

The minutes ticked past and Rio moved from being hot toward being liquefied. At last she looked up from handing over an order to see a finite number of people in line. She searched their faces, eagerly looking for the one person she hadn't seen yet today. She handed out the last rush of hot dogs until, for the first time, the line vanished.

"Holy crap." She sagged against a curved metal wall.

"Is that what you find in a heavenly toilet?" Bud wiped his forehead with a towel kept for that purpose.

"You are horrid."

"Thank you. Thank you very much. I'm here all day. How you holding up?"

"I've sweat off five pounds. And it'll probably be a long time till I eat another hot dog."

"Amen. Well, you might be interested in knowing that we've sold about six hundred of the greasy little tube steaks."

"Really? Wow. That's three thousand dollars."

"A job well done, wouldn't you say? And we have to-night and tomorrow yet."

"Good afternoon, hot dog maiden. Is this where we can purchase the famous Kennison Falls hot dogs?"

Her lips curved into a grin. David stood at the window, flanked by Kate and Stella.

"I was wondering when the Bridge Creek contingent would show up."

David grinned back, and for a moment they didn't say a word. They'd passed all week on the way to jobs, and shared brief conversations at dinner, but there'd been no more surreptitious kisses, as much as Rio wished there'd been. Even had there been time, Kate had turned herself into David's shadow when she wasn't comparing paint samples to fabric swatches with Stella.

"Three more, Bud," Rio called, then turned back. "Did you just get here?"

Kate beamed, grasped David's upper arm, and drew her-self to his side. "It's my fault, I'm afraid. I heard he was going to ride the cross-country courses this morning so he could check the lines and put up the flags, so I begged him to take me along. We had a lovely ride, but I admit I slowed him down. Even though Tully is a dream, it's been a while since I've jumped. Still, I made it through the water complex."

The thrill at seeing David sank in a pit of ugly, clawing jealousy. Kate had ridden with him? Ridden Tully, Rio's horse? *Jumped?*

The memory of David's arms around her in that water obstacle swirled through her belly and followed all the other memories into the jealousy pit. This was ridiculous. So she had a crush on David. That didn't give her private claim to him. And Tully wasn't any more hers than David was.

"Here you go." She held the hot dogs out the window.

David disengaged from Kate's hold and took the dogs. His fingers grazed Rio's, but this time she turned away from his gaze, embarrassed by her thoughts.

"You look very hot," he said.

Her mouth twitched in spite of herself. "Thanks. Best line I've heard all day."

He didn't miss a beat. "You look like you could use a cool swim."

Even Kate looked askance at that, and Rio flushed to her roots. As far as she could tell, David ignored both reactions.

"Doesn't sound half-bad," she managed to say.

"How long does Bud have you trapped in that thing?"

She checked her watch. "Another half hour. Then Claudia comes."

"We'll come back for you then?"

Her heart swelled just enough to peek out from the hole of childish envy she'd dug for it. "You don't have to worry—"

"Not worried," he said.

"Do you have things to drink back there?" Stella asked. "You look positively wilted."

"A few bottles of water. A little warm now, but wet."

"There's a lemonade booth just back where we entered the park. We'll go and get you a cold drink so by the time you're done, you'll be a little more refreshed."

She started to protest, but this was Stella being honestly kind, and the thought of something cold and tangy made her mouth water. "I would absolutely love that," she said. "Bud, would you like a lemonade? I can give you some money," she said to Stella.

"Nonsense. You're doing a lovely service to the town. Our treat."

"I'm good with the water," Bud said. "Lemonade's too sweet. But thanks."

"One lemonade it is," David said. "Be back in a jiff."

There was no way Rio could miss how Kate linked her arm through his as they sauntered off. He held his elbow stiffly, but he didn't remove her hold. Rio swallowed her anger.

Oh brother, she was in deep, pathetic trouble.

Chapter Eighteen

THAT EVENING, AFTER everyone but Bonnie was home from the park, Stella announced that she'd "done up a roast and set it in the slow cooker" before she'd left home. Dinner would be at six, and afterward they could all have a relaxing evening, perhaps even "watch a nice film on the telly."

To Rio's disappointment, Stella had pretty much usurped the dinner hour over the past week and planned it with the same flair that she planned her two room redecorations. She was a decent cook, if a little like Julia Child on crack. As much as Rio loved cooking in David's amazing kitchen, she quickly learned it was better to let Stella go it alone.

Nonetheless, she couldn't imagine a worse time than sitting around the perfect living room with perfect Katherine and bubbly Stella, staring at a movie. Worse were the quilting fabrics and paint swatches temporarily spread across a table and two chairs, ostensibly so David could have input into the colors. Rio already knew David couldn't have cared less. The only place he seemed to have any color opinion of his own was in the paint schemes for his jumps. He would simply look at his mother's suggestions and rubber-stamp them. Knowing this irritated Rio as much as losing her cooking privileges did.

She formulated possible excuses for him right up until David arrived from the barn, where he'd fit in two quick rides after getting back from town. The instant he appeared, breeches stained along the inner leg from saddle polish, hair flattened from his helmet and then finger-combed, and his soft leather belt holding in only half his shirt hem, Rio almost lost her breath. She had no explanation except that he looked ruddy and pleased and content, and as sexy as any soaked T-shirt could have made him look. She would sit through the worst movie ever made if he'd sit and watch it, too.

"Goodness, look what the wind blew in." Kate looked up from setting the kitchen table. "Smart fellow. In plenty of time to change from those barn clothes. By the time you shower, we'll be all ready."

David actually looked down at himself and shrugged. "Not that bad, is it? Change the breeches and Bob's your uncle."

"Really, David." Kate gave a polite, airy laugh. "You wouldn't want to ruin the amazing aroma of your mum's dinner with barn smells, would you? You've got plenty of time."

Bonnie interrupted the scolding by breezing in, flushed with excitement.

"Hello, Bonnie, my pet. Did you have fun at the park today?" Stella cooed at her. Bonnie, unlike Rio, was positively adored.

"It was great! I had a blast. Rio, would you care if I spent the night with Kim? Dawson's dad is home. I'd get to hang out with Gray Covey!"

Rio's heart sank. So much for a comrade to suffer with her, yet she could hardly say no.

"It's fine with me if it's all right with Kim's mom. But I didn't cook tonight, so you really should ask Stella if she'd be offended if you didn't stay for dinner."

"Goodness, no, this isn't a formal event." Stella waved her hand to dismiss the concern. "Have a wonderful time, pet."

"Just you behave yourself with that boy, young lady." Rio grinned and stuck her tongue out.

"You're completely mean." Bonnie returned it.

"Nice to know I'm not losing my touch. Oh, and sis?"

"What?"

"Have fun."

When she was gone, David put a hand on her shoulder. "You're good with her," he said. "You're relaxing a little and worrying less. It's nice to see. You okay?"

How did he seem to know just what to say?

"Yeah. About her, I am." She lowered her voice to a whisper. "As for you—I like a little barn mixed with my roast."

DAVID RETURNED TO the kitchen after defying Kate and changing without showering. He hadn't argued. Arguing never went well for him. He was used to losing control of his life with his mother. She didn't muck in his affairs when she wasn't here, so he didn't really mind giving her free rein when she was. Kate, on the other hand . . . Why she felt she had regained the authority to tell him when to shower he didn't know.

At least he had Rio. Practical with a dash of subversiveness. Her naughty little grin when she'd told him he smelled fine had delighted him to the core.

He returned to the kitchen to find Kate and his mum, but no Rio.

"I'm the luckiest man alive to have a house filled with good cooks right now." David kissed his mum on the top of her head, making her beam.

"Not much better than compliments from your son, is there?"

"We're just about ready." Kate smiled, too.

"Where's Rio?"

"She went outside. Asked if we'd be upset if she waited on dinner, too. She said she'd eaten several hot dogs and wasn't hungry."

That didn't sound right. Rio loved her food—making it and eating it.

"She's a bit of an odd thing, isn't she?" Kate asked. "You never quite know what's going to set her off."

"Set her off? Hold on. What actually happened?"

"Not a thing. We started talking about riding, and I mentioned what a wonderful jumper you had in Tully, and she got a bit testy. A few minutes later she was out the door."

"Ah," he said, although he didn't understand a thing. "She's been riding Tully, too."

"Yes, she said that." Kate shrugged. "I thought perhaps that would give us something in common."

That seemed logical. But there was nothing logical about dealing with women. Likely Tully had nothing to do with anything. And likely Rio had told the truth about not being hungry. Although that still didn't sit right. He sighed and rubbed one temple and gave up. Call him clueless.

He didn't have to say but ten words during dinner. The two women regaled him with stories of his old hometown, his mother caught him up on how things were going with the bed-and-breakfast, and Kate waxed on, as she'd done for the past week, about how fortuitous her entire trip was turning out to be. He listened with half an ear wondering how so much chat in such a perfectly appointed, cheery room could be so colorless and dull.

"You've built a lovely place here, David, in case I haven't told you. Thanks ever so for being gracious about me showing up with your mum."

Kate dragged him back into the present with the compliment.

"I'm sorry it's such a busy two weeks. I hope Mum is offering to show you 'round the area. There's a lot to see. In fact, you two should plan to take a few days and go up to Minneapolis. Stay in a posh hotel, visit the Guthrie Theater, shop at the Mall of America."

"But we couldn't do all that without you."

"I've been to the Mall. You most certainly can do it without me." He smiled.

"Never mind, we'll get time with him after the show." Stella patted Kate's hand. "Speaking of, David love, I've looked through your calendar, and I saw the weekend of September the fourth is free. I've taken the liberty of sending out a few feelers to some friends, asking if they can come for a small party. Perhaps twenty or thirty. Just something simple. Let them meet Katherine and—"

"Mum, now hang on. What the bloody hell?"

"David, really."

"Oh, sod it." He slapped his fork onto the table, making both women jump. He sighed. "I'm sorry. It's just, that's my only free weekend between now and the end of September. I wish you'd asked before making official plans."

"Nothing's set in stone," she replied, not the least bit flustered or apologetic. "But let me say, you don't have to do a thing. It's just a few hours on the Saturday, and all you need to do is show up."

"And do you know how much small little parties of the Stella Pitts-Matherson variety cost?"

"It's no problem. You know I'll help."

"Help? Mum, I know you're doing well, but you've already splashed down too much on material and paint for the bedrooms upstairs. The truth is, aside from not having the time, I need to economize. I told you that last time we talked."

"We can most certainly economize. But, pet, when have you ever worried about the odd dollar on something for your business?"

"We're not talking about my business."

"Of course we are. It never ever hurts to have your peers see how you're doing. Word of mouth goes a long way in any business."

"Mum, I'm telling you, this is not my favorite idea."

"Of course I will call off the party if you wish. I told you it's not set in stone. But all work and no play."

"Really? That's what you've got as an argument? I play plenty."

"You play not at all."

He wanted to tell her *she* played too much, but it simply wasn't true. Back in England, his mother did yeoman's work at her business. She was shrewd and used to making things happen. And people loved her.

"You're very driven," Kate added. "Remember how I told you you'd changed so drastically in Iraq? I was completely right. You did. But you've grown into that change. I like softer, more gentile David. You fit this elegant skin well now."

Elegant? Softer? Gentile? Before Iraq, Kate had thought she'd loved the real him—the him trying so hard to emulate his blustering father. To make that father proud. It had taken Iraq to show him he could never be like his father or be what his father wanted.

"This is not 'new' David," he told her. "This is who I've always been. Mum, plan this little do of yours, but I am serious—this has to be a shoestring operation. And no more surprises."

"Brilliant! I'm ecstatic, David. You'll have a great time."

He ignored the prediction and the fact that she hadn't agreed to his stipulation. He stood.

"Dinner was fantastic, Mum. Leave the cleanup and go watch the movie you recorded earlier. I'll come back and do this after I feed the horses and make sure Rio didn't get sick or something."

"I can come out with you," Kate started to stand, too.

"No, no. No need for that." That was the last thing he wanted. "Seriously, you've both been running since you arrived. Take some time to relax. Feeding will go faster by myself, and I'll come finish the movie with you later."

It wasn't that hard to convince them to stay inside. Kate had never been as outdoorsy as he and his mother were. Riding this morning and spending two hours at the park this afternoon had probably been Kate's allotment of fresh air for days.

There were always people around on Saturdays, the busiest day of the week. Although it was nearly seven, Jill was finishing up a lesson in the outdoor arena, and when he passed the door to the small arena he counted four riders. The barn, however, was quiet for the moment. Listening for any rustle that told him Rio might be somewhere there, he walked as quietly as he could along the empty row of stalls. It was time to bring in the horses and feed them, but the need to check on Rio was stronger.

He expected to find her outside. Over the past week he'd discovered she liked to hang on a fence and watch the horses. Her simple appreciation of the animals had made him see how, lately, immersed in the constant pressure cooker of running his business, he forgot that his love of horses was why he'd started this business instead of following in the riding dynasty his father had wanted to build.

At the end of the barn, he finally heard motion, and in a flash of surprise he saw Tully's head bobbing in his stall. He was already inside? One step later, David heard Rio giggle.

"You two are goofy. How is it you've never made friends before?"

He'd never heard Rio's voice so free of defensiveness. He didn't want to ruin the moment, but curiosity and a flare of desire refused to let him walk away.

"You're going to get yourself bucked right off, stupid cat."

Laughter rippled from her again, and he couldn't stay hidden. "There you are." He stepped into her view.

Thirty-one, from a perch on Tully's broad back, produced some indescribable baby cougar sound, and to David's delight, Rio giggled again.

"What a horrible cat."

"I warned you. You're creating a monster."

"She's just angry because you're interrupting her love-fest with Tully."

"I'm dreadfully sorry to Her Majesty."

The cat turned up her black nose and kneaded a circle around the horse's back.

"Yes, be nice to your minions." Rio stroked Thirty-one's mottled fur. "This is a duke of your realm. He's in charge of the laborers who bring you food. You don't want them to conspire against you."

"Are you all right?" he asked. "I can see you're completely potty, but other than that?"

She pressed a kiss between Thirty-one's ears. "I'm fine. I hope it's okay I went and got the horse. I should have asked."

"How about if, while you're here, you just treat him like he's yours? Get him any time you like."

"Really?" Her eyes shone like cut sapphires.

"If Kate ever wants to ride again, I'll find her someone else."

The pure joy in her expression faded. "That's not . . ." She sighed. "How did you know?"

"I didn't. I took a guess just now. I know Kate talked about jumping him today."

"She has every right to ride him. He's your horse, for goodness' sake. Why would I think I had a right to be proprietary?"

"Because you've always wanted a horse."

Gratitude mixed with embarrassment. "I admit it. I did get jealous. Do you really think I'm, what, potty? Is that even a word?"

"Means barmy, crazy. And yes, I think you are. But so are a hundred percent of the other people around this place. Horses get under your skin. Besides, you do well with old Tully here. He knows a good partner when he feels one."

"You don't have to make up nice things to say."

"I don't say nice things I don't mean."

She stroked at the rich whiskey-colored hair on Tully's neck. Thirty-one had curled up in a ball and now viewed the humans with a wary eye.

"What does it mean that when I got this petty, empty feeling while Kate was talking about riding him, all I wanted to do was come out and pet a horse?"

"Well, it's a dire sign, I'm afraid. Means you really are a horse person at heart."

Her face gave away her pleasure.

"But I shouldn't have blown off your mother's dinner. That was rude."

"She's fine. There's no family meal rule around here."

"It did help to come out here. It's been a strange week, and the only person I've had a chance to talk with is the police chief."

"The chief? Rio?" Concern flared in his chest.

"I've wanted to talk to you, too, but there hasn't been a free minute. Bonnie and I each got a text message from Hector. He doesn't know where we are, and the police know about the texts. Still, I feel terrible that we've put you in the middle of this. And now Kate and your mother are here, too. If there's any chance you're in jeopardy—"

He grabbed her arms and hauled her toward him, lowering his head until her eyes locked firmly onto his.

"This is where you belong right now. I utterly believe that. The Universe, God, whomever, provides sometimes without explaining His reasons. You and Bonnie are welcome guests. I don't want you ever to think otherwise. Anytime you need me, don't think twice, all right?" He released her and lifted her chin. "Promise?"

"Thanks, David. That means a lot."

"Who did you go to for advice or help at home?"

"Bonnie. My boss at the diner. A couple of friends.

But life wasn't this uncertain. I handled things day to day. That's all I could ever do."

"And you're good at it. Who taught you to be so responsible?"

She blew a rueful laugh through her lips. "Life. My dad taught me that working hard was the key to happiness. He just wasn't home that much."

"Will that crazy cat attack if I come near my—your—horse?"

Rio nuzzled the tortoiseshell fur. "You won't hurt him, will you, sweetie?"

Thirty-one meowed like a siren but didn't move. David grabbed another brush and took a spot beside Tully's hindquarters. The big horse swung his head, glanced at the humans and the cat, and returned to munching hay.

"You're not exactly a slouch at running things either," Rio said.

"My parents taught me work ethic, too. Dad's built his amazing training facility. Mum is a very hard worker; she herds around a staff of ten at her B-and-B back in England. She comes here for her holiday, though, and thinks it's time to party. She's in the throes of planning some whacking great get-together for two weeks from now. She doesn't believe my finances won't handle the strain of parties."

"Maybe because, on the surface, it looks like you're fine on money issues. It's an amazing operation."

The statement was curious not judgmental. David found it easier to talk to her than his own family.

"You can't make money boarding horses. It's impossible. But we do a lot of other things. We hold riding clinics—bring in big-name trainers to do special lessons. And the show is a huge moneymaker. Lessons and horse training are the bread and butter. But this is definitely a luxury sport. When the economy tanks, so do we. It's been a struggle the past few years."

It almost embarrassed him to admit that understatement. Very few people knew how dismal his books looked these days. Just the tax accountant he used in town. And Andy.

"I'm sorry."

Her apology sounded slightly less than sincere. The funny thing was, he understood. His idea of financial uncertainty was almost certainly a joke to her.

"Don't be. I know you understand true struggling."

"Hard is hard," she said quietly.

"Are you really doing all right?"

"Except for not knowing when I can move back to the city, I'm okay."

"Are you eager to get back? To Minneapolis?"

"I'm eager to be done with Hector and to find Paul. As welcome as you make us feel, it's not the same as having our own place. Paul would never be comfortable here, even though Bonnie is in heaven. When I told her about the insurance, she begged to move here permanently."

"I'm glad she's comfortable. What *are* you thinking comes next?"

"What I did with the insurance was a monumentally bad decision. I made the wrong choice: house payment rather than insurance premium. The insurance company doesn't care that I was prepared to pay them four weeks late. So, I'll need to pay off the property tax when that bill comes due. The city will demolish the house, and then I'll have to get rid of the lot somehow since I can't afford to build anything on it. That's why my getting any kind of job was important, and why it's important to get Hector caught so I can find us a place to live."

"Why is he so fixated on Bonnie?"

"We're all asking that." Rio sighed. "He shouldn't care about her, and he most certainly got his revenge on me. It doesn't make any sense."

"What about going out West? Have you given up on that?"

"For now. I certainly can't afford that dream." For the first time her shoulders sagged.

David's heart sank for her. He set his brush back in the grooming box and gently stopped the motion of her arm. "You know you can stay as long as you like."

"Yes. You keep saying that. But you don't know what you're offering. Even if they find Hector tomorrow, I don't know how long it'll take to find an affordable place to live."

"Rio. It's fine. And you've only just started at The Loon. Give it time."

"Then there's Bonnie who has to get into school somewhere. She's mentioned enrolling at the local high school where Kim and Dawson go. Is that a good idea?"

"Why not? It's a multi-district high school. Abby and Gray love it. Bonnie would have friends straightaway."

"As far as she's concerned, she's moved to Disney World, Neverland, and Narnia all rolled into one."

"And what about you? Where have you moved to?" He wrapped his arms around her.

She sighed, and her breath tickled the skin at his neck of his polo shirt. He shivered and she did the most extraordinary thing by running a finger along the shirt's open vee, tracing it to his breastbone and back up to his throat.

"I've moved to Willy Wonka's Chocolate Factory," she said. "There are goodies everywhere, delicious treats. But there's also danger if you take a misstep. And then there's Willy Wonka himself—so much fun and yet a little baffling and intimidating."

"Me? Intimidating?"

"Out of my league."

"If that's not the biggest load of rubbish I've heard in my life."

He didn't give her a chance to retort. He claimed her mouth with pent-up desire that flamed as if she'd touched the match to it herself. Her tongue clashed with his, and her head tilted to allow him closer. She represented everything he'd been running from for years, uncertainty, messiness, instability, and fear of rejection. But the yielding of her body brought more color, recklessness, and passion for survival than he'd felt in a very long time.

He dragged his mouth reluctantly from hers. It was still too early. Anyone could pop in and find them.

"Let's not go back to the house," he said.

"Why would you think for a second I'd do that right now?" She reached for another kiss.

"How'd you like to learn to ride bareback?"

Her eyes turned to blue moons of amusement, and she wriggled her hips against his. "Honestly? Is that what you call this in England?"

Chapter Nineteen

"Can you actually make love on a horse?"

David spluttered and tightened his arms around Rio, who rocked in front of him on Tully's broad back.

"Technically? I expect so," he said finally. "Never tried it, mind you. It's never sounded appealing. It would require gymnastics that would, at the least, take my concentration off my partner. And if the horse shied ... vital bits could be severely wounded. Look here. I meant it when I said this wasn't a euphemism for sex. Why are you being so difficult?"

Meaning suggestive and as sexy as a nymph, he thought, in growing discomfort.

"Difficult is what I do best."

He guided Tully away from the barn. He'd only intended to bring Rio to the far end of the pasture and back to calm his body from the kiss. A rational-seeming idea until he'd put it into practice. The reality was proving he'd made a gross miscalculation.

Rio squealed as Tully turned left. "His skin is slippery!"

"It slides over his muscles just like yours does. You'll get the feel for it. Let your hips sway the same way they did in the saddle."

Another mistake. Her pelvis loosened and rocked her sweet little bum straight into parts that were difficult enough for a bloke to keep safe in this sport. He placed his lips next to her ear.

"Feel how much more secure that is?"

She nodded. The joking stopped. In fact, they stopped talking altogether. Riding a horse was second nature to him, like a natural extension of his own gaits, and he spoke to Tully with unconscious cues, leaving far too much time to notice Rio's every muscle contraction and movement. If he were smart he'd ride straight back to the barn. But the growing ache lower in his body was clearing making mincemeat out of his IQ. He guided Tully across the field and didn't look back.

ANY NATURAL RIDING ability Rio possessed had disappeared the moment Tully took his first step. The security of a deep Western saddle was more evident than ever. Fortunately, what she lacked in leather beneath her was made up for by David's body behind her. He surrounded her waist with his arms, braced her back with his torso, and framed her seat with his strong thighs and legs. Slowly, with the warmth from Tully's back seeping into her muscles and the slow burn from David's touch fueling an inner fire, she relaxed. Her spine undulated with his torso, and her seat slid back into the vee of his thighs.

"I think you've got it." Low and hot his words rumbled into her ear, and shivers rushed them all the way to her stomach. "Want to go faster?"

She nodded, although the thought semi-terrified her.

"The key is to keep your hips moving just like this but faster to match the motion."

"'Kay."

She felt only a slight movement backward, maybe half an inch, in David's right thigh. Like a carousel horse, Tully's front end rose upward followed by a smooth surge forward. His hindquarters followed, lifting and pushing. He cantered onward without a single transition into the jarring trot Rio expected. A squeal of delight escaped her throat, and she gripped hard with her knees as her balance bobbled. David locked his elbows around her, and she took a glimpse down at his hands on the reins—sure, powerful, clever, tanned. The leather twined through his fingers like a complicated Mobius strip, but his grip was elastic and alive as if he held nothing more powerful than a kitten on a string.

"That's it, relax! Grab his mane." The breeze carried his voice now, as exhilarated as she felt. "Just like a rocking horse in the nursery, eh?"

She couldn't say a word as they cantered across a flat stretch of field. Her seat wasn't elegant, but David held her securely and she felt every contraction of his perfectly trained muscles. Her mind went blank except for her trust in his riding. The precision of his movements, the control of his body astounded her. This was no wild, New World cowboy ride; this was centuries of skill, the legacy of knights on chargers who swept women off their feet. David might not think sex on horseback desirable, but the field rocked by, and the slow fire inside of her burst into a bone-melting conflagration proving this was pure lovemaking—with man and wind and poetry.

Finally he bent his mouth to her ear again. "Hold on, then. Coming back is a bit less smooth."

Again the muscles in his legs tightened and a long, sexy "eaaaasy, mate," purred from his throat. Like a Lamborghini switching gears, Tully dropped from his canter to a piston-like two-beat trot. Rio flopped a little until the downshift came again, and Tully walked on as steadily as if he'd never changed gaits at all.

"Oh my gosh." Rio could barely contain herself. "I've never felt anything like that in my life." She twisted her head to look at him.

"You did great." He kissed her quickly on the side of the mouth. Then he handed her the reins. "Here. Take over."

"Oh no. I'm not—"

He ignored her and released control into her hands, snaking his arms around her waist instead. A wash of desire spread through her belly and into her limbs. A soft kiss landed on her hair, then another behind her ear.

"Don't tell a soul I went riding double without helmets," he whispered. "I feel naked without it, but it's worth the sense of danger."

"Good thing you're not really naked." Her voice rasped even to her own ears. "Who knows what I'd do then."

"I'd like to find out sometime." He pointed over her shoulder before she could respond. "Head for that gate."

The reins, instead of taking away her control, made her feel more powerful. David still cocooned her, but his legs no longer held the key to Tully's route. Instead, he let her pick the path, and his implicit trust lifted her to a high she'd never known.

"It's not so difficult this, is it?"

"Not with the perfect teacher."

"It's not teaching, it's more like dancing with the right partner."

He tightened his arms and dragged her bottom two inches backward, settling her more securely against him. A quicksilver thrill dove through her core. Before it could dissipate, he nuzzled her neck again, loosened his hold, and dragged his fingers slowly across her stomach.

"Isn't there some rule about not distracting the driver?" she whispered. "You *don't* want me closing my eyes here."

"That's right. Don't close your eyes," he commanded. "Concentrate. This is a test."

"Of what?" she croaked.

"Of your ability to resist me."

"Well, just give me an F right off the bat. I won't pass."

"You have to. We aren't at the gate yet."

"What's so special . . .?"

He halted her words by pulling her T-shirt free of her jeans and stroking her skin softly beneath the hem, up her stomach, to the fabric of her bra. She gasped when his fingers climbed one satin-covered mound and fingered the nipple.

"When you get to the gate, I'll stop."

She whimpered at his touch. "I know how to turn this horse right around."

"But you absolutely won't." He moved to her other breast, cupping it and stroking with his thumb.

"This is completely unfair. I can't touch you back."

"You have no idea how wrong you are."

She shifted restlessly.

He let go of her waist with his other hand and slipped it up to meet the first. With a hand on each of her breasts, he teased lightly until she could barely follow his directive to keep her eyes on their destination. When he buried his lips in the hollow beneath her ear and nibbled, the shock waves hit too strongly. She pulled back on the reins with a groan, and Tully halted.

"I don't want to pass this stupid test. I quit."

"Fine." He extracted his hands and, to her surprise, slipped off the horse with graceful ease. Putting his hands up for her, he tugged her down into his arms. "Hang on. Let me take his bridle off."

He unbuckled the bridle throatlatch in two seconds and pulled on the crownpiece behind Tully's ears. The horse spit the bit neatly out of his mouth and shook his head vigorously.

"You're letting him go?"

"It's all fenced. He'll come when I call him later."

He patted the big horse on the rump, and Tully ambled off until he found a patch of grass to his liking.

David hung the bridle on a tree flanking a decent-sized log jump.

"What are we doing in the middle of the field?"

He spun her fully to face him and devoured her mouth with another kiss. Her knees nearly buckled at the expertise. Just as had happened back in the barn, she barely recognized this David. The gentle acquiescent son and host was gone. In his place was a confident, skillful man—the unapologetic knight who'd brought her here.

"C'mon," he said, after ending the kiss. "What I came to show you isn't far."

He grabbed her hand. Two minutes later they passed through the gate, and twenty steps after that David led her onto a narrow path straight into the woods. The air cooled immediately, and the scent of pine tickled her nostrils. Another minute later the woods opened up slightly around a rough-hewn structure like something out of *Little House on the Prairie*.

"It's an old hunting shelter," he said, pushing open a heavy pine-slab door. "It was on the property when I bought it, and I purposely left this whole area outside the fence untouched. Most people don't know it's here."

"Do you use it for anything?"

"Only my trysts and illicit liaisons."

She whipped her head around to stare at him, and he made a face.

"Dork," she admonished.

"I haven't ever had a woman out here, if you must know. I've done a couple of poker nights by lantern light with a few fellows. I used to love camping. When things get too much now and again, I come spend the night."

The one-room miniature cabin definitely wasn't set up as any sort of love nest, but oddly enough it seemed to reflect more of David than his whole beautiful home did. A battered wooden table and three chairs sat by the room's one, small window. A single bed with a simple rail headboard made of smooth, slender logs stood against the opposite wall—a woolen Hudson's Bay blanket tucked neatly into the frame and two pillows with mismatched cases propped at its head. Three shelves held some metal dishes, a cast-iron fry pan, and a coffeepot. A can of coffee and a box of granola bars were the only food she saw. And in a far corner, beside a simple, Franklin-type stove, sat an old Western saddle, a thick saddle pad, and a bucket.

On the wall over the bed hung a picture. Of a palomino stallion.

Rio covered her mouth and stared. For an instant sorrow threatened to overwhelm her. She'd resolutely kept from dwelling on what she'd lost—but this was so similar to the picture from her room that the memories came roaring back.

"Oh love, I'm sorry." David closed the door and gathered her into his arms. "I forgot about the picture."

"It's all right."

It was—with his arms around her.

The kiss this time was nothing like the swashbuckling hero's claim-staking of minutes before. This one they sought together. Rio poured her overflowing heart into exploration. Sadness, softness, tenderness, and neediness. David accepted it all, drawing her tongue into the warmth of his mouth, kissing away the last vestiges of sadness, healing her with touch and gentleness.

They bumped into the bed frame as they lost track of space and movement. When David sat on the mattress and pulled her onto his lap, the breach in their kiss lasted barely half a second. Only when he laid back, rolled her over him and to her side, and draped one leg over both hers did she twist to free herself.

"David, oh, I don't think I'm . . ."

"Sssh." He lifted his head and combed the fingers of both hands into her hair. "I have no plans to ravage you. I didn't plan this, however deviously it might seem I've enticed you here. There's no mutual agreement, and no protection in my pocket. That's not my style, I promise."

The honest, regret-filled words brought her willingly back into his arms.

"Thank you."

"But, Lord, you are beautiful. And you make me want to forget about being a proper English duke with a successful façade to keep up."

"You make me want to have reckless fun again. I'm more worried about what that means than about you *ravaging* me."

"And you make me laugh."

"Great." She didn't really want to make him laugh.

"In all the right ways—the best ways, Rio. Plus, you make me think tattoos are gorgeous. That's what *I'm* worried about."

"Name them."

"What?"

"Name the tattoos you know I have." She smiled impishly at his widened eyes.

"Heaven help me, Arionna Montoya, I never know what to expect from you." She watched his Adam's apple bob. "The horse."

She wriggled from his hold, rolled, and unsnapped her jeans. She turned around and pulled down the waistband.

"Man," he breathed, and his finger traced the fine lines, sending goose bumps across her back. When he kissed the lowest point of the horse's neck, just above the cleft of her cheeks, a tremor set her shivering. She spun back to face him.

"Next."

"There's an owl."

She pulled off her left tennis shoe and sock and yanked up her pant leg. He smiled and kissed the owl's beak right above her ankle. Drizzles of pleasure flowed up her calf.

He went after the black-and-white stars and moon on her right side next, leaving wet tongue kisses on each star point and the horns of the moon. Heat blazed on the damp spots when he lifted his head and exposed them to air—like ice turned to fire.

"The feather," he said.

Deliberately she sat and pulled at the hem of her T-shirt. With hands shaking because it was a completely foreign act to strip slowly for a guy, she managed to work the shirt up and over her head. Brief embarrassment followed the clumsy show, and she sat before him with jeans unbuttoned and bra exposed. His eyes went straight to the subtly shaded blue-and-white feather alongside her breast, and he sat up. Without a word he worked her onto his lap, legs straddling his, and leaned forward to kiss the tattoo, curling his arms beneath hers and grasping her shoulders from behind.

She kissed his hair while he kissed her skin but couldn't maintain it when his lips followed the feather's stem into the valley between her breasts. When he nipped gently at the soft skin where the tattoo ended, her head fell back. She held him to her, reveling in the magical connection between the actual location of his mouth and the warm pulsing much lower between her legs.

"I haven't seen the others," he murmured. "You said there were six."

"The butterflies on my left foot and ankle."

She lifted the foot still clad in a shoe and David removed it. "My dad loved Monarch butterflies," she said when the tats were revealed. "His over-the-road handle was Monarch, and I guess he liked to call my mother Mrs. M. These are my most recent ones. I got them on my twenty-first birthday. I guess because I was missing Dad."

"Amazing. They nearly look alive." David held her foot in his hands and studied the butterfly with folded wings just to the outside of her foot and then the one in flight just over her ankle.

"A good tattooist is a true artist."

"So you're beginning to convince me."

"You don't need to kiss the smelly barn feet." She

giggled as he traced the delicate Monarch wings on her ticklish skin.

"Not smelly." He smiled. "I'll do it to finish the quest for number six."

She hesitated a moment, sure she wanted to show him but not sure she should. Everything was moving so quickly. "I've never shown it to anyone."

"Are you serious?"

"It's . . . personal."

"You don't have to show it now."

"I know that."

"So why me?"

"I don't know. I don't trust easily but I trust you. I'm also sure you it wasn't really as easy as you made it seem to offer me this safe place to fall." She touched his face, framed it with her palms, and lifted it to meet his eyes. "Maybe I'll regret this. But I want to show you."

"I don't want you to regret anything. I do admit, however, you have me wondering what private place you've allowed a tattoo artist to invade."

He teased her so sweetly it gave her confidence. Pulling her foot free, she knelt before him and slipped the zipper of her jeans down. She shimmied the denim and the waistband of her panties down far enough to expose her stomach, low and to the right of her navel. The stark white heart with purple highlighting was two inches tall, and a purple infinity symbol, one broken in the middle, stood out across the heart's widest section. The pair were framed by a fine green vine of leaves that trailed toward the top of her thigh.

"It's a little anticlimactic," she said, her heart thrumming with nervousness. "I was not quite five when my mother died, but sometimes I think I remember her being the only other person I ever really trusted."

He didn't say a word.

"She had a necklace with this symbol on it. I have a picture of her wearing . . ." That memory skidded to a painful stop, devoured by the memory of flames reaching for a night sky. "Shit," she said, and sank back onto her heels. She was sick to death of weeping, but tears fell again. "I'm sorry."

He folded her into a fortresslike embrace.

"This will happen often as you remember things you lost. I can't make it better, but I can tell you you're not weak."

"It's such a lost feeling."

"It is."

He sounded like he knew. She didn't want to believe he was just giving lip service to the words, but she didn't want to question him either. Uncurling herself, she swiped at her eyes and dragged in a shaky breath.

"I *used* to have a picture of my mother with the necklace on. Dad says they buried it with her, but that she always said it meant she loved the two of us forever." She rolled onto her back so he could see it again. "I broke the ends of the infinity sign because she left us too soon. It's a little silly because I really barely remember her. But what little I do remember is still the warmest feeling I have."

He bent and kissed her the tattoo, caressing her stomach, dipping into her navel with his thumb and grasping her waist. His touch wiped away the sorrow, and the heat between her legs, so close to where he played, made her groan. Every sensation that had built on the horse, and the walk to this cabin, and in the long moments he'd tortured her tattoos with teeth and tongue now swelled into need.

With consummate skill he touched the tender spot between her legs and stretched up at the same time to seal her lips with his. She moved beneath his hand and opened to the thrust of his tongue. It took only seconds to reach the edge of an abyss that completely stole her breath. For an instant she held back, forced herself not to leap, but it was too late for fear, and she let David push her over the edge. Heat, fire, electricity, and relief engulfed her as she tumbled headlong into the colors of release. From far away she heard herself cry out and, finally, as he slowed the motion of his hand, she heard David's voice, calling her back.

"Hullo," he whispered when she opened her eyes. "Did you go far away?"

"To the ends of the world." She closed her eyes again and felt the smile slip onto her lips.

"Good journey?" He nuzzled her ear. Her chin. Her throat.

She pushed him away and sat up, energy flooding her suddenly as if she'd drunk a magic elixir. "It was the most amazing place. One I've never been to before."

She kissed him and reversed their positions. With one glance she knew his body was treating him exactly as agonizingly as hers had treated her. She traced him through his breeches and relished his groan. Slowly working his belt buckle open, and even more slowly running down the zipper of his fly until she could touch him beneath it, she bent to follow her fingers with a touch from her lips.

"I think it's time you got to visit, too."

Chapter Twenty

RIO CAME CLOSE to finding an idyllic life during the beginning of that week. David and everyone else dashed around with tails on fire as final show preparations ramped up in earnest, but the connection she now felt with him remained real and electric. So real that Kate didn't bother her anymore. So real that even when David was at his most stressed and likely to bark at someone, she could make him laugh. Deep in his cocoa-infused eyes was always a secret spark showing he remembered, too.

Tuesday night, the show secretary, pressed anyone she could rope and tie into service filling envelope packets containing bib numbers and show information for the competitors. Bonnie, Kim, Kate and Stella helped. Rio, finagled her way onto Andy, David, and Dawson's group that got to mark the final cross-country course. Working outdoors—not to mention simply being with David, was infinitely more stimulating than stuffing envelopes.

On Wednesday, two flatbed trailers arrived stacked with fence panels and gates. Rio left for work while the trucks were being unloaded. When she returned in the afternoon, both indoor arenas were filled with temporary stalls, and Bonnie, Kim, and all the younger riders hopped around like rabbits labeling them with competitor names.

A dozen Port-A-Potties had been delivered and placed strategically around the barns, stables, and far end of the jumping field. With shiny stadium jumps set prism-like in the outdoor arena, and two beautiful dressage arenas, fenced with low, white chains, set up on a section of flat pasture, Bridge Creek turned into a festival grounds.

Rio also discovered that Bud and the crew at The Loon Feather would cater a competitors' party on Saturday evening. The more she learned, the more incredible the entire production seemed.

Wednesday night, David disappeared into his office in the house. Once she'd finished helping Andy with chores, Rio made her own way to the house, stunned to find the kitchen empty. For the first time in days Dinner by Stella didn't bubble on the stove or fill the room with aromas from the oven. With a frisson of anticipation, her brain went into dinner-planning mode, until she heard voices from the direction of David's office.

"It bloody well isn't fine." David's words held pent-up anger. "You can't add party flowers to my show order willy-nilly. It was already over four hundred dollars. The budget is firm."

"I've arranged to help pay for what we added," Stella replied.

"But you've helped more than enough. I am grateful, but I simply need you to come and be my mum, not my social director or my interior decorator."

"I thought you approved of the plan for the house." Stella's voice, unlike her son's, remained unfailingly even. "Ten years is the timetable you set, and we're on schedule. And we always have a party, sweetheart."

"In November. When it's slow. And this year it must be smaller."

"David, my pet, what's gone so wrong?"

"What can I do to help?" Kate's sweet, reasonable Mary Poppins voice brought another layer to the conversation. "I'll do anything I can."

"That's not what I'm asking for." He sounded the tiniest bit short with her.

"You wouldn't ask, darling. But I can offer."

Darling? Rio frowned.

"And I can handle my life fine on my own except when little surprises pop up on my voice mail, like the florist asking if they can push back the delivery date to *after* the show in order to accommodate the new order."

"I'm sorry," Stella said. "We've fixed the delivery issues. All's well."

"An extra hundred-and-fifty dollars in live plants and flowers for a four-hour get-together is not 'all's well.' You've spent a bleeding fortune on decorating. Can't a party speak for itself?"

"If that's what you wish." For the first time a hint of hurt tinged Stella's words.

"Look, Mum, I just got off the phone with the awards company. Show ribbons that should have been here last week won't be here until Friday, and they're trying to charge a rush fee. The EMT service raised their prices this year. Bud has to use a more expensive supplier for his dinner rolls because his regular went out of business. Do you see? I'm not trying to be unreasonable. I need you to stop spending money."

"We'll sort it all," Kate soothed.

"I don't want—"

The chime of the front doorbell cut off his words. Rio jumped, feeling guilty for eavesdropping in the first place, and turned toward the door as David strode out of his office.

"Rio?"

"Hi, I heard the front door."

"Yeah." He frowned and hurried past her.

Rio's jaw went slack when she saw who stood on the porch. She'd seen his pictures hundreds of times and heard his songs more than that. In the flesh, Gray Covey was both bigger-than-life and more normal-looking than on any poster or video. The woman beside him, as classically beautiful as if she'd stepped from an old Grace Kelly movie, was instantly recognizable as Kim's mother, Abby.

"David," she said. "We're so sorry to bother you, but we need your help."

"What's going on?" David ushered them in. Rio gawped.

Gray turned before answering and held his hand

out, "Hi. I'm Gray. You must be Rio. We've heard so much about you from Bonnie. I'm sorry we haven't met before now."

She took his hand, and his naturalness put her immediately at ease. "It's great to meet you. Thank you for having Bonnie over so often."

"She's delightful." Abby shook her hand, too. "Sharp and funny. She's good for both Kim and Dawson."

"Did I hear you're both staying long enough to enroll her in Quad District?" Gray asked.

"I've got an appointment at the school tomorrow."

"That's wonderful." Abby squeezed her hand. "The kids are thrilled."

"So, what's the news?" David brought them back to topic, his calm back in place.

"Jill just heard from Ben Thomlinson." Abby turned to Rio. "Her boss, a veterinarian here in town," she explained. "The police were called to a farm down near Nerstrand where they found fifty-two severely neglected horses. It sounds like they're not in very good shape, and they need to be removed immediately. We're the volunteer crew looking for help."

David groaned in sympathy.

"We know this is the worst timing for you," Gray said. "But we're running out of options. The local Hooved Animal Society has a barn that can take twelve of them. Jill and Chase and Robert can put twenty of them in their pasture. We've got room for ten, but that leaves ten that need a place. We've called several people but nobody has the space."

"Would you consider taking them temporarily?" Abby asked. "Hooved Animal will help place them. Meanwhile, Jill's organizing a team of vets to do exams over the next week."

"I . . . Of course. Yes, there's no choice, is there?"

David's hesitation had been barely noticeable, but Rio caught the uncertainty in his eye. He didn't know she'd overheard his worries just now, but she understood this meant incurring more costs.

"Thank you!" Abby threw her arms unashamedly around David's neck. "I know what an imposition this is."

"No need for thanks. Is there a plan?"

"Doc Thomlinson has a stock trailer, Jill and Chase have a three-horse, and we have ours. If you were willing to either come with your six-horse or let one of us use it, we can leave now and pick up eighteen horses. It'll take two trips each, but we'd like to start tonight. It's only about forty-five minutes away."

David's reluctance had vanished. He turned to his mother and Kate.

"What can we do?" Stella asked.

"And me, too," Rio added. "Anything you need, just ask it."

"Mum, if you'll organize a few of the boarders who are still here to move horses out of the south pasture, the one with the two shelters in it, and put them in with the geldings in the middle paddock, I'll have Andy throw half a dozen bales of hay around."

"Of course."

"Kate. There are two phone numbers in my roller file, one for Dodge City Badges and the other for Faribault Ambulance. Will you look them up, give each a ring, and confirm the orders—one for the ribbons and one for the EMT price. Be firm with the badge company—the ribbons must be here Friday morning."

"Gladly."

He met Rio's eyes next. "Would you like to come with us? You can hold trailer doors and ropes."

Her heart soared. "Sure."

"Right." His eyes softened. "Let's go."

THE COMFORT OF having Rio in the truck seat beside him was almost enough to calm David's frayed nerves. She'd waited out his silence, letting him think. At one point she covered his hand with her small, capable fingers and just squeezed. What other woman would have squelched the urge to dig for what was wrong?

"I'm sorry," he said at last.

"For what?"

"For ignoring you."

"I know you were preoccupied tonight even before Gray and Abby showed up. Are you all right?"

He stared out the window. The seven-thirty sun hung above the horizon—they had maybe ninety minutes of light left. He debated lying, but her fingers tightened and he caved.

"No."

"Oh David, what's wrong? Is it these horses?"

"Yes, but not for the reasons you think." He released a heavy sigh.

"What are the reasons?"

"I told you money is tight? Truth to tell, it's more than tight. I lost three paying boarders last month simply because the economy is so tough they sold their horses. The arena we built last summer has cost far more than the amount I was paid in insurance."

"Frickin' insurance," she mumbled and kneaded his fingers.

"No. It's more a problem with my father. In a way he's exactly like my mother. He spent last summer with me, and all I heard was, 'You'll never regret the extra touches, David. You'll justify your board rates with cracking good facilities.' You know how my mother is with the house? That's Da' with the horse facilities. They're a right pair, I'm telling you."

"You do own the place. You could tell them to butt out."

"I've always found it easier to appease them for a few weeks and then send them on their ways."

"Until now, when it's making you miserable."

"My mother *is* barking mad this trip. Because of Kate. She's trying desperately to impress the woman, and I don't know why. Well, I do. I just don't want to admit it."

"Might as well tell me about that, too."

She smiled with such warmth he believed nothing he said would upset her.

"Mum always adored Kate. She was heartbroken

when we split up and even more devastated when Kate married soon afterward. Now here she is, reunited with her dream daughter-in-law, her son is thirty-two showing no signs of producing an heir, and she had a grand idea: If she could get us together for six weeks, we'd find that old magic."

"She's said all that?"

"Not in so many words. But she's letting Kate design the rooms. She's throwing a bash to introduce her to her American friends. She points out any time she can how wonderful this place is and how far I've come. She might as well say it."

"And how does Kate feel about all this?"

"Kate wouldn't say shit if she had a mouthful of it. She's smart as a Sunday suit and rich as Midas. I haven't a clue what she hoped to accomplish by coming."

"She likes you. A lot." Rio's smile turned devilish. "If you asked her on a date, she'd go."

"Hang on." He laughed, but stared at her quizzically. "Do you *want* me to ask her out?"

"I don't own you. I can't tell you what to do."

"Well, that's brilliant, that is."

Her laughter filled the truck cab, and she swatted at his upper arm. "No, I do not want you to ask her out! And I don't want you to take her bareback riding, and I don't want her to know about the cabin. I'm pretty jealous of her, actually."

The words sent warmth to all the aching, worried parts of his mind. "Don't be jealous."

She settled back into the seat, a self-satisfied grin on

her lips. "Whatever you say. Meanwhile, we've gotten far off the main topic. So funds are tight. Welcome to my world."

There was no rancor in her words, just resigned humor.

"In all honesty, I can't afford to take on ten new horses. Not until the middle of next month when all the board checks come in. I mean, I can put them in a pasture, but I can't feed them for long. Unless I find cheaper hay very quickly. With ten extra animals, I'll be out of what I have in a week. I was pushing through for our own horses until the fifteenth. It's all a balancing act at the moment. November and December will be adventures all their own. Kim will be taking her horse back home, and Jill is talking about moving a couple of hers to their place just to economize. I could have six empty stalls by Christmas."

"That's a lot of money, isn't it?"

"To put it mildly."

"I'm sorry. Why didn't you just tell Abby it wouldn't work?"

He stared at the road, a lump of embarrassment in his chest. "First of all, it's the horses. I might be a whingeing idiot, but the animals come first. It might not be practical, but it's what an addict does. Second of all . . ."

He hesitated. She took his hand again. "Second of all, what?"

"Pure pride," he said. "I've spent a long time building this top-notch place. It's hard to admit I'm failing."

"I'm sorry, but if this is failing, David, what have I

been doing all my life? There are ways to deal with low funds. And the fact that you're putting these horses first—well, frankly, it's a relief. This is the you I've come to know and respect."

A little magic happened when she said that. He knew the relief wouldn't last; reality would kick him in the ass soon enough. But her gentle chastisement and her declaration of belief in him broke up something heavy inside. She *did* know him. After so little time, she knew he didn't crave glory the way his father did, or status the way his mother did. Something neither had ever understood.

"Thank you."

"Listen. I don't talk about this ever, mostly because I don't know what I believe anymore. But back in the day my dad would say we should always remember there's a plan to help us out of trouble. As far as he was concerned, God, or Providence, or whatever you believe in, could do miracles. I'm not sure about miracles, but I think Dad was a little bit right. Look at me. Two-pairs-of-jeans Rio is still standing."

It was the first almost-joke she'd made about her losses. In doing so, she'd struck another nerve.

"My mother used to remind me to think that way," he admitted. "She was a good, solid, outdoorsy girl. The spiritual side of her was quite strong. Now she's focused on the material. If you haven't noticed."

"I can't judge. I've been plenty fixated on the material things I lost. Maybe these horses are a blessing."

"Well, if that's not a novel way of looking at them,

I don't know what is. C'mon then, let's rescue our allotment."

THE FARM WHERE the animals had been found didn't
look so awful from the front. The house was a sixties,
mid-sized rambler. Behind it stood an ancient pole barn,
perhaps twenty by forty feet, not big enough for so many
horses, but at least an attempt at shelter. Once they all got
to the pasture area, however, the illusion shattered.

To David's surprise, Chief Hewett met them at the
property wearing his usual grim face, although it didn't
seem to be aimed at the people this time. He led them to
a herd of the most wretched animals David had ever seen.
So muddy and matted he couldn't even determine their
colors, they looked like avant-garde art—emaciated clay
sculptures in pitiful groupings.

Ben Thomlinson and Jill were already tromping
through the uneven paddock making cursory checks.
Some of the horses nickered softly. A few moved out of
touching range, and others merely followed the humans
with large, hopeful eyes. David's stomach turned.

"What the bloody hell is the story with this?" he asked
Hewett.

"Supposedly there are thirty acres out there." The
chief indicated a pasture area beyond the crowded paddock bathed in soft evening light. "The owner says he
planned to start a dude ranch like he used to ride at when
he was kid."

"Where was he a kid? The outskirts of hell?"

Hewett almost smiled. "He's in his sixties, a quiet guy. Says he's been buying horses for the past five years and collecting equipment. He just ran out of money."

"Oh good God in Heaven, and he didn't think to sell them?"

"He'll be asked a lot of questions. I promise."

"Sorry," David said. "I'm afraid I'm feeling very little charity here."

"I understand." Hewett actually clapped him briefly on the arm.

David saw Rio then, leaning against a broken board between two crumbling fence posts. She stared into the herd. He made his way to her and put a hand on her back.

"You all right?"

She turned, her mouth tight, her eyes stormy with anger. "What damages a person so badly he can do this?"

"I don't know."

"Ignorance and true psychological trauma." They both turned to find Chase behind them. He put a hand on each of their shoulders and shook his head sadly. "I don't think it's intentional cruelty. This is the same mentality that causes lonely women to become crazy cat ladies, or turns people into hoarders unable to clean their homes. Things get out of hand little by little and suddenly the person has no clue how to solve the problem."

"You're a kinder man than I am, Doc." Disgust still tainted David's emotions.

"No. I've just seen too many ugly things. If I got angry every time I'd have no soul left. I hope this man gets the punishment he deserves *and* the help he needs."

The anger drained from Rio's face. She put her arms around Chase's neck and squeezed briefly. "I'd like to be like you when I grow up."

He patted her back. "No, honey, we could use a few more Rios—stick with her."

She smiled and took David's hand. "Come on, let's go find out what we need to do to get some of these poor things home."

Chapter Twenty-One

A WELCOMING COMMITTEE of half a dozen people waited when she and David arrived at Bridge Creek with the first six horses. It had taken an hour to coax and lift the first rescuees into the four various trailers. Seventeen animals deemed most in need of help, including six Dr. Thomlinson had truly feared for and taken to his clinic, had been loaded first. Jill and Chase had three with minor lameness issues, Gray and Abby had taken two mares and three foals. David had let Rio hand choose their six. After her big speech about a higher power having a plan, she'd used no criteria other than gut feeling to pick them—nothing more than a set of eyes on one sad mare, a cocked ear on another, and a timid step forward from another.

Questions flew the moment she and David were out of the truck. David held up his hand.

"Everyone hold on. We've got six severely malnour-ished horses here. They're quite nervous, so don't get too close. We'll have plenty of time over the next few days to show them they're in a better place."

Rio heard the gasps when the first horse emerged from the trailer. It was a scrawny little paint gelding, the most sociable of the six. David handed its lead rope to Kate. The second and third were bigger animals of indeterminate color, and Andy took charge of them. The last three were quiet, huge-eyed mares.

Bonnie was delighted when David handed her one of their lead ropes. He and Rio took the last two and led the way around the back side of the barn to the pasture where Andy had spread ten bales of hay around the grass and in the two run-in sheds.

"I just used the grass hay," Andy said. "Figured if they were really in bad shape the alfalfa would be too rich."

"This is perfect. They were eating some sort of vile ditch cuttings. Thistle-filled and moldy. It'll be a miracle if they don't all colic on the pasture grass."

"Well, it's eaten down and not very nutritious this time of year," Andy replied. "They'll be fine. You did a good thing, boss."

"I think you should just put the poor creatures out of their misery." Kate handed David her lead rope when it was time for the little paint to enter the pasture.

"What?" Bonnie swung on her with enormous eyes. "Kill them?" She stroked the thin neck of the horse in her charge.

"They're so decrepit. Who knows what sort of pestilence they're carrying." Kate looked past Bonnie to David and Andy.

"That's a little extreme." Rio stared, wondering what had brought on such a reaction. Kate normally had a gentle, if aristocratic, temperament. "It's not their fault they're not beautiful."

"Beautiful has nothing to do with it." Kate's eyes censured her for the first time. "David has a lot of very expensive horses here. It would be a tragedy if something were to happen. You don't want a strangles epidemic or, God forbid, EIA."

Rio had no idea what either of those things was. She could only assume David had thought of this possibility already.

"It's not an insignificant worry, Kate," David said, to Rio's shock. "That's why we'll keep them separate until they can be vaccinated and wormed and thoroughly checked. It'll be all right."

"Are you still going to fetch more?" Stella asked. "It's getting dark."

"I'd like to," David said. "There's so much to do tomorrow. Competitors will start arriving the day after that."

"What can we do to help?"

"If Andy needs anything, help him. Did you get those messages out?" he asked Kate.

"I did. Everything's sorted."

"Brilliant, thank you."

When all six horses had their noses buried in the hay, David turned to Rio.

"You were wonderful," he said, "but it's a long process. You don't need to do it again. I can take Andy."

"I don't mind." Her heart sank at the thought of not finishing the job with him. "I'd . . . like to go back unless you'd rather I stayed here."

"No, I'd rather you come along. I just didn't want to assume you enjoyed it."

"Hard to say I enjoyed it, but it's worth this." She indicated the new residents of the pasture. "They already sound happier. I hate that the others still there don't know something better is just an hour away."

"Then by all means let's go."

BY 11:00 P.M. twelve horses, two more than the ten David had originally agreed to take, were safely in the pasture, and Rio felt like she'd just saved the world. Even though she was muddy, tired, and smelly, she would just as soon have slept on the ground beside the fence. She had no idea why, but all she wanted was to make sure they felt comfortable, safe, and cared for. David laughingly put the kibosh on sleeping with them.

"You're so tired you can barely see straight," he told her, as they stood together, watching the horses snuffle and snort, staking claims to their own places as if fearing the sudden bounty would disappear. "You'll help these guys more by getting a good night's sleep and checking on them first thing."

"Why do I care so much about them?"

He pressed a long, sweet kiss to her temple, and her eyes closed, exhaustion turning to pleasure. When they turned from the fence he took her hand. "For the same reason Kate doesn't truly get it. It's part of your DNA, unfortunately."

"Unfortunately?"

"Because it can get you in twelve half-dead horses' worth of trouble."

No regret came through in his words. He had accepted these animals as his responsibility. She could love a man who went where his heart led him.

"Will you be okay taking care of them? This definitely will get expensive."

"I'll be looking at the books pretty hard, but I can't worry about it too much until after the show. It's going to get crazier yet around here—just so you know."

"Can I look at your books with you?"

As soon as the words were out of her mouth, she bit her lip in mortification. They hadn't sounded so utterly presumptuous in her head.

"Look at my books?"

"I'm sorry. No. No, I didn't mean I wanted to see your personal finances. I only meant I'd be interested in knowing what this costs, feeding twelve horses. I . . . I struggle with my own money issues all the time, and maybe we could figure out something together. I . . . crap, that didn't sound any better. Just forget it. Sorry."

His soft chuckle surprised her. "Stop apologizing. What you're asking is a nice change from people telling me what I ought to do. I can show you what's involved if you'd really like to know."

"I wouldn't tell a soul anything."

"Do you know, I completely believe you."

His words wrapped her in a warm glow. He had an amazing ability to turn her gaffes into genuine compliments.

"I kind of wish I didn't have to work tomorrow," she said. "I'll miss the horses' first day."

"I can ask Dr. Thomlinson to come after you get home. If you'd like to hear what he has to say?"

"You'd wait? Oh, thank you."

David reached behind her neck and pulled her forward into a long, sweet kiss. "Ah, Rio," he said against her lips. "You do have it bad."

"DAMN IT, WHERE did all these people come from?" Bud looked up from the grill and his umpteenth hamburger order of the lunch rush. He'd been uncharacteristically stressed all morning. "It's Thursday, for crying out loud. Do people think it's a holiday weekend? I have to get started on the potato salad for that crazy show, and I can't buy a break."

"Busy is a good thing," Rio soothed.

"I want there to be pie and cakes left for the dinner rush. The gals at The Bread Basket are working overtime for me as it is."

"We are low on desserts." Vince nodded somberly.

Rio yawned. She'd been up since five, rising to check on the new horses before anyone else had been awake. She still had four hours left in her shift. Maybe fatigue conjured the idea; when it struck she definitely didn't have the control to assess it before opening her mouth.

"Do you have ingredients to make apple pie?"

"What?" Bud turned uncomprehending eyes on her.

"I can bake pies."

"Are you serious?"

"Yes."

"Honey, if you can bake a pie that's passable, I'll go get whatever you need myself."

"Oh no, you won't," Vince said. "You aren't leaving me on this grill alone."

Bud grinned for the first time all morning. "We'd need some apples. What I have aren't fresh enough for anything but sauce. But if you're truly serious, I'll call and have as many as you need delivered."

"How many pies do you want?" she asked.

"Three?"

"Five or six apples a pie," she said.

"I'm on my way to the phone." Bud handed Vince a long-handled spatula with a triumphant smile. "Think you can manage for five minutes, junior?"

"JUMPIN' JUDY, JOSEPH, and Mary, girl. Where'd you learn how to make a pie like this?"

Rio blushed with pleasure at the four people crammed into Bud's booth, surrounding the half-eaten pie in front of them. Claudia, Karla, Bud, and Vince dug into pieces of the warm, gooey filling.

"I think it's a good thing my Effie isn't here," Bud spoke over a mouthful of crust. "She'd be green with envy."

"That's a mighty big compliment." Claudia patted Rio's arm in congratulations. "But it's definitely deserved."

"Rio." Bud held up his empty fork, his balding head shining under the fluorescent lights and his bespectacled eyes sparkling. "What would you think of changing shifts, coming in early and making a few pies and maybe some other desserts each day?"

"Do you have any other specialties?" Vince asked. "Not that this ain't enough." He waggled his fork at the pie.

Overwhelmed, Rio took in the praise, trying to organize her thoughts so she could answer the questions coherently. Actually baking for a restaurant? She'd grilled burgers and deep-fried fish and chips, but she'd never been in charge of something as important as an eating establishment's signature desserts.

"I'm flattered," she said finally. "But are you sure? I mean, anyone can bake apple pies. Doughs and things? That's a baker's job."

"Trust me, you're a baker." Bud sat back, crossing his arms over his broad chest.

"I could try," she said. "Pies and cookies are easy enough, I guess. I can do blueberry muffins, too."

"Now *that* would save me a ton of money," Bud said. "If you came in at five or so, had a few things ready when we open, helped out with breakfast, and finished up by eleven, you'd have the afternoon free."

She thought about the horses at David's. She didn't mind getting up early. Maybe this would be a better schedule. "When would you want me to switch?"

"How 'bout tomorrow!" Bud laughed. "Claudia, you be willing to come in at two instead of four?"

"For a few pies back in the case, I'll come in whenever you like," Claudia said.

"Done," said Bud, and raised his glass of water. "Here's to our new baker."

"Until Effie returns," Rio replied and then smiled back and lifted her own glass. The new baker. Would wonders never cease?

Chapter Twenty-Two

"SO, HAY AROUND here is going for upwards of five-fifty a bale for grass and six to eight bucks a bale for the alfalfa mixes." David sat back in his desk chair and ran a hand across his mouth.

"I can see why this worries you," Rio said.

She'd learned more about hay than she'd known there was to learn. It fascinated and intimidated her to see what David had to know in order to run his business. From finding sources for hay and feed, to planning the equivalent of a county fair, to hiring help, understanding horse illnesses, and figuring out how to set his prices so he could keep customers and still make a living—he was trainer, teacher, CEO, and CFO rolled into one.

And he was right. The business was hurting.

"If those are your income/expense numbers," she continued, "and you need another twelve hundred dollars a month just for hay . . ."

"A bit short, right? Pretty much as in twelve hundred dollars short."

She acknowledged with a sigh. "Yeah. You are already not quite breaking even."

"If I could get three more boarders back, I could make that up. But this isn't the time of year people look to add four hundred dollars to their expenses. There'll be possibilities after Christmas, when parents decide to give their kids that pony they've always asked for." He smiled humorlessly. "Meanwhile, I may have to take up a bit of dishwashing."

"There have to be things to cut from the budget."

"I'm down to necessities. Things like electricity and insurance premiums have gone up. Those are not extras."

"What are these items: Friday Bonus Nights and Scholarship Fund?"

"During the summer the staff here, along with a few of the boarders, work their arses off for me. Friday nights we have a pizza, beer, and movie night—far cheaper than pay bonuses. And the scholarship fund is money to pay show registrations for three kids who wouldn't get to go to a show otherwise. Both nonnegotiable."

She nodded, her brain churning with ways those items could be cut back. But it wasn't her business. Still, when she looked at another number under "Employee salaries," she couldn't help but comment.

"This takes up a huge chunk." She pointed. "Almost four thousand a month. Is that all Andy?"

"Andy and the kids I hire for various things."

"Just wondering if you'd ever thought about cutting Andy's hours?"

"Absolutely not."

He stood with such vehemence Rio backed her chair up and stared. "Okay. Sorry," she said. "Honestly, I wasn't suggesting it. I'm just learning here."

He ran a hand through his hair, and such tiredness crossed his face that Rio stood to meet him.

"I touched a sore spot. David, I really do apologize."

He pulled her into a hug, brief but desperate. "That sore spot is Andy. You have to know that as long as I'm breathing, he's going nowhere unless he wishes it."

"That's pretty amazing loyalty."

They both sat again. "I met him two years after arriving in the States at a VFW breakfast where he was volunteering by replacing syrup bottles and filling juice glasses. He was one of the most cheerful blokes I'd ever seen but not very coordinated. For some reason we started a conversation. Discovered we'd been in Iraq at exactly the same time—almost to the dates. I was in Basra, he in Fallujah. The difference was, he'd been severely injured. That's where he lost his leg. He'd also suffered traumatic brain injury, and he was in the process of looking for work."

"You gave him a job."

"Not straight away. We simply stayed connected. I hadn't found too many fellow soldiers willing to talk. It's not much of a lark to chatter on about trauma with people who haven't been through it. Not manly to admit your nightmares. Besides that, it's amazing how many people talk a good story about supporting veterans and yet can't tolerate something like Andy's limp or slow speech. It takes a bit of effort to realize he's not slow."

"He certainly is not."

"He went through three jobs before I finally asked him to come here."

"How long ago?"

"Almost six years. After struggling for so long, he took to the work here like he was born to it. He loves the animals, and he's great with the boarders. He's the brother I never had in far more ways than one."

"I'm sorry if I sounded like I thought he wasn't important to you."

"No. I'm sorry for jumping on you. I get defensive. I identify with Andy because I couldn't have taken on a regular job when I got out either. In fact, I couldn't do a lot of things. That's what lost me Kate and drove me from England. Not many successful, happy soldiers return from that Middle-Eastern sandbox."

He leaned forward, elbows to thighs, and Rio stroked his bangs from his forehead.

"I have no way to imagine it. Were you injured, too?"

"Not physically, thank God. But I was also a thoroughly unsuccessful soldier. Ask my father, the sergeant-major. He saw minimal action in the Falklands, but he still became one of the most popular men in the British Army. He was part of a special unit that entertained and boosted morale by putting on cavalry exhibitions. A much grander military career than those of grunts like me or Andy who only got shot at."

His unmistakable bitterness surprised her. She'd

never known a more optimistic person than David. Not once had he hinted at this traumatic past.

"You don't have to talk about this if you don't want to."

"It's a long time past," he said with a sigh. "Bottom line is, neither Andy nor I had a glorious homecoming. We both lost mates. We both have scars. That Band of Brothers title is truth in our case."

"There are more stories in your eyes." She peered at him. "I won't ask you to tell them, but I'm a good listener if you ever need one."

He straightened, and his handsome cheekbones lifted in a smile of gratitude. "I really am fine. I hadn't thought about Andy's story in a while. I take him a little for granted."

"I won't suggest you let him go ever again." She offered a teasing smile.

"Best not," he agreed, and his smile returned.

"You've been telling me to stand up for myself ever since we met," she said. "You should do the same. You don't have to do anything anyone else tells you to do. Not your mother, not me. You can even be mad sometimes. It's not a sin."

"I had to learn the hard way that losing my temper never helps anything."

She shrugged. "Sometimes letting loose is like a teapot whistling—lets out the steam so you don't explode."

"You've changed since you came here, you know that?"

"I haven't changed a bit."

"Have, too. Who's the wise little bird now?"

"What? I'm not wise, you're just seeing the bossy, dictatorial real me."

"Well, you've bossed me right out of a foul mood. Even if I haven't a clue where to find enough hay I can afford to feed twelve orphaned equines."

"My dad used to sing the old Beatles song *Let it Be* to me. One line says what he used to say, 'there will be an answer.' So let it be for tonight. Enjoy your show. You said it's a moneymaker."

"But it's already part of the budget. I can't count it as—"

She set a forefinger firmly against his lips. "Stop borrowing trouble."

A chuckle rose from his throat. David spun his desk chair, grabbed her, and dragged her sideways onto his lap. "You're right," he said, lowering his mouth to hers. "I have enough trouble already."

SATURDAY NIGHT, DAVID sat back in a canvas quad chair, propped his booted feet on a picnic table bench, and closed his eyes for the first time in eighteen hours. In just a few minutes his party companions would return with second helpings from Bud's amazing-as-always barbecue feed. He took the moment of peace to thank the gods of three-day eventing, that they were done with Saturday. Cross-country day always threatened to send him to his hidden hunter's cabin with a whiskey bottle and a padlock. With a hundred riders heading out over the jumps, there was always the chance of accidents to horses or riders, bad weather, angry competitors, broken equipment. He'd dealt with every scenario at one time or another.

Today, however . . .

"Hey, wake up. You don't even ride in this shindig of yours, what have you got to be so tired about?"

"Piss off, Chase." He grinned, his eyes still closed.

"I love how he says that, *pess ohf*." Chase laughed and cuffed David's hair, leaving it flopping.

"Look who's talking, y'redneck git," David replied.

He swung his feet off the bench and winked at Jill. Really, what did he have to complain about? This was the life. A new hand ruffled through his hair and for an instant he thrilled to the touch. Then he looked into Kate's bright brown eyes, and his heart thudded back to normal.

"Poor exhausted love," she said. "You do put on quite a show."

"I'm not exhausted. I'm finally relaxing." With a gentle movement he removed her hand from his head, but before he could drop it, she entwined her fingers through his. He straightened and cleared his throat. "It's always worth the work."

Disentangling their hands, he noted her perfect manicure and the crisp short-sleeved blouse beneath a lightweight vest with some sort of velvety collar. She looked like Hollywood's version of an equestrian—not a smudge on her boots, makeup impeccable, chestnut hair perfect.

"Perhaps I'll have to make sure you get a relaxing nightcap later tonight." She wrinkled her nose suggestively in the first real flirting she'd done in ten days. It unnerved him.

"Now, Kate. Celebrating comes after it's all over. Tomorrow."

"We'll see." She patted his shoulder.

A ripple of awareness whispered up the back of his neck, and he turned to see Rio slide into a spot beside Jill. His heart galloped into a crazy beat and stayed elevated while she flicked her gaze from his face to Kate's hand and back, and he shook his head. She smiled.

The girl amazed him. *Her* touch, *her* suggestion of a nightcap would have left him ecstatic, yet she played the perfect friend. Given the right kind of damn-the-torpedoes attitude, he'd have walked straight to her side and kissed her in front of everyone, but they weren't ready. They'd both agreed. Nobody would understand the suddenness of their relationship—least of all Bonnie, she'd told him. He wasn't sure anymore they were right.

She was the prettiest thing in her jeans and faded T-shirt—the same clothing he'd seen her in two dozen times. But it didn't matter. Her curves were endlessly exciting; it didn't matter what covered them. Her blue-ocean eyes were fathomless and always searching for the next thing she needed to know. Tonight she wore her red hair down, rather than in her normal ponytail. It swirled past her shoulders, half-tamed, half-unruly, like a shimmering sunset, russet and red with shadowed highlights. She couldn't have turned him on more had she been wearing only the waning evening light.

"It went good today, boss." Andy brought his refilled plate to the table, set it down, and swung his titanium leg between the top and the bench with his hands.

"Exceedingly."

There'd been two beginner novice falls, but the kids landed like little bouncing balls. One horse had lost its rider and run off in preliminary, but the rider's pride was far more wounded than her bum. And three dozen drops of rain. Total success.

Andy scratched his head. "I was thinking—"

A gunshot-like crash and the sickening screech of metal on metal cut him off and sent everyone under the canopy into shocked silence. David's heart catapulted into his throat.

"What the hell was that?" Andy's question rang through the stunned crowd, and suddenly everyone shouted at once.

David bolted from his chair, and Rio knocked a can of pop over in her scramble to get out of her seat. Kate stared in alarm, but he didn't see whether she followed the near-stampede around the arena and toward the main drive. When they'd wound their way through two rows of cars parked alongside the barn, the source of the crash greeted them like a bad horror film. David slammed to a halt as if he'd hit an electric fence.

"Oh my! Oh no!" Rio covered her mouth.

The back end of a red Dodge pickup truck had punched clear through a corner of the barn. The truck bed had accordioned into disturbing pleats. Moaning sobs emanated from the cab.

Chase made the first move, dashing to the door of the truck. Rio ripped past David, but he caught her arm and dragged her back close to him. "Don't rush in. Let Chase make sure whoever's in there is all right."

"Tully," she whispered, her voice strangled. "That's his corner of the barn."

"He's fine." David made the promise without a clue as to whether it was true. "Come on, let's see where they went through. The tack room is there, too, maybe that buffered the stalls. Kate, Mom, keep everyone back."

It never dawned on him to leave Rio behind. She felt like a natural extension of him these days. By the time they drew even with the truck, Chase had the driver, a young woman perhaps twenty, out of the cab. Tears streamed down her cheeks, but Chase gave them a thumbs-up.

"I'm sorry. I'm so, so sorry," she cried, when she caught sight of David.

"If you're okay, that's what matters." He peered more closely at her; she wasn't one of his students or boarders. "You are all right?"

"I'll check her out," Chase said. "You go see if anything needs to be done inside."

David smiled wanly at the girl, too numb to be annoyed with her. He couldn't see past the end of the truck, so he trotted to the barn door and stared down the aisle. Even from the front he could see debris strewn across the concrete floor at the back. Snorting and restless stomping greeted him, along with a handful of whinnies as he strode into the dimmed interior and flipped on the lights.

Rio sprinted down the aisle, skirting the mess on the floor, disappearing into Tully's stall. When David reached her, she had her hands roaming over the big horse's body. "He's okay. He's fine."

His pulse eased, and he smiled through his tension. How could he not fall for a girl who went after the horse before worrying about the building? He let her tend to

Tully while he studied the detritus pushed out from the accident site. Sure enough, the truck had hit between the smaller of his two tack rooms and an empty stall he'd just Friday night filled with two dozen hay bales to make it easier to feed the new horses during the show weekend. The inside tack room door stood blown open, bits of insulation and shards of metal siding thick on the floor. Leather, broken tack boxes, and crushed saddles looked like bombing victims. When he didn't think his stomach could sink any lower, he noticed the water.

A waterline ran near ground level between the outer metal sheeting and inner wooden walls. The pipe had been sheared apart and water was rising in the corner next to the hay. At least three saddles lay in the growing puddle, and brushes, lead ropes, and bridle parts were starting to float.

"Aw no." He groaned. "Andy, we have to—"

"I'm on the shut off," he called and disappeared out the door.

David shot forward to scoop up soggy equipment as best he could. He caught sight of three more saddles beneath the truck, at least one of them flattened and pinned beneath a back tire.

Rio entered behind him. "Oh David. This is terrible."

"I need to get as much off the floor as I can. There are saddles under the truck."

She hit her knees without a word and seconds later wriggled her lithe body partway under the Dodge, arm extended. She dragged out a dripping Pessoa jumping saddle. David cringed.

Together they rescued ten saddles, at least that many bridles, and countless pieces of grooming equipment, along with two pairs of tall boots and a muddy pair of breeches. When everything had been removed to a dry section of the aisle, David finally stopped and took a good look at Rio. Everything from hair to borrowed boots dripped water. Her front was mud-streaked and plastered to her chest. All he could do was stare like a boy at his first wet T-shirt contest. A semi-hysterical laugh broke free.

"All this disaster, and the only thing I can look at are your breasts. Do you want to punch me now or lecture me later?"

"You are pretty shallow." She smiled, stepped forward to put her hands on his cheeks, and kissed him. "I'm sorry. This is awful."

"I'm not sure yet how awful. All the tack will need to be thoroughly cleaned fairly quickly so the leather doesn't mildew or get cracked. And who knows if the saddles have broken trees or other issues."

"It'll be okay."

"I expect it will."

But this felt like one blow too many. He'd told her he was one disaster from disaster. It had come sooner than he'd expected. He had insurance, but it covered the building, not necessarily equipment for those not insured. He wasn't at fault, but he had two or three very particular clients, and he could well imagine one of them finding a way to hold him responsible.

"David." Her voice reached in through his fog. "Nobody is dead. This isn't a disaster."

"Okay. If you say so."

"Come on." She took his hand and tugged on it gently. "We'll start fixing it."

THREE HOURS LATER, exhausted and numb, David dropped his head against the back of his sofa. For the first time since the accident, Rio was nowhere to be seen. Kate sat beside him while his mother buttressed her arguments for calling his father.

"You know he'll help you, David. Your father, for all his faults, is a phenomenal problem solver. Look how he turned around that barn in Kent back in the nineties. Look how he made his way to the top of his sport from nothing."

"He made it to the top by catering to sponsors, and he turns barns around by dictating stricter rules than Mussolini."

He had trouble keeping his voice calm. Of course his mother would invoke the name of the perfect and failureless Colin Pitts-Matherson. She might have divorced him, but that was only because she was smart, not because she didn't still admire him with every fiber of her female self. Everyone admired his father. Hell, he admired his father. He just couldn't stand the man.

"Oh David." Kate's voice, reasonable and modulated, grated. "Don't be so dismissive of him. I remember Colin as quite a gentleman. He won't turn his back on you if you're in this much trouble."

He wanted to shout that he was not in trouble. Unfortunately, after the fallout from tonight, both she and his mother knew that he was.

"He won't turn his back, but his help will come with a steep price. It always does. I didn't use Mussolini's name just to be funny. It'll be just like invading Ethiopia—his way or the highway."

"Just talk to him, darling." His mother came forward and sat on his other side. Instantly claustrophobia engulfed him.

"I am not calling my father."

Both women stared at him, as if they could will him into being reasonable. Kate rested her hand on his shoulder and rubbed soothingly. He shrugged from the touch but was too tired to physically move away.

"All right," his mother said at last. "You don't have to call him. I just want you to know you have family on your side."

"Thank you. But you have to let me figure this out my way."

"David?"

He looked up. Kate's hand stilled on his shoulder and turned into an icy weight as Rio slowly took the last step into the room, a sheet of paper in her hand, a sweet little wrinkle forming between her brows.

"Rio." He stood, relieved to see her. Relieved to move from Kate's touch. "How are you?"

"I'm . . . fine." The crease in her forehead deepened. "Why?"

"You got awfully down and dirty tonight. I never properly thanked you."

"No need to. We all did our parts. Stella and Kate

kept the party going so everyone had a good time. That's not something I'd have been good at. Down and dirty is much easier for me."

"I'm grateful David had some help." Kate stood and joined him again. "I'm not good at *all* with down and dirty."

The first tension he'd ever felt between the two women crackled through the air. He swallowed, ignored it, and held out his hand. "What have you got?"

She handed him the sheet of paper. "Yesterday, while you were busy with the show, I did a bunch of research. This is all new to me, and I don't actually know what I'm doing. So I hope you won't mind that I exchanged a couple of e-mails with a hay grower in Watertown, South Dakota. This came back just a little while ago."

He stared at the paper, almost unable to believe what he was reading.

"He's selling grass hay for three-fifty a bale? Alfalfa mix for five seventy-five?"

"I asked him why so inexpensive. He said he cuts three hundred acres and they had a great year. Just two hundred miles away from here they had much different weather."

"You . . . found him? How in the world?"

"I followed a few different trails, people who mentioned his name. Did you know there are online hay forums?" She grinned. "You can find anything on the Internet."

David read further. "He's delivering a semi flatbed full of hay to the western suburbs on Tuesday. He'll come here for an extra fifty cents a bale? Good lord, what is he selling? It has to be half moldy or last year's."

"Says he guarantees no mold. If you want to call him, he'll answer questions. If you aren't interested, you aren't obligated."

He was almost as stunned as when he'd first seen the smashed barn. "I can't believe you did this."

"It's not hard to look. I won't be the least offended if this isn't what you need."

"It sounds too good to be true."

"And things like that usually are, right?" Her blue eyes shone a little impishly. "But you need a little bit of luck tonight—maybe this is it. Oh, read the last line."

"'I'm willing to take two payments.'" He looked up. "Now I know this isn't real. No hay guy is going to do that."

"All you can do is call and find out, I guess."

He did a quick calculation. This could save him hundreds. And the fact that Rio had done it on her own was the most astonishing. It was such a relief that he picked her up in front of his mother and Kate and spun her around. Only with effort did he keep from kissing her.

"This is extraordinary. Thank you."

"Thank me if it turns out to be legit." Her skin flushed to compliment her hair.

"Oh, you'd better believe I will."

"You're so resourceful." Kate materialized beside him as he set Rio on the ground. "Have you run a business before?"

"No." Rio took a step back from Kate, who topped her

height by four inches. "But I've spent my life looking for bargains."

"My goodness." Kate then turned a beatific smile on him. David took his own half step back. "Do remember, love, that I, too, have means to help you if you need it. Don't settle for poor quality."

"Or . . ." Rio straightened. "He can make his own decisions. He can economize and scrabble like a normal person."

"Scrabbling leaves very little time for running a successful business," Kate replied, her voice smooth as steel. "Connections are much more efficient."

"I'm guessing we'll be doing a little bit of both," he said.

Rio stared at him, the light in her eyes sharpening, impaling him with some sort of new annoyance. She waited, for what he had no idea. He waited for her to explain. She was right about him needing to figure out his way through this, but he'd cut where he could cut and would cut more if he could find places to do it. Meanwhile, Kate was right, too. He needed to find his connections.

"I wouldn't know about the kind of connections you mean," Rio said at last, turning her laser glare on Kate. "So it's a good thing that finding and having money is your area of expertise. *He* should be the grateful one, now that he has your help."

She shocked him by spinning away from them all and heading for the kitchen. Moments later the back door opened and closed.

He had no idea what in God's name he'd done. One

minute she'd been blushing in his arms, the next shooting him death-ray eyes.

"She'll be fine," Kate said. "She's just naïve."

"Kate, leave her alone. She's only trying to help."

He looked to his mother for support, but she was staring toward the kitchen, her face set in a scowl.

Chapter Twenty-Three

RIO SEETHED ALL the way into the barn, past the tarp-covered hole in the tack stall wall and to Tully's stall beside it where the big horse munched his hay in happy equine oblivion. She stared at him through the bars until he snorted and shuffled to her, hoping for some sort of treat he couldn't find in his feed bucket. She released her irritation with a heavy sigh.

"Sorry, boy. I forgot an apple, and the feed room's kind of a mess."

Talking to him calmed her. Equine magic still astounded her even though she'd known her whole life she wanted to be around horses. The fact that the reality of something actually matched the fantasy seemed too good to be true.

Like the hay she'd found for David. Ruefully she kicked Tully's scattered hay into a neat pile fuming over Kate's words. The way moneyed people problem-solved was beyond Rio's understanding. She'd seen David's books now, and even after the briefest of looks she knew there were places he could cut further. Why would he, or anybody, think tossing more money into the hole would help?

Tully snorted again. Rio straightened. Maybe she was simply jealous. It would be nice to have a network of wealthy people to run to in a crisis. The thought of David taking such a wimpy way out, however, saddened her. She saw flashes of amazing leadership in him, like when he stood up for Andy, or even for her. The instant his family came into the picture, however, he folded like a bad poker hand.

An unexpected bump against her legs made her jump. She looked down to see Thirty-one arching against her calf.

"Hullo, you."

She picked up the little cat and its purr filled the stall. Squirming upward, Thirty-one rubbed her head hard against Rio's neck. The effect was instantaneously soothing.

With one last pat for Tully, she carried the cat out of the stall, latched the door, and leaned against the wood to nuzzle the striking orange-and-black fur. She'd never been able to consider having pets because of the time and cost commitments. That priority might have to change.

Footsteps interrupted her thoughts. The sight of her sister coming slowly down the aisle took her aback. Bonnie waved almost shyly.

"Hi," she said when she reached Rio and the cat. "I came to see if you're okay."

"Aw, thanks, but I'm fine. Why wouldn't I be?"

"I was coming down to steal some cookies, those ones you baked to try out for The Loon Feather, and I heard Kate go whacko on you. Is David in trouble?"

Rio's brows shot up in surprise. She'd never heard Bonnie say a negative word about Kate. In fact, she'd seemed enamored of the woman.

"She's not so whacko as she is rich, Bon. And David got hit hard by the recession so she thinks she has a solution. I think he just needs to economize—not all that different from what you and I do all the time. But it's hard. And don't go spreading anything around."

"I never would." Bonnie gazed at her a long moment. "That cat likes you a lot."

"Weird, huh?"

"I really like it here, Rio. I'm not sure I want to go back to Minneapolis. I thought I'd miss it, but going back feels scary now."

"Don't you miss having our own place?"

"It's strange, but I don't."

"You've made some good friends here. Like Dawson?" Rio teased.

"I don't know what to do with an ordinary guy. He's so . . . normal. He gets a little moody sometimes and doesn't say a lot. But I think he likes me."

"Boys are weird, Bonnie. Wonderful but weird. Just accept that and things will go easier." She laughed and hugged her sister with one arm. "But we can't mooch off of David much longer. We aren't helping him cut costs. We'll see how much my first paycheck is. If it's enough to pay rent and help out, then we'll work something out for a little while longer."

"You've got friends, too, you know. David likes you almost as much as Thirty-one does."

"What do you mean?" Her heart skipped a nervous beat, wondering what Bonnie suspected.

"He says it's nice having someone who likes to cook, and who likes to help in the barn."

"Oh. That." Her fears calmed again. "It's not just me. You've been doing chores, too. Still, once I figure out what our own finances truly are, we will have to find us a place."

"But then, maybe it could be around here. School starts next week."

"You're excited about that?"

"Yes."

"So . . . Hector is in the past? Once we find him, I mean?"

They hadn't heard from him in a week, and Rio didn't know whether to hope he'd finally given up or worry that he was planning something awful. Chief Hewett had returned Bonnie's phone without any information about where the calls had originated. The analysis took time, he'd told them.

"I never thought much about Hector's language, his threats, his bragging," she said. "He talked like all the other guys. Now that I've met one who doesn't . . ."

For first time since the fire, Rio said an honest-to-goodness prayer of thanks for the disaster. If in its aftermath Bonnie could see past the false strength of gang leadership, it was worth losing clothes and posters and plastic horses.

"Good for you, sis," she said. "I mean it. I'm proud of you for figuring it out."

"I think I would have anyway."

"I think so, too."

Rio pulled a saddle pad off the bar on the front of Tully's stall and dropped it on the floor. "Sit with me a minute. It's so peaceful out here. See if Thirty-one will let you hold her."

Thirty-one did. She curled into Bonnie's lap as if she knew a peace accord was needed. The air settled on them with the ozone tang of threatening rain. For a moment the barn felt like the safest place in the world.

"I was really mad at you that night. The night you dragged me to Crossroads." Bonnie took a small silvery object from her pocket and held it for Thirty-one to sniff. "I didn't want to admit in front of those older, cooler guys that I needed my big sister to come and rescue me. But I did."

Unexpected tears pricked at the corners of Rio's eyes. "Wow, Thank you. That really does help everything. I'm so sorry it had the consequences it did, but I'd do it again to keep you from Boyfriend."

"He was old, like forties old. He had very plain but scary eyes."

"You saw him? I barely got a glimpse."

"I talked to him for about two minutes. He told me Hector was lucky to have such a gorgeous girlfriend. But he didn't mean it."

"Oh, he did. Just not in a nice way."

"I know. I know what he does now." She shivered. "I'm more creeped out by him than Hector. Boyfriend was smooth, mean smooth like he was in total control. I could tell even Hector was a little afraid of him."

"Then I'm glad you're nowhere near them." She watched Bonnie turning the object she held slowly in her fingers. "What's that?"

Bonnie hesitated and then held out a square silver money clip holding an actual folded bill. "I found it outside the car when Paul and Hector brought me to meet Boyfriend. I think it's Paul's. It's got that big 'I' engraved on it. I assume for 'Inigo,' like on that belt he wears and that cap he's got. There are two one-hundred-dollar bills in here. I thought if I just kept it, Paul might try harder to find us because he'd need the money. But now, since he seems to be hiding with Hector, maybe we could just use it ourselves. He owes us that much."

Rio stared at the clip. "Where would he have gotten this much?"

"I don't know. The other weird thing is that there's a name on the back of each bill. People do that like for birthday presents and things, but to have two of them?"

Rio pulled the money free of the holder and unfolded it slowly. Just as Bonnie had said, there were two bills bearing Franklin's face and across the back of each, in what looked like plain ballpoint ink, was a girl's name.

"Keep it," Rio said, putting everything back as it had been. "You're probably right. Whenever he gets in touch, you can tell him you have it."

Bonnie rested her head on Rio's shoulder, adding more shock to the whole interaction. "I'm glad he doesn't know where we are now."

"Yeah, sweetie, I am, too. Let's hope they find him soon. I'm ready to be done thinking about him. You know what? It's been a weird day. Let's have a slumber party in my room and bring the cat. We'll sneak her in."

Bonnie laughed and gave her a tiny squeeze. "That's so naughty of you. I love it."

Naughty. Her father had always stressed what a role model she had to be for her brother and sister. She hadn't wanted the job, but once her dad was gone, she'd had no choice. Tonight it didn't seem like Bonnie needed role modeling as much as simple camaraderie. Or maybe it was Rio who needed it. Either way, a little naughty would be nice.

SHE AWOKE THE next morning to her alarm and the sound of sneezing from down the hall. She frowned, since Bonnie still slept curled up on the opposite end of the bed. The nose-blowing that followed had to be Kate. What? The regal Kate was sick? How could that be?

She shook her sister awake.

"C'mon, time to head out. You wanted to see Jill go— her division starts at eight-thirty."

"Time is it?" Bonnie mumbled.

"Seven. Where's the cat?"

As if she'd heard, Thirty-one meowed softly and padded into the room through a door opened five inches.

"Oh no, where were you?" Rio clambered out of bed and grabbed her. "Did anyone see you?"

Thirty-one jumped from her arms to the bed and nuzzled a sleepy, giggling Bonnie. "She knew it was Naughty Night. I think she was out helping us be naughty."

"She better not have been too bad."

Rio dumped the cat out the front door on the way to Stella's scones and jam. When they reached the kitchen, a surprisingly violent sneeze from gentile Kate greeted them.

"*Gesundheit*," Rio said. "Are you catching something? I'm sorry."

"No. I don't feel ill one bit," she said, reaching for a tissue from a box on the table. "It's completely allergies. I don't understand, this usually happens when there are cats or rabbits or chickens near, but David doesn't keep animals in the house. I can't figure it out."

Rio choked as if she'd swallowed a scone whole, but Bonnie covered her mouth with both hands and leaned in to Rio's ear. "On purpose," she whispered through her fingers.

Rio glared at her.

"Rio." Kate's voice made her start guiltily. "I owe you an apology for last night."

"No," she replied, relieved. "It was a strange night. Nobody really knew what to say."

"I shouldn't have disparaged you for helping. I . . . well, if I'm perfectly honest I was just a bit envious you'd been so resourceful."

Okay, now she did feel guilty. "Resourcefulness is something you learn living on a shoestring," she said. "It's had to be second nature for us."

"Do you like him?"

"Him?"

"David."

"Uh. Yes. Of course. Who wouldn't? He's one of the nicest guys I've ever met."

"I'm wondering if it's more than that. You've learned so quickly how to help him the way he needs it most. He already seems to rely on you."

Rio couldn't tell if Kate was telling the truth or being mildly catty again.

"I need to earn my way around here, that's all. I'm not used to living on charity. I intend to find any useful thing that will help until we can leave."

"I did one of the most foolish things of my life when I broke up with David all those years ago." Kate sat primly in her confessional state. "I didn't realize how wounded he was after the war. Nobody understood post-traumatic stress well then. David had been stern, decisive. The war softened him rather than hardened him, and I thought he didn't care anymore. When Stella offered me the chance to come and see him again and I realized he'd never married, it gave me hope—to make amends. I thought you should know that."

Wounded? Post-traumatic stress? The words swam in Rio's mind, making no sense. He'd admitted to being bitter about the war, but he'd never seemed unduly scarred by it. She shook her head and focused back on Kate.

"Wait. You're saying you're here to win him back?"

"I'd like to try. I thought it best if I stated my feelings to you honestly. I don't know what you're trying to start with him."

"Whatever we become is already started," she said, and hesitated. She and David had agreed to keep their attraction a secret, but this moment she wanted with her whole being to tell Lady Katherine every detail about the shiver-inducing relationship she already had with her ex-fiancé. She wanted David right there with his arms around her telling Kate she was far too late. Instead, she held in the jealousy, the desire, the recent memories of David's beautiful body next to hers. "I can't tell you what we are, but I won't stop trying to be his . . . friend."

"Fair enough. I can live with that."

Bonnie caught her eye again. This time she wasn't laughing. "What the . . .?" she mouthed.

Rio ignored her.

"I also think you should know Stella called David's father this morning. He'll be here in two days."

"But he didn't want that," Bonnie blurted.

"It's all right, pet," Stella soothed. "He doesn't know what he needs right now. His father will have some solutions, and in the end David will thank him."

"The affordable hay idea was brilliant," Kate added. "But one load of cheaper food won't solve the problems."

"It's a start," Rio protested. "Why do you insist on manipulating him?"

"David is a dreamer, not a businessman. He's made this place work with a lot of help already. He can continue on if he's willing to take the advice of those who have helped him."

Rio wanted to scream in frustration for David. "Does he know?"

"Not yet."

"He deserves fair warning. If you don't tell him I—"

She was interrupted by the buzz of her phone in her pocket—a call, not a text. She fished it out and stared at Paul's number on the illuminated screen. Her head went light.

"What?" Bonnie asked.

"Hang on, it's work," she lied.

Chapter Twenty-Four

RIO DASHED OUT the back door with no further explanation. Her heart pounded as she prayed it truly was Paul. In a tiny corner of her brain, she believed Hector didn't have the guts to talk voice to voice. It was the only thing that gave her courage to answer the phone.

"Hello?"

"My name is Inigo Montoya. You killed my father. Prepare to die."

Their corny joke brought tears to her eyes. She hadn't truly realized until that moment how worried she'd been about the jerk.

"Paul, where have you been? Where are you now?"

"I can't tell you that. Are you okay?"

"No thanks to you, *idiota*. Are you?"

"I'm with Heco."

"What the hell is wrong with you? Get away from that asshat, and tell the police you had nothing to do with the fire. And what's up with all the threatening text messages? I'm giving you the benefit of the doubt that you're not sending them."

"I have no choice, Rio. Hector isn't going to let me out of his sight until he finds you and Bonnie."

"But why? Bonnie is nothing to him. And he's gotten more than revenge for a stupid scratch down his face."

He gave an odd almost conspiratorial laugh. "Shit, girl. You should see the scratch. It's still healing. Gonna leave a good scar."

"Which is not good. He deserves to be hurt, but I don't want him to think of me whenever he looks in a mirror. He burned down our house, Paul. Isn't that enough to end your blind loyalty to him?"

"I am not loyal. I'm a fuckin' prisoner. I go along because I don't want him *thinking* I'm a prisoner. And he doesn't want Bonnie. He needs something Bonnie has."

"What?" Her senses prickled. Dread dripped into her stomach like acid.

"Something that belongs to Hector's friend."

"Who, Boyfriend? Someone needs to stop him; he's a sociopath."

A long pause followed. She didn't push. She needed this information no matter how much it scared her.

"Yes," he said quietly.

"What does Bonnie have?"

"We don't know. But BF is leaning on Heco hard. He's given him only a little more time to find Bonnie. He says she knows what she has, and he'd better get it before anyone else does or . . . he doesn't say what the consequences are."

The words should have terrified her, but somehow, in Paul's hushed, secret-agent voice they sounded more ludicrous than threatening.

"Well, it turns out I have an advantage, Inigo."

"What's that?"

"I *know* what she has."

"For God's sake, what?"

"We thought it was yours. It's a silver money clip with the initial 'I' on it."

"Damn! I need to get it from you. Where are you? We have to meet."

"No way. Not a chance until I think about this and figure out how to keep Hector and that evil, pimping Boyfriend out of it."

"Rio, come on. Get me out of this hell."

"I don't want to hear about hell, *mano*. You turned your back on us. You had to have known what Hector was planning, and you did nothing. I don't care about myself, but you owe Bonnie. She adores you. So I will do whatever it takes to keep her safe."

"You don't understand."

Rio took a calming breath and stopped pacing the back deck. She forced herself to sit in the bench rocker and keep her cool.

"Absolutely true. Are you willing to tell me where you are?"

"I told you, I can't. Hector would kill me if you went to the police. Don't go to the police, Rio, please. These guys are dangerous."

"What cop shows are you watching? That's so cliché

I'm laughing my ass off. Tell him I've already been to the police, because of his stupid ass text messages. The Minneapolis cops will find him. All we have to do is wait it out."

"What if he finds you?"

"Hector? Hah! He's not smart enough."

"Rio. You're killing me."

"I didn't get you into this mess. If you die it's on your head. Only you won't because Hector needs you. You're the best hope he has of learning where I am."

"Let's just get this over with."

"I'll think about it. But only if two things happen. First, neither Bonnie nor I gets another threatening message from him. Second, you call me sometime from a phone that Hector has no access to, and where he can't hear you. *Maybe*, we can work something out."

Another long silence followed. This one lasted nearly half a minute. It ended with a long, clear sigh.

"I don't know when that will be. He doesn't trust me. He takes my phone randomly to check texts and send them."

"That's precisely why you haven't gotten any from us. And you won't. Or any calls. Find a different phone. That's the deal."

"Okay."

"Paul. What's the 'I' on the money clip for?"

"I don't know. Nobody knows anything about Boyfriend except that if you have a debt and can get him a girl, the younger the better, he'll take care of it. He's one shadowy dude."

"He needs to go to prison with a bunch of very large,

very lonely guys. He's lower than hired assassins. If Bonnie had gone—"

"Don't." A stone-cold hiss stopped her. "I have a lot to explain about the fire, but I wasn't going to let Bonnie go with him. I'd have let them kill me first."

"Then prove it. Fix this, Paul."

"Look, I gotta go. Hector's coming in. Make sure Bonnie doesn't lose that . . . thing."

"We could send it to you."

"I suggested that. He won't let me give out even a P.O. Box that anyone could follow. It's in person or . . ."

"This is insane."

"Yeah. Just don't be stupid. Boyfriend is serious and Hector is scared. That makes him crazier than ever."

"All right. I get it." She hesitated, worry creeping back under the edges of her tough act. "Paul, be careful. Please."

"I'm fine for now."

"Thanks for letting me know you're okay."

"Yeah. I'm glad you are, too. Are you far away?"

"Yes."

"Good. I guess. Talk to you later. Say hi to Bon."

He was gone before she could ask any more questions. For several long moments she stared at the phone.

And had no idea what to do.

DAVID GLARED AT the two women in front of him and held back a curse. "Did I or did I not expressly tell you I don't wish to talk to my father?" He swung his eyes from his mother to Kate. They sat over their Monday morning coffee and oatmeal after having dropped their bombshell. Neither gave a blink, much less an apology.

"You need to talk to him," his mother said simply. "He helped you get off the ground. You have to share your difficulties."

"I do not. I paid back his loan years ago, and none of this is your business. Either of you."

Kate shrugged. "Blame me as much as your mum. I maybe pushed the hardest to call your father. I want you to succeed."

"After all these years, Kate? Just how did you come to that?"

"I understand why you're put out with me, but maybe I decided long ago I'd made a mistake by letting you go."

"Letting me go? As I recall, it was much closer to, 'David, don't let the door hit you in the arse on the way out.'"

Contrition, practiced and perfect, filled her features. "You're absolutely right. But time and experience have shown me they don't come much kinder and harder working than you."

"Well, bully for me, Kate. That doesn't mean you get to come waltzing back and make decisions for me."

"Of course not. I'm sorry. But you do know we could avoid all this completely if you'd just think about forgiving me a little and letting me help. We were good together once. We might be again." She smiled up at him like a kid asking for a new puppy—all innocence and cunning.

"Kate . . ." he warned.

"She's right, sweetheart. Maybe it's you two who should talk." His mother winked.

He ignored her. "I need you to call Da' and tell him not to come. Rio had some good ideas to start with. I'm not going to lose the farm over an accident. There's insurance."

With an eight-thousand-dollar deductible. And the young driver of the truck had had only collision, no comprehensive. At one point, he'd had that amount put away for just such an emergency, but that cushion was gone. And he wasn't going to give these two any such details. Not when the matchmaking gloves had officially come off.

"He's already booked his ticket. He was quite excited to come. Said something about this being serendipity, as a matter of fact."

"Mum." He stared, breathing heavily, gaining composure. "I don't like this."

"It's all right." She smiled. "Sit down and eat something. You had a stressful weekend."

"I'll grab a granola bar in the office in the barn. Has Rio been through here yet?"

"She's working early at the restaurant now, remember?" Kate said, as if she felt sorry for such plebian necessities.

"Damn." Disappointment stabbed swift and sharp.

"'Damn?'" Kate looked peeved. "What did you need? Maybe I can help."

"Nothing—a question about the hay bloke. I'll ask her this afternoon."

"You aren't really going to buy from a supplier three hundred miles away? That doesn't make sense."

"It does if it saves me several hundred dollars. Assuming the hay is decent."

"Big assumption."

"Perhaps." He purposefully switched subjects. "Are you two going out today?"

"No. We're painting the sewing room and doing up the curtains. We were just thinking we should get the far room done, as well. The one Rio is in. That way we'll have everything but the upstairs loo done."

He rolled his eyes. "Don't paint Rio's room without checking. She mentioned doing it herself once. Haven't a clue if she'd still like to."

"I should think *you'd* get to say," Kate replied.

"What would ever make you suggest that? I don't get a say about anything here."

He left, sorry for being so blunt, but not for finally speaking the truth. And Kate. He didn't want her sudden interest any more than he wanted his father back at Bridge Creek.

He pushed Kate out of his mind and focused his anger on his dear old da'. Colin Pitts-Matherson was half the dictator David had described and half Michael Caine dash and urbanity. He could charm or intimidate at will. During the three months he'd spent in Minnesota the past summer, he'd brought in much-needed business, but he'd overrun the place with his King Kong–sized ego. David had learned a lot—including that he'd made the right choice by not following in his father's footsteps.

He could and would never live up to the Colin P-M legend, and his mother had just driven another nail into that coffin. She'd made it excruciatingly simple. He'd suffer through trotting out one more failure in front of his father—and then it would be over. Until the next time.

"How ARE THEY doing?"

Rio's voice pulled him sweetly out of a reverie four hours later. He turned and leaned against the fence holding in his twelve new horses as she climbed onto the bottom rail and draped herself over the top one like a ginger sprite. His heart lifted in that way he still didn't understand.

"I think they're coming out of shell shock," he said. "I'm starting to see a little personality. The bay over there, he's the alpha. The two chestnut mares there are still vying for top girl. The little pinto holds his own, and your little palomino doesn't make any waves."

"She's so pretty."

They'd found the undersized three-year-old filly on their second trip. Rio had nearly cried at the wretched little thing huddled in a corner. There'd been no doubt she'd be one of their twelve.

"Look at them," she continued. "Like a microcosm of society. All colors, all vying for place and status, all just needing to be safe and have a good life. You're a good guy, you know."

"Good. Crazy. Is there a difference in this case?"

She smiled softly. "Do things feel any better in the light of a new week?"

"Well, I did contact your hay guy. He sounds legitimate so I guess that's a step toward better. I ordered three hundred and fifty bales. If I didn't thank you enough, then I say it again."

A flush blossomed beneath her dusting of freckles. "I'm glad. It's just a drop in the bucket, I know, but at this point, every little bit could help."

He fisted his hands on the fence rail and rested his chin on them. "My mother, of course, thinks if I can't solve all problems with one blow, it's a waste of time. They've called my father up from Florida."

"Kate actually told me, too. They were going to wait until he was about to arrive to tell you, but I said I'd tell you myself if they didn't do it right away. They weren't happy with me butting into your life."

"Why does that not surprise me? Well, I'm more grateful for your support than you know. All I can say is batten down your hatches. If you think my mother is a tigress, wait until you meet Colin."

"Mussolini, didn't you call him?"

"Dictator mixed with Hollywood. He could order Attila the Hun to retreat and charm him out of his woman at the same time."

"You got the charming DNA anyway."

"Oh, it's stand-up comedy time, is it?"

"Come on, you ooze charm, buster."

"Ooze, 'eh?"

"You're not terribly mean or forceful, though. More's the pity." A sudden, sultry little grin enflamed him.

"You don't know as much as you think you do."

With a growl that released all the pent-up frustrations from the weekend and the day, he encircled her waist with both arms and dragged her off the fence. She screeched and laughed uproariously as he spun her in his arms and pushed her backward. Her laughter stopped when he braced her against the side of the barn, bunched her shirt up with one impatient hand, and covered her mouth with his.

Her groans jolted his body into its hard response, and he pressed his pelvis into hers while his fingers pushed her bra up and over the round globe of her breast.

She dragged her mouth from his with a gasp when he grasped her nipple between his fingers. Her hips thrust forward and she dug into his glutes to yank him forward.

"Yessssss!"

The sibilance of her cry dove straight into his loins, and it was all he could do to stop himself searching out her zipper and his and taking her fully against the barn's cool, white metal siding.

"You're beautiful. Have I told you that?" he whispered.

"I want your shirt off."

"I want everything of yours off."

"I'm serious."

She wedged her hands between them and seconds later was working the buttons of his plaid shirt. Warmth hit his belly, cascaded down his legs, and threatened the strength of his knees when she parted the shirt and exposed his skin to her ravenous fingers. The thought they might get caught out here in the middle of the day should have been ice water on his crazed desire, but the danger only fanned the flames.

"Rio . . ." He swallowed as her lips found the sternum line between his pecs. "This is not safe."

"Too late. You started it." Her lips moved butterfly-like down his stomach. The shivers that followed hit hard and deep. "Have I ever told you *you're* beautiful?"

"You're a crazy woman."

She laughed, husky and vibrating, and continued her journey to the waistband of his breeches. His breath caught in his throat. His imagination took off to a dangerous place.

Her lips followed.

She kissed the swell of his erection, and he nearly choked. For a blissful second he allowed it, tempted to grasp her head and hold it there. Instead he groaned and dragged her up by the elbows.

"I *know* we can't get away with that here. Do you see what happens if I let my mean and forceful side have its way?"

"I love it." She pushed the shirt off his shoulders and pulled it from his arms. "Hel-lo, you magnificent man."

"Now, that's ridiculous." He grinned as she stroked his shoulders, ran her palms down his biceps and forearms, and circled his wrists.

"Your name is David, right? I believe you were friends with some guy named Michelangelo."

Their laughter bubbled joyfully, and he swapped their holds, grabbing her wrists and pinning her to the wall once more.

"You're completely mad. Where do you dredge up such nonsense?"

He released her wrists and pushed up her T-shirt with both hands this time. The breast he'd exposed earlier still awaited him, the deep bronze aureole pebbled, the nipple erect and inviting. Bending sideways he took it into his mouth, letting all the textures tease him, as if he wasn't already uncomfortable enough.

"David, David, David," she murmured, the sounds coming from deep in her throat. "I think you could make it happen just like this."

"That would make me happier than you can imagine."

With a swift, desperate motion he dropped one hand to the juncture of her thighs and pressed. Her buckled-knee reaction gratified him to his toes.

"No!" To his surprise she shoved his hand away, whimpering. "Same as you—we can't do this here."

"Let's find a place where we can."

"Tonight?"

"You really want to wait?"

"Of course not. But I'm going to. Somebody has to control your baser side."

"Rio." He pressed into her again, loving the slight abrasiveness of her shirt fabric against his skin. With both hands he cupped her cheeks and tilted her face to his. Red silk waves flowed over his fingers. Blue gemstones met his gaze. "I didn't expect this. I didn't plan any of this. Not today. Not the last three weeks. It started as pure attraction because you are beautiful. But you need to know, it's not just that anymore."

"It's not," she agreed. "Not that I know *what* it is."

"A connection."

"I want to connect tonight."

"I'll figure something out. Maybe—"

"Daaaavid!" The call from someone in the barn made them both jump guiltily.

"Crap!" Rio grabbed his shirt from the ground, shook it out, and handed it to him, then straightened her own clothing. "See. I had a sixth sense—"

He threw on the shirt and began buttoning from the bottom. She took it from the top.

"Tonight," she whispered, rose on her toes to kiss him, and disappeared around the end of the barn leaving him aching and wondrous.

Chapter Twenty-Five

ONE LOOK AT David's hard, fit body that afternoon had turned all thoughts of him as a safe, solid presence upside down. Suddenly he was sexy and dangerous, and Rio craved time with him like a suffocating woman would crave air. But if there was some cosmic plan, God, Providence, or the Universe, was being just plain cruel.

The doorbell rang at seven-fifteen that evening. When David answered it, his speechless stare and the man he let into the foyer sent her hopes for the night spiraling into disappointment. She recognized him immediately. Thick hair, the same sable brown as David's, waved across his forehead, and the same slender, muscular build filled out neat gray Dockers and a pale gray, V-neck sweater over a yellow polo with its collar preppily turned up. There was no doubt that, a full day early, Colin Pitts-Matherson had arrived.

"Da'." David finally held out his hand, which Colin

took without hesitation in an impersonal but cordial greeting.

"David."

His mother bustled to the door. "Colin? Good heavens. We were planning to fetch you tomorrow."

"Hello, Stella."

Colin embraced his ex-wife with a good deal more warmth than he'd offered his son.

"We were waitlisted for an upgrade on our scheduled flight. I got a call this morning saying some first class seats were available on today's but not ours. It seemed fortuitous to take them."

The man definitely had clout. Airlines didn't simply call the average person up and let him change his flights. And now that he was inside, he owned this room, too, with sheer presence.

"Well, come in then," Stella said. "See who else is here."

"You said you had a surprise. I, too, have brought someone along."

For the first time, Rio noticed the quiet figure behind Colin. Taller by three inches, wiry and greyhound sleek, with a broad forehead and prominent nose, he waited patiently.

"How do you do?" David shook the stranger's hand.

"Carter Maxwell," the man replied in a sonorous voice—American, not British.

"David," his father said. "Carter here might just be the answer to all your troubles."

"I have troubles?"

"Don't be obtuse. Pride and posturing have no place in a well-run business. Maxwell here has an interesting proposition for you. But we'll get to that in good time. You should know, this is very fortuitous timing."

"I see." David's face said he didn't see at all.

"Now. What's this lovely surprise I've been promised?" Colin strode into the living room, leaving his black, soft-sided suitcase next to the door.

David gestured for Carter Maxwell to follow. The man's strong, impassive face made him look butlerish—not American at all.

"I guess the surprise would be me." Kate stepped forward, her voice soft, the lift of her head self-assured, pleased.

Colin's eyes widened in unmistakable joy. "Katherine? Am I dreaming? My dear, this is the *most* marvelous surprise. I never hoped to see you as part of the family again."

"Oh Colin, I'm just a guest. I had the good fortune to run into Stella at the right time."

"Seems as if the fates are on your side all at once." Colin beamed at David. "Favoring you with perfect timing."

Rio nearly choked.

"Not interested in the fates, Da'. I have guests for you to meet, as well."

David's smile wrapped Rio in warmth. "This is Rio Montoya and her sister, Bonnie. Ladies, my father, Colin Pitts-Matherson."

Rio held out her hand. "I've heard so much about you."

"Hi." Bonnie smiled quickly.

His handshake was brief and self-assured. "Of course.

The young misfortunates. I was dreadfully sorry to hear about your home. Glad you were able to find refuge here for a time."

Rio rocked back in affronted surprise. *Misfortunates? Refuge?*

She took an unobtrusive corner seat with Bonnie while the formalities wound down in a whirl of hustle and chatter. Colin and Carter were ensconced in seats of honor, offered food and drinks, and peppered with "how are things in Florida?" questions. David was assimilated into the group like a captured human into the Star Trek Borg Collective.

Finally, Colin sat back with his coffee cup comfortably in hand, and addressed the mystery of the evening. "Why don't I have Carter explain why he's here?"

"Sure." Carter Maxwell's deep voice drew curious attention.

"I have been involved in the Eventing world for the past two decades. I competed through advanced level until I was injured two years ago. Since then, I've been sort of an itinerant teacher and clinician. Last year, I landed under the wing of your father." He looked directly at David. Rio saw only hard-edged patience on David's features.

"He's a brilliant instructor," Colin said.

Maxwell smiled his thanks. "I've learned a tremendous amount," he continued. "But my goal has always been to have a permanent facility of my own or one I could run with a partner. Your father told me about Bridge Creek and how it's the premiere stable in this area, and it sounded intriguing. When he explained about the financial issues you're having because of the economy here, I had a bold thought. I'd like to solve both our problems. I'd like to buy into your stable, David, and help you run it, as a co-owner."

In less than three seconds David's face drained of color, and Rio's breath caught in her lungs. Without warning David shot to his feet. As quickly as he'd paled, crimson flooded back into his cheeks.

"I'm sorry. Did someone give you the impression that any part of this facility is for sale? If so, he or she was quite mistaken."

"Nobody has any preconceived ideas here." Colin crossed his legs casually, as if the whole suggestion was no more than a flippant remark.

"If after you hear my offer, it isn't of interest to you, so be it. Your father is simply guiding me to potential opportunities."

"We're here to give you something to think about and, perhaps, find a way out of your current dilemma. No more than that," Colin added.

David sat cautiously back down.

"That's fine to say, Da', but you need to remember that I didn't call for your help. Your devious ex-wife did that. I don't need anything. I'm not looking for help. Or a partner."

"Very well." Colin exchanged a look with Carter that Rio couldn't decipher, almost as if something were going according to a plan. "Then we'll look forward to a relaxing few days and be on our way again."

David nodded. "I've got a new young horse I think you'll enjoy seeing. Take your time up with him."

And that was that.

An hour more passed before Rio's stubborn optimism accepted that there would be no illicit trysts that night. David, a captive to his overwhelming family's endless stories, wasn't getting away any time soon.

The conversation never waned thanks to Stella and Colin's rehash of every family moment Rio had missed in her whole life. When she saw her four-thirty alarm would go off in just under six hours if she fell asleep within ten minutes, she had to call it a night.

"I'm heading upstairs," she whispered to Bonnie.

"It's still early."

"Yeah, but I have to get up for work. You stay and eavesdrop; it's fine."

"I'm sorry, but it's kind of cool you're the new baker. Dawson says your pies are awesome. I already knew that, but . . ."

"Thanks, kid. I'll save you a piece every day for that."

She kissed the top of her sister's head and headed toward the stairs. When she passed David, the impersonality of his smile stung. That wasn't his fault—they'd made the agreement mutually. Still, when she waved her fingers and mouthed "good night," he only nodded, and she wished it didn't seem like he'd clicked back into passive mode so easily.

DAVID DESPAIRED OF ever breaking away from the troop of chattering monkeys his family and their two guests had become. It was as if they'd each arrived preprogrammed with every piece of news they'd gathered by phone, gossip, magazine, or carrier pigeon.

His heart sank further when Rio left. This was so far from what he'd promised her for tonight. He couldn't even make do with having her close as part of the family, although he was beginning to wonder why. So what if it had only been three and a half weeks? In that amount of time you could know you liked someone. A lot.

The trouble was this mess his parents had laid in his lap—described in four words:

Kate. And Carter Maxwell.

He'd stopped the latter in his tracks, but it didn't ease his mind. His father had capitulated far too quickly. Something was still up his suave and devious sleeve.

He managed to listen halfheartedly as long as Bonnie remained in her chair in the corner. Her presence reminded him Rio wasn't far away. But when Bonnie finally stood to leave half an hour behind Rio, David couldn't bear the pointless conversation without at least one of the Montoya sisters.

"Are you heading up?" he asked.

"Yeah." Bonnie smiled. "It's been nice meeting everyone, but since Rio has to get up so early, I said I'd help Andy in the barn in the morning, so it's bed for me, too."

"You two are such amazing little worker bees." Kate smiled, toothy and calm.

"It's fun. We always dreamed of having a ranch. We're enjoying it while we can."

"Good for you." Kate sat back, one leg crossed elegantly over the other. "Turn adversity into a vacation."

Even David thought that a callous comment.

"So, Bonnie," he said. "How about if I come up now and fix that window blind you had problems with?"

He countered her confused frown with an exaggerated, hopeful wink, and she caught it with an amused smile. Intelligent girl.

"Um, okay, sure. I hate to pull you away."

"It won't take long." He jumped up. "Carry on, you lot. I'll be right back."

Following Bonnie up the stairs felt like a release from prison.

"What's this about?" she asked when they neared the top.

"Shhh," he whispered. "Thank you so much, love. I was nearly ready to slit my throat."

"What? They're your parents and they're hilarious. I could listen to them all night."

"You're just hearing the funny words," he teased. "What they're actually saying is excruciating. Plus, I—" He looked at her, debating. "I wanted to come up and check on your sister."

A grin broke over her face. "I knew it. You liiiike her."

He rubbed the back of his neck. "What do you think? Is that all right? I mean, would it be all right with you if I liked her enough to, say, kiss her?"

"I don't believe for a second you haven't done that already."

"Not admitting anything until I know you approve."

"You are as weird as she is. I'm not her parent. You don't have to ask me."

"Of course not, but I know she doesn't want to upset you."

"Look, I dated a gang leader and I got into a car with a pimp. I'm not the innocent little girl she thinks I am. I know about life. Besides, you're so much better than anyone she ever hooked up with in Minneapolis."

"Thanks for that anyway."

"Come on." She took his arm firmly and dragged him toward Rio's room.

"Bonnie, I don't need—"

"Shhh." She tapped her lips firmly. He grinned while she rapped on the closed bedroom door. "Sis, are you still awake?"

"Hey, Bons. Yeah, come on in."

"Are you decent? I don't need to see you naked."

David glared at her as his pulse shot into hyper drive.

"What? What's wrong with you? Get in here before someone hears you."

"There's your invite. Go get her." Bonnie's eyes twinkled like a bloody Christmas elf while she turned the doorknob and shoved him through the doorway.

"You—"

The door closed on his reprimand, and Rio screeched. He stared at her sitting in her bed, a sheet pulled up to her chin.

"Hi," he said.

"David?"

"Believe it or not, this was entirely your sister's doing." He turned to the door. "Go to your room now, Bonnie."

"Going, going." Her muffled chortle faded down the hall.

"*Are* you decent?" he asked.

She lowered the sheet, and the surprise in her eyes warmed. She wore the same skimpy tank she'd worn on the deck the morning he'd . . . He slammed a lid on his thoughts.

"I'm not going to stay," he said unhappily. "They think I'm fixing a broken blind."

"Well, dang."

"You want me to stay?"

She patted the mattress. "You could . . . tuck me in." She blushed prettily and looked away. "Jeez, I don't say stuff like that."

"You keep saying you don't do and say all these cute little things, yet that's what I see and hear."

"You've messed up my brain. I can't think normally when you're around."

"Okay with me."

He sat. "It's still a proper fiasco down there, and I didn't know how to get away."

"I know. If you and I had simply walked out it would have been . . . awkward."

"I've spilled the beans to your sister. A little."

"Obviously. She knows you're here."

"I asked if I could kiss you."

"And?"

"She figured I already had."

He placed his palm boldly against her breast. The white feather beside it peeked out beneath his thumb. Softly he kneaded, and she sagged back onto her pillow. Her shiver passed through his hand into his chest, trapping his breath.

"Tomorrow night," he whispered. "I'll figure out how to get away."

"It's your home. Just walk."

"Okay."

He leaned forward and kissed her, loving the mint and heat of her mouth and the very faint leftover musk from the barn. She moved her tongue to his and kissed him back, languidly, as if savoring the sweetest dessert. Warning flutters deep within his belly made him stop. He couldn't afford to go further tonight.

"I'm serious," she said, catching the back of his head and pulling it back so their foreheads touched. "You stood up to your dad once tonight. You know you can do it."

"I'm tougher and meaner when I'm with you, remember?"

"Swell."

He stood up. "I'm sorry to go."

"If you knew how I felt right now, you'd be even sorrier."

"Now that was just cruel." He kissed her again and slipped away with only a promise in his eyes.

Chapter Twenty-Six

—————

"WHAT IF WE did an Irish Christmas stew?" Rio asked absently, resting on a stool beside the bakery counter, chin in palm, looking at the row of cookies, cinnamon rolls, and pies freshly displayed in the case.

Apple, blueberry, and chocolate cream. A sense of warm accomplishment filled her. Bud hadn't cared what besides apple pies she'd made, so she'd chosen what *she* wanted. And gotten praised! Now Bud was actually brain-storming menu ideas with her—new ideas for winter. He already liked the idea of a squash soup and a traditional Minnesota, meat-rich hot dish like she'd made for David her first night in his house. They'd been throwing ideas back and forth for half an hour.

"Or Swedish meatballs," she said. "A hot dish with meatballs in it."

"You ever made something like that?"

"No. But I have an idea. What if I try it out a few times

the next couple of nights and see what happens? I'll try the stew, too. We could have an employee tasting party next week after school starts."

Bud laughed. "I'm sure up for that, and I'm sure Effie will love the ideas, too. She leaves the nursing home next week and can come down for an hour or so a day. I've been telling her about you, Rio. I don't think she'll want to lose you even when she does come back to work."

His words both warmed and distressed her. Agreeing to stay on meant making decisions she'd put off since the fire. She'd assumed once Paul and Hector were found and the threat was gone, she'd be going back to Minneapolis. And after that . . .

She hadn't let herself dwell on the death of her Wyoming dream. It hurt. The Dream had been her future. She'd be lucky to afford the present once she left David's.

Maybe she didn't want to leave David's.

Not that she could stay forever. She and Bonnie were no small burden on his finances. Besides, she really did want her own place. Her own horses, her own garden, her own peace and quiet. It was all she'd ever wanted. If only her attraction to him wasn't complicating everything.

"Rio?"

"Huh? Oh Bud, I'm sorry. I went daydreaming about ingredients."

"It's nearly quittin' time for you. Have I ever thanked you for being an amazing jack-of-all-trades?" He smiled and headed back for the kitchen without waiting for her reply.

By the time she left The Loon Feather half an hour

later, her bout of depression had passed, and she fairly buzzed with excitement. Her first payday was only three days away, and she still had enough left in her meager bank account to pick up what she needed for one of her recipe ideas. She pulled out her cell phone to see if David could reserve the kitchen for her tonight, only to find she'd missed a call from him. She dialed quickly.

"Rio!" He answered within seconds, breathless.

"Hi. You okay?"

"Where are you, love?"

"Walking to my car. Heading for the grocery store." She frowned at the urgency underlying his normally calm, soothing accent.

"Could you come home instead?"

"Of course. What's wrong?"

"Bonnie's had a fright. She got some messages from Mr. Black."

Her stomach lurched. "I'll be there in fifteen minutes."

"She's all right, Rio. We're here for her, but she'd like to talk to you."

"I'm on my way."

All the way back she fretted. She should have told Chief Hewett about the call from Paul, but she hadn't. She hadn't even told Bonnie. Part of her had wanted to protect her brother until he called back. Part of her wanted to keep Bonnie from worrying. But now, with dread in her heart, she knew she'd made the wrong decision.

When she arrived home, David, Jill, Kim, Kate, Stella, and David sat gathered around Bonnie like a wagon train in defense formation, but if she'd expected to find her sister sobbing, she'd been wrong. Bonnie chatted with Stella, who held her hand nodding and smiling. Jealousy flared and Rio knelt in front of them.

"What happened, Bons?"

"More stupid texts."

"How many?"

"Three right in a row. That's what got to me. But I'm fine. He still doesn't know where we are."

Bonnie held out her phone. Rio turned it on and scrolled to the top of the list on the screen. All three messages were from Paul's number. Jealousy disintegrated in the wake of fury. How dare Paul ask her to trust him when he wouldn't do as she'd asked? She read the first text.

So you've heard from your brother. I'm disappointed Rio didn't have sense to do as he asked. You have something that doesn't belong to you, Bonnie. Text us.

"Text *us*?" Rio pressed her lips together to keep from swearing and scrolled to the next message.

I haven't heard from you yet. This is dead serious now.

She pursed her lips even more tightly.

If you don't stop listening to your sister, your brother will pay the price. And then so will you and Rio.

"That's it!" Rio stood and furiously hit the reply button. She hadn't made the wrong decision, Paul had. "I'm done screwing around with these two. I'll tell him whose dead serious now, the bast—"

"Rio. Stop."

David took the phone from her and turned it off. Rio seethed at the interruption. "I'm done waiting."

"Calm down and let's finish this without playing into

their hands. Just talk it out for a sec. What did he mean, you've heard from your brother? Bonnie didn't know either."

She pressed her thumb and forefinger into the corners of her eyes and forced a deep breath. "Two mornings ago Paul called. He claimed Hector is forcing him to cooperate. It turns out Bonnie has something Hector wants, but there's no way she could have known it. I'm sorry I didn't say anything, but Paul promised to call back. I gave him a chance to make this right."

"What do I have? He can have it whatever it is!"

"That money clip."

A gasp escaped Bonnie's open mouth. "It's Heco's?"

"No. It's Boyfriend's."

She paled.

"I'm completely lost," said Kate.

David peered into her eyes and put a hand on each shoulder. Comfort flowed from his fingertips. Briefly, Rio told the story she'd gotten from Paul.

"I warned Paul he was on his own if either Bonnie or I got another threatening text. Well, I was wrong. He's worn me down. Give me the phone and let me get the stupid money clip back so Hector will lay off."

"Just wait," David said. "I've called the police. Chief Hewett will be out here within the hour."

"You what!" Rio glared at him. "You had no right to call on my behalf."

"I made them call," Bonnie said. "But why didn't you tell me about this? If I'd known I wouldn't have been so scared at first."

"I didn't want you to deal with it yet. And I didn't

want you to think it was okay to call Paul yourself. I forget you're not a child in all this. I really am sorry. I made the wrong choice. Again."

Bonnie slipped her arms around her and hugged her. "No, you didn't."

Rio's tears slipped free for the first time.

Chief Hewett arrived half an hour later. A dark blue Ford pulled in behind his cruiser, normal-looking outside but with a barrier behind the front seat and a light mounted on the dash inside the driver's door. The driver emerged, wearing a plain suit. A uniformed officer exited the passenger side.

"Good afternoon." Chief Hewett nodded his hatless head as he approached the deck. "Everybody okay here?"

"We are," Rio said.

"I have reinforcements today," he continued. The other two men joined him. "Detective James Peterson and Officer Dan Crowley from the Minneapolis Police Department."

They shook hands all around.

"We understand you have some information about a man known on the streets as Boyfriend," the detective said. "We're very interested in anything you can tell us."

"We don't know much about him," Rio said. "My brother has claimed Boyfriend wants something he lost and my sister found."

"Your brother is Paul Montoya?"

"Yes."

"Tell me more."

She recounted the story again, answering questions

as best she could. Bonnie produced the offending money clip, and Detective Peterson examined it almost gleefully.

"Could you identify this Boyfriend if you ever saw him again?"

"Sure," said Bonnie. "I sat right next to him."

"Can you describe him?"

"He's older, maybe in his early forties. A white guy, kind of distinguished looking."

"Tall? Short?"

She bit her lip. "I don't know for sure, I never saw him standing. He didn't seem all that big. Just a normal size. He wasn't, like, super-scary or anything, but I got nervous when I saw how old he was. I'd thought he was a friend of Hector's."

Detective Peterson reached into a breast pocket and took out a photo. He handed it to Bonnie and Rio looked over her shoulder. The man in the picture wore a blue-striped dress shirt with an open collar. Sandy-gray hair waved around his ears. It looked like an official portrait of some kind.

"That's him," Bonnie said without hesitation.

The three police officers looked about as unprofessionally happy as cops could get.

Peterson smiled at Bonnie. "Miss Montoya, do you know you're the first young woman to escape this man before he actually took her away to work for him? You're very, very lucky. And we're grateful for your help. Would you be willing to testify against this man in court?"

"Wait a second." Rio leaped in. "She doesn't know anything about his operation or whatever it is he does."

"I understand. All we'd need is an ID under oath."

"I could do that." Bonnie lifted her eyes defiantly. "I'm really the only one who got away?"

"We have two witnesses who've worked for him, but they're too fearful to help. Boyfriend is threatening and usually careful to the point of invisibility. He has a network of small-time gang leaders, like Hector Black, who take most of the heat for him. We're reasonably certain that if Mr. Black started the fire at your home, it was under duress from Boyfriend."

"So you know who he is?"

"We have a very good idea now, thanks to you. This is our first positive ID. His cover is that he's an upstanding member of the community, and he's desperate to keep his Boyfriend identity a secret."

"So we can leave the money clip with you and be done with it. Except for her testifying?" Rio indicated the clip in Peterson's hands.

"I'm hoping we can get you to help with one other thing, and that's finding Hector Black. I'd like you to arrange a meeting with him so we can follow you and grab him, as well."

Oh no. No way.

"This sounds too much like TV. I'm not into wires and stakeouts. And Bonnie sure isn't doing any such thing."

Officer Crowley, a young, beak-nosed man with a friendly demeanor, laughed. "No wires, no drama. We'll be right there with you, nab him, and if he confirms the clip belongs to Boyfriend, we've got them both."

"When would I do it?"

"Now that we have this information, we don't want to lose the opportunity," Peterson said. "I'd say let's get this done, but you need to tell us when you're ready."

Rio glanced around the small crowd. Everyone, even Kate, who looked wilted and terrified for the first time in Rio's memory, stood ready to support them. Enough was enough.

"All right. Tell me what I should do."

Chapter Twenty-Seven

"You ready to try it?" David waggled his brows at her from his saddle, and Rio gave Tully's neck a pat for courage.

"What's the worst that can happen?" she replied. "I'll break an arm and Hector can sign my cast tomorrow."

It was the first she'd mentioned the meeting they'd set up earlier that afternoon. Since then, Bonnie had skipped off to Dawson's, and David had kept Rio occupied by giving her an official cantering lesson on Tully. He'd helped make Irish Stew for dinner, then sent his mother and the others to town for a last party shopping trip. And now, Rio was about to test her newly learned riding skills.

They reached the start point of a long, straight galloping lane through some trees. When in her life had a day ever been so full of disjointed adventures? From baking pies and planning a police sting, to riding off across the hills on a dream horse.

"Ride the same way you did in the arena. If he picks up more speed than you want, straighten up, gather the reins, and squeeze your legs to slow him."

Squeeze to stop. Riding was completely counterintuitive.

"Okay."

"And no racing." He laughed.

"Really? You think?"

"I'll stay beside you. You'll be fine."

Her transition into the trot wasn't beautiful, and her cues for cantering were so floppy she felt sorry for poor Tully, but the big gelding read her mind anyway and launched into the three-beat canter gait. For a moment she floundered, but after five or six strides she caught the rhythm, and she understood why people wrote that riding felt like flying.

David cantered Gomer along beside them and shot her a wide smile. "You look great!"

She fixed her eyes straight ahead but grinned. "It's fun!"

"Best fun in the world."

He rode in a Western saddle like hers this time, wearing jeans rather than breeches, cowboy boots rather than his tall boots, and a bonus—a pair of full-leg, suede chaps. No fringes, no fancy stitching, just utilitarian, form-fitting sexy chaps. Not even helmets could spoil the picture of her cowboy come to life.

They halted at the far end of the pasture just as they had the last time, and Rio let out a whoop. "Amazing!"

"Anybody ever tell you how sexy you look on a horse?"

"All the time."

"It's nice to see you having that much fun."

They walked the horses along the fence line until they reached the familiar gate at the back of the property.

"You do know this is what I had in mind all along, right?" he asked.

Little sizzles ignited at the memory of the shack on the other side of the fence.

They untacked the horses, threw the saddles and blankets over the top board of the fence, and hung the bridles over the saddle horns. David grabbed a set of saddlebags from behind his cantle.

"Whatcha got?" Rio asked.

"A loaf of bread, a jug of wine. And chocolate, because I've heard it will release a woman's inhibitions."

"I have no inhibitions."

"That bodes very well." He kissed her but pulled away before she could deepen it.

The little cabin hadn't changed. Rio fluffed her hair to get rid of the helmet flatness and walked the perimeter of the room, taking more time this visit to check out the shelves, the dusty window, the table, and the old stove. When she turned back, David stood with his back against the door, watching, smiling.

"Man, you're pretty."

Her stomach fluttered. "You aren't too bad either. With your hair a little mussed like it is, that saddlebag over your shoulder . . . those chaps. If you took off your shirt you'd look just like the cowboy I used to have on my wall."

Obvious pleasure pulled the corners of his lips upward. "We have the compliments well in hand. Excellent."

"I know what you're trying to do—keep me from being nervous about tomorrow. But I'm fine."

"Not frightened?"

"Apprehensive, but not scared. We're meeting in a safe place that Paul chose. He won't do anything."

"I think you're amazingly brave. I'm quite proud of you."

She didn't know how to respond. She wasn't brave; she was desperate to be done with this and . . . and what? Go back home? Where was home?

"I've had a lot of help . . ."

She stopped midsentence and stared. David hadn't moved, but he grasped the hem of his gray T-shirt with both hands and drew it up and over his head. It landed on the floor in a heap.

"Best I can do," he said.

His best beat the lost cowboy from her old wall by miles. She didn't speak. She barely kept drool off her chin.

"Not good enough, 'eh?" His teasing grin turned the flutters in her stomach into full-fledged trembles of excitement.

His hands dropped to the small buckle at the front of the chaps. Wordlessly he pulled the leather strap free of the buckle prong, then he bent forward and slid a zipper down the outside of the left leg. He did the same to the right. He pulled the chaps off with the slow flair of a Chippendale dancer.

"You've got to be kidding me," Rio whispered, her throat dry. "Are you *trying* to turn me on?"

His brows arched. "Is it working?"

"It's been working for the past three days."

He strode to her in three steps as if his patience had evaporated, hauled her against his bare chest, and sent his fingers diving into her hair. The heat of his kiss flowed over her, melting her will, her knees, and their kiss into delectable sweetness. She explored his back, kneading and stroking the broad muscles, then she smoothed down his tapered waist and gripped the seat of his jeans.

"Now who's trying to turn whom on?"

"I do love your proper grammar."

"Dukes must have it."

"There's no duke here. Just some hot American cowboy."

He released her, stepped back slightly for balance, and lifted her into his arms. "We're going to build a fire and then pretend it's a campfire. If you want cowboy . . ."

"I don't see anything to build a fire with."

"Leave it to me."

He did seem able to build a fire out of nothing. With one match, a piece of paper towel, and a pile of dry bark stashed behind the stove, he set the fire blazing in minutes.

"How *did* you learn all this? Really, I mean."

"Mum started it. She was a fanatic outdoorswoman in her youth. And when we lived in Yorkshire when I was a boy, Mum took me into the woods and out onto the moors to hunt partridge and grouse and to hike. I was good at it, and I enjoyed pitting myself against the elements. I read everything I could get my hands on about survival. She put me in Scouts and I got chances to practice skills there.

"Then Da' moved us to Kent, where he started his barn, and I met an old army man turned gamekeeper for our neighbors. Taft, we called him. Before he passed on he taught me more about navigation, tracking, and scouting than anyone else wanted to learn. I think he's, perhaps, the smartest bloke I've ever met."

"Did you ever consider making this your career somehow?"

"No. I had enough of survival living in Iraq."

"Something happened there, didn't it?"

"Lots of things happened."

"But something that wounded you. As badly in your own way as Andy is wounded."

"Hardly."

"You can tell me anything, you know."

"It's not worth talking about so I don't often. My commander in Basra learned pretty quickly I could find my way around almost anywhere a little easier than the average soldier. I became a night scout and a guide on the rare occasions we traveled from the main camp. It was no glory job. I wasn't after glory. I just wanted to get out of there alive."

"What's wrong with that?"

"One night, my lieutenant got us assigned to an important scouting mission into the desert fifty miles out of the city. He took eight men with him, me included.

We'd got decent intelligence about an insurgent cell that had been terrorizing the city for six months. Once underway, I got a very strong sense of where the terrorist group would *not* stay overnight, because I'd studied the area as thoroughly as I could. But my gut feeling didn't match the intel. When it came time to choose a bivouac, I completely disagreed with my CO."

"What did you do?"

"Stuck stubbornly to my guts. Along with half the group I refused to follow the lieutenant. Rather a Fletcher Christian moment, or so the army decided. Dishonorable discharges for the lot of us. So you see, all my expertise did was get us into trouble. Now I stay out of trouble."

There had to be more. The story ending had too much glibness, too much gloss from practiced telling.

"That's not all there is, though."

"Oh, that's pretty much the story. C'mon, forget Iraq. Check out the saddlebags."

He handed her the pouches, and she reluctantly let the discussion go, digging into the bags, producing a bottle of the Minnesota white wine they'd shared on the first trail ride weeks ago, two gourmet chocolate bars, and four scones from breakfast that morning.

"A feast," she said.

"Yes. And as soon as I open this bottle, a toast to having it without benefit of my meddling family that means well but oftentimes have to be endured."

"Why?" she asked, unwrapping a scone and stealing a corner with a lick of her lips. "I mean, why do you have to endure them? This is your place. They should abide by *your* rules."

"You've asked that before, but it's complicated. I've fought many a battle with my parents over the years, and I always lose. In truth I could have a stubborn temper when I was young. Cheeky was too mild a word for me. And it got me in nothing but trouble."

"Carried over into Iraq?" she teased.

The teasing went over like a curse in church. "I do suppose," he replied a little curtly and set to opening the wine.

She touched his arm. "David, I'm sorry. I was joking."

The smile he offered lacked a few degrees of warmth. "I know. And it's hard to understand, I'm sure. It's just that, long ago I learned the best way to get 'round my parents was to appear I was doing what they wished. So, a few weeks a year I let them boss me around until they go home and then I do things my way."

"But bringing in someone who offers to buy half your property? That's not just a little meddling."

"No. You are right."

"But your dad backed off, right?"

"He did. You know, I had a long chat with him and that Maxwell chap today. He's actually a pretty astute guy, old Carter. Had some good ideas. Some of his clientele would follow him back and forth to and from Florida, and turns out he could fill the barn without trouble."

"Wait. You aren't considering this?"

"No, not seriously. This place is my life. I don't want to share it. It was merely interesting to listen to him. A couple of his ideas would certainly solve some issues around here."

He popped the cork out of the bottle and pulled two hard plastic juice glasses from the bags.

"Ooh, elegant." She held them while he poured. "You are a true romantic."

He grunted. "Would you believe I heard those exact words from my father today? 'You're too much of a romantic,' he said. 'Nothing ever runs in a vacuum. We all need help.'"

"He's right. But you have lots of help. People revere you, in case you don't know. You're a good guy. Sometimes too good." She raised her glass. "I say, let's drink to being a little not-so-nice. Like Fletcher Christian."

He knocked his glass to hers with a bright, plastic click, but his eyes seemed focused. Far away.

"Are you okay?" she asked.

He set his glass down and pulled her onto his lap as he sank onto a wooden chair. It creaked with the weight. "I'm always okay when you're around."

She feathered his hair through her hands. "Except, you're suddenly somewhere else."

"No. No. There's just so much going on. Guess it's hitting me."

She snuggled her hips against him but massaged his bare shoulders, hard and slowly. "You're truly worried. Things are even worse than you told me."

"Needing eight thousand dollars to fix the barn doesn't help. I already have a fifteen-thousand-dollar loan because of the arena."

"It's a gorgeous arena," she offered.

It was. Wood interior, full wall mirrors, permanent bleachers—a premiere indoor arena.

"State of the art. Made to Da's specifications."

"Why?"

He didn't answer. Instead his brow furrowed and he pulled away. He looked slightly miffed. "The loan was dirt cheap with the disaster relief rates. I had minimal debt at the time, and it definitely enhances the value of the property. But I didn't come here to justify my actions or my relationship with my father."

Chastised, she tried to halt his deteriorating mood. It needed boosting fast or the reason they'd raced to this cabin would no longer exist. "I'm sorry. I'm not trying to pick on you."

"There's just a lot of second-guessing of my decisions where my family is concerned."

"You don't have to let me bully you either, you know. You don't have to be so nice to everyone. Ignore me." She smoothed at his hair.

He caught her hand. "You really seem to have something against nice guys. You know that?"

"What are you talking about?"

"Kate has the same problem. All those years ago she thought I'd lost my edge. Now *you* think I'm too nice."

The last thing she wanted was to be compared to Kate.

"You're wrong. I think your niceness makes you pretty close to perfect. I'd never known men like you existed. But I've just heard stories about what an amazing survivalist you are, and I don't think I've ever seen you apply it to your own life. You tell me to stand up for myself. You tell Bonnie to be strong. You say you even told your lieutenant in Basra to take a hike. But all I've ever seen you do is dance when your mother or father says dance. I was cheering inside when you told Carter no last night. Now you're even waffling about that."

He dropped her hand and stood, causing her to slide off his lap.

"First of all, I asked you to leave Iraq alone. Second, what would it matter to you if I did waffle? What if my decision changed and I thought it was a *good* idea to let Carter Maxwell buy into Bridge Creek?"

"Practically? I'd understand why you'd want to get out of debt. Honestly? I'd think you were selling out a dream. I'd like to have a fairy godfather around when it comes time to pay the property taxes on a house that doesn't exist for land I can't imagine anyone will want to buy. I'll be eating Ramen noodles and working any hours I can find, scrabbling like the rest of the great unwashed until I can even pretend to go after my dream."

She hadn't realized how tight her voice had grown until she finished and David stood staring. "So I'm not struggling enough for you, is that it?"

"You're not struggling at all."

The man was clueless. Gorgeous, talented, pulse-poundingly hot, but clueless.

"Well, that's lovely, that is. Here I thought you were the only one who supported me."

"This is a ridiculous conversation, David. You've run Bridge Creek perfectly well without ever having asked my opinion, so don't. As for my support—you have it. I love this place. I'll call hay guys from here to Mexico if you want me to. But ask me if you've struggled? Hell, no. You've got the luxury of giving up."

"Where did this side of you come from?" His eyes flashed with wounded pride.

Nobody in her old neighborhood would wonder about this brutally honest Rio. She supposed she'd never shown it to him.

"I've been on good behavior," she said, all too truthfully. "But from where I stand, I think I'm a better survival expert than you are."

Wounded pride turned to bright anger, but nothing about it caused fear of him, nor did it curb her annoyance. Even so, desire flew hot and hard through her veins. He grasped her by the upper arms and hauled her to him. With crushing decisiveness he covered her mouth with his and plundered until his kiss forced her head back and drew the strength from her legs.

For a moment she believed they'd have their tryst after all, and then he pulled his lips from hers and released her, swaying in the aftermath.

"You meet with Paul tomorrow. Get through that, and we'll talk."

THE NEXT MORNING, although Rio tried to talk him out of it, David refused to let her go meet with Paul without him. He accompanied her and Chief Hewett, whose presence was a surprise in and of itself, to Minneapolis and the rendezvous with Detective Peterson even though Rio said little, didn't touch him, or look for reassurance, the entire seventy-five-minute drive into the city. The tension between them had only grown, and it didn't help that the whole situation felt like an episode of *Law & Order* that had been written for Inspector Clouseau.

Two blocks from the restaurant where Paul had agreed to show up with Hector, Peterson, dressed as Hewett was in nondescript plainclothes, met them with overblown enthusiasm. "I can't thank you enough for helping with this, Miss Montoya. We could be putting an end to something that can legitimately be called a reign of terror. Even Hector Black doesn't know who he's dealing with in the case of Boyfriend."

"You do what you have to do," Rio said.

"This shouldn't take more than ten minutes." The inspector touched her on the shoulder. "Just talk like you normally would. All Hector has to do is admit the money clip is the one they want."

"Shouldn't there be some sort of signal if she gets in trouble?" David asked, immediately feeling three pairs of incredulous eyes on him, as if he'd asked whether she should tap dance naked if she needed help.

Unexpectedly Rio grinned, returning for one moment to her normal, confident self. She rose on tiptoe and kissed him softly beside the mouth.

"You know exactly what to do with mistreated horses, right? I promise I know what to do with angry boys."

"You'll be careful?"

"I'll be fine. So will Hector if I don't kill him when I see him."

He grinned back. "All right. Have at them, my menacing little ginger bird. I'll be here."

A feeling of dread he didn't show engulfed him. It unnerved him to worry this much about someone else— normally such protective apprehension was reserved for his animals. He followed Peterson and Hewett to the opposite side of the street, where their view was unobstructed. Rio checked her watch and leaned against the storefront's plate-glass window. After only five excruciating minutes, David had no idea how real stakeouts ever got conducted.

Suddenly, finally, Rio was not alone. Paul Montoya arrived, his tight black T-shirt and black jeans standouts in the sea of normal, colorful, late summer colors. To David's surprise, Rio threw her arms around him, and Paul buried his face in her shoulder.

When they finally parted, an earnest conversation began. Many head shakes on her part and much gesticulating on his seemed to get them nowhere, until Rio dug into her pocket and pulled out what had to be the clip.

"Good, good," Peterson murmured.

Rio held it out of Paul's reach. At last Paul turned, made a "come" motion, and a gaunt, leather-jacketed figure slunk into view, hands thrust into his pockets, prominent cheeks sallow.

Rio's mouth began moving before Hector got close enough to interact. From their vantage point half a block and a street width away, David and the policemen could hear raised voices, but no words. Without warning, Rio and Hector sprang at each other, and Paul jumped between them, splaying a hand on their chests to push them apart. David's heart leaped into his throat, and he lunged as well. Hewett caught his arm.

"Easy, man," he said. "She's fine. She's the aggressor."

"Daft little idiot," David said.

"She's tough. And it looks like her brother can handle it."

"I thought you mistrusted her." David turned in amazement.

"She's proven herself more than trustworthy," he said quietly. "I care a lot that she and her sister don't get hurt, and I just want to get her home safely."

Home.

David wondered if that slip of Hewett's tongue could ever be true, or if Rio would always be a child of the city. Or if it was her Wild West dream that would come true.

More raised voices floated across the street. Hector grabbed for Rio's hand, but she yanked it violently away and stepped back. The first clear words traveled from the scene.

"Fuck you, bitch."

David shot forward again, his blood boiling. Again Hewett grabbed him.

"David . . ." he warned.

"If he touches her . . ."

"Leave it to us," Peterson said.

Once more, Rio's mouth moved in mile-a-second lecture mode. Finally Hector seemed to calm and, to

David's surprise, Rio pointed across the street directly toward their position. Both police officers looked at each other in confusion. This was not in any plan. All she was supposed to do was glance their way when Hector had given the word. Instead she waved them over.

"I'm going alone," Peterson said. "Hewett, back me up. Matherson, stay out of the way."

David had no reason to argue with the detective's directive, but he didn't like it. He hadn't analyzed the incident in Basra for years, but he'd pulled it out of hiding last night and the memory sat in the forefront, fresh and painful. He had supposedly learned from it—learned not to blow, not to rage. He knew he should sit on his figurative ass and wait. But his senses tingled with apprehension— the knowledge something was wrong—the same feeling he'd had that desert night so long ago.

Peterson headed across the street at a leisurely stroll. Hewett circled to the left, and David peered at the threesome across the road. Rio had her hand protectively over the clasp of her purse where she'd stuffed the clip. Paul stared at Peterson, and as the officer neared them seemed to grow taller in suspicion. Suddenly David knew exactly what was going to happen. Rio had told them she had friends with her. Peterson was a good actor, but the wrong age to be a friend of Rio's. Hector was going to figure out the entire ruse, and Rio was going to get hurt.

David moved in the opposite direction from Hewett and trotted through the crowd until he could cross the street without Hector seeing him. Peterson had nearly made it to Rio's side when Hector bellowed "Stop!"

"You bee-atch, you brought the cops."

"This is just a friend of mine," Rio replied angrily. "Don't be an idiot."

In one swift move Hector grabbed her wrist, twisted it, and trapped her against his chest. Like Wolverine unsheathing his blades, he flashed a knife at Peterson. "You stay away from me or I'll cut her, I swear. I'm not going anywhere with you."

"Heco, give it up," Paul said.

"Shut the piehole, Inigo. You set this up."

"He had nothing to do with it," Rio said, struggling. "And the police want Boyfriend, not you."

"That's right," Peterson soothed. "Just put the knife away, Hector. Hurting someone won't help your case."

David crept closer, hugging the building. Hector cranked a little harder on his hold, and Rio squeaked in discomfort. Red flared behind David's eyes, but he held his breath.

"Just stay away," Hector said.

"You're a complete, brainless jerk," Rio hissed at him.

"Shut up." He tightened his grip again.

This time Rio growled at him like Thirty-one did when she was pissed. She lifted a foot, cocked it, and landed a heel kick directly below Hector's knee.

He yowled and loosened his hold enough for her to sink to the sidewalk. Hector made a grab, caught a fistful of her fiery hair, and David launched himself at Hector's legs. As they both hit the pavement, David caught a glimpse of Peterson swooping in to envelope Rio, Paul chopping at Hector's wrist, and the knife flying free.

Then he concentrated on the struggling body beneath him.

The boy fought like a caged coyote, rangy, tough, and agile. David couldn't keep the grip on Hector's legs, so he crawled over him and lay flat, holding him down with body weight. The next thing he knew, Hewett was pulling him off the boy, and Peterson had a knee in Hector's kidney.

"Asshole, get off of me!"

"Close your mouth, Mr. Black." Peterson sounded like he was ordering coffee, but he ground his knee in harder.

When Hector quit struggling and groaned, Peterson let up the pressure, stood, and hauled Hector to his feet. Like a lightning bolt, Hector wrenched, swung, and connected with Peterson's jaw.

"Fuck!" the detective yelled. He retained his hold for another second, until Hector chopped at his wrist.

The instant he was free, Hector dashed past David like a greyhound and disappeared between two buildings. Hewett charged after him.

"You won't find him," Paul said. "He knows every hole in every back alley on Lake Street. I know where he'll go. I'll talk some sense into him."

Rio grabbed her brother by the T-shirt front. "Just tell us now where he is."

"I can't," he said. "I wouldn't live a day if I ratted him out now."

"Damn it all to hell," Peterson spat, rubbing his jaw. "We had the little bastard." He glared at David. "Didn't I tell you to stay across the street?"

"You did. And you missed all the signs that everything was headed sixes and sevens. He'd have run long before he did and taken Rio with him."

"We're trained for this. We'd have had him."

David looked at Rio, but she had her eyes glued on Paul. Since he'd been promised immunity, she released his shirt. "If you don't call me tonight, it'll be years before you talk to Bonnie again. I mean it." She cuffed him on the arm.

Without a word he sprinted in the opposite direction from Hector.

"Are you all right?" David put one hand on Rio's shoulder.

She nodded but didn't look fine. "Thank you," she all but whispered, and her eyes lowered uncharacteristically.

She barely looked at him after that. He couldn't tell if she was angry or distracted or actually hurt, but her lack of connection added ten pounds to the weight in his heart. He couldn't win. Not in Basra. Not in Minneapolis. Both times he'd averted disaster, but only by disobeying orders because the commanders and the detectives were so bloody vain they couldn't see beyond their own embarrassment.

"The big question is whether you got Hector to identify the clip," Peterson said, wagging his injured jaw slowly back and forth.

Rio pulled the phone from her pocket. "I think he did. He saw the money clip and said Boyfriend would quit bugging us if he got it back. He also told me Boyfriend ordered the fire but it wasn't meant to get so big, it was simply supposed to distract us so Paul could go in and look for the clip without Bonnie knowing."

Peterson took her phone and swiped the screen. With one touch a muffled voice came through the voice recorder. He listened and smiled with grim relief. "Bingo."

"Sorry. I lost him." Tanner Hewett returned, breathing hard. "Little devil slipped into some black hole somewhere." He looked David in the eye. "I wish you'd left him to me, though. I could have tackled and cuffed him."

That did it. Rio still refused to look at him, and even though her physical status now bordered on the shaky, David turned his back to her and glared at the officers. "You know what? Bugger the whole bloody lot of you."

Chapter Twenty-Eight

DAVID STALKED INTO the barn at 11:00 a.m. the next day and strode to where Rio stood watch over the little palomino rescue filly that had been quarantined earlier that morning. The rest of the horses had been cleared as healthy. This one, Rio's favorite, had contracted a severe rhinovirus that, in her weakened state, had become life-threatening.

She expected David to ignore her as he'd done for the past eighteen hours, and the truth was, she wouldn't blame him. He'd come along to the meeting with Paul just to keep an eye on her—and thank God he had. But he'd been chastised by the police, and she'd followed it up with . . . nothing. Barely a thank-you. The truth was she honestly didn't know how to face him. She'd nearly gotten him hurt, and that scared her to death. She'd clearly made him angry at the little cabin the night before. He confused her and annoyed her and turned her on and stripped her of all her natural defenses and bravado.

Until she figured out where and if he fit into her life, she was a wicked wimp.

"There's nothing we can do but give the drugs a chance to work," he said, stopping beside her. "I'd like you to go get a jacket and saddle up Tully."

She peered in surprise at the small, unreadable spark of warmth in his eyes. Amusement? Forgiveness? A peace offering?

"It's not cold. I don't need a jacket."

"You will. It's my concession."

"To what?"

"To surviving on less than a fortune."

"You don't need to prove anything—"

"On the contrary. You've made it pretty clear, as have the police, that I need to stick to what I know. Time to prove that I can."

She scrambled for excuses, not at all certain what his motives were.

"We can't leave the filly."

"We can. Andy is every bit as competent as I would be."

"But Bonnie . . ."

"Bonnie and Dawson are going to a movie, and then Kim is having some sort of before-school-starts sleepover."

"Oh, that's right."

"My parents, Carter, and Kate are going into Minneapolis to eat and to pick up some last-minute things for Mum's bash tomorrow night. I declined to go along. I have a different menu in mind."

"I don't know about this."

"You don't need to be nervous, but you will have to dredge up a little trust." She studied him, but his eyes and voice never wavered.

"Fine. What else should I pack?"

"Oh no, there's no packing. As I said, you can bring a jacket. Or a sweatshirt."

She didn't know how to react, but in a way it was a relief not to know. Maybe a few hours "lost" in the woods would get whatever was bugging them out of their systems.

Forty minutes later they rode from Bridge Creek in a direction she'd never gone. Aimed somewhere between town, the state park, and the little hunter's cabin, they passed through grassland void of trees. She'd tied a sweatshirt to the saddle. Tully felt familiar and solid beneath her. The warm August air smelling of grass, clover, and sunshine enveloped her, and the swish of the horses' legs and occasional snort that jingled their bridles filled her with a sense of adventure, so she stopped worrying about David's plan.

He named the birds that fluttered out of the long grasses—redwing blackbirds, robins, meadowlarks. He showed her how to follow the trajectory of the sun and why it meant they were traveling southeast. The first hour passed in a pleasant haze of sunshine and late summer.

"How are you doing?" he asked when they turned from their pathless meander toward a thick woods. They beckoned with cool shade. "Need a rest?"

"I'm good for a while longer."

He offered her a genuine smile. "Have to call you Iron Britches from now on, won't we? I knew you were a natural horsewoman."

"Thanks. That's a big compliment coming from you."

"Hey, you don't get 'em if you don't earn 'em."

She took a fortifying breath and plunged into the waters that frightened her. "Are you still angry with me?"

"I've never been angry with you."

"I didn't stick up for you out loud yesterday."

His face tightened slightly. "No. But you're whole and safe, and that's the only thing I care about. Cloth-headed detectives be damned."

"David, I'm sorry. I was wrong. The police were wrong. What you did was the bravest thing anyone's ever done for me. I just . . ."

He turned Gomer directly across Tully's path and halted. Tully snorted and reversed a step. "Just what?"

"It's stupid."

"I don't care."

She hesitated another moment and sighed. "I was angry—at me for dragging you into the ugly world I grew up in, and at you for stupidly putting yourself in danger because of me. I wanted the police to be right so I'd have a reason to stay angry and selfish and hold on to my fear and embarrassment. I didn't like that you'd seen the real me. I know it doesn't make sense."

"It doesn't. You think I haven't seen the real you? The Rio who stood up to Hector is the Rio I've come to admire—tough, unafraid, spit-in-your-eye."

"That's lovely. A fantastic image."

"You are fantastic. A woman of a thousand talents and I'm quite sure you don't know it."

"I could say the same about you." They rode silently. A crazy stray tear she couldn't explain threatened to expose her relief, her fear, her sadness. She wiped it surreptitiously with the back of a hand. "I'm sorry," she said. "You were right yesterday. Hector might have dragged me with him. Thank you. The police should have heard me say that."

He smiled softly. "Thanks."

"Where are we going?"

"An hour further."

"To do what?"

"To survive."

He refused to give any other details. They stopped once to dismount and stretch and let the horses snuffle in the sparse grass beneath the trees of an ever-thickening woods. If someone had told Rio, the lifelong city girl, that her Minnesota had a place so devoid of civilization this close to a town she'd have written him off as crazy, but the place David had brought her barely had paths through the trees, much less a discernable destination.

Three and a half hours into the ride he stopped, looked around their tangled surroundings, and nodded. "This'll do."

"That's it. No more games. Do for what?"

"Our restaurant, hotel, and entertainment rolled into one."

A jolt of excitement rippled down her spine, followed by a shot of terror. "Hotel?"

"Told you this required a little trust."

"How about a little blanket?" The slightest sarcasm crept into her words as reality sank in. "Or water? You know, the stuff you can't live without?"

"You just have to be a little tougher and meaner than the woods. Or wherever you're lost. I can be tough and mean, that's the point of this."

"What if I just say I believe tough, mean you can get us through this and we simply go home?"

"I'd say, you're welcome to mount up and head back. I've stayed alone in the woods. But I'd miss you."

"And you know I won't because I'd be lost within twenty feet."

Once again he simply smiled.

They spent the first hour getting the horses tethered to trees and scouting an area about a hundred feet around them for types of plants, trees, and ground smoothness. He explained why he'd chosen this spot—for its handful of full-canopied trees that would offer some shelter if it rained, combined with taller pines that left a carpet of soft needles on open ground smooth enough to sleep on.

"What about animals and cold?"

"Fire, sweatshirts, and, if necessary, body heat."

"There's the first line that might be worthy of a travel poster."

Following his instructions, she cleared the ground and made a bare circle for a fire. She gathered tinder and kindling and delighted in the fragile little white flower blossoms she uncovered. The last of the summer anemones, he told her.

"Do you honestly not know where we are?"

"We're in a privately owned, two-hundred-and-sixty-acre woods between a wetlands preserve and the state park. I know the owner."

"So you aren't lost, but I am."

"Pretty much. Come on, let's take the horses for a drink. There's a stream nearby as I recall."

The stream tumbled clear and pristine through the shade, the same one that wound through the Glen Butte State Park and eventually created the actual Kennison Falls. Rio hadn't thought once about thirst until she watched Tully and Gomer swallowing their huge draughts of the cool water.

"Can't we just dunk our noses in and drink, too?"

"No. It's fairly clean, but there's still bacteria that make it unsafe."

"It doesn't hurt the horses?"

"Different makeup in their guts."

"So what do we do, tap trees?" She scowled.

"Under dire circumstances. Or we wait for morning and find dew-covered leaves to suck on."

"Very funny."

"All right, you can also cheat again and bring along a little device like this."

From his belt, he unhooked a mesh bag Rio hadn't noticed and took out an eight-inch-tall cylinder with a clear tube attached. He filled the cylinder with creek water and a few minutes later handed her a little nylon cup full of cold, crisp, filtered water.

"Wow!"

"Nice gadget, 'eh?"

"Who knew water could be so delicious? Can it squeeze out a nice, juicy burger?"

He laughed. "Sorry. But if you want to eat, we can go hunting."

"Hunting? For what?"

"Squirrel or rabbit maybe. Gophers aren't really worth it."

"Kill bunnies? No way!" Her stomach twisted at the thought. To her chagrin, he laughed again.

"You didn't complain about the steaks we've eaten or the roast you cut up to put in the stew."

"Yeah, but I didn't have to kill it."

"That's hypocritical."

"I don't think so. I can't build roads, but I drive on them. I have someone else make my clothing—I don't go naked. So what if I prefer someone else to catch and kill the meat?"

"Fair enough. But would you starve to death rather than do the hunting?"

"I won't starve in twelve hours."

"It's the principle."

"Fine." She frowned. "How are you going to hunt this rabbit and/or squirrel? Do you have a gun tucked somewhere, too?"

"Just a MacGyver bit of string and my pocketknife."

"No fair. How come I didn't get tools?"

"Because your job this trip is to learn how to use them."

She should have been thoroughly put off by his attitude. Instead the tug of attraction hit harder than ever.

Once they returned to their camp spot, David knelt, and for the third time in her life, Rio watched him build a perfect fire. He left her alone for almost an hour afterward with instructions on how to keep the fire going but not let it get too big. She stuck to her task diligently and found the solitude with only the flames' crackle to keep her company to be a deep joy she'd never imagined. It only confirmed the thought that she was meant to be a pioneer woman somewhere with no city craziness encroaching on her. Her old vision of a small solitary ranch somewhere in Wyoming surfaced for the first time in weeks. If only she could drag David with her . . .

Whoa.

She shook the thought away and tried to ignore the heavy desire settling into her body like a sudden flu. Whether it came from thinking about leaving him or just plain thinking about him she couldn't tell . . .

"You ready for dinner?"

She turned as he came through the trees like Daniel Boone with a rabbit hanging upside down in his hands.

"Oh gosh." She covered her mouth in surprise and stared despite herself.

"C'mon," he said. "You faced down a gang member with a knife. This is just an old rabbit."

"How do you *know* he's old?"

"Because he's big, a little gray in the paws, and slow enough that he fell for my snare. Want to help me skin him?"

"No!"

"I think this is the first time I've seen you remotely squeamish."

"I think this is the first time I've seen you remotely . . ."

"A killer?"

"No. A caveman."

"I'll take that as a compliment. If you don't want to dress the rabbit, you can go scout us up two long, sturdy sticks that we can sharpen for roasting the meat. I'll take care of this."

In the end, pride and a little shame at her weakness made her stay and watch the cleaning process. After David made the first slits Rio's squeamishness dissipated, and she marveled at the way he shucked off the fur and skin with neat, efficient strokes of his knife point and then cut the meat into long strips.

Twenty minutes later Rio held her first strip of roasted rabbit tentatively in front of her mouth. For the first time since she'd seen the dead animal in David's hand, she quailed just a little. She felt like she should say a prayer of thanks to the animal's spirit like the American Indians did.

"Thank you, rabbit," she said out loud, expecting David to laugh again.

"Amen," he said.

He took a bite of his and closed his eyes. His lips, full and sensual, pursed with pleasure. Rio licked her own lips in preparation and took a generous bite. The meat was a little stringy and slightly gamey but still moist and sweet. David searched her face expectantly.

"It's not bad," she admitted.

"A little different from hamburger."

"A lot different, you mean."

They finished their first pieces. David took her stick and skewered another raw strip. It sizzled immediately when she held it over the coals.

"Did you have to kill things and eat them in Iraq?" she asked absently, turning her stick.

When he didn't answer, she looked up from her stick and found him staring into the flames, every feature tightening as if he was attempting to shutter out the question and any that might follow.

She studied him silently. Here he was in self-described tough and mean mode, yet the vulnerability wrapped around him nearly cried out to be acknowledged. As often as she'd been annoyed at his indulgence toward his family, she'd never seen him fragile. She'd made him tell her about Iraq the other night, and ever since then . . .

She laid her stick and its partially cooked meat aside. Scootching across the pine needle floor, she grasped his arm.

"This trip tonight," she said slowly. "This sudden need to prove you're tough. It's about Iraq, but it's not about the discharge. It's the part of the story you didn't tell me in the cabin, isn't it?"

He relaxed as if he'd come unstuck. His sad smile held multiple other emotions: gratitude, ruefulness, but mostly resignation.

"I guess it is at that. I don't tell the story anymore."

"Well, buster, you do tonight."

Amusement tinged the light in his eyes. "That was rather unequivocal."

"Just gotta be tougher and meaner than the survivalist." She laughed at his scowl. "Come on, get on with dinner and start talkin'."

He picked up his roasting stick, nodded for her to do the same, and when the meat sizzled again, he took a deep starting breath.

"You know ninety percent of the story. I did disobey orders, and I did get dishonorably discharged."

"But what really happened?"

"I was a quiet kid, sensitive my mum said, and observant, but it drove my father crazy that his son didn't have the killer instincts he thought it took to get ahead in life. So, when I was a teen, for a while I tried to cultivate Da's no-bullshit personality. And, maybe for a while, he thought I might make it."

He stopped and checked the rabbit. Satisfied, he set his aside to cool. Rio did the same.

"When it came to the army, I got lots of advice about how to advance. How to be tough at the right times, how to be invaluable. But after being in the thick of things, I didn't want any of that."

"You just wanted to get out alive," Rio said.

"That's right. Get home. The only goal. I did my job. In fact, I did whatever was asked. Until that night."

"Then it had to have been something you felt awfully strongly about not doing."

"To put it mildly. When it came time to find a place to bivouac, the lieutenant ordered us to go west, since the insurgents had been spotted days before to the east. There were caves, as well. Protection, he said. But I'd been studying the Iraqis' movements over months. I knew in my gut they'd gone for the caves, too. I not only disagreed with the decision, I argued. Vehemently. I'd decided to adopt my father's take-no-prisoners attitude, and I ended up calling the lieutenant arrogant, shortsighted, and unfit for leadership."

"*You* did?"

"Oh, I certainly did." His grimace conveyed the pain of memory. "I went well *beyond* what my father might have done. Even had I capitulated as I ought to have, there still would have been charges of insubordination. But I was so utterly convinced I was right."

"What happened?"

"Three men followed me." He paused and rubbed his mouth. "Three went with the CO. That night, all four of them were stabbed in their sleep."

The stark words might have been stabbings to her own heart. An intense wash of dizziness threatened to send her head down toward her knees. "Oh God, no," she whispered.

"We found them the next afternoon."

"I don't . . . oh God, you *found* them?"

"I admit, that was hellish."

"I don't even know what to say . . . Sorry isn't nearly a good enough word."

"It was inadequate then, as well."

"And now you live with it? You bury it and deal with it when it pops up like this?"

"I've dealt with it. It's in the past."

"I don't know. It's pretty much in the here and now, wouldn't you say?"

"I made my peace with what the army did. You can't

have soldiers disobeying orders on a hunch every five minutes, can you?"

"But your commanding officer was wrong. The ultimate kind of wrong. He brought you along to do exactly what you did."

"But the decision was ultimately his."

"Okay, even if I accept that, why wasn't your family, Kate especially, weak with relief that you didn't die? That you were smart enough to stay alive?"

"She and my father thought I came back changed."

"No. Really?" Rio's eyes shot angry sapphire sparks. "How unforgiveable."

He pulled his stick out of the fire and leaned it against a tree root so the meat could cool. "I learned a lesson in Iraq. Keep your mouth shut. Don't argue. If I'd have kept my cool, I could have talked the CO into coming with me. He dug in because I dug in."

"You can't possibly know that."

"I know it. I've learned it after the fact. I learn it every day. Nod and smile. Works like a charm. As for Kate, she wanted someone with a sterling record and a forceful nature who could become as successful as my father had. My record was no longer sterling. I was all but unemployable in the U.K., what with the dodgy discharge papers. Kate hated that blot on my character.

"After she left me, I tried again with my father. I made one trip following him on a U.S. tour of guest clinics and lessons. When he came to Minnesota I happened to see this place for sale. I made a decision in less than a flash and never looked back."

"You gave up your citizenship to stay here?"

"My act of anger and defiance against the British military, my father, and no doubt Kate. And I've never for a moment regretted it. I love it here."

"But none of this is wimpy. Why do you let them, us, think of you as mild-mannered and easygoing?"

"Because I am. I'm not my father. Maybe I'm *wimpy* with my family, but I told you, it's easier to nod and smile and let them go home believing they're still influencing my life. I don't care what they *think*. They live a long way away."

"And you don't think your father is proud of you."

"I don't know what my father is." For the first time, his voice gained an edge, dull but definite, and Rio heard all the longing of a son looking for his father's approval. She wasn't sure David even knew it was there.

"Why did you react so strongly that night in Iraq, do you think?"

"Because I was scared shitless?"

"Yes. So forgive yourself."

"Done a long time ago."

"You know what? I don't think that's true."

Chapter Twenty-Nine

"YOU'RE A LITTLE heavy into the pop psychology to-night." David looked more amused than upset, and Rio rubbed his shoulder, kissing his bicep with a smile.

"Because I feel responsible for dredging this up. I'm sorry I made you talk about it the other night."

"You don't need to be. I really don't talk about it. But it wasn't so hard. With you."

"What can I do to make it better?"

His eyes shone as if he were preparing to make a joke. Then they softened to a moment of seriousness. "Understand that I need to deal with my parents the way I do. Ignore the blot on my copybook—as my gran used to say."

"There's no blot to ignore. This is how I know you haven't forgiven yourself. And you can't forgive yourself until you forgive your father. So deal with them however you want. But promise to be nice to yourself, too. You can't be down on people I like."

The flash of humor returned. "So you like me again?"

"Yeah," she sighed. "I guess. Can we kiss and make up now?"

A grin lifted the corners of his mouth, and a familiar fire lit his eyes for the first time since their awkward night at the little cabin. An unexpected but welcome flash of pure desire blazed through her stomach and landed, pulsing, deep in some untouchable spot. He took her roasting stick from her hands without speaking.

"What do you want?" she teased.

He answered with his lips and tongue. One large, sure hand lifted her hair to cup the back of her head and pull her against him. Hard and delving, his kiss melted her faster than fire could have, tasting wild like the food he'd caught and smelling of pine and smoke and tangy male perspiration. Every desire liquefied within her and rushed like water over a broken dam to the aching point between her legs.

Mewling with impatience, she found her way onto his lap, never breaking the searching kiss while arching her belly into his.

Their kiss, succulent, punctuated with quiet and not-so-quiet groans and escalated breathing, intensified every sensation until she believed the simple friction of their bodies sliding naturally against each other would be enough to send her flying over a cliff of pleasure. Then his free hand slipped under her T-shirt, and his hard, round fingertips slid up her torso, scalding her skin, meeting the bottom of her bra and pushing it out of the way like it was no more barrier than a soap bubble. His thumb found the tip of her breast and she broke their kiss for the first time, gasping in pleasure.

"You like that?" he rasped.

"Duh," she whispered.

He lay back and expertly switched their positions, cradling her body from the hard ground and hovering above her, his eyes smoky in the evening light now slanting through the trees. She stroked his cheek, roughened with a day's growth of beard, handsome with its strong cheekbones. He closed his eyes.

"Thank you," he said.

"What for?"

"For waiting. This is what you deserve—not petulant lovemaking from a man in bloody crisis mode."

She giggled at the formality. "I love it when you speak Duke to me. So proper."

He lifted her shirt, exposing the breast he'd been caressing. "Yeah? Well, here's your proper right here."

He laid her onto the carpet of pine needles and slid down her body until his mouth found her nipple. She cried out at the array of fireworks shooting through her body as first one breast and then the other received lavish attention. He followed with tickled kisses and nips between her breasts and down her stomach, making her buck as she squirmed to get away. He held her captive and blew raspberries onto her skin. Squealing laughter rang into the trees.

"Ticklish, are we?" He lifted his head, his grin limned with devilish intent.

"Yes, yes. Stop!" He blew another wet kiss next to her belly button. "Stop!"

He shimmied back up her body, cupping her breast and stopping her helpless laughter with a kiss.

"I suppose it's true, we never finished dinner."

She wanted nothing more to do with roasted rabbit. In his arms she was full, satisfied, and convinced he could keep them both that way. Insanely she wanted to bind herself to this man who seemed deeper, more pain-filled, and yet more loving and trustworthy than her own family ever had. After just this brief time, after this small dip into the pool of his life, she wanted to jump off into the deepest water and let him be her lifesaver.

"I only want dessert."

"Hmmm." He kissed her ear. "Cliché but most agreeable."

He pushed to his feet, tugged her up after him, and swung her into another deep, thirsty kiss. Kissing her all the way, he pushed her toward the horses' tack set neatly beneath a tree. Parting from her long enough to grab the two woolen saddle blankets, he locked lips again, walked them back to the fire, unfolded the blankets, and spread them on the ground with the horsehair-covered sides down.

"Bob's your uncle," he said. "Fit for a king."

"I'm not greedy. A duke will do."

"You really have to stop calling me that. I'm starting to believe I'm actual royalty."

"Fine by me."

They sank to their knees on the blankets. Both his hands this time slipped up her sides and in a fluid motion he shucked off her shirt like silk from satin.

Equally gracefully he divested her of the lacy bra beneath it.

His gaze caressed her almost physically, and every inch of her skin dimpled into goose bumps and hard peaks. Hot, masculine hands spanned her rib cage, and his thumbs found her nipples again.

"Gorgeous."

"Let me see you."

She followed his lead and tugged off his T-shirt. The effort left his thick hair mussed and his eyes luminous. Tipping forward, she pressed her lips to the soft patch of hair on his chest, then kissed her way up to the hollow of his throat. His taste was sweet and salt, rough and manly, different from anyone she'd ever known. Serious, playful, and soul-deep exciting.

He fumbled with her waistband, unsnapping her fly, rasping down the zipper, and sending anticipatory chills dancing down her thighs. When the jeans flapped open, he plunged his fingers past the waistband to her seat, curling them over the curves of her glutes, kneading into the muscles and pulling her closer with each pulse of his hands.

With a final tug he locked her against the long length of his erection, and everything inside her shimmered to a standstill with the exception of a flight of exquisite butterflies that left trails of feathery sparks along her body.

"Nearly perfect," he whispered.

Everything he touched turned to sensation and every sensation fed the desire that was fast becoming craving. They collapsed together onto the blankets and the wool only added stimulation to her sensitized skin. His tongue circled in her mouth, stroking the tender surfaces. Quivering, she roamed his shoulders, his back, and his muscular arms with desperate fingers. Finally she forced her hand between them and found the snap to his jeans. It took a little perseverance, but once she had his zipper down, she reached past the denim and stroked him through the cotton of his boxers.

He groaned, and she couldn't rush her boots off or wriggle out of her jeans fast enough. Once naked, she bent tor David's boots and yanked them off, first the left and then the right, and tossed them unceremoniously into the trees. Seconds after that, he peeled off his jeans and grabbed her to him, his long male body rough and glorious against hers.

There was not enough time and yet all the time in the world to explore the new places, textures, feelings of each other. His body was a magnificent toy, full of hard planes and soft spots, dark hair, and firm skin. Everything she touched made her shiver.

But she didn't want to be far enough away from him to explore for long. She wanted him around her and in her and with her. She threw one leg over his hip, and his fingers found her softest and most sensitive spot. Lightning struck again and again as he explored the dampness at the juncture of her legs with a long, talented finger. She pushed reluctantly away and grasped his length with confidence, glorying in the power she could wield over him.

They played, they teased. He traced her tattoos and she loved how he touched her. How even in his ardor and foreplay, without words, he promised never to hurt her. She loved that she knew it without question.

Without warning, playing wasn't enough.

Desire like a tsunami slammed her from head to core, leaving her trembling in his arms.

"Now," she begged. The first words either had spoken in long minutes.

He rolled to his side, grabbed his jeans and dug in a pocket, then rolled back with a foil square.

"More supplies you sneaked past me." She kissed him. "My prepared Scout."

"They did *not* teach us this in Scouting." His grin only heightened her need. "And just so you know. I didn't believe we'd get anywhere near this point tonight. But since we've been dangerous together from the start, I didn't dare leave without these."

She watched with trembling fascination while he rolled on the protection, astounded by her erotic reaction. "Is now still a good time?" he teased into her ear, returning to her and draping himself over her body.

"Five minutes ago would have been better."

He entered her slowly, and she arched into him, feeling his fullness as if it had been a missing part of her. The rhythm came so easily, so wondrously, at first it was like playing all over again. Their foreheads bumped, he kissed her nose, her eyes. She laughed softly with hitching breath. They made the pleasure last—forced it to last—as they rocked together in a heated dance as old as time. And then, the fire slammed them both without warning.

He cried into her cries. The reds, blues, golds, and whites of the powerful orgasm carried her away from her body, only to bring her crashing back with wave after wave of licking heat. David drove, his muscles rock firm, his breath hot on her face, sweet in her nostrils. But she couldn't concentrate, couldn't control the waves that just kept crashing until, at last, tears of relief and utter joy flowed down her cheeks, dousing the flames into hot, glowing embers.

SOMETIME IN THE night she'd wrapped herself back around him like a child around a teddy bear. David yawned and smiled into her hair, surprisingly comfortable. Rio's sweatshirt still covered their shoulders, his zippered hoodie their feet. They'd dressed reluctantly in the light of the campfire, but the nights were cool now, and sleeping naked in the woods even with a fire was a poor idea no matter how much he would have loved waking her at midnight to re-create what they'd shared.

The sky glowed pewter and purple, indicating dawn was less than an hour away. David didn't want to wake her. Her red hair tumbled across her face like the remnants of their fire from last night. All her wariness had vanished, leaving only peace on her features. How she'd turned him inside out last night, he didn't know. His only explanation was that somehow he felt whole when they were together. Or else she was exactly the wood nymph she appeared to be in sleep.

"Rio?" He smoothed the hair out of her eyes. "Love? Wake up."

She awoke immediately, her blue eyes filled with disoriented concern.

"It's all right. Everything's fine," he said.

Her features relaxed into a smile. "Hi."

"How does a ride sound?"

"Now?" Her sleepy incredulity made him laugh.

"No, not for five whole minutes."

"Oh, all right then." She kissed him on the corner of the mouth and closed her eyes, snuggling back into his side.

Forty-five minutes later, with the campsite looking exactly as it had when they'd arrived, they rode into a clearing and tethered Gomer and Tully to trees at the bottom of a twenty-five-foot rise. Rio followed him to the top where they could see out to the horizon. He marveled at her acceptance of this entire night—a rash and arrogant plan he'd put into action just to assuage the resurgence of guilt and inadequacy he should have fully buried long ago. The tough inner city girl, with no experience at this whatsoever, was following without a whimper. And healing him without a question.

Maybe her dream of solitude and self-sufficiency wasn't so far-fetched after all. She'd probably do fine. But the thought of her pursuing any dream that took her away filled him with dread.

"Oh David, look!"

He'd seen the sunrise countless times, as a boy learning to camp, as a hiker with his mother, as a soldier in the deserts of Iraq. But he'd never seen it along with a face as full of wonder as Rio's. She watched the colors spread through the eastern sky, yellow, pink, and purple studded with sapphire, as if she'd been given sight for the first time.

"Pretty, 'eh?"

He sat behind her, legs spread, regretting the position as soon as she leaned back.

"It's miraculous. Oh, look at the colors!"

The sun's fireball rose slowly at first, then it floated fully over the horizon and sent the shadow colors fleeing in the power of its yellow-and-white light. After five minutes it blazed fully in a fresh, pale-blue sky.

"Thank you," Rio whispered, as if he'd given her the sun as a personal present.

"Are you anxious to get back to the farm?"

"Why?"

"I've a whole list of sights to show you as long as we're out here. And I think I know where there are some wild raspberries for breakfast."

"It sounds too good to be true."

"Then spend the day with me, my love, and I'll prove it's not."

She craned her neck, and her lush lips pecked him on the cheek, soft as down, powerful as a stun gun. "I can't think of a more perfect idea."

Chapter Thirty

"Just be prepared. We could be buggered with my mother."

Rio halted Tully beside Gomer and laughed. "There's still an hour before anyone comes for the party. It's not like she gave me any real jobs to do."

They'd spent the day wandering an area of waterfalls and creeks, a limestone-walled river valley, and countless wooded nooks and crannies. Although her body now ached from hours in the saddle, it also glowed—from an impulsive lunch of little sustenance but sweeter lovemaking than the night before. No guilt over being away while party prep took place was going to ruin her newfound happiness.

"Where the devil have you two been?" Colin, pouring himself a generous glass of wine, greeted them in the kitchen, more amusement than chastisement in his question. "Your mother's been beside herself."

"I'm sure she has things well in hand without me," David said. "We were delayed."

Colin shrugged, and his eyes lit on Rio. His gaze narrowed, and she swore a flicker of a smile threatened his lips. "Get up to your rooms and change before the bloody gauntlet of Minnesota's most impressive dressers is assembled, touch wood Stella doesn't see you along the way, and if you show up cheerful and ready, you might escape all hell."

Rio groaned internally. She'd known she would have to find something that approximated party clothing, but she hadn't done it.

"I have nothing to change into," she said when Colin had left the room. "I'll just—"

"Well, well. The prodigal children. Where *did* you two run off to?"

Rio looked up to find Kate in a tea-length cocktail dress of olive green, the bodice and plunging neckline encrusted with gold and green gems and sequins. On anyone else the color could have been sickly. On Katherine it stunned.

Her elegant eyes shot arrows of disapproval—directly at Rio.

"Hullo, Kate," David replied cheerfully. "I took Rio to see some sights on the other side of the state park, and darkness came on more quickly than we'd figured. We found a safe place to overnight and then, in truth, we didn't hurry back. You know how much I was looking forward to this."

"What's going on?" Stella bustled in next and stopped short.

"Hey, Mum. Here we are, just in time for the do."

"You do realize I nearly called our lovely local constable." She assessed them sharply as if trying to decide whether to send them to their rooms or simply scold them. "At least you had manners enough to let your man Andy know you'd taken the horses. And I know you can take care of yourself in the direst of conditions. But I really could have used your help earlier, David." She sighed and shook her head. "Well, nothing for it. Go and change, and then help your father with moving the chairs."

Rio bit back a snort. So it was both a scolding *and* a trip to their rooms.

"Stella, let me stay in here and take on the kitchen coordination," Rio said. "I really have nothing appropriate to wear, and I'm perfectly happy to fill platters and coffeepots."

"Pish-tosh," she replied without a blink. "Kate can help you find something to wear. There are dresses I've left here, in your room, in fact. Kate, love, you can do her up in a snap."

"Of course."

Kate looked as if she'd rather do anything else, and Rio's resentment swelled for the first time. "I really don't think I need—"

"Mum," David interrupted. "You have to let Rio do as she pleases."

Rio smiled with gratitude. Kate did, too. "I agree," she said. "Rio, you do whatever you wish."

It didn't take a rocket scientist to see Kate wasn't worried for a second about Rio's feelings or comfort. She would have David as an escort all evening if Rio acted as kitchen servant. Petulance and possessiveness trumped Rio's pride in a rush.

"Actually," she said. "If you'll show me the dresses, I'd like to try to them."

Kate couldn't hide the puckered scowl of her surprise, but David grinned in obvious happiness, and that made following Kate's regally draped backside up the stairs worth letting Stella win. Rio would have to owe David one. She hadn't stood up to uber-mother either.

Once in her room, Rio showed Kate the dresses she'd noticed her first night and not thought of since. Kate studied the two for only a moment before picking the black-and-white sequins.

"This will bring out your red hair."

"You don't have to hide away up here with me, Kate. I can dress myself."

"Let's see how it fits. I work with clothing and know a few tricks. After that I'll leave you alone."

Rio sighed, with a sudden welling of nerves. "I lied. I'm the last girl who knows how to dress for a party. I'm sorry you got forced into this, but I really do appreciate the help."

Kate said nothing for a long moment, looking from Rio to the dress and back. Finally she shook her head. "Nobody forced me. You're a natural beauty, Rio. I can see why David would be attracted."

"It's not what . . ." She stopped herself. It definitely *was* exactly what Kate thought, and Rio was tired of hiding it. "It's mutual," she said, for the first time.

"I'm not surprised. Look, Rio, I'll be honest. I'm not giving up on getting him back."

"Understood."

She said nothing more. It might be fun to fight for someone she wanted. And, despite herself, she found that Kate's ministrations, which could have been obnoxious, were fun, too. The black-and-white dress flowed opulently to just above Rio's ankles. Although it was two inches too big around, Kate sent Rio to shower "in five minutes, no more," and took a raft of safety pins expertly to the side seams.

There was no time to dry Rio's thick red locks, so Kate sat her in a chair and set to braiding, ending up with a gorgeous inverted French braid so pretty Rio honestly thought she'd never take it out. Kate finished with the barest hint of mineral foundation and some lip color.

"Voila." Kate stood back. Barely twenty minutes had passed. "Have a look."

The inside of one wardrobe door held a full-length mirror. Rio dared a glance and caught her own breath. The dress, white with beaded flowers over one shoulder, now hugged her snugly, accentuating her bustline and flowing softly, hombrelike, into silver, deep gray, and then black where it flared gently around her legs. She couldn't resist one twirl.

"Wow," she said. "Bibbidi-bobbidi-boo, Fairy Godmother."

Kate laughed. "A little enhancement of what was already there, that's all. Come on, let's go to a party."

IT WASN'T THAT Rio didn't appreciate compliments as much as the next girl, but the response throughout the evening to her metamorphosis was so overwhelming it made her wonder just how pitiful she looked under normal circumstances. First Bonnie, dressed herself in a pretty blue sundress from Kim's closet, then Stella, then David, fell over themselves raving about the dress, the shoes—also Stella's—the braid.

She tolerated it exactly the way she tolerated Carter, who captured her several times to regale her with his past, present, and future plans, convincing her he'd one day make it big on ego alone. She also endured Kate's opening salvos in her war on David, flirting openly, dragging him from person to person collecting introductions. Despite that, he never left Rio alone, and he never let Kate trap him alone, but he belonged in the group the way he belonged with his horses, while she, attractive enough in her borrowed clothes, felt like Thirty-one at the Westminster Dog Show.

Throughout the night she smiled and nodded, and drank her new favorite Minnesota wine wondering how Stella Pitts-Matherson from six thousand miles away had made so many friends. At last, three-fourths of the way through the evening, David took her elbow while she was in the middle of hearing an excruciating diatribe on land, taxes, and foxhunting with Stella and Colin and three members of a hunt club outside the city. She couldn't have been more relieved.

"I'm afraid I have to steal Rio from you. We're needed in the barn." David smiled, but his features held a tightness that set worry gnawing at Rio's stomach.

"The barn, David, really?" asked his mother.

"Yes. We'll be back shortly."

"But you have your man for barn work," she insisted.

"Mother. I'm afraid you'll have to excuse us anyway."

Rio thought she'd drop her teeth—right before she cheered. He'd not only stood up, he hadn't even apologized.

"Is something wrong?" she asked.

"I'll tell you on the way."

At the back door she swapped Stella's black sandals for her barn-grubby tennis shoes and threw on the sweatshirt she and David had slept under the night before. The night breeze held a hint of early fall and lifted the hem of her dress in a teasing swirl.

In the barn she found their weak and bedraggled palomino filly flat on her side in a stall and Ben Thomlinson bent over her with a stethoscope. The first round of antibiotics clearly hadn't helped, and cold gripped Rio's heart. David had warned her not to give any of the rescue horses names until they were all declared healthy and fine. It was too risky to become attached.

He'd pack her off for Crazytown if he knew she'd named all twelve and kept them in her mind like a litany: Lacey-Rain-Hank and Digger, Amber-Jewel-Cricket-Dot, Harpo-Zeppo-Zeke . . .

And Glory.

That had always been the name of her fantasy palomino, the one she'd one day own. This ravaged little horse met none of her dream qualifications, yet Rio had known from the first that the filly needed a name worthy of hope.

"She went down about two hours ago," David told her.

"Is she going to be all right?"

Dr. Thomlinson stroked Glory's neck and stood. "Her vitals are okay. We need to give these new drugs time to work. But, Rio, sometimes, even when we do everything right in starting to feed starved horses, their systems simply can't handle the changes. I'd say she's got a slightly better than fifty-fifty chance."

David ran a hand roughly through his hair. Rio's eyes welled. "What should we do?" she asked.

"Watch her. If she tries to stand, encourage her but don't force her. Our goal is for her to stand and support herself."

Ben left soon after that, and a sense of helplessness replaced Rio's sadness. David encircled her shoulders and kissed above her ear.

"Sometimes having animals means dealing with losing them."

"We won't lose her." She had no expertise on which to base such a prediction, but she proclaimed it adamantly anyway.

"All right. I believe you. We can leave her for a little while. We should get back."

"You go." She glanced up at him. "Please, let me stay a little while."

"You sure?"

"Just don't tell your mother where I am with her dress."

He tugged on her braid and smiled, then pulled just hard enough to tilt her head back. Hot and sweet, he slipped a kiss onto her lips. "Don't worry about my mother."

As soon as he was gone, too, Rio stole into the make-shift tack room and grabbed a saddle pad. She slid open Glory's stall door, spread the pad on the shavings, and sat by the filly's head. Softly she stroked the shaggy cheeks and tender muzzle and crooned words of comfort. Time floated past without so much as tapping her on the shoulder.

SHE AWOKE WITH a gasp and shot to her seat in the dark, blinking for orientation. The air hung thick and pungent with sawdust and ammonia. She scrubbed her eyes, re-membering where she was.

Glory.

She found the filly's warm head and heard her breath-ing noisily. When a small body moved beside her she startled, ready to scream at a mouse or worse until Thirty-one meowed and brushed along her arm, purring like a little cougar.

"Kitty! Oh man, you scared me." She scooped up the cat and nuzzled her. "I haven't spent much time with you lately, have I? It's nice of you to come and take care of us. How's Glory?"

As if answering, Glory gave a rumbling whicker.

"Hey you," Rio cooed. "That was awfully nice to hear."

Thirty-one stepped to the filly and rubbed back and forth along her long, white-blazed face. Glory snorted and raised her head, snuffling at the visitor. Then she threw her head and neck sideways and rolled onto her belly like a dog.

"Good girl!" Rio crowed. "Look at you. You're half-way up."

She knelt beside the horse and scrubbed her neck with eager, encouraging fingertips. For several minutes Glory leaned into the touch, her eyes no longer dull. Then her energy flagged, and she grunted, rolling again to her side, her head pressed against Rio's thighs. Thirty-one sprang to Glory's shoulder and found a spot she could knead and turn into a roost. The horse sighed. The cat blinked.

Rio scritched beneath Thirty-one's chin, amazed. "A horse whispering cat. What a rockin' girl you are."

She settled back into the shavings with no idea what time it was. Nobody had come to wake her so it couldn't be awfully late. Her eyelids drooped, and she propped herself against Glory's neck. The intelligent thing would be to go back to the house, and yet the need to stay held her captive. Sleepiness finally won, and her chin dropped to her chest.

Voices woke her. Once more she fought through the fog of sleep and found herself curled in a ball in the front corner of the stall. It was still dark, but she could see Thirty-one lying between her and Glory, and she could see the filly once again on her belly with her legs tucked comfortably beneath her. She nickered when Rio pushed herself up.

The voices still drifted from far down the aisle near the doorway, but identifying David and Kate took no guesswork. Rio's cheeks heated. They could not find her still in Stella's cocktail dress, sleeping in shavings with a sick horse. She stood, frantic with groggy embarrassment. The dress skirt hung bedraggled and coated with wood shavings, her hands reeked of horse, and her tongue tasted like a bird's nest.

"She wasn't in her room. She must still be in here," David said.

"No," Kate replied. "She must be asleep in some corner of the house. She hated the party, you know. And nobody is mad enough to stay five hours in a malodorous barn in dress clothing."

She had hated the party. But she'd have gone back. Five hours? David had let her stay here until two in the morning?

"No telling what Rio might do. She's a unique woman."

"She's a strange girl, David," Kate countered. "Not remotely the sort you fall for."

"In the past that was certainly true."

Desperately Rio eyed the door across the aisle. She didn't want to hear another word. But she'd have to cross in full view.

"It's true *now*, David. You can't send a little street girl, no matter how practical she is, onto the Internet to solve this latest crisis. You need a real solution. You need real capital."

"Rio is hardly a little girl. And practicality is sometimes a rare commodity."

One point for you, dear David. But what crisis? Her heart raced anew.

"Then be practical. You can't absorb this. What did the lawyer say again? Twenty-five thousand?"

"For medical costs, yes. But I'm not remotely worried about the frivolous suit—she unquestionably backed into my barn in an area where parking was clearly marked and perfectly level, unlike what she's claiming."

"But you have to retain a lawyer regardless. For goodness' sake, let me help you. You know I have the means."

"Absolutely not. You know that's a terrible idea, generous as it is."

Rio listened in growing dismay.

"Then what would you suggest as the solution? You seem to be addicted to, even attracted to, hard luck stories at the moment—your own most of all. And Rio Montoya and her sister are not helping you focus. What are we doing out here worrying about her?"

"Kate. Rio and Bonnie are special. I don't want to hurt her by—"

"Then, sweetheart," Kate interrupted. "If you don't want her hurt, get her away from this mess. Be smart."

Tell her. Tell her it'll hurt you more to send me away.

"Rio has nothing to do with this mess. She can't help, it's true, but I'm fond of her. I'll think of something; there's still Maxwell's offer."

Fond of her? Rio's heart took a full-on knife stab so painful that tears threatened. And Carter Maxwell? David couldn't. He would never really sell out . . .

"He seems a decent fellow," David continued. "I don't know yet that I think he's the answer, but isn't it just possible working with him might be better than accumulating more debt?"

Never. David. He's arrogant. He's not like you. You can't. Tell Kate you can find a way. We can find a way.

Their voices faded, and Rio guessed they'd gone into the ruined tack room. Pressing her luck, she rolled the stall door open two inches and peered down an empty aisle. Grabbing Thirty-one, she slipped out and fled to the back of the barn into the deepest corner, not quite making it to the back door.

"It certainly looks to me as if you can prove your case." Kate and David returned to the aisle.

"You see? The lawsuit has absolutely no legs; it's simply annoying. Let's check the filly and see if Rio's there. I don't hold out a lot of hope for that little horse."

That stupid, simple line broke the dam holding back Rio's tears. How dare David give up? British understatement be damned. How dare he reduce what they'd shared to *fondness* of her?

"Bugger all, would you look at that!" David's astonishment cut through her pain. "She's up!"

Up? Rio's sad and confused heart gave a surprised leap of hope.

"Oh David, but she's so thin. The poor thing. Just put her out of her misery."

Rio held back a cry of indignation. Of all the uncaring—Suddenly, hiding seemed ridiculous. Why should she care whether Kate saw her caring for the horse? Kate needed a big dose of reality.

"Absolutely not," David said. "This is the happiest thing that's happened in two days."

The knife twisted. Intellectually Rio knew he spoke only of the farm. But nothing felt intellectual while she hid like an idiot in the dark.

Glory nickered. Rio swiped away her tears.

"Where's Rio, girl?" David rolled open the stall door.

"Does she know about you? She'll be more than a little relieved."

"You know, love ..." Kate turned on a surprising Marilyn Monroe breathiness. "There are things even more exciting than a recovering horse. And there are women, like me, who've learned their lessons and seen their mistakes. I would love a chance to make you see the person who *is* waiting for you in the barn."

Silence fell. David grunted. Kate made a soft, succulent humming sound. Rio's tears vanished in a red haze. Thoughtlessly, she stepped from the shadows.

They didn't see her at first, but she saw the kiss. Then David pushed Kate away and staggered backward.

"What the hell?" he demanded.

"Remember how good it used to be?"

"For God's sake, Katherine. What gave you the idea I'd welcome *that*? I've welcomed you as a guest and an old friend. But—"

He saw her.

"Rio!"

"Well, isn't this a surprise?" Her pure anger filtered out the rejection she'd just heard him dole out to Kate.

"It certainly was," he agreed, and spun to embrace her. "Are you all right? Where were you, love? I was worried."

Being held by him in front of Kate should have been Rio's dream come true, but she struggled in his arms.

"Oh really," Kate said, glaring. "You can't possibly be serious about this."

"How serious we are has nothing to do with you thinking you can kiss me when I haven't invited it."

"Is that right?" Rio broke free. "Well, maybe we aren't that serious about *this* after all. Especially since *this* doesn't even have a name."

"What the hell, Rio? Keeping us a secret was done for you. For both of us. We both agreed. What do you want me to say?"

"You already said it. I happen to have heard." She turned to Kate. "Remember you told me you weren't going to give up fighting for him? Well, I think I might now be a teensy point ahead in the war. At least he's *fond* of me."

She left them both staring and made herself walk calmly out of the barn.

Chapter Thirty-One

SHE APPROACHED HIM slowly, tentatively. It nearly killed David to see such defeat in Rio's demeanor and such wariness of him.

"Hi," she said, joining him at the little palomino's stall door.

"'lo."

"Glory."

He looked at her, not understanding.

"That's her name. You told me not to give her one, but I did anyhow."

She hadn't lost all her spirit, he thought gratefully. "It's a perfect name."

She watched Glory munching her hay for a moment, then leaned sideways on the door. "I'm sorry. David. Really. I was out of line last night."

"Well, you did see me kissing another woman."

"I saw another woman kissing you. I'm pretty

sure, after what I heard you say to her, there was a difference."

He smiled. "There was. And Kate knows I'm not interested in having it happen again."

"She had a right to fight for you. She warned me she was going to do it."

"Well, nobody warned me. I'm sorry, too, Rio. I didn't mean for that to happen."

She nodded, resignation and uncertainty still in her eyes. He cupped her chin and tilted her sweet face upward.

"I told her I loved you."

That shocked her out of her melancholy. "You did?"

"Rio. Don't you know that in England 'fond' is slang for love?"

Her nostrils flared and her lips pursed as she stared at him, uncertain for only a second. "It is not."

"It is. I should know," he said. "I'm ready to tell the world how I feel if you are. I'm sorry I didn't last night."

"You were right, though. We'd agreed all along not to tell. I was just so angry she got her lips on you I refused to listen. I was mad, too, that she was still talking about Carter Maxwell."

"Carter Maxwell," he repeated, his body weighed down by the very words. Never had a perfect solution to a problem been so incredibly unpalatable. "Believe me, Rio, I don't want to share this place with him."

"But you're thinking about it?"

"It would be stupid not to think about all possible options." He gathered her into an embrace to comfort himself as much as her. "I meant it. I don't *want* to share my farm."

"I'm glad."

Glory nickered as David braced her against the stall wall and captured her mouth in a deep, hot makeup kiss.

"Oh, excuse me, I'm so sorry." The man under discussion stepped through the door and averted his eyes from the kiss but didn't leave.

"Morning, Maxwell," David replied.

"I'm about to take a short ride into town with your father, but I wanted to give you this first." He handed David several sheets of paper. "I know you're only considering my proposal, but I'm not above pitching as hard as I can. These are owners who'd be willing to board with me."

David perused the list, flipping pages and scowling. "Twenty-five names," he said. "I have only five open stalls."

"You have at least six or eight boarders who aren't serious about competing. Sending them to more appropriate trainers would free up all those stalls. Then you can charge what this facility is worth and your cash flow immediately improves."

"I would never ask my loyal clients to leave." David held Rio tightly around the shoulders though she tried to wriggle free.

"These are simply suggestions," Carter said amiably. "Just making sure you know I have plenty of potential for creating income."

"Noted and appreciated."

"All right, boys," Rio said. "I'm taking Bonnie shopping. You two have a lovely talk."

She didn't mean it. David kissed her again, hoping the public display would soften her just a little, but she was getting good at walking away.

BONNIE STARTED SCHOOL the next day in new clothes purchased with Rio's first paycheck. After so much time feeling destitute, the act of providing for her family again thrilled her.

Rio arrived at work late after arranging to see Bonnie off the first day.

"Hav hav sum pie. Wekkom, kom in. Hav hav s-pie." Cotton hopped around her perch like someone had given her pie all right, laced with caffeine.

"Have some pie, Cotton," she repeated.

"How-dee, Stray-jer."

Lester burst into "Colonel Bogey."

It was like coming home. She'd grown to love The Loon Feather.

"Got her off okay?" Bud asked, as she rounded the counter from the dining room now filling with breakfast customers.

"I did. She was so excited."

"And you? Feeling any better?"

"Better?"

"You've been pretty down the past few days. Been worried about you, but I figured you were just concerned about Bonnie."

She lowered her eyes, filtering the sympathetic words through embarrassment. "It's true, and believe me, it's nice to have you and The Loon for comfort."

"We're glad you like it here. We like having you." Claudia appeared from the office behind the kitchen pushing another woman in a wheelchair. Rio recognized the plump lady with the salt-and-pepper hair and the effusive smile immediately, even though she'd never met her.

"Effie!"

"It's so good to meet you at last, Rio." Effie held out her hands and took both of Rio's. "I didn't quite believe you were real, I've heard so many good things."

"Oh, please tell me you didn't listen to them all."

"I don't think my Bud would fib about a cook. Besides, I had a slice of your pie for breakfast. I have nothing to teach you, young lady, and everything to be worried about."

She didn't look worried. The fog Rio had lived under all week, lifted slightly.

"We're all here to celebrate this." Bud handed her a pretty, fall-themed menu insert.

"What?"

Claudia pointed to the heading "Limited Time Fall Specials." Beneath it were Rio's two dishes. "Time to put all our testing on the line."

For the first time in days Rio grinned easily. "It's pretty much a dream come true."

"Well, let's get started," Bud said. "It'll get plenty real awfully fast."

The first batches of Irish Stew and the new meatball casserole were ready by 11:30 a.m., and the first compliments came in with the first orders. Rio took her turn out front to help Claudia when Vince arrived to help in back. The day hummed along like perfect choreography.

"Hi, Rio!"

She looked up from the register to see Nora Pint waiting for a seat. She'd been into Nora's tattoo parlor just to check out her artwork, and Nora came regularly to The Loon for lunch. Theirs was turning into an easy friendship.

"Hey, Nora. How's business?"

"Always slow come fall, but okay. I heard about your new lunch specials and had to come check 'em out."

Her face, broad-cheeked and guileless, registered pleasure even before she sat down.

"And to think I ever bemoaned small-town gossip." Rio smiled. "Is your brother coming?"

"Damian? Yes, but he's finishing up an intricate skull with a bandana eye patch and a pink rose in its teeth."

"Yikes. C'mon and wait. There's a good window table left."

"Hey, is there some woman staying out with David these days? And a tall, thin man. Slightly Ichabod Crane–ish only nicer looking?"

"Yeah," Rio replied. "A couple of other houseguests. Why?"

"Tiffany at the bakery said they stopped in earlier and bought out her entire supply of doughnuts. Told her they were celebrating because Ichabod agreed to be David's partner. What's that about?"

Nora might as well have blown a cannonball into her gut. "Rio?"

"I . . . sorry. I have no idea what David's up to," she lied. "If I . . . hear anything, I'll let you know."

She knew absolutely she had no moral authority to be pissed off. This was David's decision. Nonetheless, she was beyond pissed off. He was surrendering before he'd even begun to fight.

"What's the matter, honey?" Claudia asked when Rio brought Nora's order to the counter.

"Nothing," she said. Mortified, she felt a tear roll down her cheek.

"Come with me."

Claudia pulled her into the office and closed the door. "Something big just happened," she said. "Tell me."

What difference would it make if she did tell? You trusted people, told them things, and they went away. Or they lied. Or they tried to sell their sisters to gangland pimps. Rio spilled her entire story—from the troubles with Hector, to the failed sting, to her weekend with David. And she had to hint, disloyally, about David's troubles, too, in order to explain about Carter.

"And this hurts because I've fallen in love with him," she finished.

The words surprised her a little. But only a little. They were true.

"He's a good man, Rio. And you're a good woman. You'd complement each other."

"He told me he wouldn't sell out. And, yes, it's his decision. But why tell me a lie?"

"Maybe he didn't. Maybe he's had some time to decide it isn't a bad idea for him."

"Maybe."

Claudia stroked Rio's hair. "I can't tell you what to do or how to love. But say a little prayer, right now. Just ask for guidance and then let it go out into the Universe."

"Prayers." Rio scoffed. "I lived on prayers when my dad would go out on the road. Or Paul would go out with his friends. Not too sure about prayers."

"You'd be surprised at what a little faith can do."

"Well. All I care about is knowing what to do. I don't want to leave David's. I don't want to stay. I can't afford my own place yet. I used to be good at problem-solving."

"So ask for the problem to be solved. What the heck, right?"

Rio laughed. Claudia's doctrine seemed to be as rigid as her long, gray, hippie braid. And yet, it felt strong and genuine.

"All right. For you I'll try anything."

A sharp knock on the door ended their conversation. Claudia opened the door and Rio half-jokingly turned her eyes upward. "Okay," she said. "If You've got a solution, now's pretty much the time."

"Hey, Rio." Bud stood in the doorway. "There's a customer out here insisting on speaking to the cook."

Chapter Thirty-Two

THE CUSTOMER'S NAME was Don Sterling. His thick brush mustache gave him a Sam-Elliott-in-handsome-middle-age look, but he spoke like an East Coast businessman. He had three plates in front of him and an expression of sublime enjoyment on his face. The first thing he did was hand Rio a business card.

"It's nice to meet you. They tell me you're the cook behind these dishes."

"Yes."

"Serendipity brought me here," he said. "But I think you may be the person I'm looking for." His mustache lifted and he held out his hand.

"I . . . don't understand." She shook it and, at his invitation, sat across from him.

"I run a ranch near Sheridan, Wyoming. The Coyote Creek. We cater to guests—a fancy of way of saying it's a dude ranch. We're pretty successful, but last year we suffered a devastating fire and have just rebuilt."

Rio's mouth went dry and her pulse nearly suffocated her. Fire? Wyoming? Was this a joke?

"My old chef and his assistant recently retired. I have a new head chef, but I need someone fresh, someone with down-home cooking skills, to work with him. I'm finishing a road trip and happened to stop here for lunch. Honestly? This is some of the best-tasting, hearty food I've come across. You aren't by any chance looking for a change in jobs, are you?"

Rio looked around for hidden cameras.

"I . . . hadn't been looking. But, Mr. Sterling, I'm not a chef. I've worked in diners. I have no formal training."

"I have staff to train you. But if you developed these recipes on your own, you have the raw talent I'd love to nurture."

THE KITCHEN FLOOR creaked beneath his pacing. David looked at the clock for the fiftieth time in half an hour. Bonnie was due home any time, and Rio wouldn't miss that. She should have been home two hours ago, and today, of all days, he'd been counting on having the afternoon with her.

Not that he was looking forward to what he had to say. But he had to get to her before Kate or Carter did.

She entered, finally, five minutes later, laden with a bakery box and a Mylar balloon. He grinned just seeing her, but the dull question in her eyes sent his hopeful mood plummeting. He'd had his speech all planned. But she already knew.

"Good day?" he asked.

"Great day." She set her box on the counter and tied the balloon to a drawer handle. "And I understand you've had a momentous day yourself."

Too calm. She was far too calm. "Rio, forgive me. I've been waiting here all afternoon to tell you what's going on. How did you find out?"

"Kate and Carter spilled the beans at The Bread Basket, and that's all it takes. I work at Kennison Falls Gossip Central, remember."

"Can we talk about this? It's not what you think."

"David. I have absolutely no say in what business decisions you make. You don't have to talk to me about anything."

"I think we've shared far too much for that to be true." He took one of her arms and pulled her close. "I do not take us for granted. I don't take making love with you last weekend for granted either. You've given me so much more than you know, and you're invested in this place. I understand why you're upset."

"Thank you." A softening in her features sent her color higher.

Lord, she was beautiful. He slipped a kiss onto her cherry lips. She even tasted like cherries, and apples, and vanilla. She kissed him back, so sweetly it shouldn't have meant anything, but his body responded as it always did—coming to full alert, hungry for the next step. But she pulled away.

"It's a trial is all. Six months. Just a lease. If it works, we'll move forward."

"It sounds well-planned and perfect for you."

"But you don't really think it is."

She put a finger on his lips. "I told you. It doesn't matter."

"It matters to me."

"Why?"

"Because—" He stopped, surprised at what he was going to say. "Because I've come to care about all your opinions. I care about you."

That certainly hadn't come out right. Too stiff and formal. But he didn't know what right was. Her ideas and enthusiasm always gave him confidence. But Kate had been right, too. All the phone calls in the world wouldn't find enough discounted hay and merchandise to make a difference. And he couldn't give Rio any kind of life if he didn't fix his troubles.

"I got a job offer."

Her words jolted him out of his thoughts. "A what? What kind of offer?"

"If it's legitimate, it's my dream on a silver platter."

The Cinderella story she wove after that sounded shady as hell to him. When she mentioned salary and benefits, panic hit his system. He could lose her to this nonsense.

"That's utter madness, Rio. You can't do something that foolish."

Wrong words again. She stiffened and backed away. "Why would you say that? I've told you more about my dreams than anyone."

"But a bloke appearing out of nowhere with a ranch,

and a cooking job, and an arse-load of money? Can't you see the stranger with the candy here? Maybe he goes around the country spinning this little fable and enticing unsuspecting women to some completely different kind of ranch."

"For crying out loud. I'm not brainless. I'm not packing up and striking out tomorrow. I wasn't even promised a job. I'd have to apply. It's just something to look into." She let the words simmer momentarily. "Hmmm. Where have I heard that speech before?"

"Rio. Don't. Stay with me. Let's see where this goes. Us."

He could see the conflict in her eyes just as Bonnie burst into the room with Dawson right behind her.

"Hey! Welcome home." Rio's brightness returned, but David saw it for the cover-up it was. "How was Day One?"

"Fantastic!" Bonnie hopped to the kitchen island and gave her sister a quick hug. Then she surprised David by giving him the same. "Would you believe a school without metal detectors? And they let you go outside for lunch. And my precalc teacher is a hunk."

"Nice," Dawson said, ogling the box Rio had brought home. "I'm right here."

"You're hot," Bonnie said. "There's a difference."

"All right, you two. Happy first day of school. Have some cake. Where's Kim?" Rio nodded for Dawson to open the box.

"Already in the barn," Bonnie said.

"Chocolate," Dawson murmured, obviously in love.

"Look who I found!"

Everyone turned, wide-eyed, when Stella entered from the living room with Chief Hewett behind her.

"Can a cop with news join the party?" he asked.

David had never seen the man with a full smile. He stuck out his hand. "You look like a cop with good news."

"Most of it is."

Before the chief could start, David's father and Carter rushed through the back door. "We saw a police car," Carter began, and stopped at the sight of Hewett holding court in the kitchen.

"Is everything quite all right?" his father asked.

"Good. Everyone's here," Hewett said. "This affects the entire household. Minneapolis police picked up a Mr. Jeffrey Iverson this morning in his science classroom at a suburban high school north of Minneapolis. Mr. Iverson was, in fact, Minnesota's Teacher of the Year four years ago."

"Iverson," Rio said, setting a hand over her heart. "The money clip."

"Yes, ma'am." The chief grinned. "He also has an alleged alias."

"Boyfriend," she whispered.

"I thought you'd all want to know. Bonnie, you'll be contacted soon now about making your official identification."

"Okay!"

"This is wonderful, thank you," Rio said. "What about Hector and Paul?"

"Well, that's my bad news. We have evidence Mr.

Black left the city, perhaps the state. Your brother hasn't been seen."

"Could I try to call him?"

David didn't want her anywhere near her brother, nor did he want Bonnie to find any reason to help or forgive Hector, so his heart fell when Hewett agreed.

"It might be good for him to know Iverson's been taken into custody. Perhaps Paul still knows how to contact Mr. Black."

"I'll call him now and put it on speaker phone in case he says something you need."

She dialed Paul's number with visibly trembling hands and closed her eyes as if in prayer.

"Hello—" The voice David had only heard a handful of times answered.

"Paul! Paul, is—"

"—my name is Inigo Montoya. You killed my father. Prepare to die if you don't leave a message, man."

Everybody groaned while Rio waited for the beep. "Paul? Call me. If you haven't heard, the police have Boyfriend in custody. It's true. Tell Hector. Please? And please call."

When she hung up Tanner Hewett smiled at her. "He'll call you back, I'm sure of it. Just let me know when he does. We'll find him and get him some help."

"*Will* he go to prison?"

"Honestly? He's an accessory to arson. But much will depend on his testimony and what he's willing to do to break ties with the gang. I can't promise anything. But I'll help."

"I don't know how to thank you," Rio said.

SHE WAS WORTHLESS the rest of the day, every nerve frayed waiting and praying for Paul to call. She'd gone so far as to open a novel in her room when her cell phone finally buzzed in her pocket. Digging it out, she went limp with relief at the number.

"Paul!"

"Rio. That was the truth? They got the asshole?"

"The police talked to me in person."

"You aren't just setting me up with the cops again?"

Her heart went out to him despite herself. "I can't promise you're done with the police, but it won't be me who turns you in. Hector, though? I'd hang him from the nearest lynching tree."

"I don't know where he is. He split after the last run-in. He don't want to get caught."

"Can you at least get him a message to say Boyfriend can't hurt him?"

"I can try. Where are you? Where's Bonnie?"

She looked around the bare bones space that had been her sanctuary for five weeks. "I'm not telling you until Hector is caught. But if he's really disappeared, I'll meet you somewhere. I've been worried."

"You don't hafta worry." A hint of the old Paul came through his exhaustion.

"Where are *you*?" she asked.

"A friend of Juan's cousin has a place out on the other side of Lake Calhoun. I haven't seen nobody in the Browns and Whites in two weeks. I'm a freakin' upstanding citizen. I really want to see Bonnie."

"Inigo, you big dumb jerk. You'd better be dang sure you're telling me the truth if you want to see her. She's truly safe for the first time in her life."

Silence and then, "That's good. That's real good. I'll call you in a couple of days."

"It better be you who does the calling."

A soft chuckle filled the space between them. "Bye, *Mamacita*."

Rio slumped into the chair next to the small table that held her laptop. She didn't use the computer for much. News. Gathering information about cheap hay ... She wriggled the mouse and stared absently at the wallpaper—a running, gold-and-flaxen palomino.

She wondered if her little filly would ever look like this. She had a fighting chance now, but Rio might never know.

Or did she really have to leave?

The phone call with Paul had shaken everything back up. Her life in Minneapolis wasn't truly finished. Perhaps Paul wouldn't be able to travel to Wyoming. She didn't exactly have the job. There were so many things she'd miss if she left Bridge Creek. Glory. Andy. Thirty-one ... David. Oh David.

She moved the mouse again, and her eyes lit on the mail icon. The number four stared back at her. Curiously, she opened her inbox, and her stomach lurched. The top three e-mails were from Coyote Creek Ranch. She hovered over the first message, and clicked.

Dear Rio. We were extremely impressed with your résumé and your letter. I hope you've had time to explore

*our website and learn a little about our facility. We'd like
to offer you . . .*

Her hand flew to her mouth.

Well. Damn.

"NO! THERE'S NO discussion." Bonnie shot laser-hot fury
across the kitchen from her narrowed black eyes. "You
said it yourself. We lost that dream. We have to start new.
Well, I've started new. I love this school. I love Dawson.
I'm not going anywhere."

"It's the answer to all our problems."

"I don't have problems, Rio. You didn't either. What
happened to make you so unhappy again?"

"I'm not unhappy."

Rio had expected anger, but this was not the petulant
foot-stomping of an immature teen. This was an angry
young woman making valid arguments.

"We have the perfect setup here. This *could* be our
answer, you know."

"We cannot stay here forever. One way or another, we
need to stand on our own. Give us a chance, Bons."

"You take this chance." She turned. "I'm not going
with you."

"Bonnie!"

She ignored the call, stalked out of the room, and seconds later banged out her anger on the stair treads heading for her room. Rio rested her elbows on the island and
buried her face in her hands.

"She needs a firmer hand you know." Kate rested

a perfect hip against the kitchen door and folded her arms.

"Excuse me? You were eavesdropping?"

"It seems to happen a lot around here," she countered.

"Well, this is none of your business."

"She's always allowed to do exactly as she pleases," Kate continued. "And nobody likes that she's still got potential contact with gang members, or that you're talking with your brother, who could bring them all to the doorstep."

"Are you *blaming* my sister for our situation?"

"I'm saying she's had way too much exposure to violence and she talks to you like a bratty child. If I were in charge, she'd be going to a private school for extremely bright girls."

"Thank God you're not in charge."

"I'm not alone in this. We've talked about it."

"We?"

"Stella. Colin. David."

"I don't believe you."

And she didn't. This was Kate. Still spoiled, still flirting with David, still Bonnie's ideal. Kate would like nothing better than for Rio to leave. She'd say anything.

"What's going on?" David entered clad in the tight gray T-shirt Rio liked best on him, his breeches, and his chaps. She went weak in the knees before she steeled herself. "I just saw your sister do the oddest thing," he said. "She climbed out her window and ran off down the road."

"What?" Rio turned reflexively toward the door.

"Did you just see Bonnie climb down the side of the

house, or am I mad as a March hare?" Stella popped in, confused and laughing.

"What did I tell you?" Kate asked. "She's out of control."

"For cripes' sake, Kate. I'm not sending Bonnie to a private girl's school. Didn't you ever sneak out a window when you were a kid?"

"Certainly not."

Rio threw up her hands. "Well, that shouldn't surprise me, I guess. You ought to try it. Might loosen you up a little."

"David, haven't we all said that Bonnie needs some time in a good private school?"

"Private schools are wonderful, nurturing places, pet," Stella said.

David frowned. "I agreed that Bonnie is worth putting anywhere she'll be safe and protected. If that's a private school, I'm all for it."

"All for it!" Rio glared at him. "Are you serious?"

"Aren't you serious about protecting her?"

Rio couldn't even get angry. Things had gone from bad to out-of-control in this house. She was outmaneuvered, outplanned, outgunned. She'd promised to let David deal with his family as he needed to, but they'd brainwashed him and that would last long after they were gone. Furiously, she grabbed the letter from Coyote Creek off the counter where Bonnie had left it and shoved it in David's hands.

"This is where she'll be safe, David. No need to worry about a private school, which I damn well can't afford anyway. I'm going to accept the job. I'm giving Bud two weeks' notice tomorrow. Bonnie and her dangerous criminal groupies will be safely out of your hair soon enough."

DAVID TURNED IN utter confusion to Kate and his mother once Rio had gone. "What did you say to her?" he asked.

"The truth," Kate replied. "Her sister is out of control. David, you said yourself that you didn't like her being in touch with the old gang members. She's fighting to stay with them."

He looked at his mother beseechingly.

"Love," she said. "Bonnie's a sweet girl. She deserves better than her sister can give her."

"That's enough," he commanded. He'd never seen this side of his mother. He'd never paid any attention to the way she manipulated him or anyone else. But Kate was his mother on steroids. And suddenly, he knew he didn't have to pamper either of them anymore. Nor did he have to be mean to be firm. He almost laughed as he took his mother by the shoulders. "Stella Pitts-Matherson, you evil old blouse. You are not welcome to speak that way of a girl I've become very close to. Rio is an amazing woman, and she's raised Bonnie to be that sweet girl you talk of.

"Katherine. You've become hard since I knew you. I'm sorry if I ever gave you reason to think you could win me back, but you cannot. Ever. I moved on long ago. Now, I would love to have you stay for your full time here, another two weeks, is it? Or, and I say this with all firmness, the decorating budget is exhausted, the parties are over. If you feel like you could get more done back in England,

I'll dip into the scholarship budget to help pay for a ticket switch. I love you both—do whatever makes the most sense. Now I'm going to find Rio and, I hope, Bonnie, before they run away from home."

HE WAS TOO late. The trust he'd built had been breached—Rio's family had been violated. He couldn't explain away to Rio's satisfaction what he'd said about Bonnie. Although his mother and Kate elected to leave early and seemed relieved to do so, David couldn't convince Rio to stay.

Ten days after his mother flew out, Rio stood by her car beside her furious sister, two small suitcases, and Thirty-one. There was no sense in leaving the cat. She'd captured Rio's heart, and vice versa, in a way David had failed to do.

"I will miss the hell out of you," he said, checking to where Bonnie sobbed in Dawson's embrace.

"I wouldn't have survived this without you," she said. "You know that's true."

"Don't go," he said, for the thousandth time.

"We have different visions," she replied for the thousandth and first. "I need this. God knows it'll be good for Bonnie, too. She'll figure it out."

She reached up on tiptoes then and kissed him before he could do it. She made it aching and hot and deep. She choked on her tears when she pulled away.

"I hope it's what you want it to be," he made himself say.

"It will be. I hope the same for your partnership."

He didn't reply.

She hugged Andy. She hugged Dawson. She hugged Kim. And watching her drive away was like having a thousand tears to the edges of his heart—not lethal but permanently crippling and excruciatingly painful. When he finally turned away, his father was watching the dust tail with pensive eyes.

Chapter Thirty-Three

COLIN STAYED THREE weeks longer than the women, but he was leaving at last. David watched with little emotion as his father approached. Three more hours and David would leave for Minneapolis-Saint Paul International. Then he'd spend the night with Chase at Crossroads. Where *she'd* come into his life, triggered an avalanche of change, and, nine weeks later, left him down one cat and a fully functioning heart but up one partner.

A very bad trade.

But the eight-thousand-dollar deductible on his insurance claim had been paid, and the hole in the barn existed no more. Rio had been right. People with connections simply snapped their fingers and trouble evaporated.

"So, your Good Samaritan act with the rescue horses has paid off." His father joined him at the fence. The horses were still scruffy and most far too ribby, but each had a shine back in its eye and they'd all started to play—nipping and chasing—like healthy horses. He wished Rio could see the changes.

"They'll be fine now," he said. "The two already adopted are doing well."

"That little chestnut has some potential," his father said.

"And that gray." David pointed.

"Agreed."

"So." Colin's hesitation was uncharacteristic. "I'm off to England for Christmas."

"Oh?"

"Your mum's invited me."

"Get off it, Da'."

"Right, yeah?"

Didn't that bloody well figure? Even old Colin would get his happily-ever-after.

"Just don't send me any details."

"I thought perhaps you'd like to join us."

The whole request made no sense to his brain. "Da', thanks. But I don't think the finances will bear that yet. Go. Make nice with me mum. You two never should have split."

His father grunted. "Best thing for it at the time." After a moment's silence he shrugged into the distance. "Have you heard from her?"

David knew exactly who he meant. "Very little. Dawson hears from Bonnie, who's miserable. However, the job is legitimate and busy. The ranch is huge. And they have horses to ride."

A stab of sadness hit at that. He'd known there'd be holes when she left. He hadn't foreseen how deep they'd be or that he'd fall into one pretty much every other minute.

"Sounds like what she wanted, doesn't it?" Colin nodded. "So, almost time to go. You're making your way with young Carter, then?"

Barely, David thought. "He's a hard-arse. Needs a bit of polish and some people skills, but he's got talent. He's you without understanding."

"You think I have understanding? There's a shock."

"I said you don't understand me, not everything."

"True. I stopped understanding you when you cocked up your discharge—"

"Don't. Don't you dare . . ." But Rio's words came to him again: "You'll never forgive your father until you forgive yourself." Lord, how he'd been trying. "You know what, no. I hope you do bring that up again one day—when you want to know what really happened. To me. Not to you."

A sharp voice carried from inside the barn. "That's it, Mr. Manning. We no longer have need of your help here."

David exchanged a confused look with his father but then anger blazed through his gut. He sprinted to the barn and found Andy and Carter faced off like two school yard bullies, purple-faced and huffing. A bucket lay sideways on the floor, grain splattered across the aisle.

"What the bloody hell is going on?" David demanded.

"This man of yours can't follow simple directions. He was about to overfeed this horse by three times what it should get. It's not his first mistake. And he's rude and slow. You need to economize around here. You start with him."

Andy said nothing. He stared at the ground, fists clenched, jaw twitching. Bruce Banner about to become Hulk. "Why do you let them walk all over you?" Rio had asked. "Where's the great survivalist?"

Damn, she'd been too right. He'd tried so hard to gain acceptance from his family over the years that he'd cheated himself. He'd learned it from his mother. And with his father he'd nearly sold his soul to the devil to gain acceptance. For the first time he saw the answer to every one of his problems clearly. It would be better to lose the farm than lose his self-respect. Than to lose Rio.

"Carter. You've just overstepped your place by a margin too great to make up. As of this moment I'm reneging on our agreement."

"Now, wait just a minute." Carter sputtered like a dying car. "We have a legally binding contract. I'm not going anywhere."

"I'll have a lawyer here in half an hour, you flaming idiot. How dare you presume you have the right to fire my staff. For your information, if there was a mistake made, it wasn't Andy's. He's worked here for years and never once mistaken amounts of anything. That's your bloody horse, you check the feeding instructions. They will be wrong."

"Now, cool it down, laddie." His father stepped in. "This is not a disaster. Just a misunderstanding."

"Sod off," David said. Their fragile goodwill disintegrated

"I've got money invested in this place," Carter spat.

"You'll get every penny back. So pack your bags and find yourself the first available ticket. Head back with your mentor here. Keep the act together."

"That's uncalled for—" Colin began.

"No, Da'. I'll tell you what's uncalled for—letting you convince me to slink around like a second-class Pitts-Matherson for most of my life. You say I lost some sort of manliness or honor in the army. Wrong. I *gained* honor and bravery when I defied that lieutenant's stupid, ignorant order in the first place. What lost it again was listening to the army's rot when they threw me off and then listening to yours when you told me how disappointing I was.

"The best thing I've ever done is buy this place. It's mine. I built it. But still I've let Mum turn it into her personal dollhouse. And let you keep coming 'round to tell me it's not quite good enough."

"Oh, now I—"

"No." He held up a hand. "Rio was right. She was always right. This is a showplace that's crumbling under its own weight. The economy can't sustain it in this form. Rio might scrimp and find unorthodox ways out of trouble, but at least she's fighting for her dream. So, sod the pair of you. I'm about to go fight for mine."

Neither man said a word. David started down the aisle and then turned.

"Be ready in two hours, Da'. Andy, you're getting a raise."

"David."

"What? *Colin.*"

"I knew I liked that girl."

RIO SAT BACK in the Adirondack chair on the minis-
cule porch of her cabin. She pulled a wool blanket more
tightly around her shoulders and listened to the wind
howl through the hills behind her new home. To the front
of the cabin, two football fields distant, the main ranch
house glowed in the eight o'clock dark.

Idyllic.

Everything she'd ever dreamed of having hunkered
around her in a big, unbelievable package as perfect as
if she'd designed it herself. The Bighorn Mountains were
not high and craggy like the pictures of the Rockies, but
rolling and mysterious, rising up in unexpected places,
steeped in history.

Coyote Creek comprised ten thousand acres. Two
hundred head of cattle roamed the pastures, ready to be
herded by visitors. Rio had seen bighorn sheep, elk, and
mule deer. Birds filled the grasslands. And quiet? She'd
hit the jackpot on quiet. Hours and hours of it after she
left work.

Bonnie detested it just like she detested Rio. She'd
started school this week after ten days of moving and getting settled. Sheridan was forty minutes away, the little
towns of Story, Buffalo, and Gillette surrounded them.
School was a forty-five-minute bus ride. Rio told herself
she could handle Bonnie's anger; it would cool. The freedom and the safety were worth it.

Paul had turned himself in and, in exchange for giving up Hector, received a shortened sentence in a minimum-security facility. He'd done the right thing. Another reason to be thankful.

To top it off, the job was a dream. She'd already learned more than she'd known there was to learn. She'd ransacked the Internet to supplement her list of memorized family recipes, and she'd sold the ranch kitchen on four of them. Her co-workers were smart and talented, and they accepted her and even respected her.

But they didn't love her.

She didn't need their love, of course. She'd come for the solitude, the landscape devoid of bustle, smelly cars, screaming neighbors, and insane family members. Admittedly, things were too quiet sometimes. Business and crowds would pick up over the holidays, they told her, when there would be Christmas guests, hayrides, and sleigh bells.

Idyllic.

Thirty-one crept out of the neat, sparsely furnished cabin. Even the cat had mellowed in the two weeks since arriving. She clung to Rio and Bonnie and had her fill of field mice and birds to chase. Rio picked her up and snuggled her under the blanket. Life was . . . good.

The headlights that swung into her short driveway shattered the peacefulness and sent her pulse racing. Nobody came here at night. Nobody drove the property at nine-thirty. She stood and let the blanket heap to the ground. A chair scraped inside and seconds later Bonnie stood beside her.

"Who's that?"

"No idea."

"Should we lock the door?"

How ridiculous was that? Rio thought. She'd come from a gang-infested city where she'd walked the streets in inkier darkness than this. Here she was, in the quietest place she'd ever been, scared of one car.

"It's probably Don. He said he'd keep an eye out while we settled in."

The headlights blinked off.

Seconds later the dome light shone weakly as the driver's door opened. She couldn't stop the irrational fear, despite her assurances to Bonnie, that Jason's hockey mask was about to glow into view. Then the passenger door followed suit. No one said a word. Both doors closed at the same time.

Bonnie screamed first.

"Dawson? My gosh, it's Dawson!"

She leaped the three steps to the ground and flew toward the car. *Dawson?* And then a face did appear out of the colorless night. No hockey mask, just a familiar perfect smile and a smile shadowed by a handsome, unfamiliar tan cowboy hat.

"I don't expect a welcome anything like that one, but maybe a hullo?"

She muffled a gasp with one hand, and Thirty-one jumped from her hold to the blanket. She sprang to the porch railing and rubbed against David's shoulder. He snorted in amazement.

"Get that, will ya? What did you do to the cat?"

Pure joy freed itself inside of her, and she began to laugh. In one stride she picked up the cat and moved her out of the way.

"David," she whimpered, leaning over the low railing and wrapping her arms around his neck, knocking the hat back on his head in her eagerness.

"Hey you, rancher girl. There are a few things I realized I didn't get to say to you before you left."

"Yeah? No, wait, don't say them yet." She broke away, crossed to the stairs, and followed Bonnie's lead by leaping onto the lawn. He was beside her in less than a second and lifted her off the ground so she could wrap her legs around him. "Now," she said.

"I love you. I told Kate. But I never said it to you."

She laughed again. "You came all this way just for that?"

"Just for that. And a few other things."

"What's with the cowboy hat? No, shhh. My turn first." She kissed him, long and a little desperately. If this was a dream, she wanted to be sure and get it in. She pulled back, taking his bottom lip with her between her teeth and letting it go with a soft scrape. "I love you, too."

"You do?"

"I loved you the minute you clotheslined my brother the first night at Crossroads. And then you opened that gorgeous mouth and spoke like a fairy-tale prince. I was a goner."

"I only loved your hair." He laughed and kissed her—one quick taste. "And your eyes. And that feistiness and stubbornness. And bravery. The rest I took my time with."

"So what are you doing here? And . . . hold on, where did the other two go?"

"They don't want to see this. We're the old farts. They're off snogging behind the house."

"I don't want to hear that."

"Then hear this. You asked why the hat. You've always wanted a cowboy, and even though I'm far from one, I'll stay here with you, Arionna Montoya. I don't care about some stupid ten-year plan I made. I don't care about Bridge Creek if giving it up would mean I could keep you in my life. It took an army, a scrawny horse, a gorgeous redhead, and ten long years to show me I don't need more money as much as I need you. If this is your dream, then it's my dream. I'll start over."

"I hate my dream. My dream stinks." She laughed again.

"Excuse me?"

"I didn't know. I'd never been alone. Do you have any idea how lonely being alone is? I don't need solitude—not like this. Security—that's what I found with you. We were in turmoil, but the ground was rock steady. Your family is crazy, but at least it isn't going anywhere. I found people who don't leave you because there's trouble. They don't take advantage of you. They want you."

"Will you be my family, then?"

"Will you be mine? I'll even try to get along with Crazy Carter."

"Carter was an idiot. He's packed off back to Florida. I'm back to having debt up to my eyeballs, so you have your scrimping and saving work cut out for you."

"Finally. Something I'm good at."

"Madam, you are good at so very many things."

He squeezed her to him. Heat sluiced through her veins. "I don't think we can do this here. Not with those two in this little place. It's cute, but far from soundproof."

"Then how soon can you quit your new job? There's actually one room in my house you've never seen."

"Your bedroom."

"Precisely."

"How did your mum decorate that?"

"I wouldn't let her near it. It's painted beige. It's got some store-bought greenish, bluish, stripy curtain things on the window, and it's an unholy mess."

"Does it have a bed?"

"King-sized. Quite comfortable, actually."

"It sounds heavenly."

She kissed him again. This one took off on a timeline of its own, leaving them both out of breath.

"Can you two knock it off?" Dawson's voice barely fazed them. They both turned their heads, cheek resting against cheek. "We want to go inside, it's cold out here."

"It is?" David asked.

"Hadn't noticed," Rio added.

"Blech," said Bonnie.

"You two go right ahead." David straightened their kiss back out. "We're still discussing the future."

Epilogue

THE CHRISTMAS TREE sparkled against the picture window in the living room, its backdrop a postcard-perfect fall of fresh snow. Rio never tired of the lights in every shimmering color, and the glass ornaments, discount-store frugal but richly colored and plentiful. Her favorite decoration was the long garland of popcorn and cranberries they'd spent three nights stringing.

Cinnamon wafted from the kitchen where the rolls still baked for brunch in half an hour. A bayberry candle burned on the mantle, and the tree still offered up its sprucey fragrance.

Bonnie tore into a present, her fourth of the morning, with the maturity of a five-year-old and squealed when she revealed a pair of paddock boots just like the ones Rio had opened minutes before.

"Thank you, David. Thank you so much!"

"You're official now. Helmets, boots, breeches. No excuses not to be on the next Olympic team."

"Okay. Sure." She rose and gave him a huge hug. "Thanks, soon-to-be brother-in-law."

Rio grinned and stared at her present—the tangible sign Bonnie's statement was true. The promise of hundred Christmas mornings to come, according to the note that had lain in the box beside it. The diamond on her ring finger caught the brilliance from the tree lights and made a tiny Christmas rainbow on the wall. It still took her breath away.

"I have one more for you." David leaned across the couch and kissed her.

"No, David, you've given me too much already. I—"

The peal of the doorbell cut off her protest.

"Paul!" Bonnie jumped up, still clad in her pajamas and robe, and raced to the door. Five minutes later, their brother stood in the room, slightly sheepish, but smiling.

"Sorry I'm late," he said. "It's a long drive in the snow."

He'd been out of prison for three weeks. Hector, on the other hand, wouldn't be celebrating Christmas outside Stillwater Correctional Facility for ten to fifteen years. Boyfriend was awaiting trial without bail.

Rio hugged her brother tightly. David shook his hand. Paul held out a bag with three gifts in it.

"Not much," he said. "Thanks for letting me come."

"Don't be silly. You didn't need to bring anything."

They hung his jacket on the banister and ushered him to the armchair. Bonnie opened a set of notebooks and a fountain pen. David unwrapped a scarf with a Union

Jack on one end and an American flag on the other, which made him crow with delight. Rio's box was a fair amount bigger.

"What on earth?"

She unwrapped it slowly, savoring the moment with her family as much as the gift, until the box was open. Several wads of newspaper later, she covered her mouth and muffled a cry. In her hands was a vintage Breyer horse, exactly like the one she'd lost in the fire.

"Oh Paul. No way! Wherever did you find one?"

"It's not a random one," he said. "It's The One. It's yours."

"Mine? But . . . how?" Bewildered, she lost her words.

"I meant it when I told you there was never supposed to be a big fire. I didn't know he was going to use gasoline. It was just going to be a little paper fire to scare you and get Bonnie out so Hector could find that money clip. But I had a bad feeling. I snuck into your room before the time Hector was supposed to start the fire. I couldn't get all the horses, but I got about a dozen. The others are in the car outside."

Tears flowed so hard she couldn't speak.

"I know you thought we were never a family, Rio, but we were. We are, I hope. Thank you for not hating me."

She wiped her eyes and wrapped herself into his embrace. When he released her, David shook Paul's hand again, then took Rio back into his embrace.

"Okay, my last gift. I told you once that I didn't understand why anyone would get a tattoo, but I've fallen for a woman with half a dozen of them. They are as much a part of you as your red hair, your blue eyes, and your brave, unfailing heart. I know now exactly why you have them—because they keep parts of your life alive. Am I right?"

She nodded. He held out his left arm and slowly rolled up the short sleeve. Rio gasped. Encircling his bicep lay a tattooed band created from interlocked red, white, and blue infinity symbols.

She leapt into his embrace, and he held her, as closely as the brandchapter-new promise on his arm. "David, you did this for me?"

"The symbol centers are all connected love. No broken futures. Crazy families, crabby cats, rescued palominos, and all, Rio, this is forever."

She covered her eyes and the tears of joy she couldn't stop, but David gently pried her fingers free and held them tightly. Thirty-one meowed and twined in a figure eight through their legs as a long, endless kiss sealed the promise.

Continue reading for an excerpt from

THE RANCHER AND THE ROCK STAR

and

RESCUED BY A STRANGER

Available now!

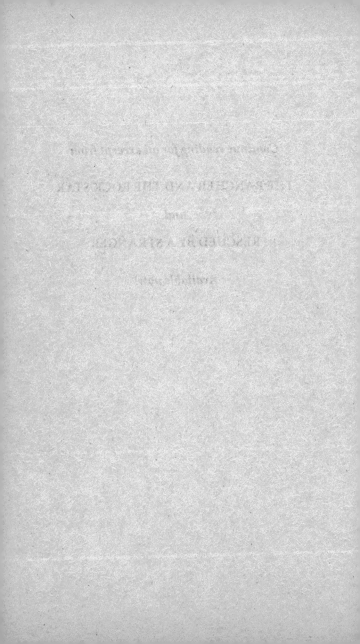

An Excerpt from

THE RANCHER AND THE ROCK STAR

FATE WAS A nasty flirt.

Gray Covey dropped his forehead to the steering wheel of his rented Chevy Malibu and sighed, a plaintive release of breath, like a balloon with a pinhole leak. He had no idea what he'd done to her, but Fate had been after him for months. After this last wrong turn in her twisted maze, he knew she'd finally trapped him.

The long, pitted road before him wasn't described in the useless directions scribbled on the slip of paper in his hand. Neither were the two branches fanning left and right fifty yards away. And being lost wasn't enough. Oh-ho, no. On top of everything, Fate had hung an angry, bruise-colored sky about to unleash enough water to terrify Noah.

He lifted his eyes, rubbing the creases above his brow. As he prepared to admit defeat, the edge of a small sign to the left caught his eye, and his first small hope sparked.

Inching the Malibu over the washboard road, he pulled up to the hand-lettered sign he'd been told to look for. Hope flared into gratitude.

Hallelujah. *Jabberwicki Ranch.*

Still unable to believe someone would give a piece of property such a stupid-ass name, he stopped short of laughing. Half an hour ago, a dour attendant named Dewey at the only gas station in Kennison Falls, Minnesota, had made it clear nobody in the town of eight hundred souls laughed at anything Abby Stadtler–related. The woman Gray sought was no less than revered.

And yet . . .

The saintly Abby Stadtler was harboring a missing child.

His.

He rolled past the Jibberjabber sign, stopping at side-by-side black mailboxes. *A. Stadtler—Jabberwicki* and *E. Mertz.* Ethel Mertz. What?

Alice in Wonderland meets *I Love Lucy*?

"You've got to be kidding me." He spoke out loud without meaning to. Out of habit he checked over his shoulder to make sure he hadn't been followed and overheard.

This explained why Dawson had been so hard to find—he'd fallen down a friggin' rabbit hole. The sophomoric humor helped him remember he was only half serious about throttling his runaway son to within an inch of his life. And it kept him distanced from emotions that had been scraped raw in the past weeks. His current jinxed concert tour aside, between his mother's worsening illness, moving her to the care facility, and Dawson's disappearance within days of that, life lately had been sorely lacking in humor.

Except, maybe, for Ariel. In his ex-wife's case, all he could do was laugh. "They've found Dawson," she'd announced on the phone the night before in her clipped British accent. "But unless you want the authorities to fetch him, you'll have to pick him up, darling. I can't leave Europe with the baby."

Of course not. After all, only six weeks had passed since their son's disappearance—nobody could make arrangements for a two-year-old on such short notice.

Gray had not been about to let the police "fetch" his son, nor had he wanted to alert Dawson and send the boy running again. So here he was in Jabbitybobbits, Minnesota, despite the monumental nightmare he'd caused by leaving his manager, his baffled band members, and eighteen thousand fans in the lurch.

Well, what the hell? It was just Fate adding another hilarious disaster to the worst tour in rock history. Re-focusing, he looked left toward a homey log house, then right into a thick stand of pine and oak. Which fork led to Ethel Mertz and which to The Jabberwock's ranch?

Eeny, meeny, miny . . . He couldn't get lost if he stayed right. Slowly he drove toward the trees and didn't see the diminutive, elderly woman staring at him until he'd drawn even with where she stood in an opulent flower garden near the road. For a moment he considered stopping, but her assessing glower and the stern set to her square-jowled face convinced him to settle for an impersonal wave and continue around the gentle curve through the woods. He hoped the dour watchwoman wasn't the much-adored Abby Stadtler.

The house he *hoped* belonged to Jabberwocket ... *Ranch?* didn't appear until he was in its front yard—an old, two-story farmhouse painted non-traditional Guinness brown with windows and doors trimmed in blue and white. A disheveled patch of shaggy, colorful wildflowers, much less immaculate than the garden he'd just passed, stretched along one side.

The growl of thunder greeted Gray as he exited the car, and he looked with concern at smoke-bellied thunderheads piling high. The end-of-May breeze smelled wet and thick. In front of a small garage stood an older, red Explorer, and on his left a short stone path led to a porch wrapping two sides of the house.

After mounting two loose steps, he faced a pair of dusty saddles, the kind with big, sturdy horns in front, sitting on sawhorses, and several flowerpots in various stages of being planted. A small square of black electrical tape covered the doorbell. He knocked, got no answer, then knocked again. Several minutes later he returned to the driveway, searching his surroundings. Down another gravel slope, a couple hundred yards away, stood a vintage barn, its white paint worn and the haymow window boarded-up from the inside. He sighed and climbed back into his car.

Heady scents of hay, sawdust, and animals hung in the heavy air when he left the Malibu once again. To his delight, a golden retriever loped toward him with lolling tongue and giant doggy smile. "Hey fella." Gray scratched the dog's ears. "Got a boss around here somewhere?"

A muffled *thunk* answered. Ahead, backed up against the open door of the barn, stood a flatbed trailer loaded high with spring-green hay. The golden led him to the wagon front, and a pair of small, gloved hands emerged from inside the barn, grabbed the twine on one bale, and yanked it out of sight. Intrigued, he watched until the owner of the hands popped from the dim barn interior. She placed her palms on the flatbed and, in one graceful movement, hoisted her long-legged body to a stand. Reaching for a top-tier bale, she dragged on it, toppling the entire stack. Gray's brows lifted in appreciation.

"Afternoon," he called.

Her startled cry rang more like a bell than a screech of fear, but she stared at him with her mouth in a pretty *oh* and her chest heaving. "Jeez Louise!" she said at last. "You scared me half to death!"

Flawless skin was flushed with exertion, and her round, bright eyes flashed uncertainty. A thick, soft pile of chestnut made a haphazard bun atop her head, but long wisps of hair had escaped and swung to her shoulders. Her face stopped Gray's thoughts dead. It was not the toughened visage he'd have expected of a woman who chucked hay bales like a longshoreman. The elegant, doe-eyed face belonged in a magazine, not a barn.

"I'm really sorry," he said.

A rumpled, hay-flecked, flannel shirt hung loose over body-hugging, faded jeans that had suffered one nicely-placed rip across her left thigh. He braced for the inevitable squeal of recognition.

"Can I help you with something?" She squinted at him for a few seconds, but rather than squeal, she shook her head and pulled down another stack of hay.

"Are you Abby Stadtler?"

"Yes." She continued dragging bales, and he sighed in relief.

"I'm looking for my son."

That stopped her. "Son?" Her eyes took on a glint of protectiveness. "Who are you?"

That stopped him. For an instant his vanity stung, but the freedom of unaccustomed anonymity hit, and he allowed a private grin. "David Graham." He used his official alias. "Pleased to meet you."

"Likewise," she said. "Excuse my rudeness, but this hay has to get in that barn before the storm hits. I can't help you with your son. I don't know anybody named Graham."

Abby Stadtler hopped to the ground. The plaid shirt swung open to reveal a bright blue tank top hugging a curvy hip. "My boy isn't Graham," he said, meeting her eyes, which were unlike anything he'd ever seen. Greenish? Blue-ish? "He's Dawson. Dawson Covey."

"I know a Dawson. His last name is Cooper."

He tamped down a flicker of irritation, as she grabbed twine, swung a bale, and took two steps to dump it in the barn. There was not a single sound of exertion—or any hint she was taking him seriously.

"Yes, that would be my devious son." He held onto a pleasant tone. "Cooper is his grandmother's name."

"And why would he use a different name?"

As she turned the interrogation on him, a rope of tension twisting down his neck knotted between his shoulder blades and threatened to stiffen him top to toe. He willed his fingers to uncurl, one-by-one. "Because he's sixteen years old, he's pissed off at his mother and is hiding from me. He's also sharp as a knife blade, so it's taken us a while to find him. You've obviously never had teenagers."

An immediate illusion of height accompanied the steeling of her spine, and the soft, nameless color of her eyes turned to stormy aquamarine. "You shouldn't make assumptions." She tossed another hay bale, and Gray took a step backward.

"I apologize. I only meant you don't look old enough to have teenagers." That was true.

"If that was an attempt at getting yourself off the hook, it was smooth but ineffective." The sharpest prickles left her voice.

Finally, she stopped tossing and crossed her arms. The rolled-up sleeves on her overshirt exposed slender forearms with sexy lines of definition curved along the muscle.

Gray produced his best version of a devilish grin. "Dang. I usually have better luck with a silver tongue."

"I'll just bet. Look, Mr. Graham." She hesitated. "Wait a minute. Did you say sixteen?"

"Yup. My Dawson is sixteen. How old is yours?"

She didn't respond to the humor. "Eighteen. We definitely have some confusion here. I hired a young man six weeks ago to help around the farm. He'll be leaving for home in another month. Colorado."

Gray snorted. "He'll be leaving for Colorado over my dead body."

"Mr. Graham." Her voice flashed with annoyance to match her eyes. "I think you have the wrong Dawson. People must have mixed up the information they gave you."

"I do not have the wrong Dawson." Slamming his palm on the wooden bed of the hay wagon hard enough to cause flakes of alfalfa, and Abby Stadtler, to jump, the humor Gray had been using so desperately as a shield disintegrated. His make-nice smiles hardened into anger lines he could feel. "Look, Madam Jabberingwickets, or whatever the hell this place is called. You've got my son." He jabbed his fingers into a back pocket, yanked out his wallet, and flipped through the three pictures that were part of its meager contents. "Tell me this isn't the little con artist you call Dawson Cooper."

The photo was two years old, but it did the trick. Abby leaned over it with skepticism, and then her shoulders sagged. "Oh no."

"Oh yes."

"I, I'm sorry."

He gave her points for the apology, although she looked for all the world as if she didn't want to give it. "It's all right." He calmed his voice. "All I want is to find my son."

"I've never heard Dawson mention a father. He's talked about his mother in New York."

In a stinging sort of way that made sense, Dawson wouldn't want to mention his dad's notoriety. He jammed the wallet back into his pocket. "She's not in New York. They live in London, and he packed up and left his private school just after Easter last month. Didn't you check him out before letting him move in?"

Anger flared in her face again. For some reason, Gray found the rising and falling storms in her seawater eyes knee-weakening. "You *really* need to stop making judgments. What you just said was condescending and insulting."

She turned her back and grabbed another hay bale, tossing it willy-nilly into a pile along with the others already in the barn. This one went a fair distance with the steam of her anger behind it. He couldn't help but grin in admiration. Abby Stadtler was soft and enticing as a chocolate éclair on the outside, with TNT instead of custard beneath the surface.

"Look, I don't know you . . ."

"That's right." Her fuse obviously still sparked, she clambered onto the wagon again. "For your information, your son had a New York driver's license, references from a past employer, and a personal reference. No, I didn't do an FBI background check on him. Up until now, I've had no reason to suspect I needed to. I don't know where you come from, but around here we try our hardest to believe the best of people."

Gray scarcely heard beyond the fact Dawson had come up with faked reference documents. He didn't know whether to be horrified or impressed as hell.

"I . . . That's amazing." He tried finding some amusement in her face, but she kept yanking hay bales from the pile, her back flexing, captivating him. He wondered where Mr. Stadtler was. "Abby . . . Mrs. Stadtler." He struggled not to anger her again. "I told you my son is smart. I forgot how smart. He's pulled off a professional-level scam here, and I can't tell you how grateful I am he came to a safe place like this."

She threw a glance over her shoulder, her eyes no longer sizzling. "He's a good boy, Mr. Graham, even now that I know the truth. Not that he won't get a proper lecture."

The very first hint of humor tinged her voice, and Gray grinned back, relief sweet in his chest. "You'd be justified. So, where is he?" Realization struck him. "Why isn't he helping?"

"He isn't here."

His attention snapped back to her. "Excuse me?"

"He and Kim are gone for the weekend."

"Gone! Gone?" Gray balled his fists and wanted to hurl a hay bale across the barn himself. "Gone where? And who the—" He took a deep breath. "Who is Kim?"

"The teenager you thought it obvious I never had." This time her eyes danced with a hint of laughter, and if her newfound cheerfulness hadn't come at his expense he'd have found the crinkled corners of her eyes appealing.

"When will he be back from wherever he went? With your teenage daughter." He forced his voice to stay modulated and pleasant.

"They've been on a retreat with the church youth group all week. They'll be back tomorrow late morning."

"Tomorrow?" *Another day?* Gray lost his hold on calm. "Damn it!"

He stalked from the hay wagon. The cloying air pressed heavier with every step, and the clouds encroached, purple and black. Thunder reverberated, close, angry. He had another show in Chicago tomorrow night. No way could he miss it, too. What would Chris do when he found out tonight's gig hadn't needed to be canceled at all?

Slipping his hand into the pocket of his leather blazer, he fumbled for a pack of cigarettes. He hated them. He was down to half a pack a day, but times like this he despaired of ever kicking the habit. With automatic skill he drew one out, flicked his lighter flame against the end of the cigarette, and took a drag.

The idea of Chris Boyle on a rant made Gray swear under his breath again. Everything came down to money for his manager. Sometimes Gray felt like no more than a wind-up monkey who waddled onstage, banged its cymbals together, made the crowd screech, and raked in the dough. He dug his fingers through his hair and started a vicious second drag—

Thwack!

The cigarette flew from his lips as if a bullwhip had snatched it, and he choked on air and smoke.

"Are you really this phenomenally stupid?" Abby, her face florid, her posture like a boxer ready to jab, ground her boot toe into the smoldering cigarette until shattered pulp remained.

"What the . . .?" He stared at the ruins then into her furious eyes.

"This is a barn. Fifty feet away is a wagon loaded with hay. Do you have any idea what a gust of wind could do with one of your stupid ashes?"

"Oh, damn, Abby, Mrs. . . . Abby. I'm sorry." Contrition twisted his gut.

He *hadn't* considered the danger before lighting up. Her gaze drilled into his, and regret gave way to a slow roll of deep, unexpected attraction. Earlier they'd been separated by hay and irritation, but now they were separated by nothing but five inches of steamy, sultry air. An asinine string of thoughts ran through his brain: how smooth her cheek was up close; how the middle of her pupil was soft and calm like the eye of a hurricane; how much he wished he had a breath mint.

"It won't happen again."

Along with his sudden, inappropriate desire came an image of Fate laughing as he got pummeled by Mr. Abby Stadtler—who probably always carried breath mints. Then, without warning, Abby's face drained of color. Slowly, she covered her mouth with one slender hand.

ABBY PRESSED SO hard against her lips she could almost feel pulses in her fingertips—ten runaway jackhammers. Every clue, every suspicion, crashed over her as she stared at the earnest-eyed man before her. How in the world had she missed it? What was he doing in her farmyard?

When he said, "It won't happen again," his thick brows furrowed in honest apology, his rich baritone was suddenly, obviously, as familiar as her daughter's voice. And his pale blue eyes were ones she'd seen as many times as she'd entered her child's bedroom, only this time they mesmerized in person, not from a dozen posters on Kim's walls.

He'd given it away himself. "Dawson Covey."

Oh, Lord, she'd slapped a cigarette from Gray Covey's mouth.

Strangled laughter caught at her throat. This was far from the meeting fantasized by ten thousand adoring women at any given time. What did you say to a rock legend after you'd called him a liar? She dropped her hands from her mouth. "You—"

His face changed. The instant before she'd recognized him, he'd shown honest contrition. Now his mouth slipped into a strange, plastic smile, automatic, a little self-satisfied. Her annoyance sparked. It reminded her why, despite his knee-weakening looks, he'd irritated her with his assumptions and attitude. All at once, she didn't want to give him the satisfaction of fawning over his identity.

"Sorry." She forced herself to spin away and pull off a fib. "I just got a mental picture of my barn going up in flames. I accept your apology. But know this. If it *does* happen again, I won't be knocking the cigarette out of your mouth. I'll be drowning it with you attached."

Ignoring his celebrity left her uplifted, as if she was going against nature—something her practical streak rarely allowed. She half-expected him to protest with wounded pride but, in fact, he remained silent until she was back at the hay wagon.

"You're funny even when you're mad," he said. "I guess I consider myself lucky."

"My daughter wouldn't say I'm funny." She half-grinned, although her back was to him.

"Speaking of your daughter and, by association it seems, my son. I don't suppose there's any way of getting them home early? I was hoping to take him with me tonight."

Irritation seized her again, and she glared over her shoulder. Her breath caught now that she recognized who he was, but she shook it off. "Dawson's been living here for almost six weeks. Won't it be kinder to give him time to adjust?"

"You do understand he's a runaway, right?" His voice lifted a notch in irritation. "You have no claim to him. Not to mention, a lot of people have been put out by your . . . employee."

"Put out? How about worried? Has anyone been worried in all the time it took to locate him?" Immediately Abby regretted the thoughtless words. Gray's features stilled, and his eyes iced. "I'm sorry. That was rude of me . . ."

The first plop of rain hit her dead on the nose, followed by a second on her head. Her heart sank. She'd let herself get distracted, and now she risked losing the eighty bales of hay still on the rack if they got soaked.

"Crap, crap, crap." For half a second she waffled between Gray and the hay wagon. She groaned and chose the hay. "I'm sorry. Can you finish this discussion from the barn?"

Two more fat drops left splotches on her shoulders, and she hoisted herself back up onto the wagon. Normally, she didn't mind stacking hay. It taxed her body while anesthetizing her brain. But even if she threw as hard as she could she wouldn't beat this storm.

"I worried about him." Gray's voice held as much promise of thunder as the storm.

"I didn't mean that." She pulled two stacks of bales into heaps with one movement, and they banged into her legs, nearly knocking her off balance. More rain splashed her cheeks. "At least, I didn't mean it to sound so harsh."

"Let's just call us even for assumptions. The point is, I flew from Chicago and am missing work to be here. I'm sure this will sound even crasser to you, but I have appointments I can't miss. My job involves more than just me and a boss."

Two bales. Three. Four.

"So you thought you'd simply grab your son and, what, take him to work with you?"

"As a matter of fact, that's exactly what I thought. I'm his father. I have considered what's best for him."

Five. Six. Seven. Abby heaved the hay just far enough to get it into the barn door. She could stack it later. Her arms started to sting from their exaggerated motions, but she knew how to ignore the discomfort.

"I'm sure that's true." She grunted with exertion. "But wouldn't you like to know why he ran away in the first place, before you haul him off again?"

"Lady." His taut voice caused her to look into his angry face. "I don't know if you think you're some sort of pop psychiatrist, but I'm not the sixteen-year-old here. I know why my son ran and, frankly, I don't blame him. But, it's not your business, and I don't have the freedom to hang around waiting for him to come back."

The drops fell faster, and the breeze picked up. An eerie twilight settled over the farm.

"Seems to me you do what you have to do where your children are concerned. Sacrifice. Ask yourself what your priorities are." She tossed harder. The tender alfalfa leaves in the fragrant bundles glistened with moisture. In ten minutes the bales would be soaked deep. The rain saturated her shirt, and the tendrils escaping her loose chignon clung to her cheeks.

"You're something, you know that? You warn me about making assumptions then tell me my priorities are screwed up. Who the hell do you think you are?"

The knife-blade edge to his voice made her stop and blink. She'd concentrated so hard on fighting the rain that she'd forgotten her actual fight with the person next to her. Lecture mode always seemed to slip out when she multi-tasked, but Gray's glare of unequivocal anger told her she'd stepped over the line. Although the water beating into her hay made her cringe, she looked him in the eye.

"I'm sorry," she began, but something fluttered in her chest, and she caught her breath in surprise. He didn't look exactly like any picture of him she'd ever seen— and Kim had scrapbooks full of clippings and magazine photos. Three dimensions served him incredibly well. "You're right." She reined in her emotions. "I've grown fond of your son, Mr. . . . Graham. But I don't have the right to be protective of him."

The anger drained from his eyes, but his body remained a study of sculpted seriousness. Cocoa-colored hair feathered back from his forehead and framed his high cheekbones with thick locks that kissed his collar. A chiseled Adam's apple bobbed when he swallowed, and Abby's stomach fluttered again. If the rock-and-roll lifestyle was supposed to ravage a body, Gray Covey's hadn't paid attention to the rule.

Unable to ignore her hay any longer, she pulled her gaze from Gray's, jumped off the wagon, and began dragging bales. This time her back muscles whined with every surge.

"I don't suppose you could wait to finish until this passes?" he asked. He held up his palm to show he knew the answer. The rain on the old barn roof drummed like the backbeat on one of his songs. A flash of lightning slashed the dark sky, and thunder followed mere seconds later. He shucked off his leather jacket. "Aw, hell."

An Excerpt from

RESCUED BY A STRANGER

THE DOG IN the middle of the road was all legs and mottled black patches. It stood still beside the yellow center-line, a good fifty feet away but too close to ignore, and Jill Carpenter eased off the accelerator of her Chevy Suburban.

"Get out of the way, sweetie," she murmured, switching her foot to the brake.

Because she'd worked at the only vet clinic in Kennison Falls since junior high school, she knew most of the dogs in the area. This one, however, was shabbily unfamiliar. And stubbornly unmoving. It stared at her with a mutt-in-the-headlights look that didn't bode well.

Finally, twenty feet from the unblinking animal, Jill blared her horn and stomped her brakes until the anti-lock system grabbed, and loose pebbles pinged the chassis like buckshot. At the very last moment the dog leaped—directly in front of her.

Accidents supposedly happened in slow motion, but no leisurely parade of her life played before her eyes. The jerk of her steering wheel, her shriek, a blur of darting, raggedy fur, and the boulder of dread dropping into the pit of her stomach all happened in something under five nanoseconds.

Then her stomach dropped again as it followed the nose of her truck across the narrow county road and down a six-foot ditch. The Suburban gave a carnival-ride fishtail, its rear axle grinding in protest. Something warm spurted into her face, and she came to rest parallel to the road on the steep ditch bank, wedged in precarious place against a slender maple sapling.

For a moment, all she noticed was her own wheezing breath—her lungs forcing twice as much carbon dioxide out as they sucked oxygen in.

Had she missed the dog? She was sure she had. Please let her have missed the dog. Her heart pounded in concern until she peered out her windshield, shifted to see better, and the Suburban rocked. The dog's fate was forgotten in a gasp.

The world was sideways.

Something sticky ran down one cheek, and an old Counting Crows song filled the truck interior. The turn signal *ploink-ploinked* to the music like a metronome. Through the windshield and up to her right she could see the edge of the road. To her left through her driver's window lay the bottom of the ditch three feet below. All she'd have to do was shift the wrong way, and she'd be roof down, hanging from her seat belt.

A flurry of sailor-approved words charged through her mind, but her frantic heartbeat choked them off before they turned into sound—almost certainly a good thing, since the air stream caused by swearing would probably be enough to roll her. She pressed her lips together and tried to slow her respiration. Her shoulder, jammed against the door, ached slightly, her seat belt effectively throttled her, but as far as she could tell, she hadn't hit her head.

The Creature, her un-pet name for the vehicle she'd detested since buying it, growled as if angry its spinning back tire wasn't getting anywhere. "Crap!" Jill shot her arm forward, ignoring the pinch of her seat belt, and turned the key.

The truck rocked again, the Crows quit Counting, and the turn signal halted its irritating pinging. At last time stopped whizzing past like an old Super 8 movie, and her thoughts careened into each other with a little less force.

This was definitely going to wreck an already no-good, very bad day.

Sudden pounding startled her, rocking the SUV again. She swiveled her head to the passenger window and let loose a terrified scream. Pressed to the glass was a smoosh-nosed, flattened-featured face. Jill squeezed her eyes shut.

"Ma'am? Ma'am? Can you hear me?" The window-pane muffled the gargoyle's voice.

Slowly Jill forced her eyes open, and the face pulled back. Her panic dissipated as the nose unflattened, lengthening into straightness with perfect oval flares at its tip, and divided a strong, masculine face into two flawless halves. Inky, disheveled bangs fell across deep furrows in his forehead. For an instant Jill forgot her straits, and her mouth went dry. A brilliant sculptor somewhere was missing his masterwork.

"Can you get the window down?" he shouted, refocusing her attention on the phone in his hand. "I'm calling 911. Can you tell me where you're hurt?"

Intense navy-blue eyes pierced her for answers, her pulse accelerated, and embarrassed heat infused her face. "No!" she called. Shaking off her adrenaline-fueled hormones and forcing her brain to function, Jill turned her key once more to activate the accessory system and twisted to punch the window button, jostling The Creature. "No!" she gasped again, as the glass whirred into the door frame. "No calls. I'm fine."

"You are not fine, honey. Stay still now." His drawl was comforting and sing-songy—born of the South.

Truly confused, Jill watched him swipe the face of his phone. He might be the best-looking Samaritan between her predicament and the Iowa border, but although she *was* balanced pretty precariously, his intensity was a tick past overreactive.

"Honestly. All I need is to get out of this murderous truck without rolling it on top of me."

His eyes switched from worry to the kind of sympathy a person used when about to impart bad news. "I'm afraid your face and the front of your shirt tell a different story. You're in shock."

She peered down at herself. At first she gasped at the bright red splotches staining her white tank top. She touched her cheek and brought a red fingertip away. Strangled laughter replaced her shock. He reached for her and made the Suburban wobble.

"Don't lean!" She choked. "Seriously, don't! I'm not bleeding to death, I swear."

His eyes narrowed. "Are you bleeding not to death?"

"No." She stuck her red-coated finger into her mouth and, with the other hand, scooped up a half-dozen French fries caught between her hip and the door. She'd picked them up not ten minutes ago from The Loon Feather Café in town, and Effie had put three little paper cups of ketchup in the take-out tray. Eating fries while driving—another of her vices, along with owning too many horses, flightiness in all things, and swerving to avoid dumb dogs in the road. Gingerly she held up the flat, empty, red-checkered box. "It's only Type A Heinz," she said. "See? No 911 needed. Besides, this is rural Rice County, and it'd take the rescue guys twenty minutes to find me. Is the dog all right?"

"Dog?"

"The one I swerved to miss. You didn't see an injured dog?"

His indigo eyes performed a laser scan from her head to her toes. They settled on her face and softened. "It must have disappeared. I wasn't watching it since I was prayin' to all the angels while you barreled down this ditch."

"But it didn't get hit?"

"I'm pretty sure it didn't get hit," he repeated gently. "You really all right? The dog isn't exactly important at the moment. Nothing hurts? Did you black out?"

Jill let out a breath of relief. This morning, the docs at Southwater Vet Clinic had put down two families' beloved dogs and a young client's show horse. Knowing the stray in the road had survived didn't balance the scales, but it helped a little.

"I just didn't want the dog to be dead. Nothing hurts. I didn't black out. All I want is to get out of my homicidal truck."

"Homicidal?" He laughed and took a step back. "Are you blaming your poor stuck truck for this?"

"Poor truck?" Jill glanced around her seat to see how she dared start extricating herself. The first thing she did was unlatch the seat belt, and the pressure on her arm eased. "This is The Creature. She's a diva. Any other vehicle would *not* have kept going left after I cranked the wheel back to the right." She looked at the man. "She'd kill me outright, but who else would pour college loan money into her like I do?"

The right side of his upper lip, as perfectly sculpted as the rest of his features, lifted in an Elvis-y half grin—a cute-on-handsome action that made Jill's mouth go parched again.

"Sounds like we'd best get you out before Lizzie Borden the truck here changes her mind." His warm, humor-filled voice calmed with its hypnotic Southern cadence.

"I'd be very, very good with that," she replied.

"Let's try the door." He reached for the handle.

"No! Wait. Don't! Whenever I move the whole thing rocks. I—"

"Okay, it's okay." He held up his hands. "I'll look first and see how solid she's sitting."

He stepped away and walked slowly around the front of the Suburban. Jill took the time to regroup. She wasn't a wimp, dang it. This was stupid. The man already believed she was half-baked. She needed to stop whining and simply crawl out. And she had to get the stupid truck out of this stupid ditch or she'd miss the most important riding lesson of her life. Maybe if she could see how to straighten her wheels she could just drive—

"She isn't hanging on by a lot, you're right." He returned to the window. "But you should be able to ease out this way. I'll open the door very carefully. Trust me."

Trust him? For all she knew he had a handgun in his pocket, a twelve-page rap sheet, and a mug shot at the post office. "Fine." She grimaced. "Just don't mug me until I'm fully out. One crisis at a time."

His slightly nasal laugh flowed between them, as musical as his voice. "Gotta love a woman who's funny in the face of adversity."

Funny? This merely kept her from weeping. In addition to causing expense for which there was no money, this accident was messing up two appointments she couldn't afford to miss.

"I'm not being funny." She wriggled out from behind the steering wheel. "On the other hand, if you murder me right here I'll have a great excuse for being late." She edged to the passenger side and glanced at her watch. "Make that very late."

"Lizzie here didn't murder you, and I'm not going to either."

He tugged on the door and it hit the slope, barely opening ten inches. Jill was small, but not that small.

"Great. Just awesome." She eyed the stranger dubiously.

"I'm afraid it's out the window for you." He shrugged.

"Well, this gets better and better." She simply wanted out, and she reached for the oversized tote she used as purse, clothing bag, and carry-all. "Would you toss this on the ground? I hope that stupid dog appreciates its life."

"It's on its knees thanking—"

"All the angels?" she teased.

"Yes, ma'am." The return of his Elvis grin sent a flutter through her belly. He hefted her striped, leather-handled bag and grunted. "Lord love a monkey, what have you got in here? Car parts?"

"Riding boots." She reached for the top of the window opening and suddenly heard what he'd said. "*What?*"

"Sorry, my granddaddy's saying. Gotta admit"—he grunted—"didn't expect you to say boots."

"Only because you don't know me," she muttered.

"Let's go then. We can do getting-to-know-you once you're free."

The easiest way out was headfirst, since it caused the least amount of wiggling. But halfway out, with her torso flopped over the door frame and her knees hovering above the passenger seat, The Creature slowly swung its nose downward. She shrieked.

"Got you!" Strong hands caught her beneath the armpits.

The Creature spun left and spit her from the window.

The momentum squirted her out and propelled the stranger backward. One second Jill's shoe toes skimmed the window frame, the next she sprawled atop a very long, very hard male body. He grabbed her and held the back of her head expertly, as if people fell on him all the time and he knew precisely what to do.

"Sorry. Sorry. I'm okay. Are you okay?" Her words were muffled in his shoulder.

She should move.

He should move.

Instead, his chest rose and fell beneath her, and his breath warmed the top of her head. His fingers formed a firm brace at the base of her neck, and he lay like a stone beneath her. When she finally made the tiniest effort to roll away, his free hand planted itself on her hip.

"No," he commanded in a hoarse whisper.

No?

"Relax. Make sure you're all in one piece."

She certainly didn't know this guy well enough to relax in a reverse missionary position with him ... but the pleasant musk of masculine perspiration prickled her nose and mingled with the redolent scent of his leather jacket. Her eyelids floated closed in spite of herself, and she went all but limp with relief. When he relaxed, too, however, she couldn't ignore his long, lean form beneath her or the intense pressure gathering low in her body. She tried to concentrate on the fact that nothing bad was happening while he held her—no accidents, no animals dying, no worry she was late for—

"Oh my gosh!" She jerked hard against his hold.

Immediately he released her, gave her shoulder a squeeze, and a mini-explosion of sparks raced for every nerve ending in her body. She pushed onto her hands and stared into eyes as calm as a waveless lake.

"Hi," he said, his mouth only inches from hers. "I'm Chase Preston. Nice to meet you."

She rolled off him laughing and sat up on the incline. "Hi, back. I'm Jill Carpenter. How can I thank you for rescuing me?"

He waved dismissively. "You'd have figured out how to escape, Jill Carpenter, but glad I could help."

He sat up, too, and stuck out his hand, but Jill was almost afraid to take it. Her stomach dipped in antici-pation at the sight of his long, clever-looking e knHe-HisHiTheThefingers and knuckles flanked by prominent tendons. At last, she let his grip engulf hers, as warm and comforting as his full-body hold had been. When he rocked to a stand he pulled her along, and her body rose with no more effort than surfacing from buoyant water.

She tried to smile—to thank him by holding their clasped hands a second longer, but after a final, slow squeeze, he let his fingers slide free.

"Now that you're safe, it's time to find you a way out of this ditch. Is there anyone you can call way out here in rural whatever county?"

Jill took her first good look at The Creature, and her heart sank. She'd harbored the ghostly hope that, once free, she'd see how to drive it from the ditch. It hadn't been a very strong hope, but now it was dashed beyond any stretch of imagination. The Creature's grille touched the bottom of the ditch, one rear tire had spun a bald patch into the grass, and the passenger side corner hovered six inches off the ground. It wasn't going anywhere under its own power. Anger at her predicament started a slow burn.

Jill grabbed the bag Chase had set on the hillside, the anger heating up as reality smacked her in the face. How was this fair? For once it had seemed her dream would have a fighting chance, but oh no. With short, angry stomps she marched up the steep slope, and when she reached the road after working up to full-fledged fury, she nearly crashed into a gleaming, silver-and-red motorcycle. She glimpsed the intricate Triumph logo on the gas tank and jumped back. Motorcycles were not her thing.

"So, who can you call?"

She stopped short of snapping at him, dropped her bag, and pressed her fingertips against her eyes to hide her frustration. "Dewey's Garage and Gas in town." She sighed.

"Can I take you there? Or call for you?"

"No. I have my phone, and you've helped too much already. Believe me, Dewey knows this truck. He won't be at all surprised he has to tow her out of a ditch."

"Then give him a call. I'll wait with you."

She started to object. Being rescued was far out of her realm of experience, but the man's presence had a calming, spell-like effect on her worry and her anger. She found Dewey's number and punched the call button. A familiar voice came answered. "Dewey Mitchell."

She explained her problem and waited for Dewey to calculate his ETA.

"I'm out delivering some fuel, and it'll take forty-five minutes or so to get back to the tow truck. Sorry I'm not closer."

Disappointment spread through her like chills. "I'll take you as soon as I can get you, Dewey. Thanks." She described where she was and hung up.

"He could be an hour." She tried desperately to hide her rekindled anger. Of all the days for disaster to hit . . . "All he said was he'll hurry."

She plopped to her seat in the grass beside the road. Her consultation with a brand-new riding student was supposed to start in five minutes, but the bigger issue was Colin Pitts-Matherson. The visiting coach of the U.S. Equestrian Eventing Team was not known for magnanimity. As a talent scout would for any sport, he'd asked for one chance to see her perform. He'd expect to see her ride. In forty-five minutes. With no sob-story excuse about a dog in the road. Her shot at an Olympic dream could well be resting in the ditch along with The Creature's hood ornament.

A mellow rustling of clothing distracted her, and something heavy draped across her shoulders, steeping the air in a scent she recognized as his, even after this short time. Chase squatted in front of her and drew the jacket securely around her body. She stared at him, mesmerized and annoyed in equal measure.

"What the heck?"

"You're shivering. I don't want to see you go into shock."

Chase now wore only a soft, heathery-gray Henley, fitted to his broad pecs like superhero Lycra. A smear of ketchup marred the front, and she couldn't stop her fingers from brushing at it. The juxtaposition of fur-soft brushed cotton over the hard wall of muscle behind it made her quiver.

Oh brother.

She shoved at him with all her strength. He barely moved.

"For crying out loud!" She tried to fling the jacket off, but he held it firmly in place. "I'm missing two important appointments while I'm sitting here on my ass, and I can't get help for an hour. I'm not in shock. I'm majorly pissed off."

When she quit struggling, he released his hold on the jacket, grasped her chin gently, and studied her face.

"I'm sorry." His voice tightened. "First responder training from an old job. It's habit." He released her chin. An odd emptiness replaced his touch. "Let me take you to your appointment. You'll get there safely and on time. The truck's not going anywhere until it's towed."

"But I'm going six miles in the opposite direction of where you were going. I can call my boss to come get me."

"Heck, six miles? That's barely spittin' distance after what I've done the last two days."

A swirl of nervousness circled through her chest. She wouldn't climb aboard a motorcycle with someone she knew, much less a random stranger—despite the fact that he'd rescued her butt and had a phenomenal body.

"That's very nice of you," she said. "You've gone above and beyond, but I'll give David a call."

"You sure? I can have you there in ten minutes."

Or he could have her splatted like a dead raccoon on the asphalt in thirty seconds.

"Oh, I'm pretty sure." She nodded emphatically.

A eureka-moment smile blossomed on his lips. "Hey. You aren't afraid of a little ol' motorcycle?"

Over her shoulder, she took in the Triumph with a serious eye. Its crimson gas tank and chrome fenders shone in the sunshine, and although she knew next to nothing about motorcycles—except that when someone wiped out at fifty miles per hour he wound up half-mangled and in casts in the hospital, scaring his kids half to death—she could tell this one was not new.

"It's a good-looking machine," she allowed. "It's gotta be an older model?"

"Vintage is what the bike geeks call it. It's a '75 Bonneville. Belongs to my grandfather actually, his pride and joy. Would you believe he bought it right here in Minnesota? When I decided to come this way, he thought the old girl should have a road trip home."

"Ooo-kay, there's not much of a story in *that* teaser." She lifted her eyes and got a wink.

"Hop on and I'll tell it to you."

"Now, that sounds like a bad biker boy's version of 'come see my etchings.'"

"I'll have to remember that." His laugh added to the warmth emanating from his jacket.

"How far *have* you come in two days?"

"From Memphis."

She let out a low, appreciative whistle. "How much farther are you going?"

"I'm not entirely sure. I'm heading for a town somewhere around here called Northfield."

"Oh, it's *close*. Maybe fifteen miles once you go through Kennison Falls."

His Elvis smile enchanted her as always. "That's very, very good news."

He stood and held out his hand to pull her to her feet. Jill brushed away a smudge of dust on her thigh. She wasn't wary by nature, and strangers weren't rare. Kennison Falls, Minnesota got enough through-traffic to keep the local merchants in good business. But leather-jacketed bikers with gorgeous, penetrating eyes were not the norm.

She wished she could control the sudden pounding of her pulse, but tangled as she was in his eyes, his accent, and her ridiculous fear, containing her heartbeat was a lost cause.

"My mama warned me about taking rides from strangers."

"I won't let the big, bad Triumph hurt you, you know."

She closed her eyes and took another deep breath. "This is nuts."

He peered at her. "You really are scared."

"Always was." She forced herself not to look embarrassed. "Even when my father had one."

He didn't tease or even comment. From the seat, he picked up a black, shiny-visored helmet and held it out to her. "You can wear this. It possesses the power to keep you safe. Put your arms into the jacket, too, that's more protection."

Twice, now, he'd promised to protect her. Something primitive finally calmed her nerves, if only slightly. With resignation she pulled the helmet over her head. It fit like a fishbowl and dimmed the light like three pairs of sunglasses.

Chase rapped on the hard shell while she snapped the chinstrap.

"Where's your bag of boots?" He chuckled.

She grabbed it from the grass, and he plopped it atop a small duffel, pushing them to the metal tail behind the seat and stretching a bungee cord around both bags. He flipped down the passenger foot pegs and swung his leg over the seat.

"Squeeze on," he said blithely, and she did. The padded seat cushioned her better than her best riding saddle did, but there was no life beneath her, no living thing to partner with. "Put your feet on the rests here over the pipes. Don't let them dangle—the metal gets good and hot. Hang on to me or hold that strap on the seat. And don't worry."

She flipped up the visor. "I ride horses not Hogs. You can reason with a horse. And they're smart enough to keep from doing stupid things because they don't want to die any more than I do." She snapped the visor back in place.

"Well, this isn't a Hog, it's a Triumph. And, honey, I'm smart enough to know I don't want to die either." He laughed and shifted one hip to bring a boot heel down on the kick-starter.

The bike answered with a grumpy rumble but didn't catch. He stomped again. The Bonneville sprang to life, vibrating beneath Jill like a purring lion. The pulsations went through her like electrical current.

"One more thing," he called, twisting over his shoulder. "Lean with me into the turns. It won't be your instinct, but it'll be safer. Ready?"

She clutched the seat strap, and the motorcycle rolled forward a foot. Chase let out the clutch. With a slight jolt, and a tilt to the right, the bike roared onto the road.

They picked up speed like a launched rocket, and Jill swayed from side to side, her wimpy grip on the leather seat strap not nearly secure enough to keep her stable. As they followed a curve to the left and the bike leaned, she held in a screech, squeezed her eyes shut, and threw her arms around Chase's waist. Immediately her torso quit swaying.

Don't crash. Don't crash. Don't crash. The mantra played through her mind until, finally, they'd been underway long enough that the silliness of her fear hit home. She opened her eyes and watched familiar sights flash past in an unfamiliar way. The wind whipped at Chase's jacket, but sheltered in its folds she felt no chill. Beneath her hands, Chase's stomach muscles contracted and flexed as he moved as one with the motorcycle. Hanging on to him was like pressing up against a safe, brick wall. It took a second for her to comprehend when his fingers pried gently at hers, wiggling and loosening her grip.

"Relax!" he called over his shoulder, the word barely audible as it whizzed past her helmeted ear with the wind.

She hadn't realized how tightly she'd been squeezing. With effort, she pulled her hands apart and let go, grasping for a hold on the leather again, but he caught one hand and tugged her arm forward, patting it when the hold was just right. A hard shiver rolled through her body and then, for the first time, Jill found the ability to relax as he'd commanded. Beneath her hold, he came to life, not a brick wall at all but a supple, tensile lifeline.

"Be ready to tell me where to turn," he shouted again. "I've got you. Trust me."

About the Author

Lizbeth Selvig writes fun, heartwarming contemporary romantic fiction. Her debut novel, *The Rancher and the Rock Star,* was released in 2012. Her second, *Rescued by a Stranger* is a 2014 RWA RITA® Award nominee. Lizbeth lives in Minnesota with her best friend (aka her husband), a hyperactive border collie, and a gray Arabian gelding. After working as a newspaper journalist and magazine editor, and raising an equine veterinarian daughter and a talented musician son, Lizbeth entered Romance Writers of America's Golden Heart® contest in 2010 with *The Rancher and the Rock Star* (then titled *Songbird*) and won the Single Title Contemporary category. In her spare time, she loves to hike, quilt, read, horseback ride, and spend time with her new granddaughter. She also has four-legged grandchildren—more than twenty—including a wallaby, two alpacas, a donkey, a pig, a sugar glider, and many dogs, cats, and horses (pics of all appear on her website www.lizbethselvig.com). She loves connecting with all her readers.

Give in to your impulses . . .
Read on for a sneak peek at eight brand-new
e-book original tales of romance
from Avon Books.
Available now wherever e-books are sold.

THE COWBOY AND THE ANGEL

By T. J. Kline

FINDING MISS McFARLAND

THE WALLFLOWER WEDDING SERIES

By Vivienne Lorret

TAKE THE KEY AND LOCK HER UP

By Lena Diaz

DYLAN'S REDEMPTION

BOOK THREE: THE McBRIDES

By Jennifer Ryan

SINFUL REWARDS 1
A Billionaires and Bikers Novella
By Cynthia Sax

WHATEVER IT TAKES
A Trust No One Novel
By Dixie Lee Brown

HARD TO HOLD ON TO
A Hard Ink Novella
By Laura Kaye

KISS ME, CAPTAIN
A French Kiss Novel
By Gwen Jones

An Excerpt from

THE COWBOY AND THE ANGEL
By T. J. Kline

From author T. J. Kline comes the stunning
follow-up to *Rodeo Queen*. Reporter
Angela McCallister needs the scoop of her career
in order to save her father from the bad decisions
that have depleted their savings. When the
opportunity to spend a week at the
Findley Brothers ranch arises, she sees a chance
to get a behind-the-scenes scoop on rodeo. That
certainly doesn't include kissing the devastatingly
handsome and charming cowboy Derek Chandler,
who insists on calling her "Angel."

"Angela, call on line three."

"Can't you just handle it, Joe? I don't have time for this B.S." It was probably just another stupid mom calling, hoping Angela would feature her daughter's viral video in some feel-good news story. When was she ever going to get her break and find some hard-hitting news?

"They asked for you."

Angela sighed. Maybe if she left them listening to that horrible elevator music long enough, they'd hang up. Joe edged closer to her desk.

"Just pick up the damn phone and see what they want."

"Fine." She glared at him as she punched the button. The look she gave him belied the sweet tone of her voice. "Angela McCallister, how can I help you?"

Joe leaned against her cubical wall, listening to her part of the conversation. She waved at him irritably. It wasn't always easy when your boss was your oldest friend, and ex-boyfriend. He quirked a brow at her.

Go away, she mouthed.

"Are you really looking for new stories?"

She assumed the male voice on the line was talking about the calls the station ran at the ends of several news programs asking for stories of interest. Most of them wound up in her mental "ignore" file, but once in a while she'd found one worth pursuing.

"We're always looking for events and stories of interest to our local viewers." She rolled her eyes, reciting the words Joe had taught her early on in her career as a reporter. She was tired of pretending any of this sucking up was getting her anywhere. Viewers only saw her as a pretty face.

"I have a lead that might interest you." She didn't answer, waiting for the caller to elaborate. "There's a rodeo coming to town, and they are full of animal cruelty and abuse."

This didn't sound like a feel-good piece. The caller had her attention now. "Do you have proof?"

The voice gave a bitter laugh, sounding vaguely familiar. "Have you ever seen a rodeo? Electric prods, cinches wrapped around genitals, sharp objects placed under saddles to get horses to buck . . . it's all there."

She listened as the caller detailed several incidents at nearby rodeos where animals had to be euthanized due to injuries. Angela arched a brow, taking notes as the man gave her several websites she could research that backed the accusations.

"Can I contact you for more information?" She heard him hemming. "You don't have to give me your name. Maybe just a phone number or an email address where I can reach you?" The caller gave her both. "Do you mind if I ask one more question—why me?"

"Because you seem like you care about animal rights. That story you did about the stray kittens and the way you found them a home, it really showed who you were inside."

Angela barely remembered the story other than that Joe had forced it on her when she'd asked for one about a local politician sleeping with his secretary, reminding her that viewers saw her as their small-town sweetheart. She'd found herself reporting about a litter of stray kittens, smiling at the animal shelter as families adopted their favorites, and Jennifer Michaels had broken the infidelity story and was now anchoring at a station in Los Angeles. She was tired of this innocent, girl-next-door act.

"I'll see what I can do," she promised, deciding how to best pitch this story to Joe and whether it would be worth it at all.

An Excerpt from

FINDING MISS McFARLAND
The Wallflower Wedding Series
by Vivienne Lorret

Delany McFarland is on the hunt for a husband—
preferably one who needs her embarrassingly large
dowry more than a dutiful wife. Griffin Croft
hasn't been able to get Miss McFarland out of his
mind, but now that she's determined to hand over
her fortune to a rake, Griffin knows he must step
in. Yet when his noble intentions flee in a moment
of unexpected passion, his true course becomes
clear: tame Delaney's wild heart and save her from
a fate worse than death . . . a life without love.

She *had* been purposely avoiding him.

Griffin clasped his hands behind his back and began to pace around her in a circle. "Do you have spies informing you on my whereabouts at all times, or only for social gatherings?"

Miss McFarland watched his movements for a moment, but then she pursed those pink lips and smoothed the front of her cream gown. "I do what I must to avoid being seen at the same function with you. Until recently, I imagined we shared this unspoken agreement."

"Rumormongers rarely remember innocent bystanders."

She scoffed. "How nice for you."

"Yes, and until recently, I was under the impression that I came and went of my own accord. That my decisions were mine alone. Instead, I learn that every choice I make falls under your scrutiny." He was more agitated than angered. Not to mention intrigued and unaccountably aroused by her admission. During a season packed full of social engagements, she must require daily reports of his activities. Which begged the question, how often did she think of him? "Shall I quiz you on how I take my tea? Or if my valet prefers to tie my cravat into a barrel knot or horse collar?"

"I do not know, nor do I care, how you take your tea, Mr.

Croft," she said, and he clenched his teeth to keep from asking her to say it once more. "However, since I am something of an expert on fashion, I'd say that the elegant fall of the mail coach knot you're wearing this evening suits the structure of your face. The sapphire pin could make one imagine that your eyes are blue—"

"But you know differently."

Her cheeks went pink before she drew in a breath and settled her hand over her middle. Before he could stop the thought, he wondered whether she was experiencing the *fluttering* his sister had mentioned.

"You are determined to be disagreeable. I have made my attempts at civility, but now I am quite through with you. If you'll excuse me . . ." She started forward to leave.

He blocked her path, unable to forget what he'd heard when he first arrived. "I cannot let you go without a dire warning for your own benefit."

"If this is in regard to what you overheard—when you were eavesdropping on a *private matter*—I won't hear it."

He doubted she would listen to him if he meant to warn her about a great hole in the earth directly in her path either, but his conscience demanded he speak the words nonetheless. "Montwood is a desperate man, and you have put yourself in his power."

Her eyes flashed. "*That* is where you are wrong. I am the one with the fortune, ergo the one with the power."

How little she knew of men. "And what of your reputation?"

Her laugh did nothing to amuse him. "What I have left of my reputation will remain unscathed. He is not interested in my person. He only needs my fortune. In addition, as a second son, he does not require an heir; therefore, our living apart should not cause a problem with his family. And should he need *companionship*, he is free to find it elsewhere, so long as he's discreet."

"You sell yourself so easily, believing your worth is nothing more than your father's account ledger," he growled, his temper getting the better of him. He'd never lost control of it before, but for some reason this tested his limits. If *he* could see she was more than a sum of wealth, then *she* should damn well put a higher value on herself. "If you were my sister, I'd lock you in a convent for the rest of your days."

Miss McFarland stepped forward and pressed the tip of her manicured finger in between the buttons of his waistcoat. "I am *not* your sister, Mr. Croft. And thank the heavens for that gift, too. I can barely stand to be in the same room with you. You make it impossible to breathe, let alone think. Neither my lungs nor my stomach recalls how to function. Not only that, but you cause this terrible crackling sensation beneath my skin, and it feels like I'm about to catch fire." Her lips parted, and her small bosom rose and fell with each breath. "I do believe I loathe you to the very core of your being, Mr. Croft."

Somewhere between the first *Mis-ter-Croft* and the last, he'd lost all sense.

Because in the very next moment, he gripped her shoulders, hauled her against him, and crushed his mouth to hers.

An Excerpt from

TAKE THE KEY AND LOCK HER UP

by Lena Diaz

As a trained assassin for EXIT Inc—a top-secret
mercenary group—Devlin "Devil" Buchanan isn't
afraid to take justice into his own hands. But with
EXIT Inc closing in and several women's lives on
the line, Detective Emily O'Malley and Devlin
must work together to find the missing women and
clear both their names before time runs out . . .
and their key to freedom is thrown away.

"I want to talk to you about what you do at EXIT."

"No."

She blinked. "No?" Her cell phone beeped. She grabbed it impatiently and took the call. A few seconds later she shoved the phone back in her pocket. "Tuck's outside. The SWAT team is set up and ready to cover us in case those two yokels decide to start shooting again. The area is secure. Let's go." She headed toward the door.

"Wait."

She turned, her brows raised in question.

He braced his legs in a wide stance and crossed his arms. "If I'm not under arrest, there's no reason for me to go to the police station."

Her mouth firmed into a tight line. "You're not under arrest only if you agree to the deal I offered. The man who killed Shannon Garrett and the unidentified victims in that basement is holding at least two other women right now, doing God only knows what to them. All I'm asking is that you answer some questions to help me find them, so I can save their lives. Doesn't that mean anything to you?"

Of course it did. But he also knew Kelly Parker, and anyone with her, couldn't be saved by Emily and her fellow cops. It was becoming increasingly clear that Kelly was the bait in a trap to catch *him*. The killer would keep her alive, maybe even provide proof of life at some point, to lure Devlin to wherever she was being held. Did he care about her suffering? Absolutely. Which meant he had to come up with a plan to save her without charging full steam ahead and getting himself killed. Because once the killer eliminated his main prey—Devlin—he'd have no reason to keep either of the women alive.

He braced himself for his next lie. If Emily thought he was bad to supposedly get a woman pregnant and abandon her, she was going to despise him after this next one.

"Finding and saving those women is your job," he said. "I have other things to do that are a lot more fun than sitting in an interrogation room."

The shocked, disgusted look that crossed her face was no worse than the way he felt inside. Like a jerk, and a damn coward. But if sacrificing his pride kept her safe, so be it. He had to get outside and offer himself as bait to lead his enemies away from the diner before she went out the front. He strode past her to the bathroom door.

"Stop, Devlin, or I'll shoot."

He slowly turned around. Seeing his sexy little detective pointing a gun at him again seemed every kind of wrong, especially when his blood was still raging from the hot kiss they'd just shared.

"Seriously?" he said, faking shock. "You're drawing on an unarmed man? *Again*? What will Drier say about that? Or Alex? I smell a lawsuit."

She stomped her foot in frustration.

The urge to laugh at her childish action had him clenching his teeth. She was the perfect blend of innocence, naiveté, and just plain stubbornness. Before he did something they'd both regret—like kissing her again—he slipped out of the bathroom.

A quick side trip through the kitchen too quickly for anyone to even question his presence, and he was down the back hallway, standing at the rear exit. Now all he had to do was make it to some kind of cover—without getting shot—and lead Cougar and his handler away from Emily, all without a weapon of his own to return fire.

Simple. No problem. He shook his head and cursed his decision to go to the police station this morning. Then again, if he hadn't, he wouldn't have gotten to kiss Emily. If he were killed in the next few minutes, at least he'd die with that intoxicating memory still lingering on his lips.

He cracked the door open and scanned the nearby buildings. Then he flung the door wide and took off running.

An Excerpt from

DYLAN'S REDEMPTION
Book Three: The McBrides
by Jennifer Ryan

From *New York Times* bestselling author Jennifer
Ryan, the McBrides of Fallbrook return with
Dylan McBride, the new sheriff. Jessie Thompson
had one hell of a week. Dylan McBride, the boy
she loved, skipped town without a word. Then her
drunk of a father tried to kill her, and she fled
Fallbrook, vowing never to return. Eight years
later, her father is dead, and Jessie reluctantly
goes home—only to come face-to-face with
the man who shattered her heart. A man who,
for nearly a decade, believed she was dead.

Standing over her sleeping brother, she held the pitcher in one hand and the cup of coffee in the other. She poured the cold water over her brother's face and chest. He sat bolt upright and yelled, "What the hell!"

Brian held a hand to his dripping head and one to his stomach. He probably had a splitting headache to go with his rotten gut. As far as Jessie was concerned, he deserved both.

"Good morning, brother. Nice of you to rise and shine."

Brian wiped a hand over his wet face and turned to sit on the sodden couch. His blurry eyes found Jessie standing over him. His mouth dropped open, and his eyes went round before he gained his voice.

"You're dead. I've hit that bottom people talk about. I'm dreaming, hallucinating after a night of drinking. It can't be you. You're gone and it's all my fault." He covered his face with his hands. Tears filled his voice, his pain and sorrow sharp and piercing. She refused to let it get to her, despite her guilt for making him believe she'd died. Brian needed a good ass-kicking, not a sympathetic ear.

"You're going to wish I died when I get through with you, you miserable drunk. What the hell happened to you?" She handed over the mug of coffee and shoved it up to his mouth to make him take a sip. Reality setting in, he needed the coffee and a shower before he'd concentrate and focus on her and what she had in store for him.

"Don't yell, my head is killing me." He pressed the heel of his hand to his eye, probably hoping his brain wouldn't explode.

Jessie sat on the coffee table in front of her brother, between his knees, and leaned forward with her elbows braced on her thighs.

"Listen to me, brother dear. It's past time you cleaned up your act. Starting today, you are going to quit drinking yourself into a stupor. You're going to take care of your wife and child. You're going to show up for work on Monday morning clear eyed and ready to earn an honest day's pay."

"Work? I don't have any job lined up for Monday."

"Yes, you do. I gave Marilee the information. You report to James on Monday at the new housing development going up on the outskirts of town. You'll earn a decent paycheck and have medical benefits for your family.

"The old man left you the house. I'll go over tomorrow after the funeral to see what needs to be done to make it livable for you and Marilee. I, big brother, am going to make you be the man you used to be, because I can't stand to see you turn into the next Buddy Thompson. You got that?" She'd yelled it at him to get his attention and to reinforce the fact that he'd created his condition. His eyes rolled back in his head, and he groaned in pain, all the reward she needed.

"If you don't show up for work on Monday, I'm coming after you. And I'll keep coming until you get it through that thick head of yours: you are not him. You're better than that. So get your ass up, take a shower, mow the lawn, kiss your wife, tell her you love her and you aren't going to be this asshole you've turned into anymore. You hear me?"

"Your voice is ringing in my head." He stared into his coffee cup, but glanced up to say, "You look good. Life's apparently turned out all right for you."

Jessie shrugged that off, focused more on the lost look in Brian's round, sad eyes.

"I thought you died that night. I left and he killed you. Where have you been?"

"Around. Mostly Solomon. I have a house about twenty miles outside of Fallbrook."

"You do?" The surprise lit his face.

"I started my life over. It's time you did the same."

An Excerpt from

SINFUL REWARDS 1
A Billionaires and Bikers Novella
by Cynthia Sax

Belinda "Bee" Carter is a good girl; at least, that's
what she tells herself. And a good girl deserves
a nice guy—just like the gorgeous and moody
billionaire Nicolas Rainer. Or so she thinks,
until she takes a look through her telescope
and sees a naked, tattooed man on the balcony
across the courtyard. He has been watching
her, and that makes him all the more enticing.
But when a mysterious and anonymous text
message dares her to do something bad, she
must decide if she is really the good girl she has
always claimed to be, or if she's willing to risk
everything for her secret fantasy of being watched.

An Avon Red Novella

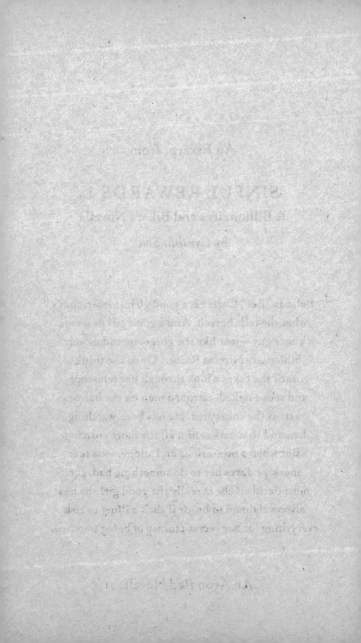

I'd told Cyndi I'd never use it, that it was an instrument purchased by perverts to spy on their neighbors. She'd laughed and called me a prude, not knowing that I was one of those perverts, that I secretly yearned to watch and be watched, to care and be cared for.

If I'm cautious, and I'm always cautious, she'll never realize I used her telescope this morning. I swing the tube toward the bench and adjust the knob, bringing the mysterious object into focus.

It's a phone. Nicolas's phone. I bounce on the balls of my feet. This is a sign, another declaration from fate that we belong together. I'll return Nicolas's much-needed device to him. As a thank you, he'll invite me to dinner. We'll talk. He'll realize how perfect I am for him, fall in love with me, marry me.

Cyndi will find a fiancé also—everyone loves her—and we'll have a double wedding, as sisters of the heart often do. It'll be the first wedding my family has had in generations.

Everyone will watch us as we walk down the aisle. I'll wear a strapless white Vera Wang mermaid gown with organza and lace details, crystal and pearl embroidery accents, the bodice fitted, and the skirt hemmed for my shorter height. My hair will be swept up. My shoes—

Voices murmur outside the condo's door, the sound piercing my delightful daydream. I swing the telescope upward, not wanting to be caught using it. The snippets of conversation drift away.

I don't relax. If the telescope isn't positioned in the same way as it was last night, Cyndi will realize I've been using it. She'll tease me about being a fellow pervert, sharing the story, embellished for dramatic effect, with her stern, serious dad—or, worse, with Angel, that snobby friend of hers.

I'll die. It'll be worse than being the butt of jokes in high school because that ridicule was about my clothes and this will center on the part of my soul I've always kept hidden. It'll also be the truth, and I won't be able to deny it. I am a pervert.

I have to return the telescope to its original position. This is the only acceptable solution. I tap the metal tube.

Last night, my man-crazy roommate was giggling over the new guy in three-eleven north. The previous occupant was a gray-haired, bowtie-wearing tax auditor, his luxurious accommodations supplied by Nicolas. The most exciting thing he ever did was drink his tea on the balcony.

According to Cyndi, the new occupant is a delicious piece of man candy—tattooed, buff, and head-to-toe lickable. He was completing armcurls outside, and she enthusiastically counted his reps, oohing and aahing over his bulging biceps, calling to me to take a look.

I resisted that temptation, focusing on making macaroni and cheese for the two of us, the recipe snagged from the diner my mom works in. After we scarfed down dinner, Cyndi licking her plate clean, she left for the club and hasn't returned.

Three-eleven north is the mirror condo to ours. I

straighten the telescope. That position looks about right, but then, the imitation UGGs I bought in my second year of college looked about right also. The first time I wore the boots in the rain, the sheepskin fell apart, leaving me barefoot in Economics 201.

Unwilling to risk Cyndi's friendship on "about right," I gaze through the eyepiece. The view consists of rippling golden planes, almost like . . .

Tanned skin pulled over defined abs.

I blink. It can't be. I take another look. A perfect pearl of perspiration clings to a puckered scar. The drop elongates more and more, stretching, snapping. It trickles downward, navigating the swells and valleys of a man's honed torso.

No. I straighten. This is wrong. I shouldn't watch our sexy neighbor as he stands on his balcony. If anyone catches me . . .

Parts 1 and 2 available now!

An Excerpt from

WHATEVER IT TAKES
A Trust No One Novel

by Dixie Lee Brown

Assassin Alex Morgan will do anything to save
an innocent life—especially if it means rescuing
a child from a hell like the one she endured. But
going undercover as husband and wife, with
none other than the disarmingly sexy Detective
Nate Sanders, may be a little more togetherness
than she can handle. Nate's willing to face
anything if it means protecting Alex. She may
have been on her own once, but Nate has one
more mission: to stay by her side—forever.

What was Alex doing in that bar? She had to be following him. It was too much of a coincidence any other way. Nate nearly flinched when he replayed the image of her dropping Daniels and then turning on those goons getting ready to shoot up the bar. Shit! Was she suicidal along with everything else? Anger, tinged with dread, did a slow burn under his collar. He needed to know what motivated Alex Morgan . . . and he needed to know now.

He clenched his teeth, whipped his bike into an alley, and cut the engine. If she was bent on getting herself killed, there was no fucking way it was happening on his turf.

She dismounted, uncertainty in her expression. As soon as she stepped out of the way, he swung his leg over and got in her face. "Take it off." He pointed to the helmet.

Not waiting for her to remove it all the way, he started in. "What in the name of all that's holy were you thinking back there? You could have gotten yourself killed."

A sad smile swept her face and something in her eyes—a momentary hardening—gave him a clue to the answer he was fairly certain she'd never speak aloud. Ty had told him the highlights of her story. Joe had freed Alex from a life of slavery in a dark, dismal hole in Hong Kong. From the haunted look in her eyes, however, Nate would bet she hadn't completely dealt with the aftermath. His first impression had been more right than he wanted to admit. It was quite likely that she nursed a dangerous little death wish, and that's what had prompted her actions at the bar.

His anger receded, and a wave of protectiveness rolled over him, but he was powerless to take away the pain staring back at him. He could make a stab at shielding her from the world, but how could he stop the hell that raged inside this woman? Why did she matter so much to him? Hell, logic flew out the window a long time ago. He didn't know why—only that she *did*. With frustration driving him, he stepped closer, pushing her against the bike. Her moist lips drew his gaze, and an overwhelming desire to kiss her set fire to his blood.

She stiffened and wariness flooded her eyes.

He should have stopped there, but another step put him in contact with her, and he was burning with need. He pulled her closer and gently slid his fingers through her hair, then stroked his thumb across her bottom lip.

Her breath escaped in uneven gasps and a tiny bit of tongue appeared, sliding quickly over the lip he'd just touched. Fear, trepidation, longing paraded across her face. Ty's warning sounded in his ears again—she was dangerous, maybe even disturbed—but even if that was true, Nate wasn't sure it made any difference to him.

"Don't be afraid." *Shit!* Immediately, he regretted his words. This woman wasn't afraid of anything. Distrustful . . . yes. Afraid? He didn't even want to know what could scare her.

Her eyes softened and warmed, and she stepped into him, pressing her firm body against his. He caught her around the waist and aligned his hips to hers. Ignoring the words of caution in his head, he bent ever so slowly and covered her mouth with his. Softly caressing her lips and tasting her sweetness, he forgot for a moment that they stood in an alley in a questionable area of Portland, that he barely knew this woman, and that they'd just left the scene of a real-life nightmare.

He'd longed to kiss her since the first time they'd met. She'd insulted his car that day, and not even that had been enough to get his mind off her lips. Good timing or bad—kissing her and holding her in his arms was long overdue.

An Excerpt from

HARD TO HOLD ON TO
A Hard Ink Novella
by Laura Kaye

From *New York Times* and *USA Today* bestselling author Laura Kaye comes a hot, sexy novella to tie in with her Hard Ink series. When "Easy" meets Jenna, he has finally found someone to care for, and he will do anything to keep her safe.

As the black F150 truck shot through the night-darkened streets of one of Baltimore's grittiest neighborhoods, Edward Cantrell cradled the unconscious woman in his arms like she was the only thing tethering him to life. And right at this moment, she was.

Jenna Dean was bloodied and bruised after having been kidnapped by the worst sort of trash the day before, but she was still an incredibly beautiful woman. And saving her from the clutches of a known drug dealer and human trafficker was without question the most important thing he'd done in more than a year.

He should have felt happy—or at least happier—but those feelings were foreign countries for Easy. Had been for a long time.

Easy, for his initials: E.C. The nickname had been the brainchild years before of Shane McCallan, one of his Army Special Forces teammates, who now sat at the other end of the big back seat, wrapped so far around Jenna's older sister, Sara, that they might need the Jaws of Life to pull them apart. Not that Easy blamed them. When you walked through fire and somehow came out the other side in one piece, you gave thanks and held tight to the things that mattered.

Because too often, when shit got critical, the ones you loved didn't make it out the other side. And then you wished you'd given more thanks and held on harder before the fires ever started raging around you in the first place.

Easy would fucking know.

The pickup paused as a gate *whirr*ed out of the way, then the tires crunched over gravel and came to a rough stop. Easy lifted his gaze from Jenna's fire-red hair and too-pale face to find that they were home—or, at least, where he was calling home right now. Out his window, the redbrick industrial building housing Hard Ink Tattoo loomed in the darkness, punctuated here and there by the headlights of some of the Raven Riders bikers who'd helped Easy and his teammates rescue Jenna and take down the gangbangers who'd grabbed her.

Talk about strange bedfellows.

Five former Green Berets and twenty-odd members of an outlaw motorcycle club. Then again, maybe not so strange. Easy and his buddies had been drummed out of the Army under suspicious, other-than-honorable circumstances. Disgraced, dishonored, disowned. Didn't matter that his team had been seriously set up for a big fall. In the eyes of the US government and the world, the five of them weren't any better than the bikers they'd allied themselves with so that they'd have a fighting chance against the much bigger and better-armed Church gang. And, when you cut right down to it, maybe his guys weren't any better. After all, they'd gone total vigilante in their effort to clear their names, identify and take down their enemies, and clean up the collateral damage that occurred along the way.

Like Jenna.

"Easy? *Easy?* Hey, *E?*"

An Excerpt from

KISS ME, CAPTAIN
A French Kiss Novel

by Gwen Jones

In the fun and sexy follow-up to *Wanted: Wife*,
French billionaire and CEO of Mercier Shipping
Marcel Mercier puts his playboy lifestyle
on hold to handle a PR nightmare in the
US, but sparks fly when he meets the
passionate captain of his newest ship . . .

Penn's Landing Pier
Philadelphia
Independence Day, 5:32 AM

"Of course I realize he's your brother-in-law," Dani said, grinning most maliciously as she dragged the chains across the deck to the mainmast. "In fact I'm counting on it as my express delivery system." She wrapped a double length of chain around her waist. "My apologies for shamelessly exploiting you."

"Seriously?" Julie laughed. "Trust me, I'll try not to feel compromised."

"Like me," Dani said, her hair as red as the bloody blister of a sun rising over the Delaware. She yanked another length of chain around the mast. "But what can *I* do. I'm just a *woman*."

"And I'm just a media whore," Julie said. "And a bastard is a bastard is a bastard." She nodded to her cameraman, flexing her shoulders as she leveled her gaze into the lens. "How far would you go to save *your* job?"

Two days later
L'hôtel Croisette Beach
Cannes

Pineapple, Marcel Mercier deduced, drifting awake under the noonday sun. A woman's scent was always the first thing he noticed, as in the subtle fragrance of her soap, her perfumed pulse points, the lingering vestiges of her shampoo.

Mon Dieu. How he loved women.

"Marcel," he heard, feeling a silky leg slide against his own.

He opened his eyes to his *objet d'affection* for the past three days. "Bébé . . ." he growled, brushing his lips across hers as she curled into him.

"Marcel, *mon amour*," she cooed, fairly beaming with joy. "*Tu m'as fait tellement heureuse.*"

"What?" he said, nuzzling her neck. Her pineapple scent was driving him insane.

She slid her hand between his legs. "I *said* you've made me very happy." Then she smiled. No—*beamed*.

He froze, mid-nibble. Oh no. Oh *no*.

She kissed him, her eyes bright. "I don't care what Paris says—I'm wearing my *grand-mère*'s Brussels lace to our wedding. You wouldn't mind, would you?"

He stared at her. Had he really gone and done what he swore he'd never do again? He really needed to lay off the absinthe cocktails. "Mirabel, I didn't mean to—"

"Why did you leave me last night?" she said, falling back against the chaise, her bare breasts heaving above the tiny triangle of her string bikini bottom. "You left so fast the maids are still scrubbing scorch marks from the carpet."

Merde. He really ought to get his *dard* registered as a lethal weapon. He affected an immediate blitheness. "I had to take a call," he said—his standard alibi—raking his gaze over her. She really was quite the babe. "I didn't want to wake you."

All at once she went to full-blown *en garde*, shoving her face into his. "*Really.* More like you couldn't wait to get away from me. And after last night? After what you asked me?" Her enormous breasts rose, fell, her gaze slicing into his. "You said . . . You. *Loved. Me.*"

Had he? *Christ.* He needed to diffuse this. So he switched gears, summoning all his powers of seduction. "Mirabel. *Chère.*" He smiled—lethally, he knew—cradling her chin as he nipped the corner of her mouth. "But that call turned into another, then three, and before you knew it . . ." He traced his finger over the bloom of her breasts and down into the sweet, sweet cavern between them, his tongue edging her lip until she shivered like an ingénue. "You know damn well there's only one way to wake a gorgeous girl like you."

"You should've come back," she said softly, a bit disarmed, though the edge still lingered in her voice. "You just should have." She barely breathed it.

"How, *bébé?*" He licked the hollow behind her ear, and when she jolted, Marcel nearly snickered in triumph. Watching women falling *for* him nearly outranked falling *into* them. "Should I have slipped under the door?" he said, feathering kisses across her jawline. "Or maybe climbed up the balcony, calling 'Juliet? Juliet?'"

She arched her neck and sighed, a deep blush staining her overripe breasts. Marcel fought a rush of disappointment.

Truly, they were all so predictable. A bit of adulatory stroking and it was like they performed on cue. She pressed against his chest as he tugged the bikini string at her hip, her mouth opening in a tiny gasp.

"Mar-*cel* . . ." she purred.

He sighed inwardly. It was almost *too* easy. And that was the scary part.